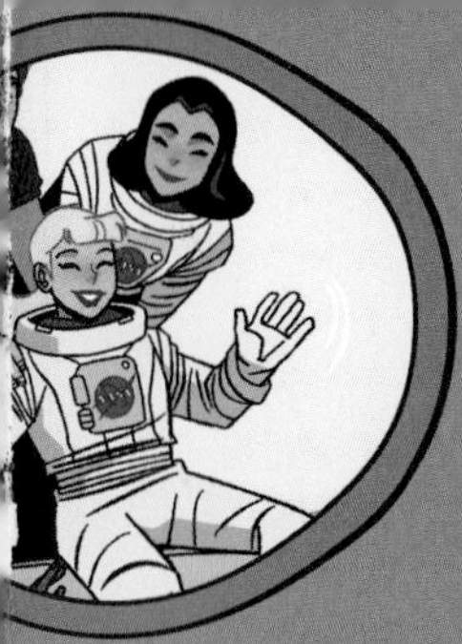

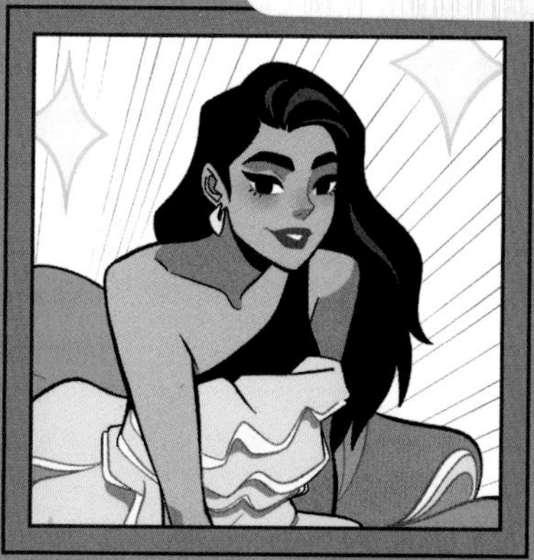

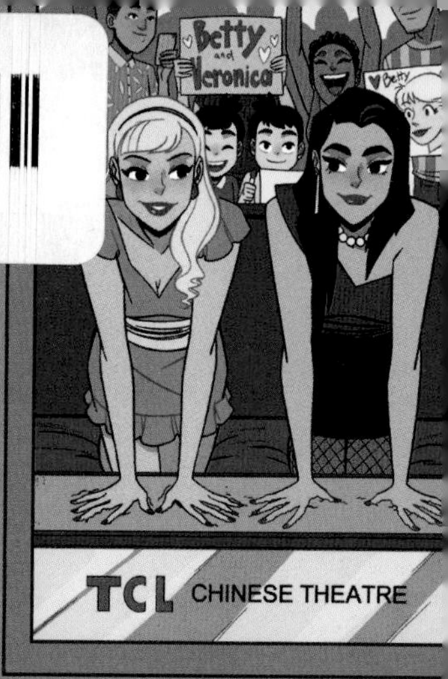
Betty and Veronica
TCL CHINESE THEATRE

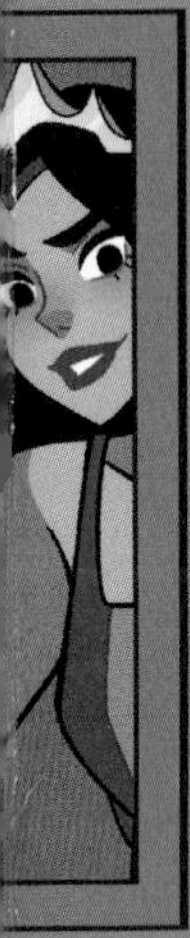

BETTY and VERONICA®

The Bond of Friendship

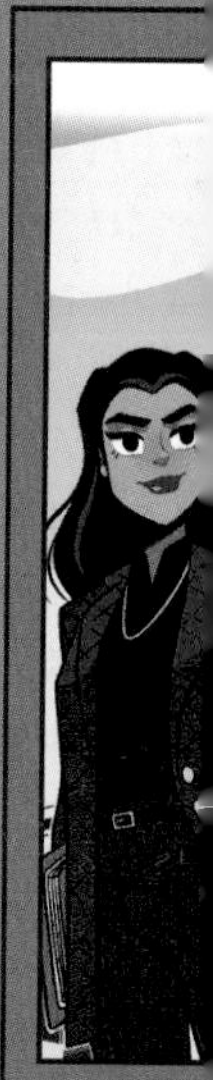

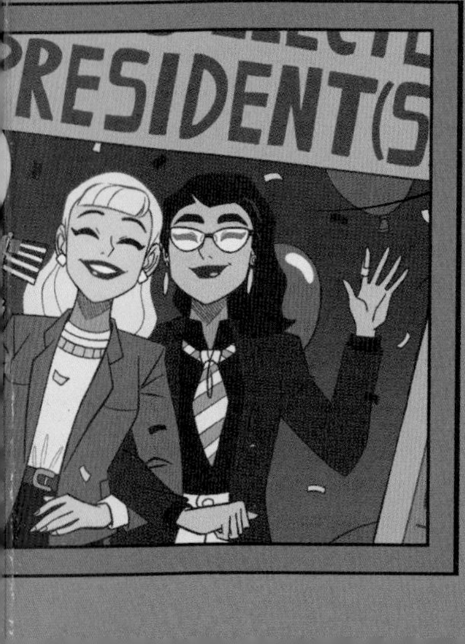
PRESIDENT(S

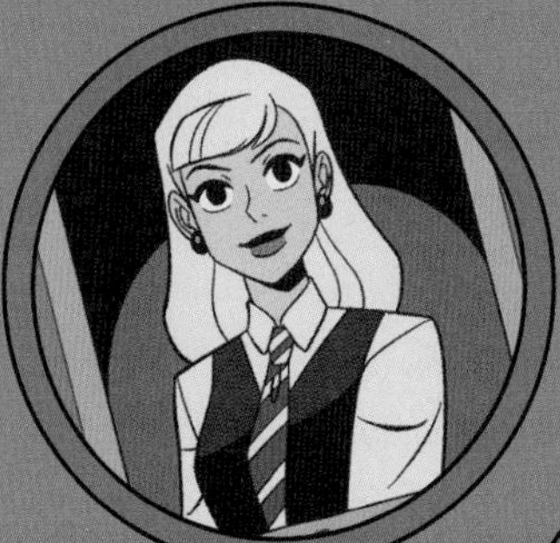

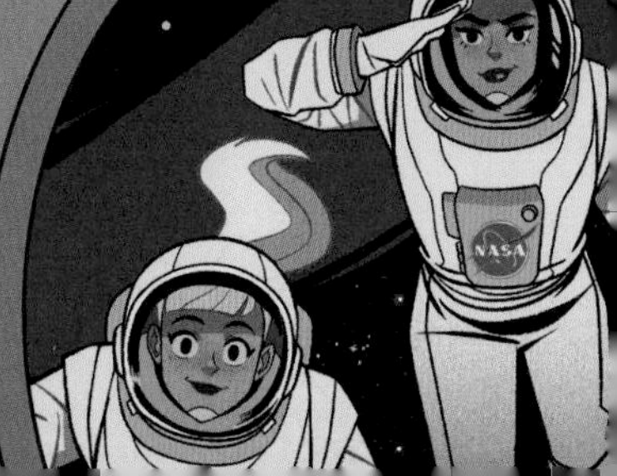
NASA

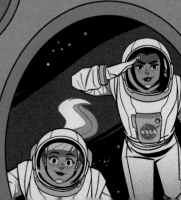

Written By
Jamie Lee Rotante

Illustrated by
Brittney Williams

Colors by
Matt Herms

Letters by
Jack Morelli

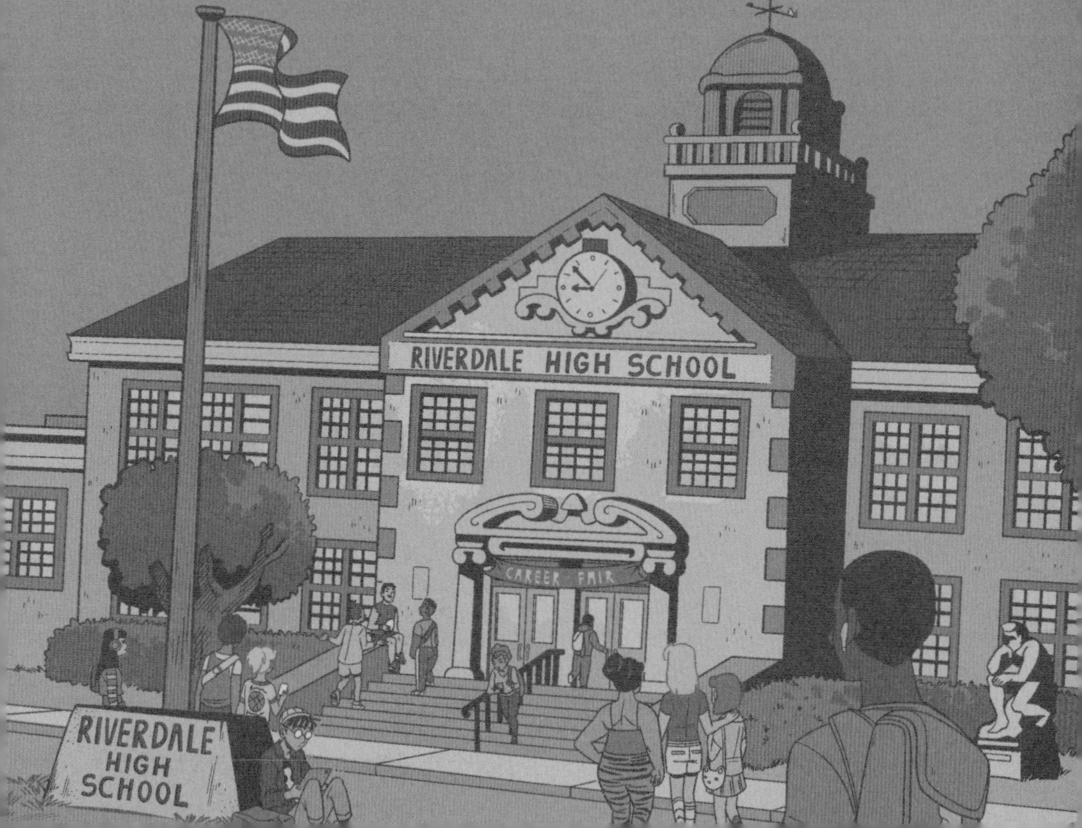
RIVERDALE HIGH SCHOOL
CAREER FAIR
RIVERDALE HIGH SCHOOL

Cover by
Brittney Williams

Designer
Kari McLachlan

Editors
Alex Segura &
Vincent Lovallo

Assistant Editor
Stephen Oswald

Publisher / Co-CEO: Jon Goldwater
Co-President / Editor-In-Chief: Victor Gorelick
Co-President: Mike Pellerito
Co-President: Alex Segura
Chief Creative Officer: Roberto Aguirre-Sacasa
Chief Operating Officer: William Mooar
Chief Financial Officer: Robert Wintle
Director: Jonathan Betancourt
Art Director: Vincent Lovallo
Production Manager: Stephen Oswald
Lead Designer: Kari McLachlan
Editor/Proofreader: Jamie Lee Rotante
Co-CEO: Nancy Silberkleit

ISBN: 978-1-64576-985-9

TABLE of CONTENTS

PROLOGUE

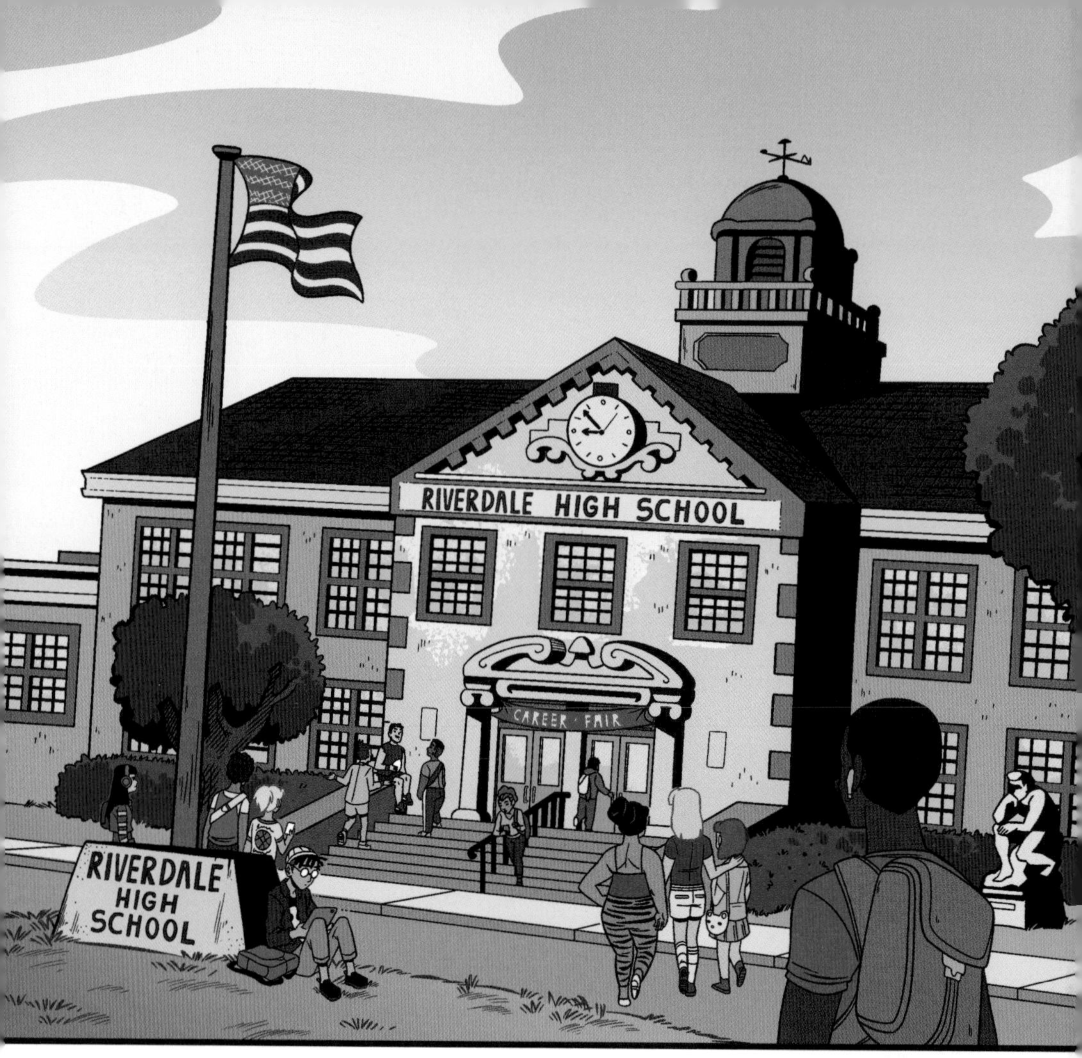
RIVERDALE HIGH SCHOOL
CAREER · FAIR
RIVERDALE HIGH SCHOOL

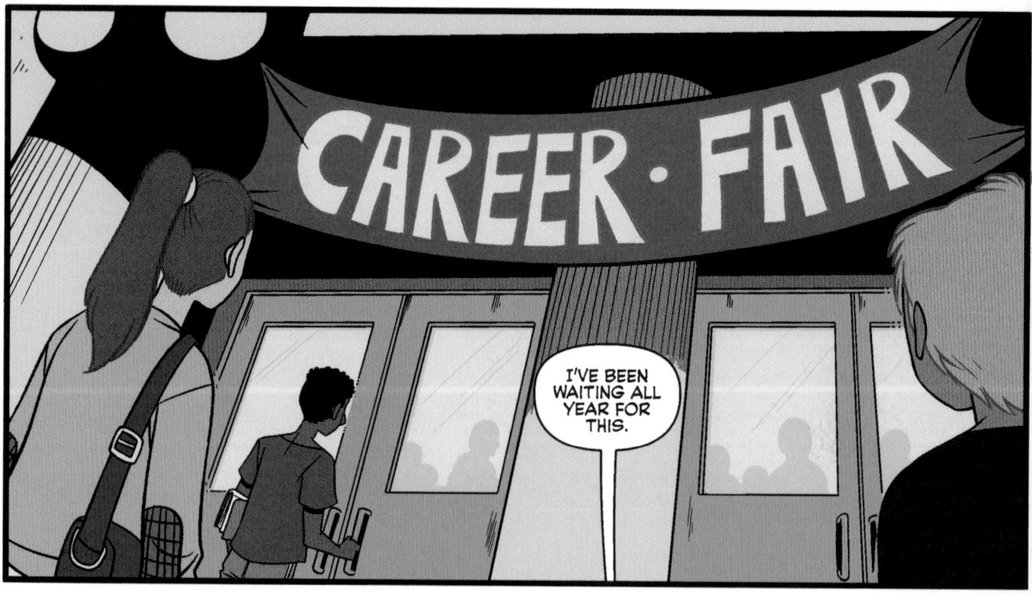
CAREER · FAIR
I'VE BEEN WAITING ALL YEAR FOR THIS.

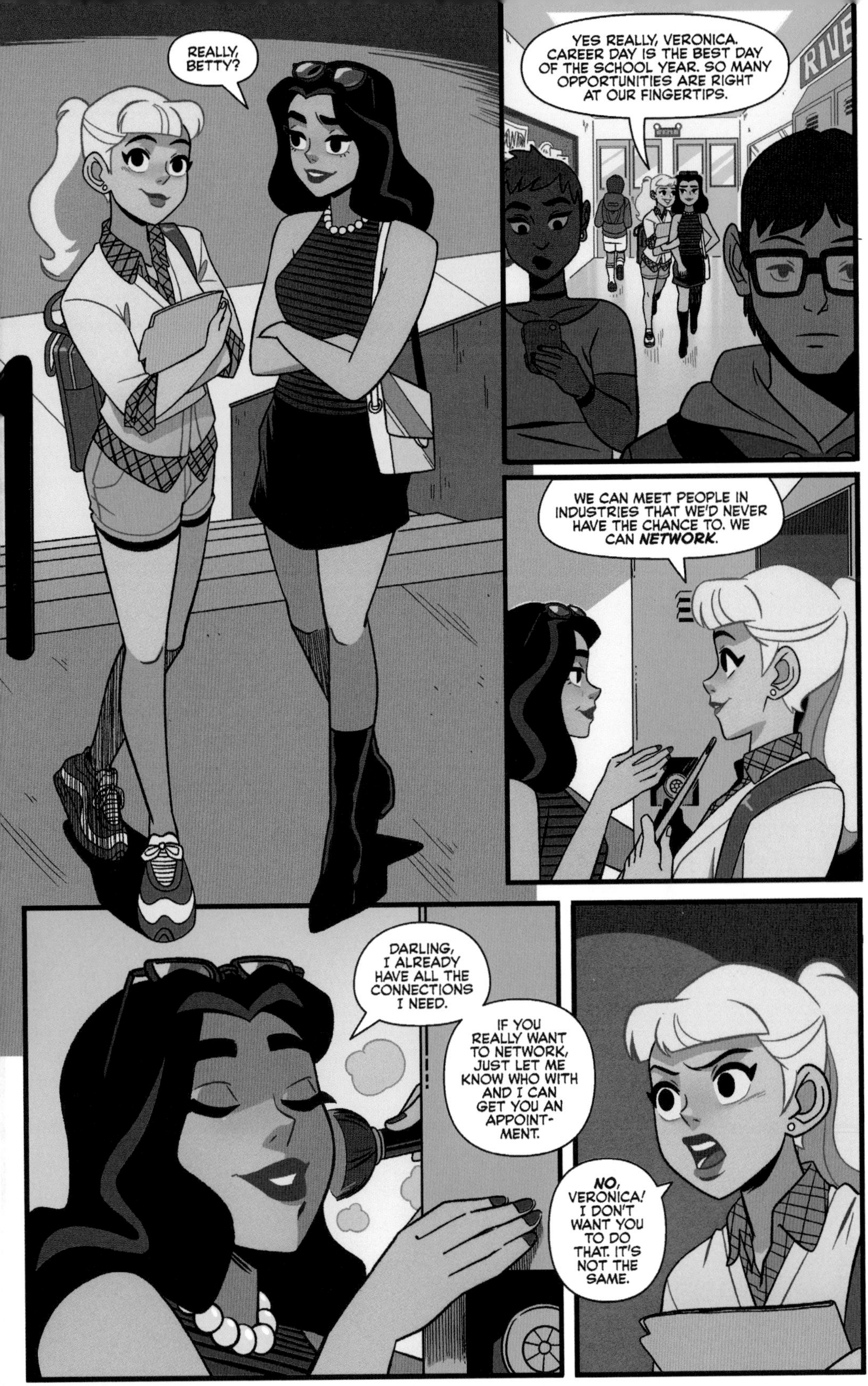
REALLY, BETTY?
YES REALLY, VERONICA. CAREER DAY IS THE BEST DAY OF THE SCHOOL YEAR. SO MANY OPPORTUNITIES ARE RIGHT AT OUR FINGERTIPS.
WE CAN MEET PEOPLE IN INDUSTRIES THAT WE'D NEVER HAVE THE CHANCE TO. WE CAN ***NETWORK***.
DARLING, I ALREADY HAVE ALL THE CONNECTIONS I NEED.
IF YOU REALLY WANT TO NETWORK, JUST LET ME KNOW WHO WITH AND I CAN GET YOU AN APPOINT-MENT.
NO, VERONICA! I DON'T WANT YOU TO DO THAT. IT'S NOT THE SAME.

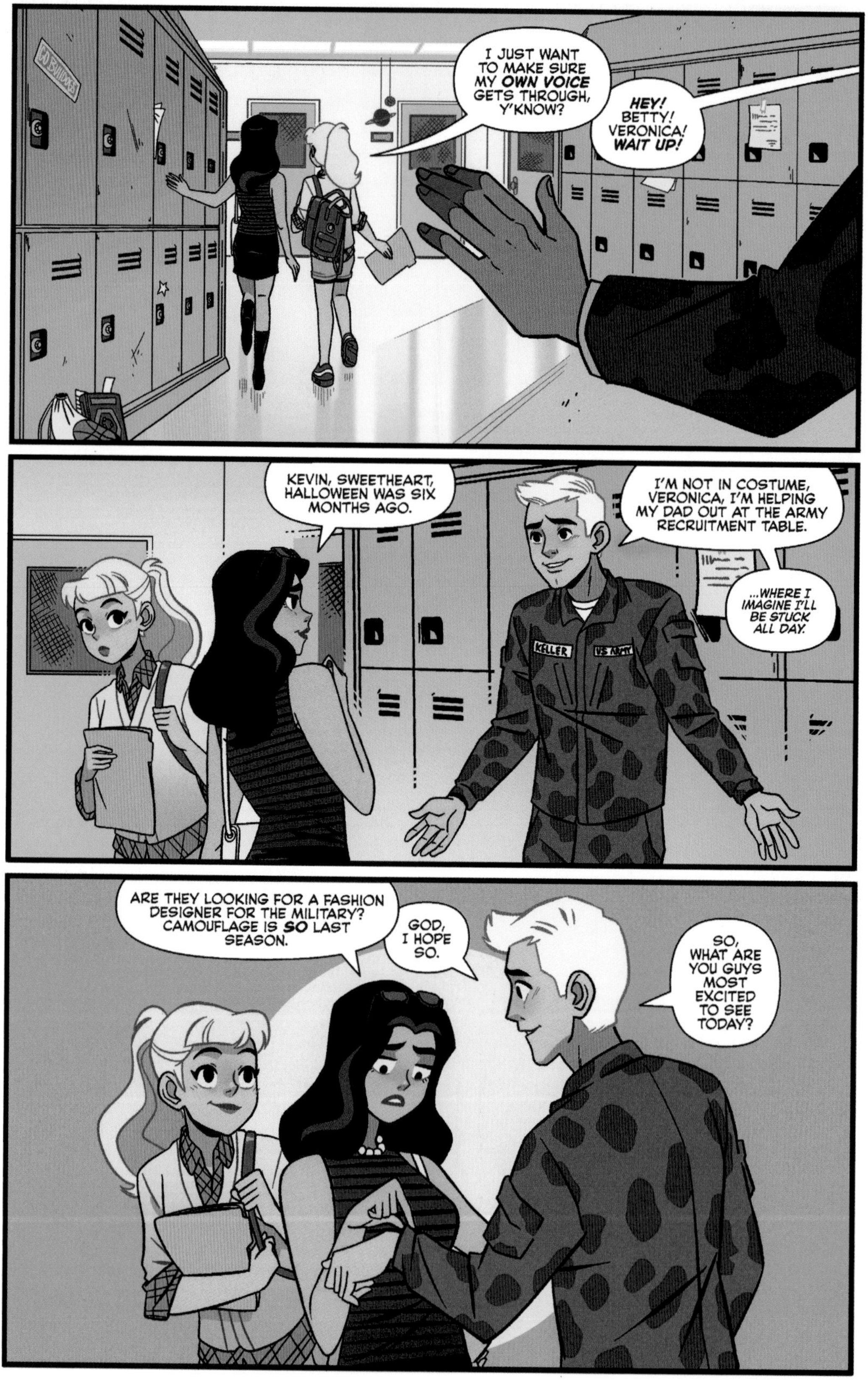
I JUST WANT TO MAKE SURE MY *OWN VOICE* GETS THROUGH, Y'KNOW?
HEY! BETTY! VERONICA! ***WAIT UP!***
KEVIN, SWEETHEART, HALLOWEEN WAS SIX MONTHS AGO.
I'M NOT IN COSTUME, VERONICA, I'M HELPING MY DAD OUT AT THE ARMY RECRUITMENT TABLE.
...WHERE I IMAGINE I'LL BE STUCK ALL DAY.
KELLER
US ARMY
ARE THEY LOOKING FOR A FASHION DESIGNER FOR THE MILITARY? CAMOUFLAGE IS ***SO*** LAST SEASON.
GOD, I HOPE SO.
SO, WHAT ARE YOU GUYS MOST EXCITED TO SEE TODAY?

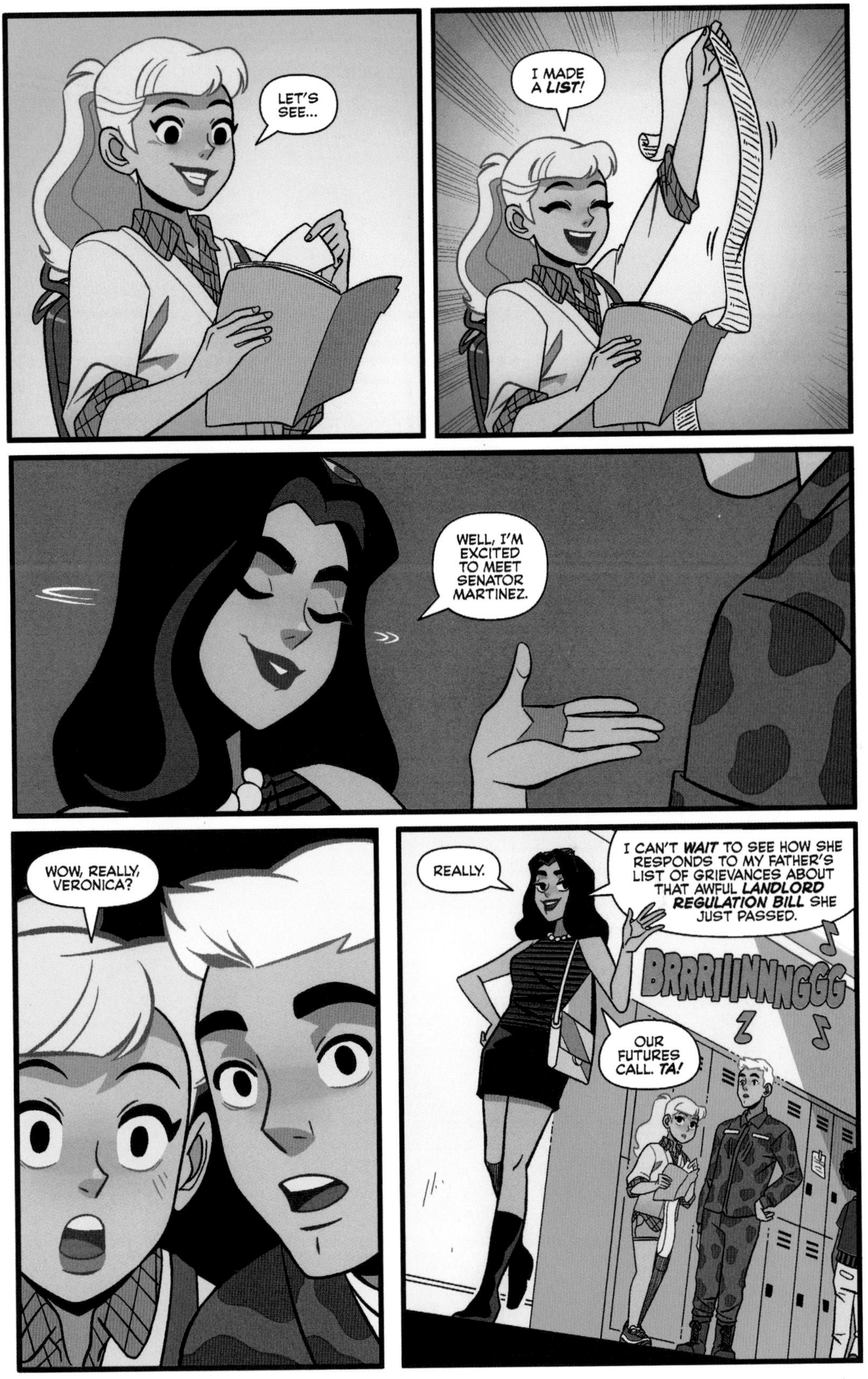
LET'S SEE...
I MADE A *LIST*!
WELL, I'M EXCITED TO MEET SENATOR MARTINEZ.
WOW, REALLY, VERONICA?
REALLY.
I CAN'T *WAIT* TO SEE HOW SHE RESPONDS TO MY FATHER'S LIST OF GRIEVANCES ABOUT THAT AWFUL *LANDLORD REGULATION BILL* SHE JUST PASSED.
BRRRIIINNNGGG
OUR FUTURES CALL. *TA!*

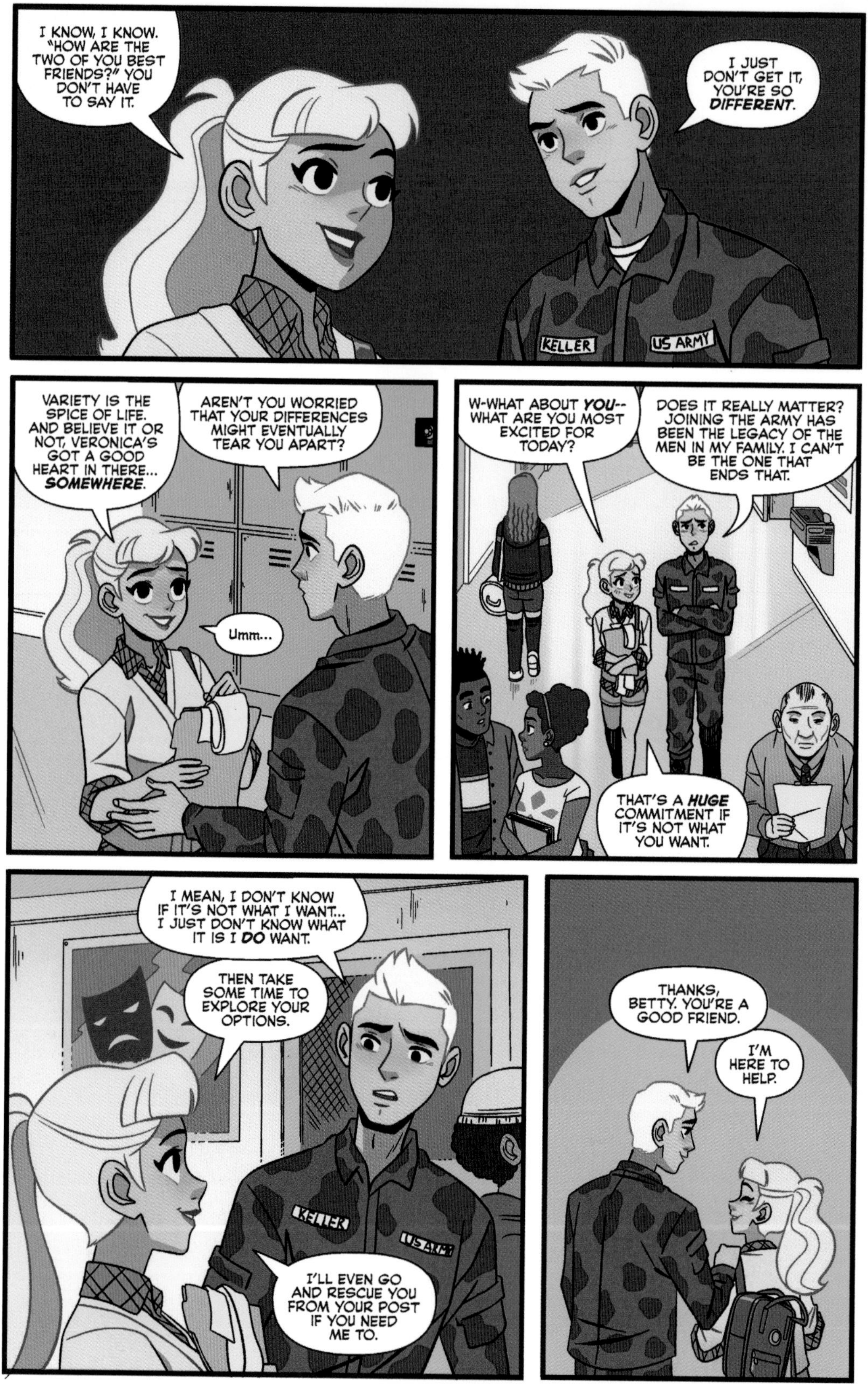
I KNOW, I KNOW. "HOW ARE THE TWO OF YOU BEST FRIENDS?" YOU DON'T HAVE TO SAY IT.
I JUST DON'T GET IT, YOU'RE SO *DIFFERENT*.
KELLER
US ARMY
VARIETY IS THE SPICE OF LIFE. AND BELIEVE IT OR NOT, VERONICA'S GOT A GOOD HEART IN THERE... *SOMEWHERE*.
AREN'T YOU WORRIED THAT YOUR DIFFERENCES MIGHT EVENTUALLY TEAR YOU APART?
Umm...
W-WHAT ABOUT *YOU*-- WHAT ARE YOU MOST EXCITED FOR TODAY?
DOES IT REALLY MATTER? JOINING THE ARMY HAS BEEN THE LEGACY OF THE MEN IN MY FAMILY. I CAN'T BE THE ONE THAT ENDS THAT.
THAT'S A *HUGE* COMMITMENT IF IT'S NOT WHAT YOU WANT.
I MEAN, I DON'T KNOW IF IT'S NOT WHAT I WANT... I JUST DON'T KNOW WHAT IT IS I *DO* WANT.
THEN TAKE SOME TIME TO EXPLORE YOUR OPTIONS.
KELLER
US ARMY
I'LL EVEN GO AND RESCUE YOU FROM YOUR POST IF YOU NEED ME TO.
THANKS, BETTY. YOU'RE A GOOD FRIEND.
I'M HERE TO HELP.

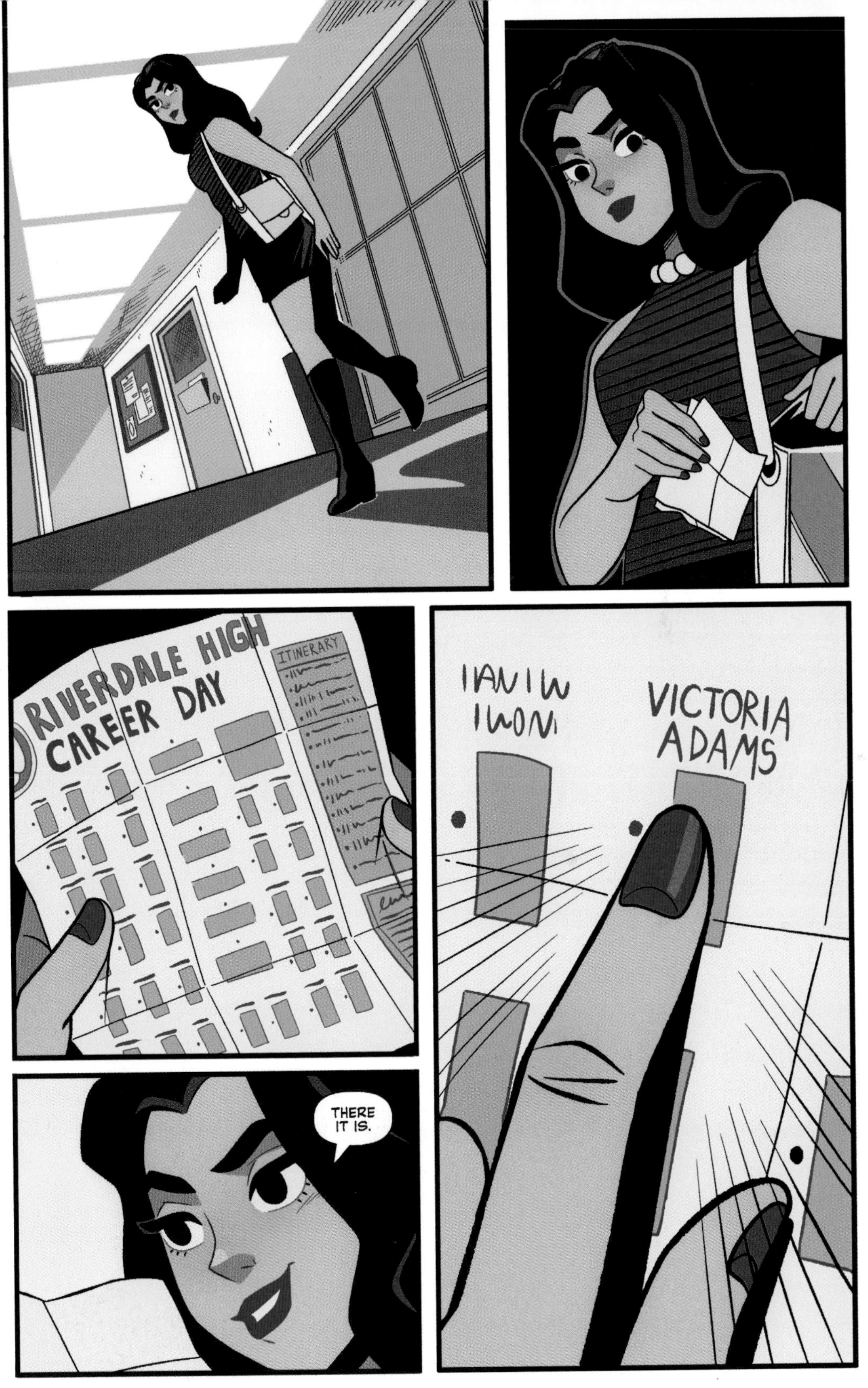
RIVERDALE HIGH
CAREER DAY
ITINERARY
VICTORIA
ADAMS
THERE IT IS.

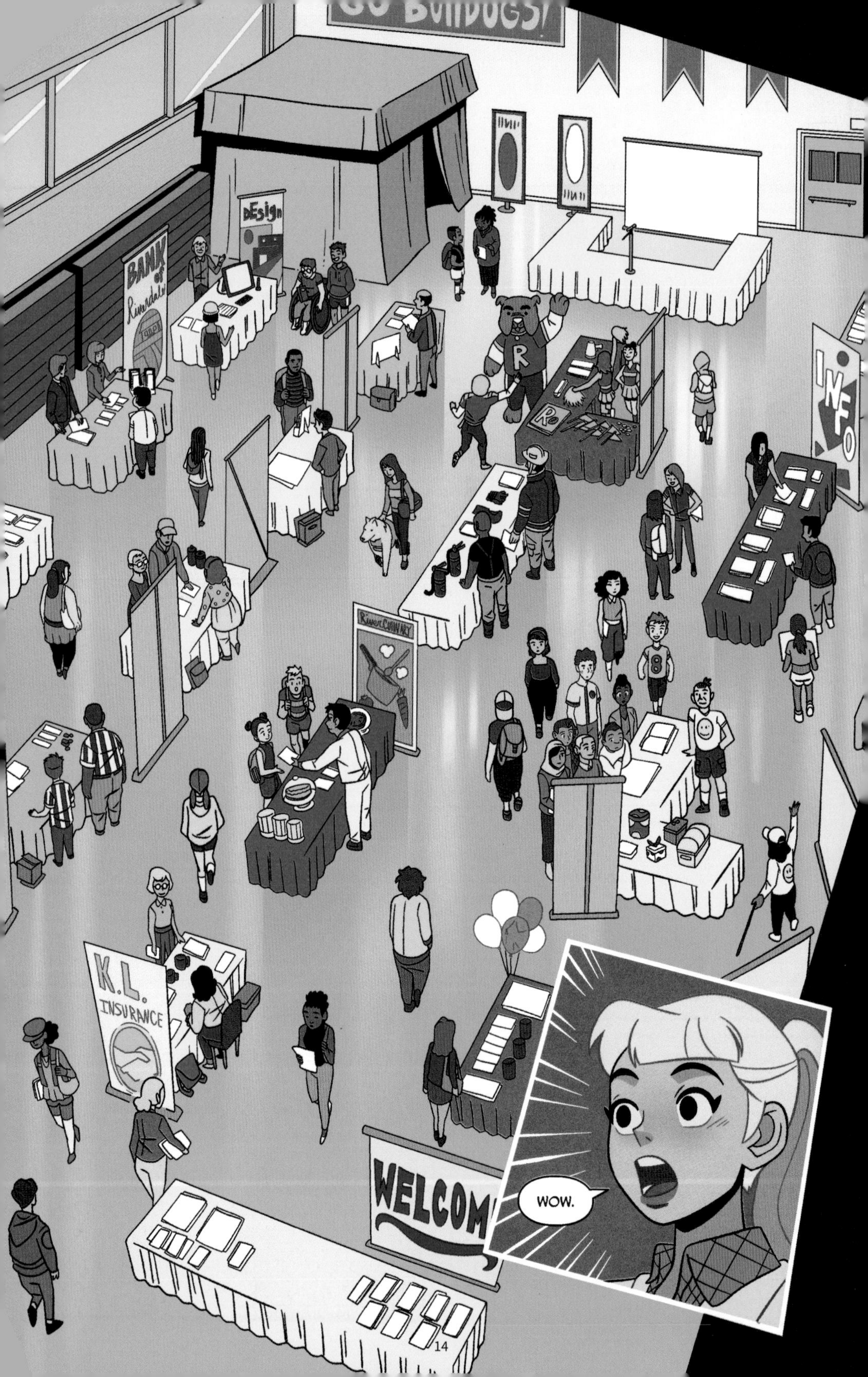
GO BULLDOGS!
DESign
BANK of Riverdale
INFO
River CULINARY
K.L. INSURANCE
WELCOM
WOW.

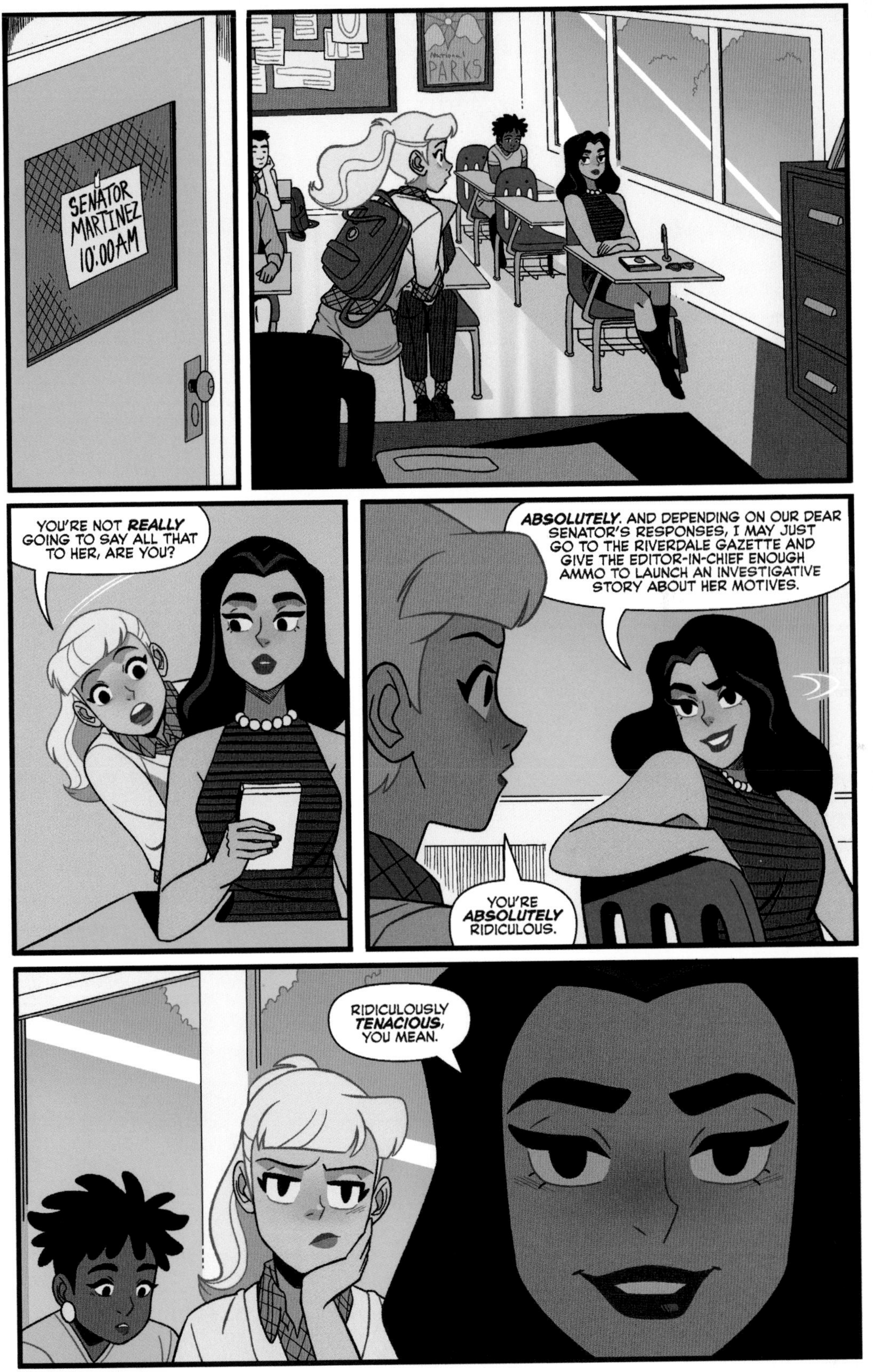
SENATOR MARTINEZ 10:00AM
National PARKS
YOU'RE NOT REALLY GOING TO SAY ALL THAT TO HER, ARE YOU?
ABSOLUTELY. AND DEPENDING ON OUR DEAR SENATOR'S RESPONSES, I MAY JUST GO TO THE RIVERDALE GAZETTE AND GIVE THE EDITOR-IN-CHIEF ENOUGH AMMO TO LAUNCH AN INVESTIGATIVE STORY ABOUT HER MOTIVES.
YOU'RE ABSOLUTELY RIDICULOUS.
RIDICULOUSLY TENACIOUS, YOU MEAN.

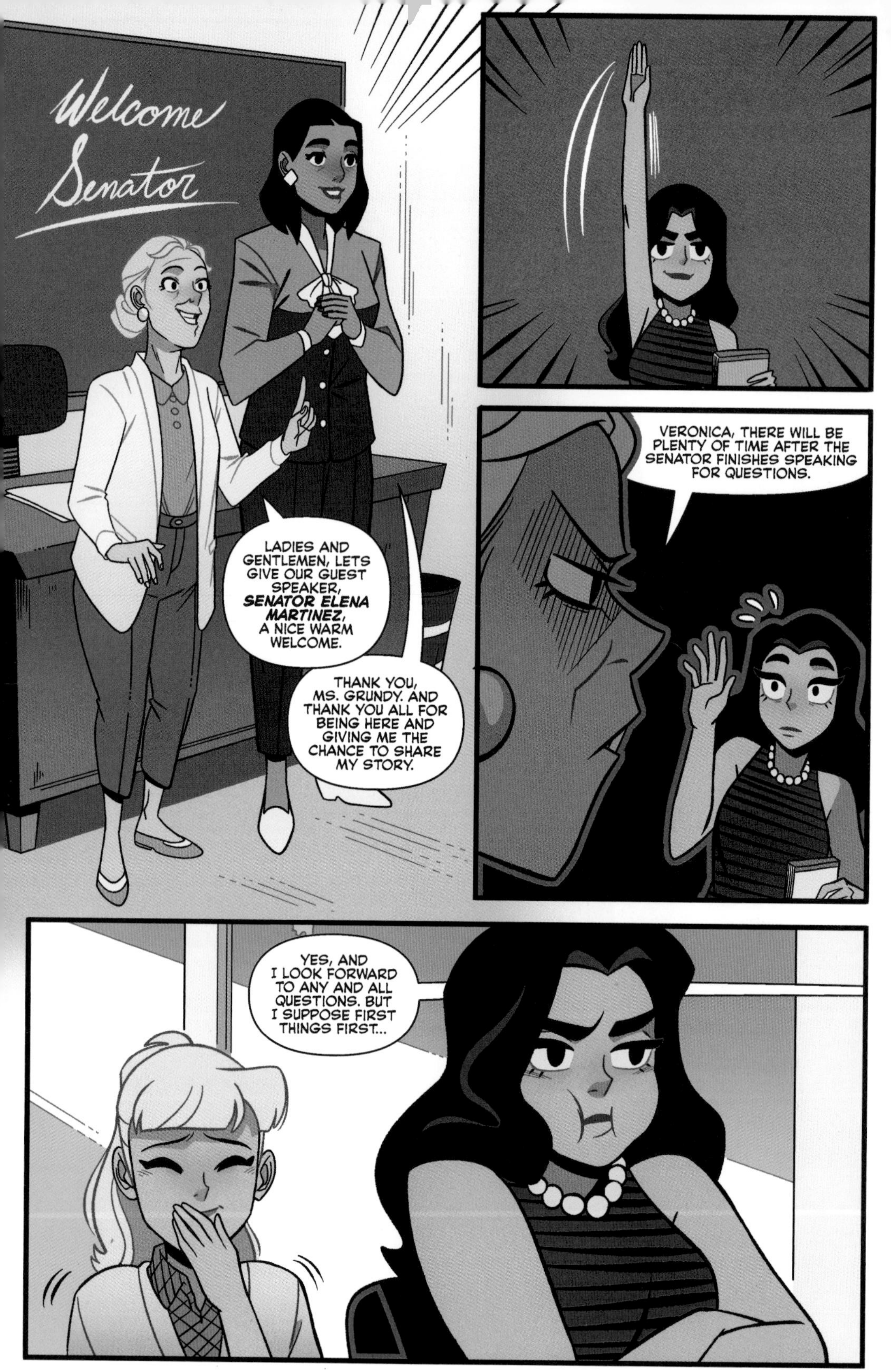
Welcome Senator
LADIES AND GENTLEMEN, LETS GIVE OUR GUEST SPEAKER, **SENATOR ELENA MARTINEZ**, A NICE WARM WELCOME.
THANK YOU, MS. GRUNDY. AND THANK YOU ALL FOR BEING HERE AND GIVING ME THE CHANCE TO SHARE MY STORY.
VERONICA, THERE WILL BE PLENTY OF TIME AFTER THE SENATOR FINISHES SPEAKING FOR QUESTIONS.
YES, AND I LOOK FORWARD TO ANY AND ALL QUESTIONS. BUT I SUPPOSE FIRST THINGS FIRST...

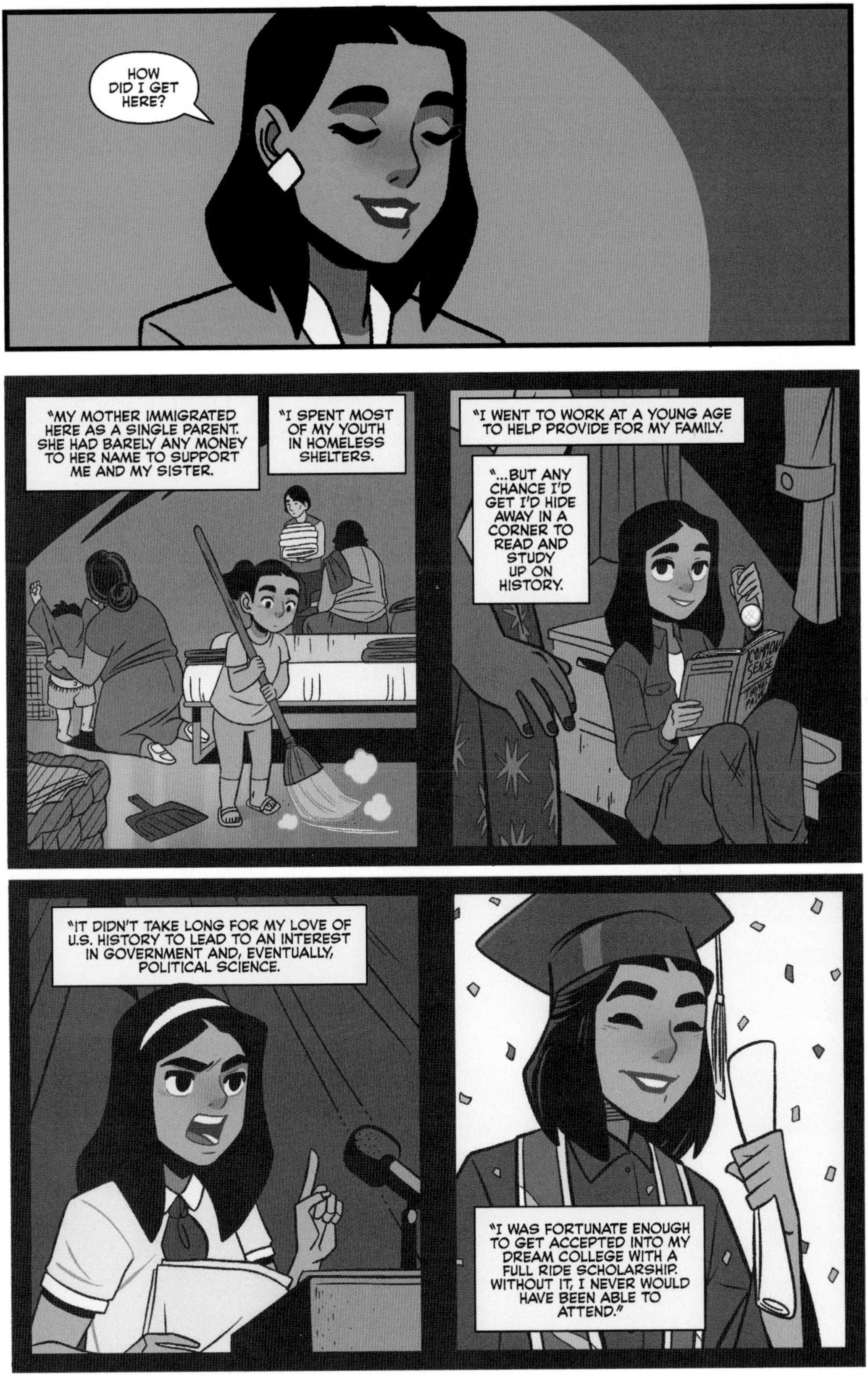
HOW DID I GET HERE?
"MY MOTHER IMMIGRATED HERE AS A SINGLE PARENT. SHE HAD BARELY ANY MONEY TO HER NAME TO SUPPORT ME AND MY SISTER.
"I SPENT MOST OF MY YOUTH IN HOMELESS SHELTERS.
"I WENT TO WORK AT A YOUNG AGE TO HELP PROVIDE FOR MY FAMILY.
"...BUT ANY CHANCE I'D GET I'D HIDE AWAY IN A CORNER TO READ AND STUDY UP ON HISTORY.
"IT DIDN'T TAKE LONG FOR MY LOVE OF U.S. HISTORY TO LEAD TO AN INTEREST IN GOVERNMENT AND, EVENTUALLY, POLITICAL SCIENCE.
"I WAS FORTUNATE ENOUGH TO GET ACCEPTED INTO MY DREAM COLLEGE WITH A FULL RIDE SCHOLARSHIP. WITHOUT IT, I NEVER WOULD HAVE BEEN ABLE TO ATTEND."

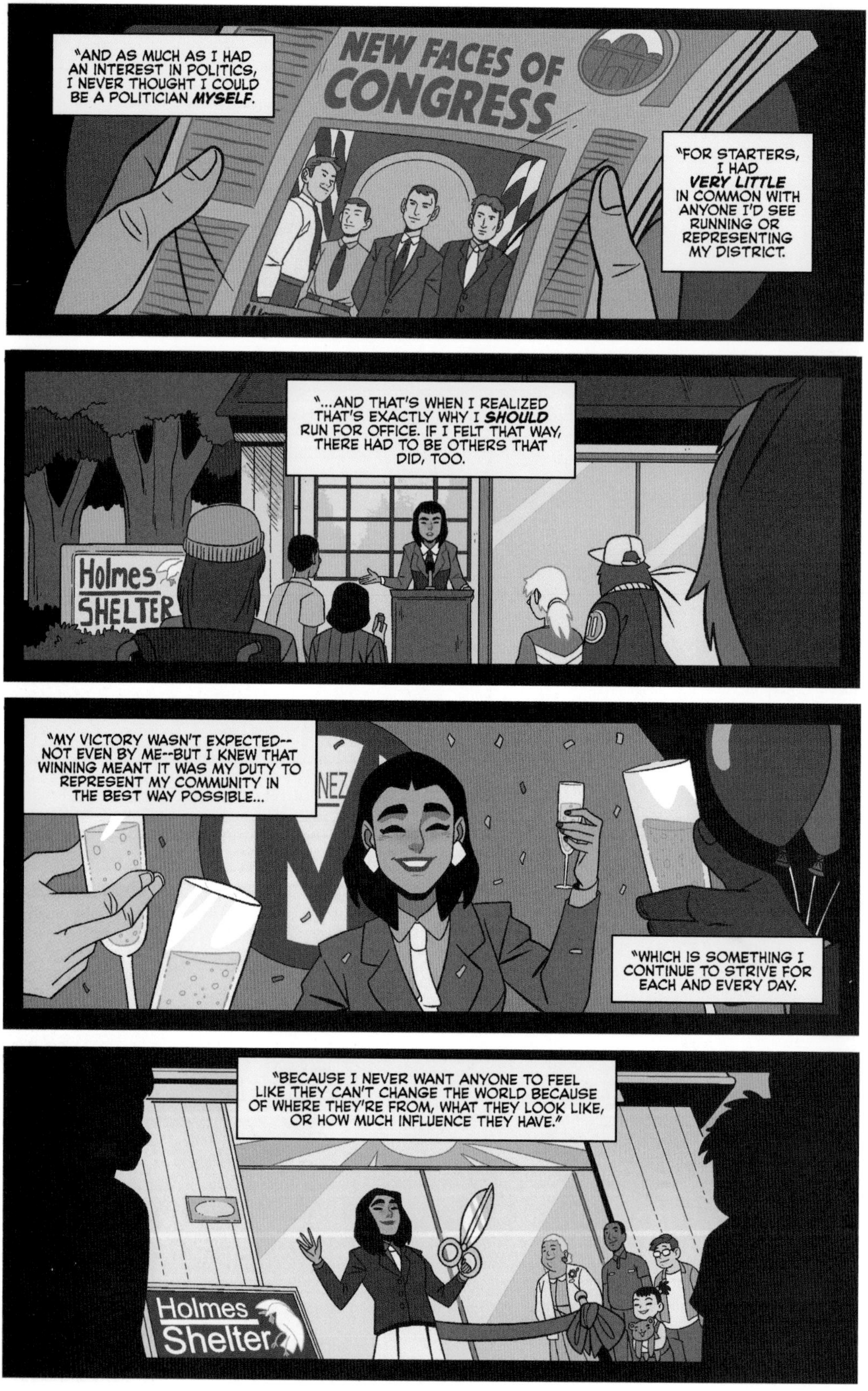
"AND AS MUCH AS I HAD AN INTEREST IN POLITICS, I NEVER THOUGHT I COULD BE A POLITICIAN *MYSELF*.
NEW FACES OF CONGRESS
"FOR STARTERS, I HAD *VERY LITTLE* IN COMMON WITH ANYONE I'D SEE RUNNING OR REPRESENTING MY DISTRICT.
"...AND THAT'S WHEN I REALIZED THAT'S EXACTLY WHY I *SHOULD* RUN FOR OFFICE. IF I FELT THAT WAY, THERE HAD TO BE OTHERS THAT DID, TOO.
Holmes SHELTER
"MY VICTORY WASN'T EXPECTED--NOT EVEN BY ME--BUT I KNEW THAT WINNING MEANT IT WAS MY DUTY TO REPRESENT MY COMMUNITY IN THE BEST WAY POSSIBLE...
"WHICH IS SOMETHING I CONTINUE TO STRIVE FOR EACH AND EVERY DAY.
"BECAUSE I NEVER WANT ANYONE TO FEEL LIKE THEY CAN'T CHANGE THE WORLD BECAUSE OF WHERE THEY'RE FROM, WHAT THEY LOOK LIKE, OR HOW MUCH INFLUENCE THEY HAVE."
Holmes Shelter

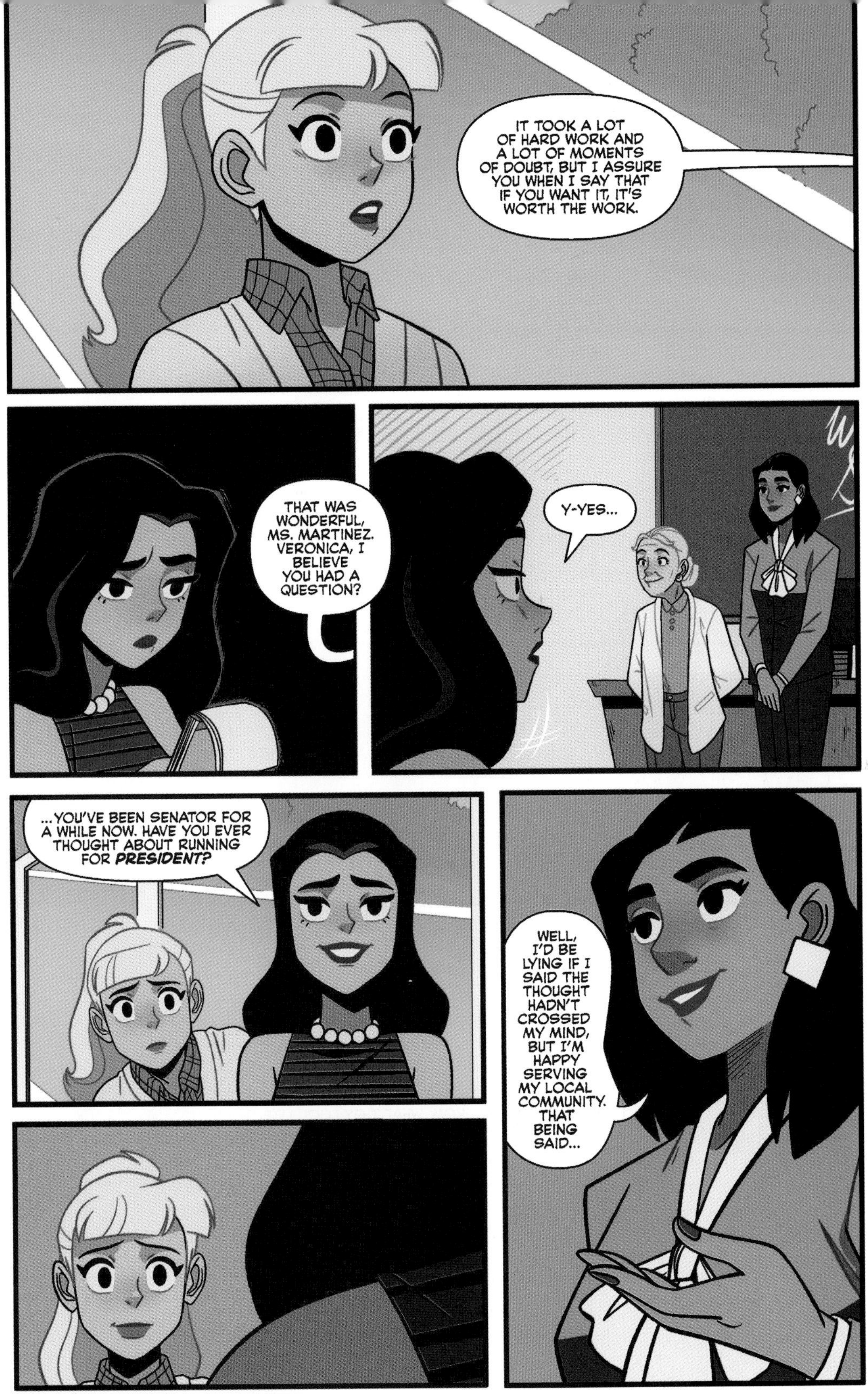
IT TOOK A LOT OF HARD WORK AND A LOT OF MOMENTS OF DOUBT, BUT I ASSURE YOU WHEN I SAY THAT IF YOU WANT IT, IT'S WORTH THE WORK.
THAT WAS WONDERFUL, MS. MARTINEZ. VERONICA, I BELIEVE YOU HAD A QUESTION?
Y-YES...
...YOU'VE BEEN SENATOR FOR A WHILE NOW. HAVE YOU EVER THOUGHT ABOUT RUNNING FOR ***PRESIDENT?***
WELL, I'D BE LYING IF I SAID THE THOUGHT HADN'T CROSSED MY MIND, BUT I'M HAPPY SERVING MY LOCAL COMMUNITY. THAT BEING SAID...

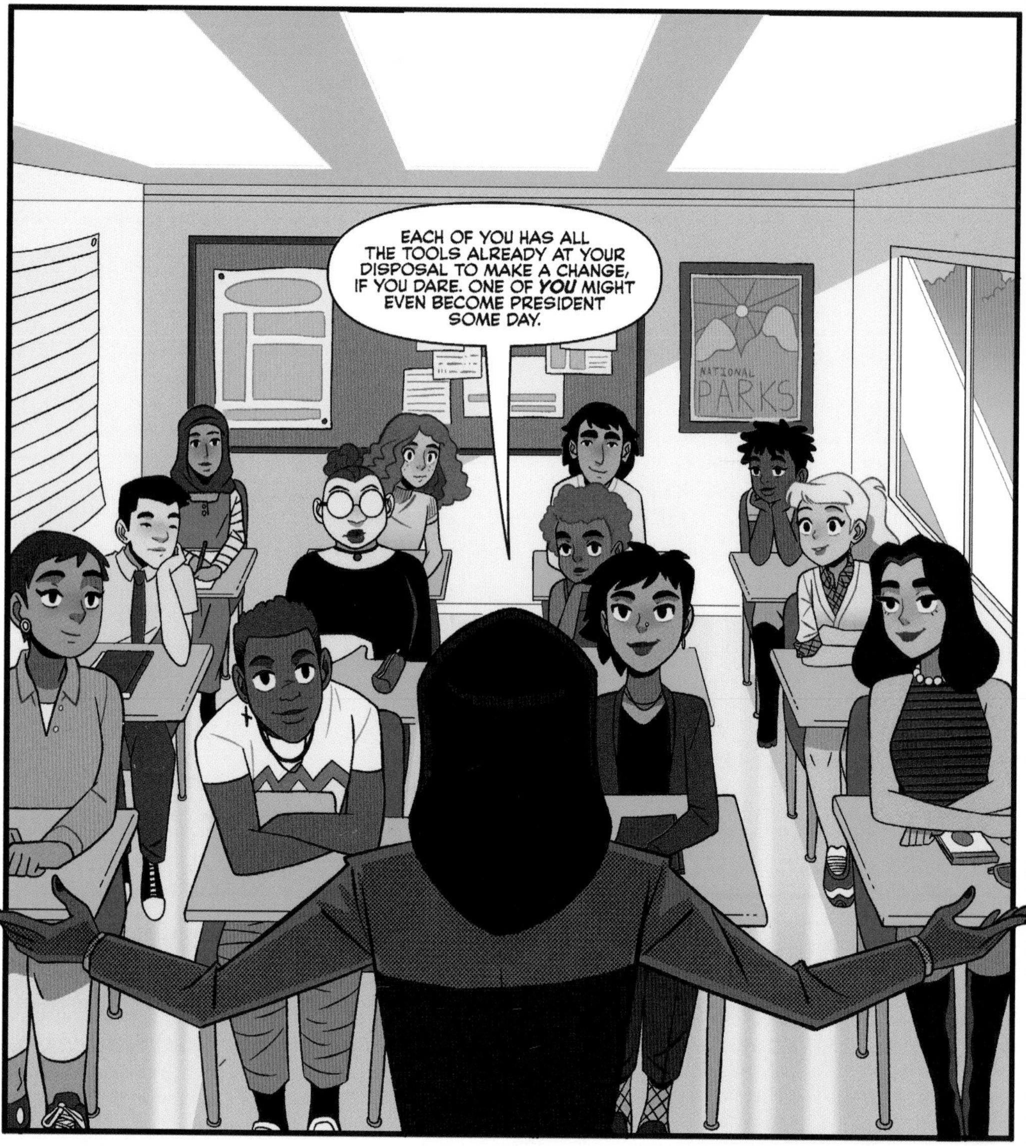
EACH OF YOU HAS ALL THE TOOLS ALREADY AT YOUR DISPOSAL TO MAKE A CHANGE, IF YOU DARE. ONE OF *YOU* MIGHT EVEN BECOME PRESIDENT SOME DAY.
NATIONAL PARKS

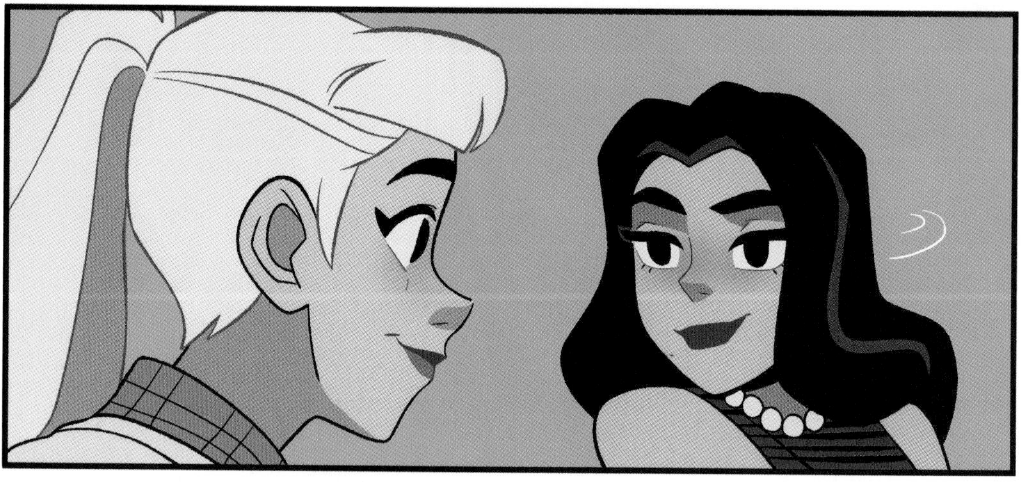

CHAPTER ONE

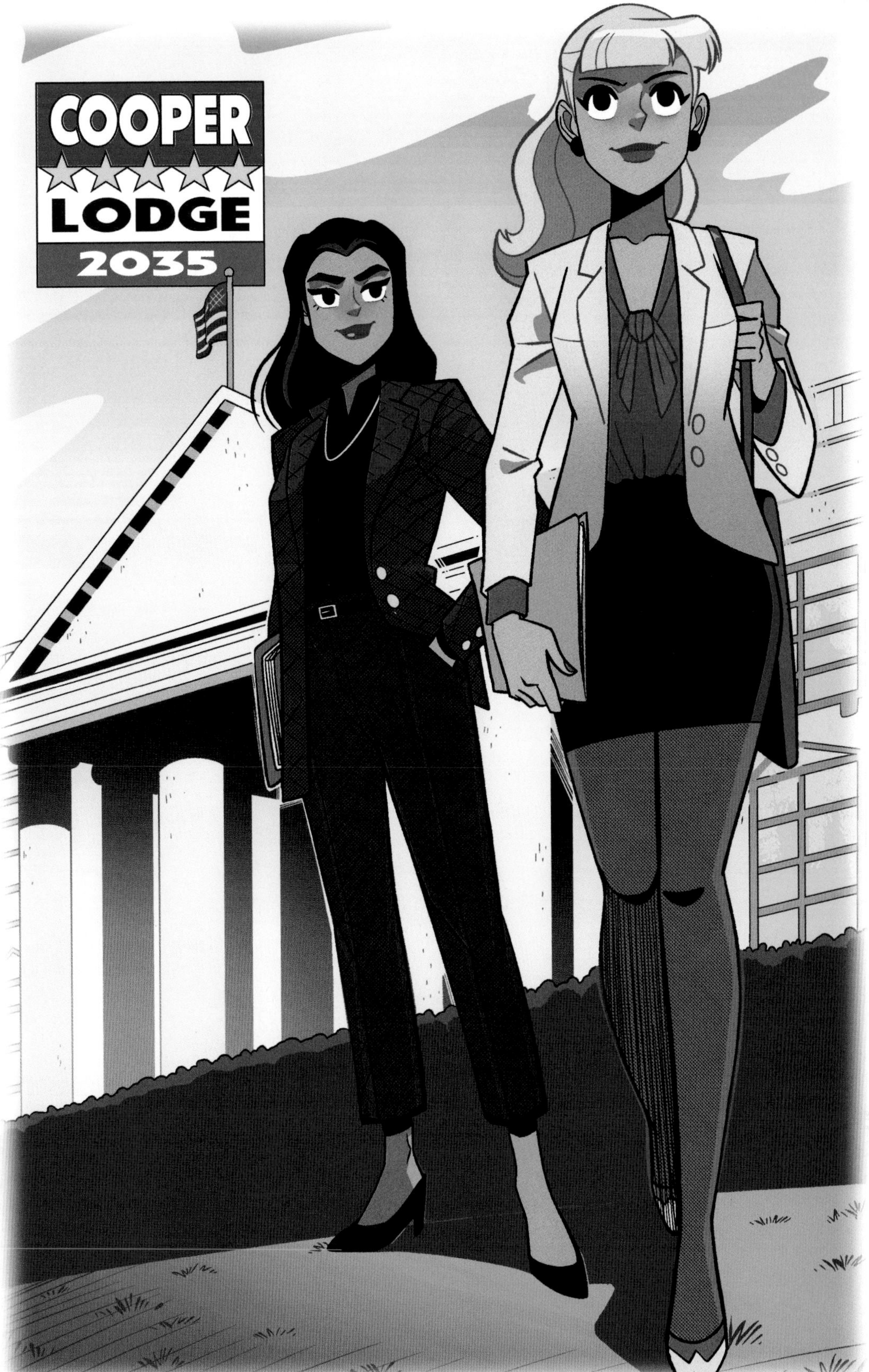
COOPER
LODGE
2035

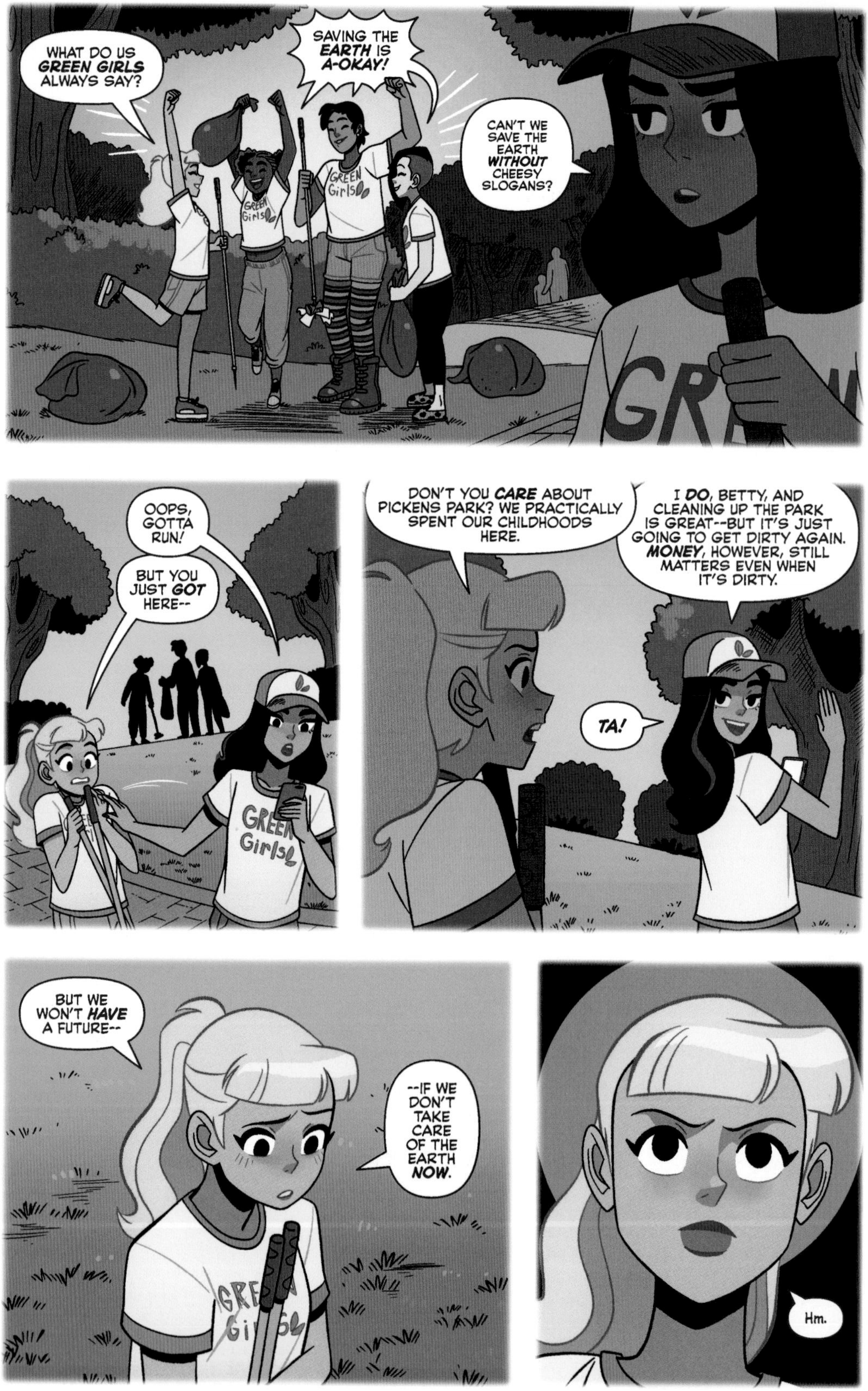
WHAT DO US GREEN GIRLS ALWAYS SAY?
SAVING THE EARTH IS A-OKAY!
CAN'T WE SAVE THE EARTH WITHOUT CHEESY SLOGANS?
OOPS, GOTTA RUN!
BUT YOU JUST GOT HERE--
DON'T YOU CARE ABOUT PICKENS PARK? WE PRACTICALLY SPENT OUR CHILDHOODS HERE.
I DO, BETTY, AND CLEANING UP THE PARK IS GREAT--BUT IT'S JUST GOING TO GET DIRTY AGAIN. MONEY, HOWEVER, STILL MATTERS EVEN WHEN IT'S DIRTY.
TA!
BUT WE WON'T HAVE A FUTURE--
--IF WE DON'T TAKE CARE OF THE EARTH NOW.
Hm.

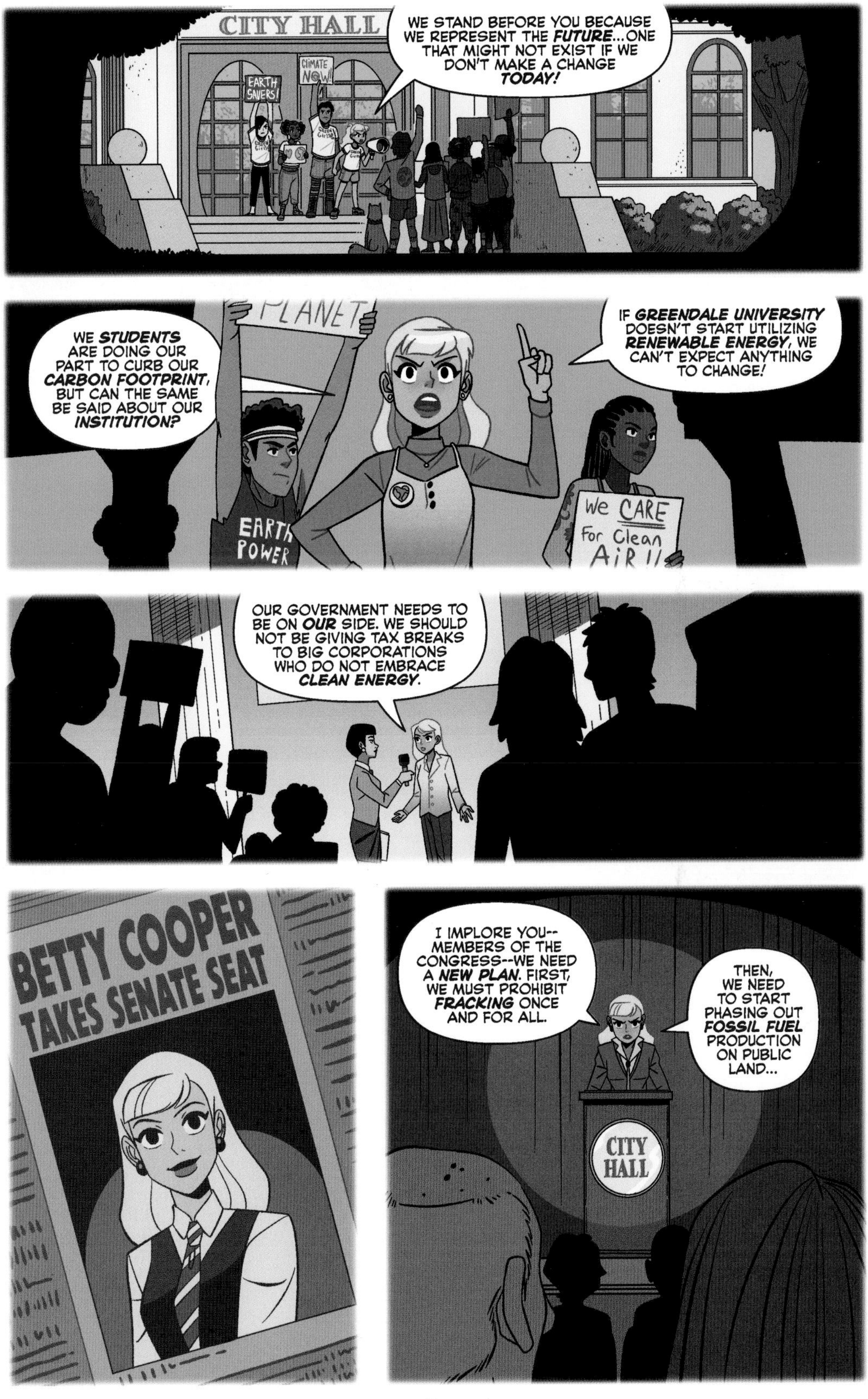
CITY HALL
EARTH SAVERS!
CLIMATE NOW!
WE STAND BEFORE YOU BECAUSE WE REPRESENT THE ***FUTURE***...ONE THAT MIGHT NOT EXIST IF WE DON'T MAKE A CHANGE ***TODAY!***
PLANET
WE ***STUDENTS*** ARE DOING OUR PART TO CURB OUR ***CARBON FOOTPRINT***, BUT CAN THE SAME BE SAID ABOUT OUR ***INSTITUTION?***
IF ***GREENDALE UNIVERSITY*** DOESN'T START UTILIZING ***RENEWABLE ENERGY***, WE CAN'T EXPECT ANYTHING TO CHANGE!
EARTH POWER
We CARE For Clean AiR !!
OUR GOVERNMENT NEEDS TO BE ON ***OUR*** SIDE. WE SHOULD NOT BE GIVING TAX BREAKS TO BIG CORPORATIONS WHO DO NOT EMBRACE ***CLEAN ENERGY***.
BETTY COOPER TAKES SENATE SEAT
I IMPLORE YOU-- MEMBERS OF THE CONGRESS--WE NEED A ***NEW PLAN***. FIRST, WE MUST PROHIBIT ***FRACKING*** ONCE AND FOR ALL.
THEN, WE NEED TO START PHASING OUT ***FOSSIL FUEL*** PRODUCTION ON PUBLIC LAND...
CITY HALL

YES, BERNARD? NO! **NO!** NO--DON'T TAKE THE PROFIT, I WANT THE **COMPOUNDING GROWTH!**

GREEN Girls?

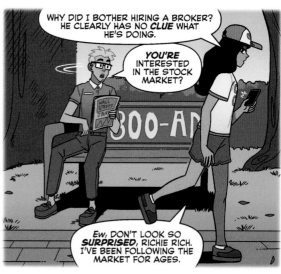

WHY DID I BOTHER HIRING A BROKER? HE CLEARLY HAS NO **CLUE** WHAT HE'S DOING.

YOU'RE INTERESTED IN THE STOCK MARKET?

WALL STREET TOUR

300-A

Ew, DON'T LOOK SO **SURPRISED,** RICHIE RICH. I'VE BEEN FOLLOWING THE MARKET FOR AGES.

THE NAME'S **LONNIE EASTERMAN**-- AND I THINK YOU MIGHT BE INTERESTED IN THIS.

WOW, IT HAS A WATERMARK AND EVERYTHING.

Young Business Professionals of Riverdale High

OKAY, FUTURE FINANCIAL GURUS, WHAT'S THE FIRST ORDER OF BUSINESS?

LOOKS LIKE **SOMEONE** GOT LOST ON HER WAY TO DRAMA CLUB.

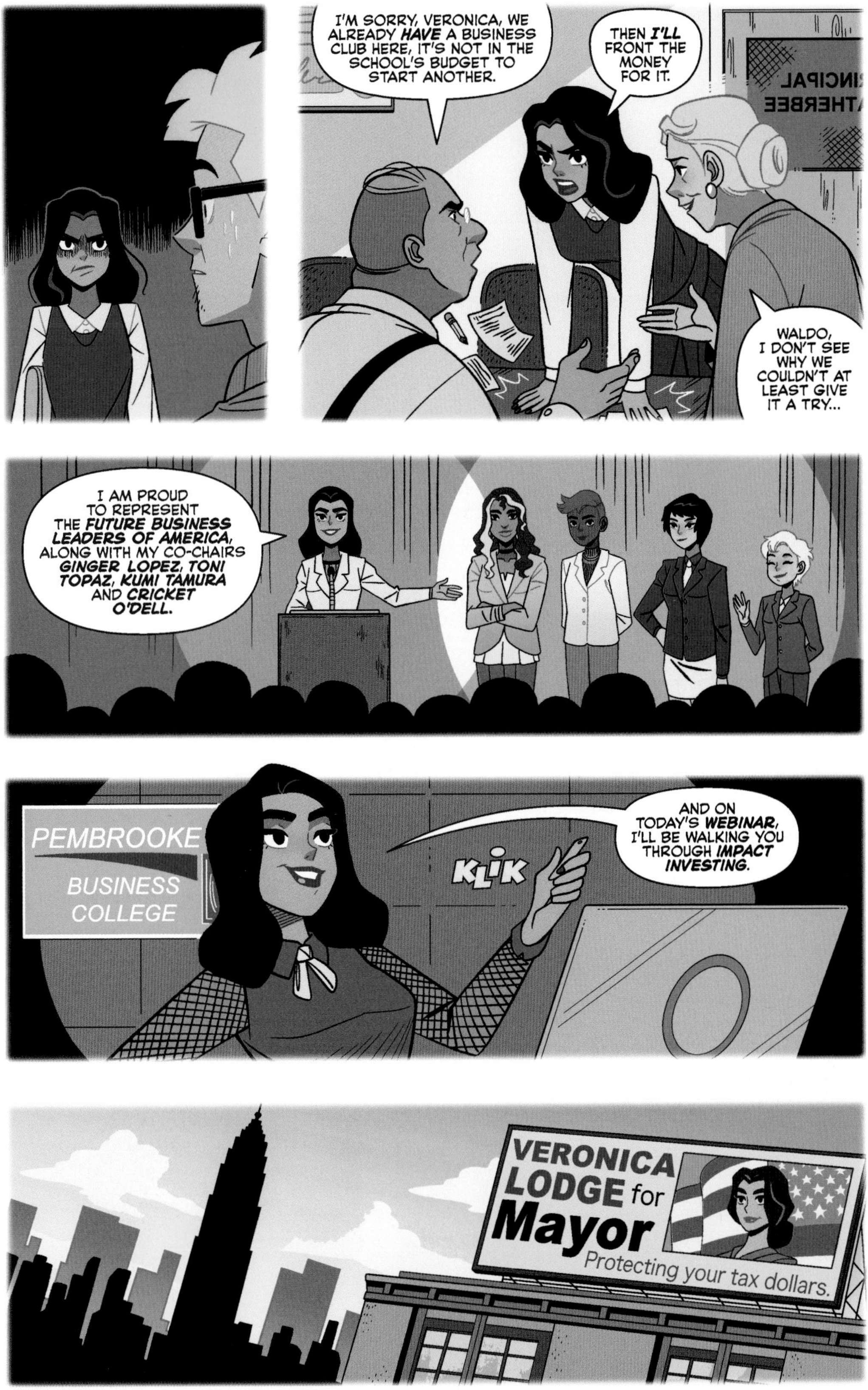
I'M SORRY, VERONICA, WE ALREADY HAVE A BUSINESS CLUB HERE, IT'S NOT IN THE SCHOOL'S BUDGET TO START ANOTHER.
THEN I'LL FRONT THE MONEY FOR IT.
RINCIPAL
ATHERBEE
WALDO, I DON'T SEE WHY WE COULDN'T AT LEAST GIVE IT A TRY...
I AM PROUD TO REPRESENT THE FUTURE BUSINESS LEADERS OF AMERICA, ALONG WITH MY CO-CHAIRS GINGER LOPEZ, TONI TOPAZ, KUMI TAMURA AND CRICKET O'DELL.
PEMBROOKE
BUSINESS COLLEGE
KLIK
AND ON TODAY'S WEBINAR, I'LL BE WALKING YOU THROUGH IMPACT INVESTING.
VERONICA LODGE for Mayor
Protecting your tax dollars.

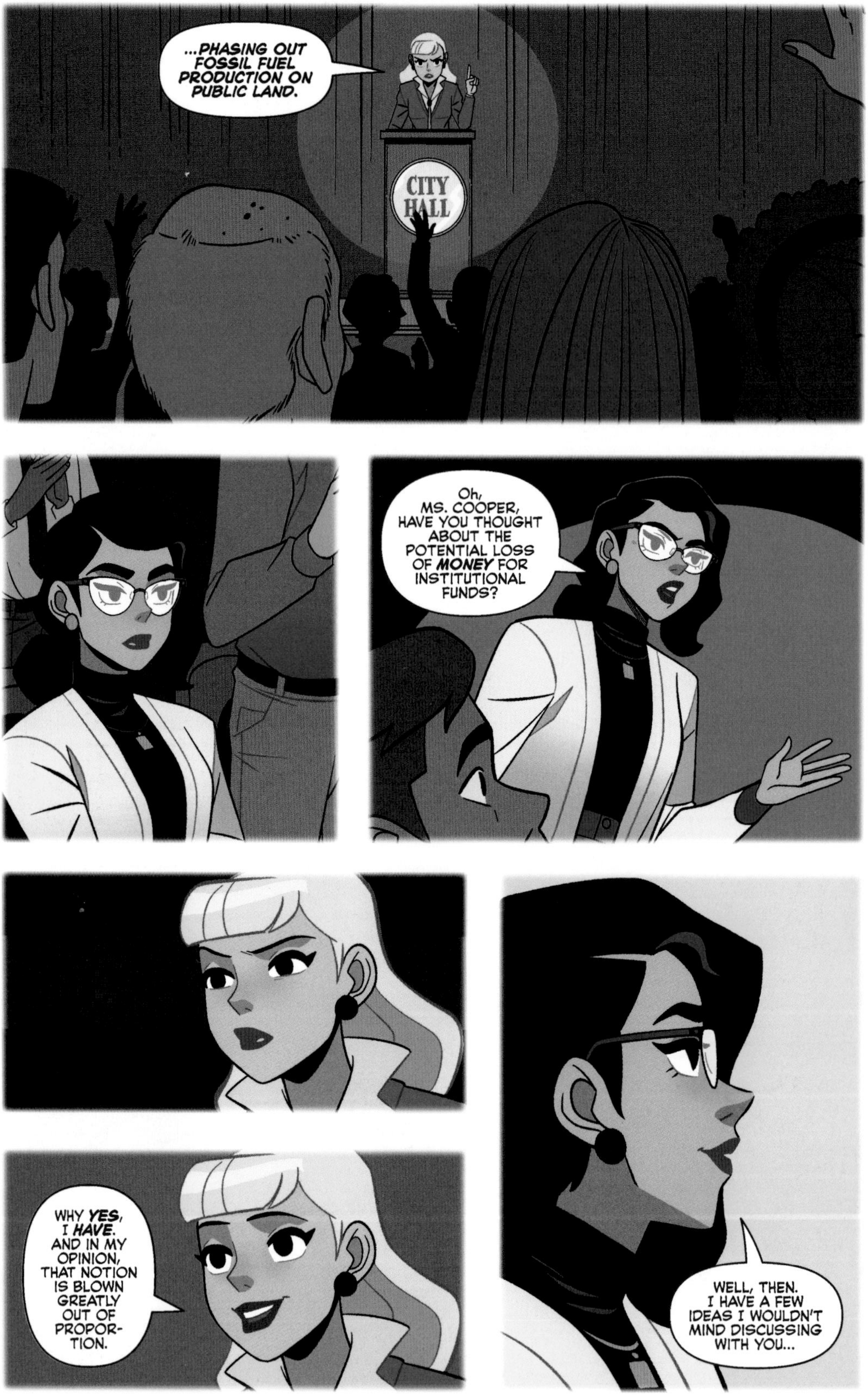
...PHASING OUT FOSSIL FUEL PRODUCTION ON PUBLIC LAND.
CITY HALL
Oh, MS. COOPER, HAVE YOU THOUGHT ABOUT THE POTENTIAL LOSS OF MONEY FOR INSTITUTIONAL FUNDS?
WHY YES, I HAVE. AND IN MY OPINION, THAT NOTION IS BLOWN GREATLY OUT OF PROPOR-TION.
WELL, THEN. I HAVE A FEW IDEAS I WOULDN'T MIND DISCUSSING WITH YOU...

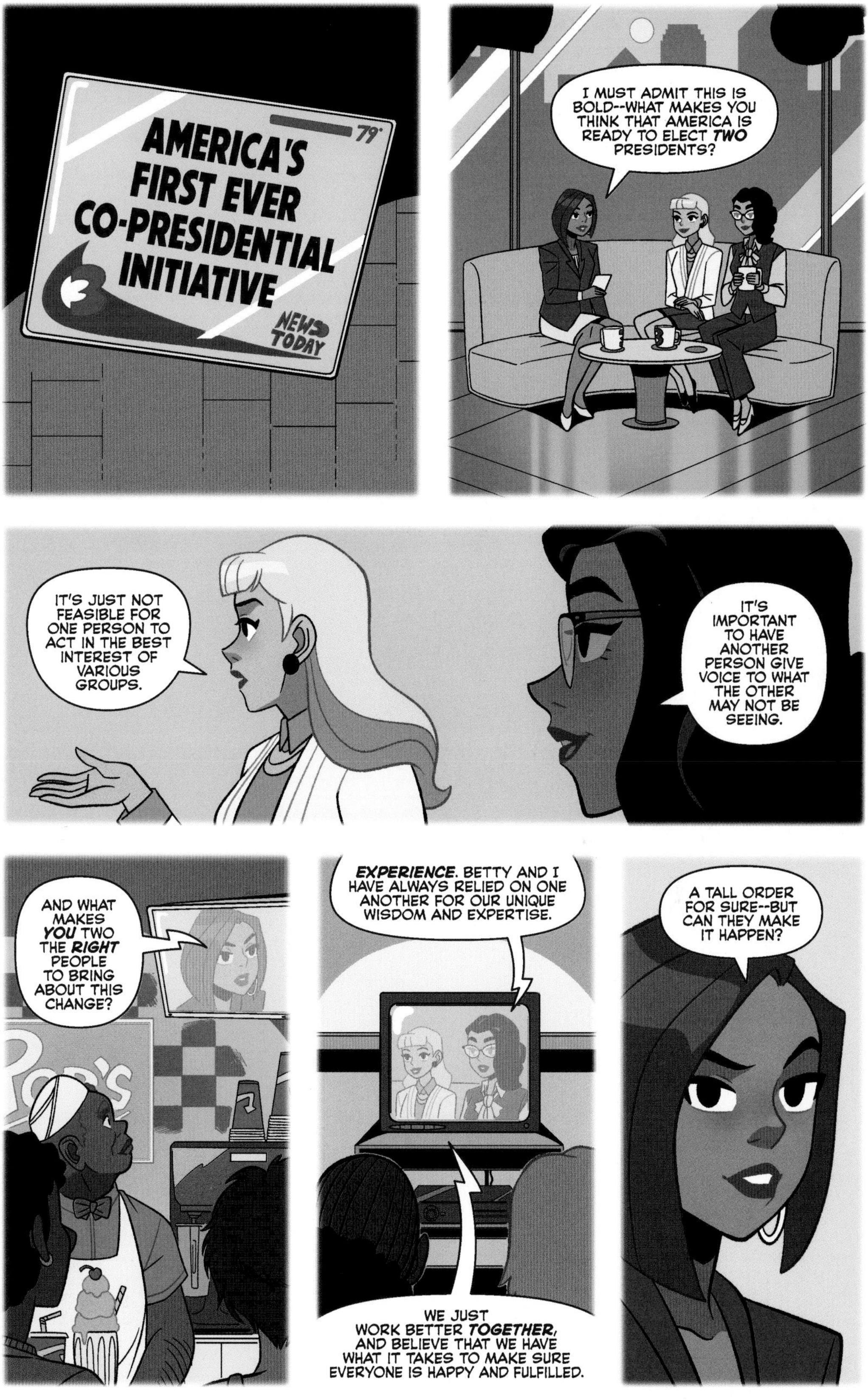
AMERICA'S FIRST EVER CO-PRESIDENTIAL INITIATIVE
79°
NEWS TODAY
I MUST ADMIT THIS IS BOLD--WHAT MAKES YOU THINK THAT AMERICA IS READY TO ELECT *TWO* PRESIDENTS?
IT'S JUST NOT FEASIBLE FOR ONE PERSON TO ACT IN THE BEST INTEREST OF VARIOUS GROUPS.
IT'S IMPORTANT TO HAVE ANOTHER PERSON GIVE VOICE TO WHAT THE OTHER MAY NOT BE SEEING.
AND WHAT MAKES *YOU* TWO THE *RIGHT* PEOPLE TO BRING ABOUT THIS CHANGE?
EXPERIENCE. BETTY AND I HAVE ALWAYS RELIED ON ONE ANOTHER FOR OUR UNIQUE WISDOM AND EXPERTISE.
WE JUST WORK BETTER *TOGETHER*, AND BELIEVE THAT WE HAVE WHAT IT TAKES TO MAKE SURE EVERYONE IS HAPPY AND FULFILLED.
A TALL ORDER FOR SURE--BUT CAN THEY MAKE IT HAPPEN?

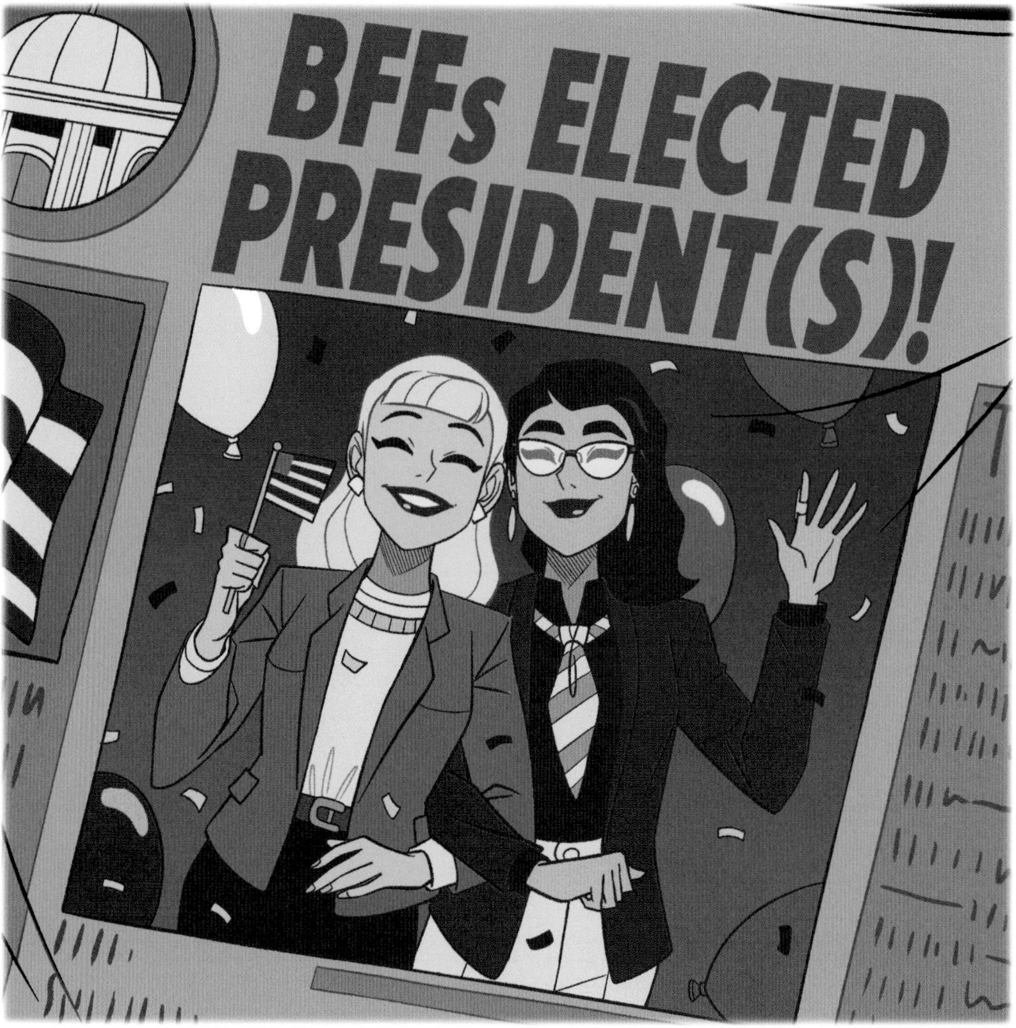
BFFs ELECTED PRESIDENT(S)!

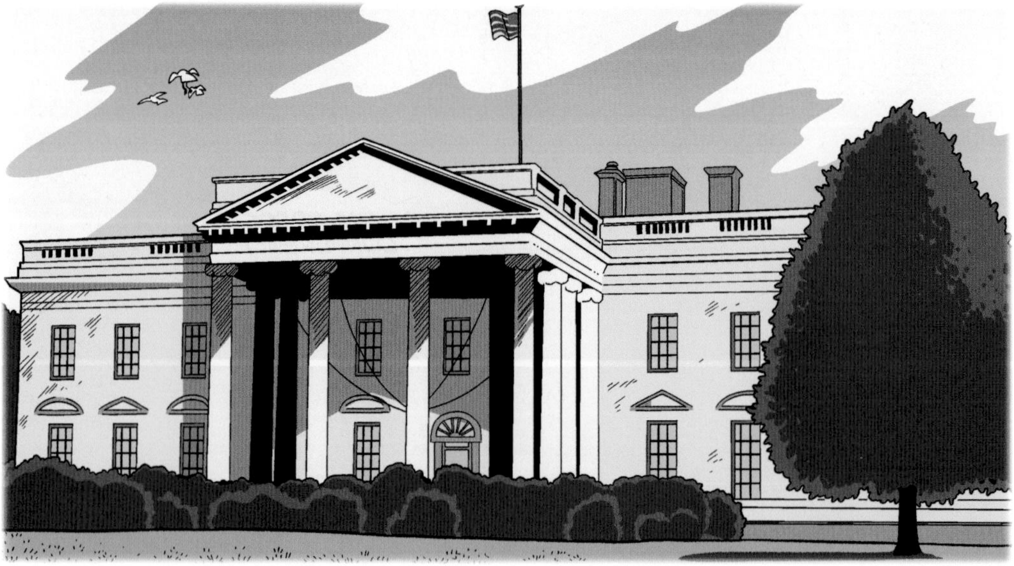

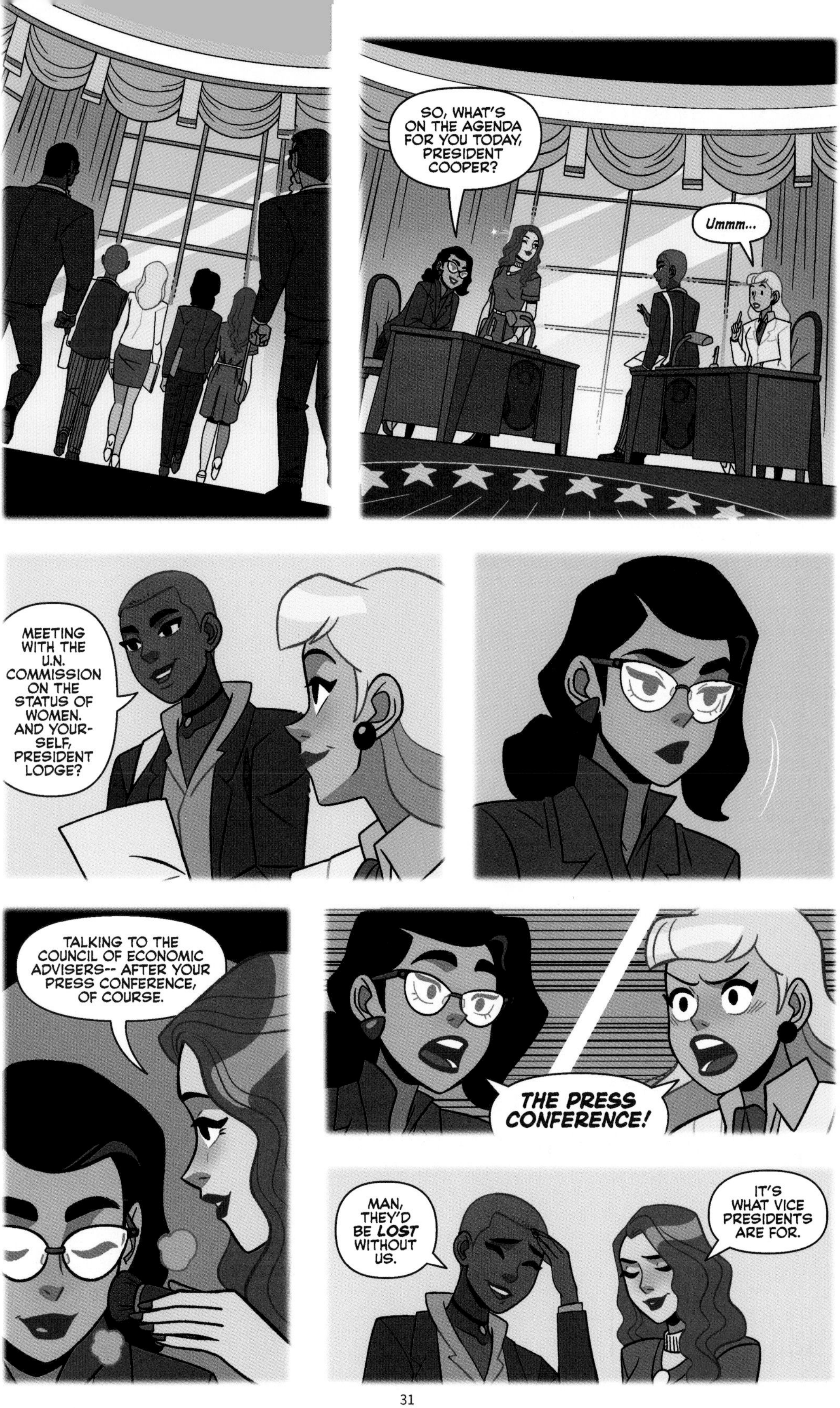
SO, WHAT'S ON THE AGENDA FOR YOU TODAY, PRESIDENT COOPER?
Ummm...
MEETING WITH THE U.N. COMMISSION ON THE STATUS OF WOMEN. AND YOURSELF, PRESIDENT LODGE?
TALKING TO THE COUNCIL OF ECONOMIC ADVISERS-- AFTER YOUR PRESS CONFERENCE, OF COURSE.
THE PRESS CONFERENCE!
MAN, THEY'D BE LOST WITHOUT US.
IT'S WHAT VICE PRESIDENTS ARE FOR.

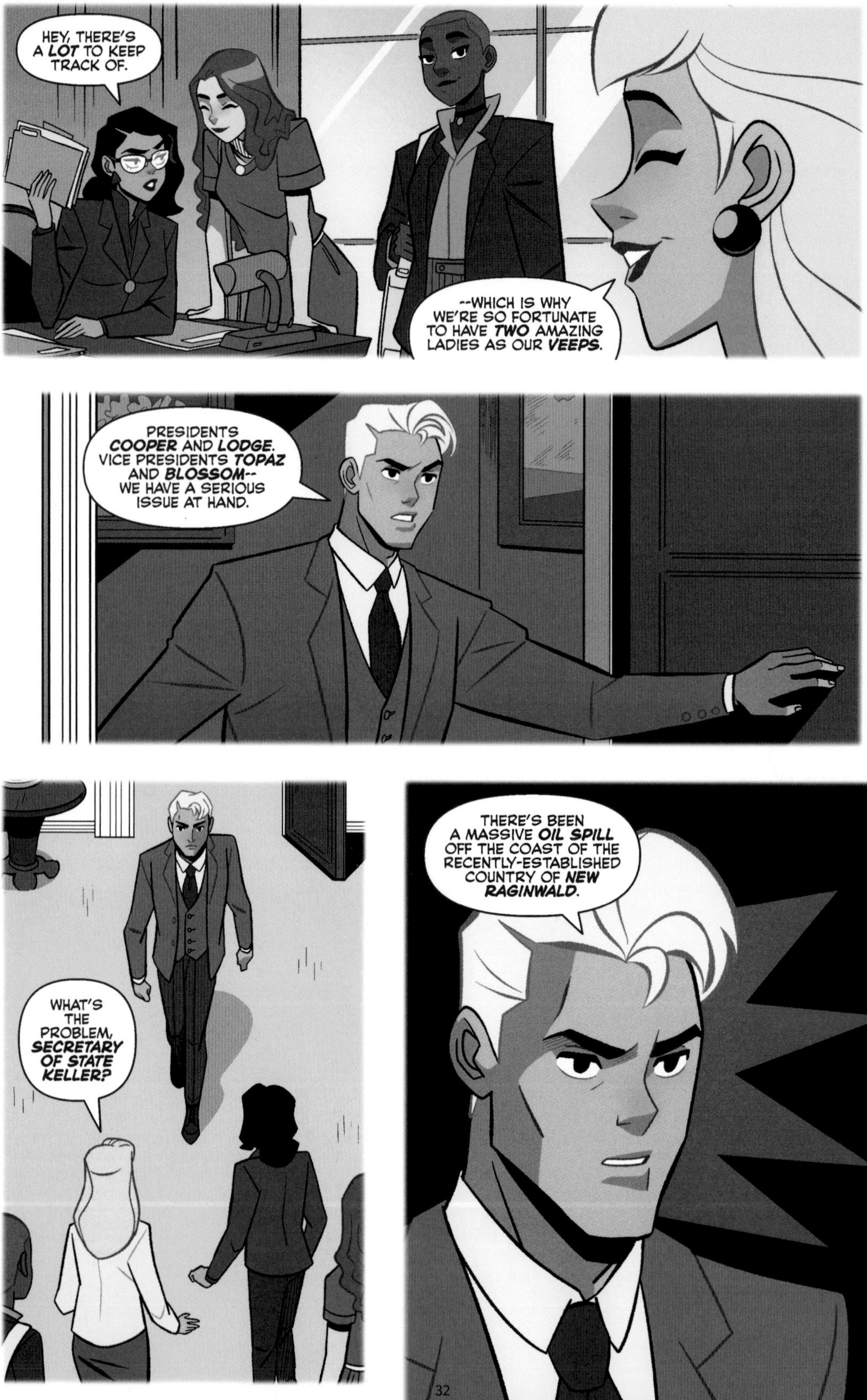
HEY, THERE'S A LOT TO KEEP TRACK OF.
--WHICH IS WHY WE'RE SO FORTUNATE TO HAVE TWO AMAZING LADIES AS OUR VEEPS.
PRESIDENTS COOPER AND LODGE. VICE PRESIDENTS TOPAZ AND BLOSSOM-- WE HAVE A SERIOUS ISSUE AT HAND.
WHAT'S THE PROBLEM, SECRETARY OF STATE KELLER?
THERE'S BEEN A MASSIVE OIL SPILL OFF THE COAST OF THE RECENTLY-ESTABLISHED COUNTRY OF NEW RAGINWALD.

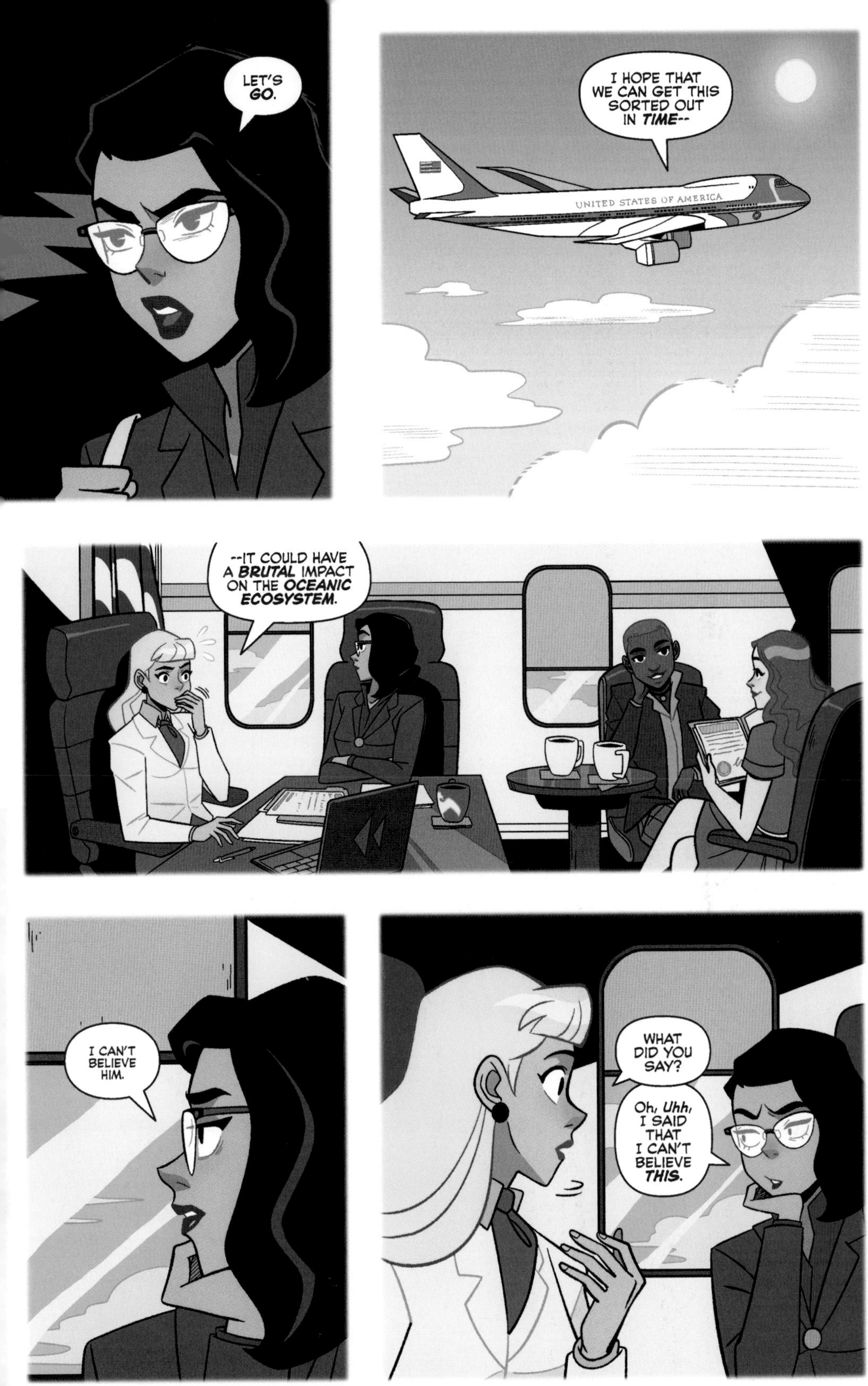
LET'S GO.
I HOPE THAT WE CAN GET THIS SORTED OUT IN TIME--
UNITED STATES OF AMERICA
--IT COULD HAVE A BRUTAL IMPACT ON THE OCEANIC ECOSYSTEM.
I CAN'T BELIEVE HIM.
WHAT DID YOU SAY?
Oh, Uhh, I SAID THAT I CAN'T BELIEVE THIS.

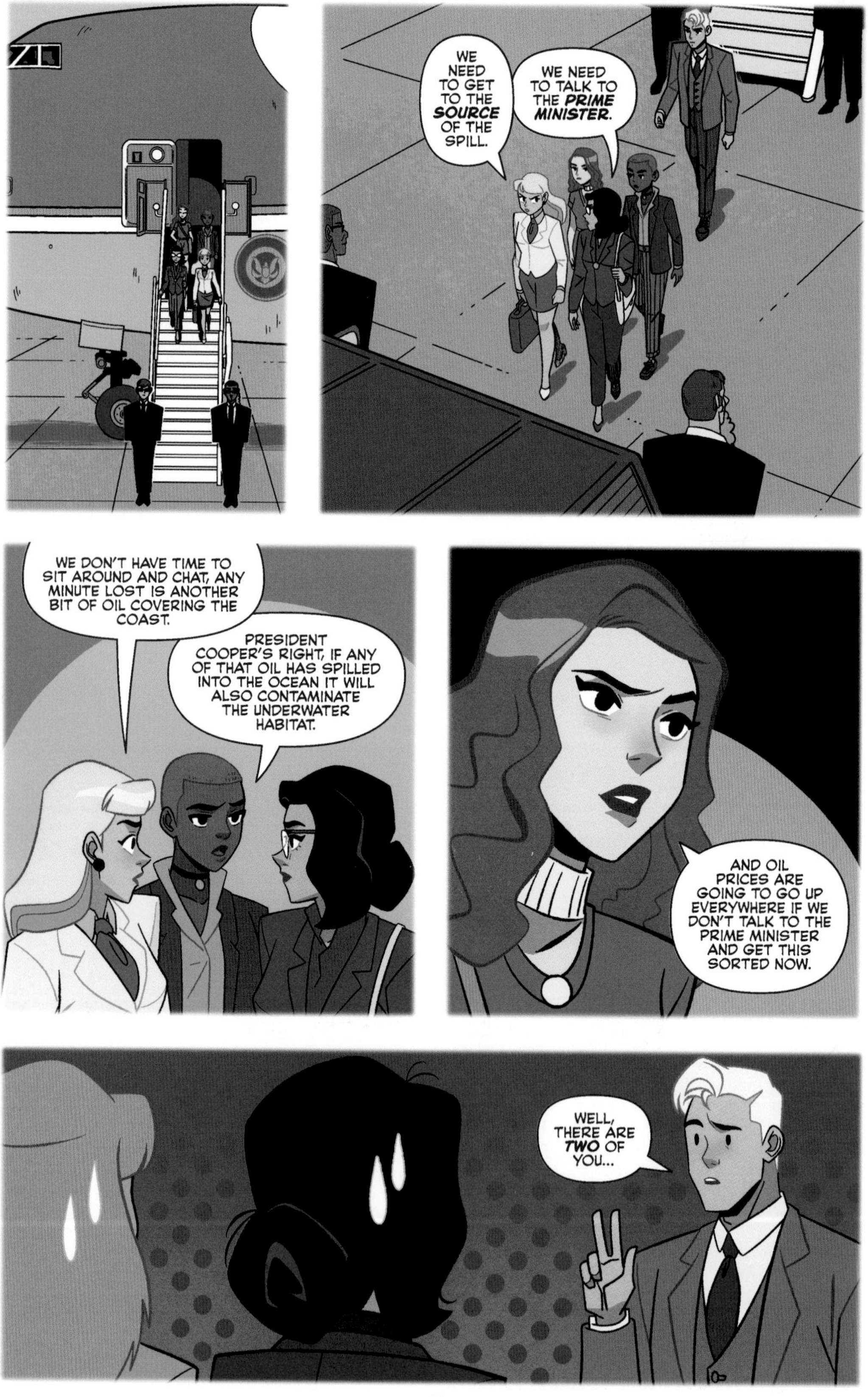

WE NEED TO GET TO THE **SOURCE** OF THE SPILL.
WE NEED TO TALK TO THE ***PRIME MINISTER***.
WE DON'T HAVE TIME TO SIT AROUND AND CHAT, ANY MINUTE LOST IS ANOTHER BIT OF OIL COVERING THE COAST.
PRESIDENT COOPER'S RIGHT, IF ANY OF THAT OIL HAS SPILLED INTO THE OCEAN IT WILL ALSO CONTAMINATE THE UNDERWATER HABITAT.
AND OIL PRICES ARE GOING TO GO UP EVERYWHERE IF WE DON'T TALK TO THE PRIME MINISTER AND GET THIS SORTED NOW.
WELL, THERE ARE ***TWO*** OF YOU...

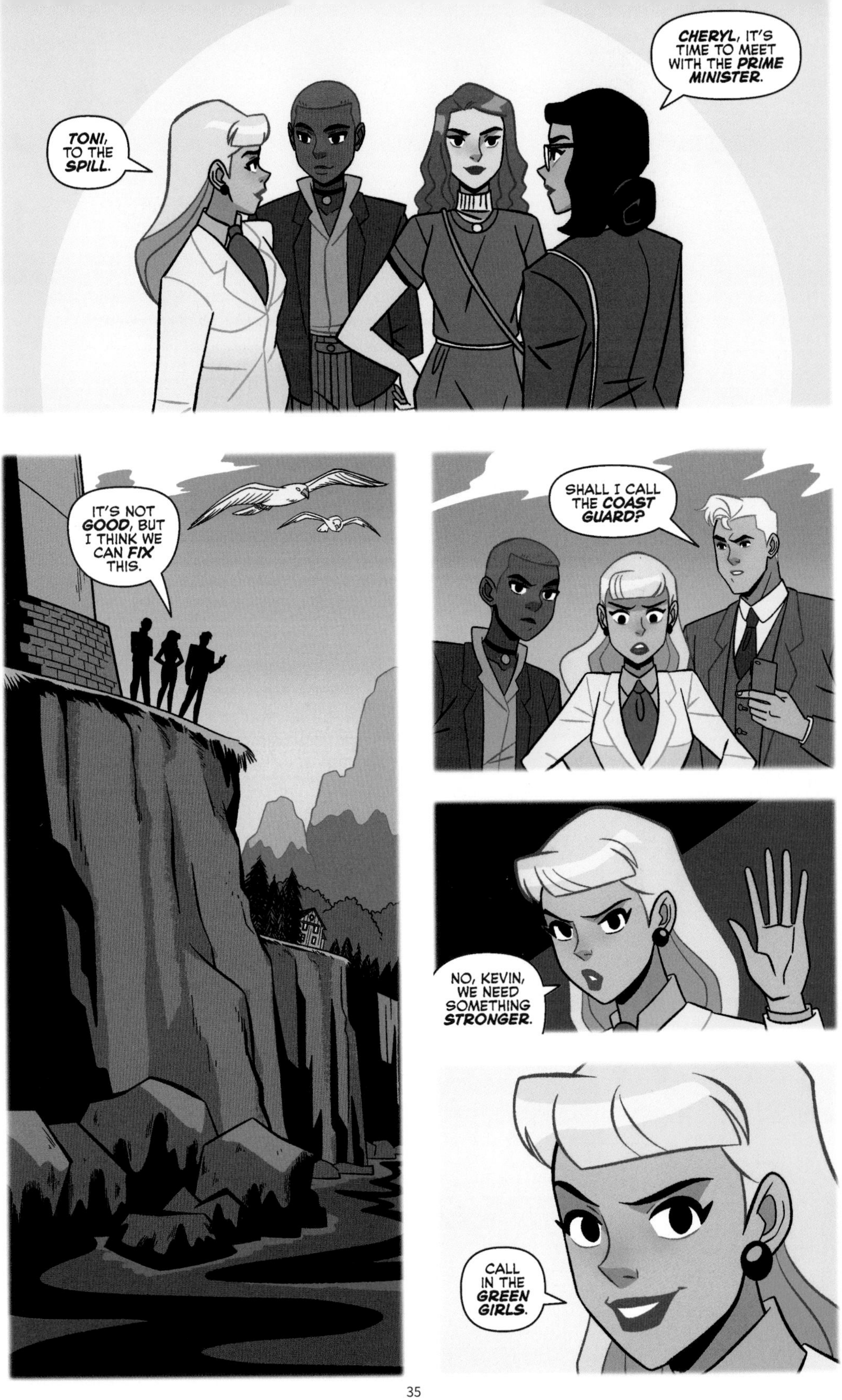
TONI, TO THE SPILL.
CHERYL, IT'S TIME TO MEET WITH THE PRIME MINISTER.
IT'S NOT GOOD, BUT I THINK WE CAN FIX THIS.
SHALL I CALL THE COAST GUARD?
NO, KEVIN, WE NEED SOMETHING STRONGER.
CALL IN THE GREEN GIRLS.

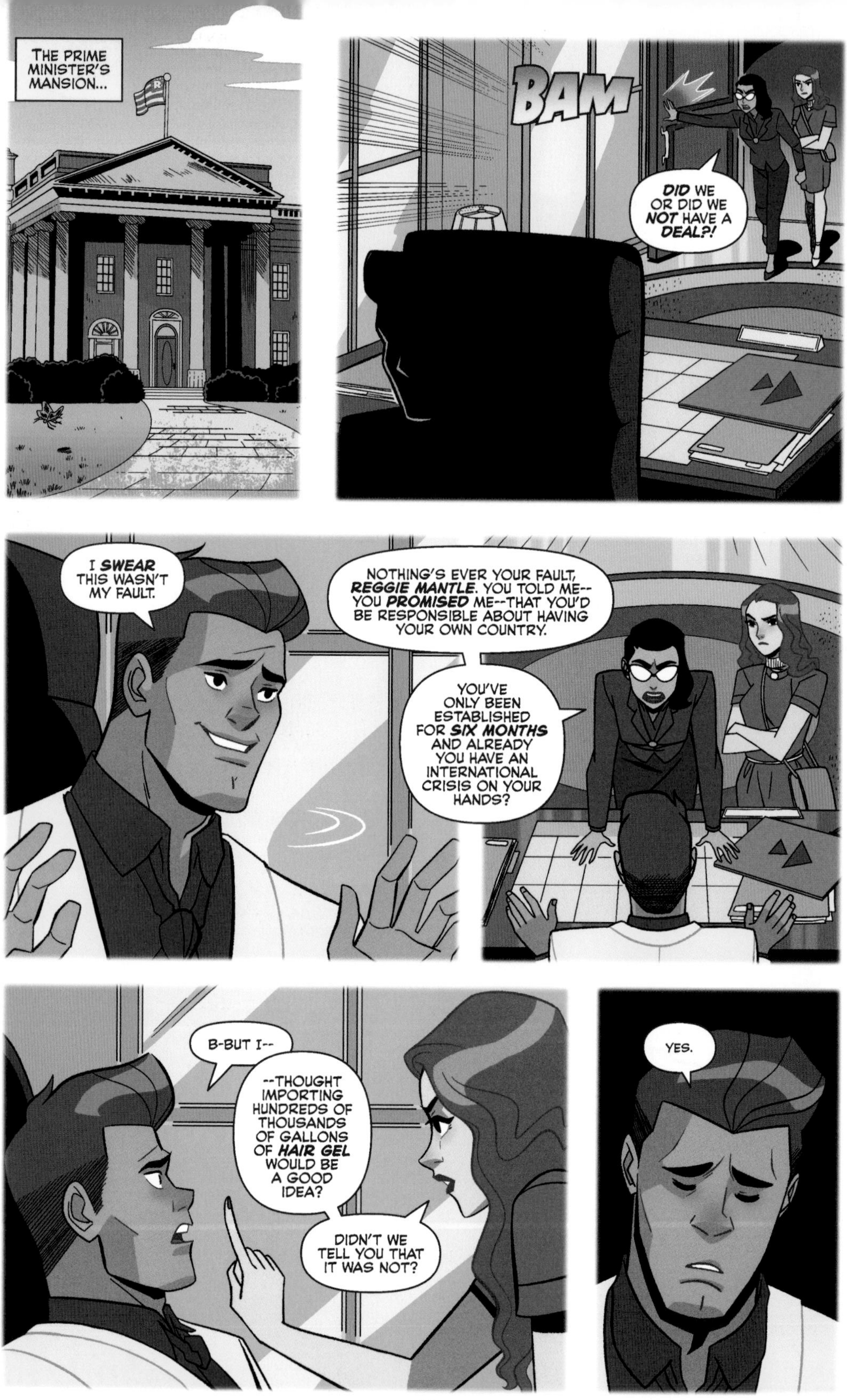
THE PRIME MINISTER'S MANSION...
BAM
DID WE OR DID WE NOT HAVE A DEAL?!
I SWEAR THIS WASN'T MY FAULT.
NOTHING'S EVER YOUR FAULT, REGGIE MANTLE. YOU TOLD ME--YOU PROMISED ME--THAT YOU'D BE RESPONSIBLE ABOUT HAVING YOUR OWN COUNTRY.
YOU'VE ONLY BEEN ESTABLISHED FOR SIX MONTHS AND ALREADY YOU HAVE AN INTERNATIONAL CRISIS ON YOUR HANDS?
B-BUT I--
--THOUGHT IMPORTING HUNDREDS OF THOUSANDS OF GALLONS OF HAIR GEL WOULD BE A GOOD IDEA?
DIDN'T WE TELL YOU THAT IT WAS NOT?
YES.

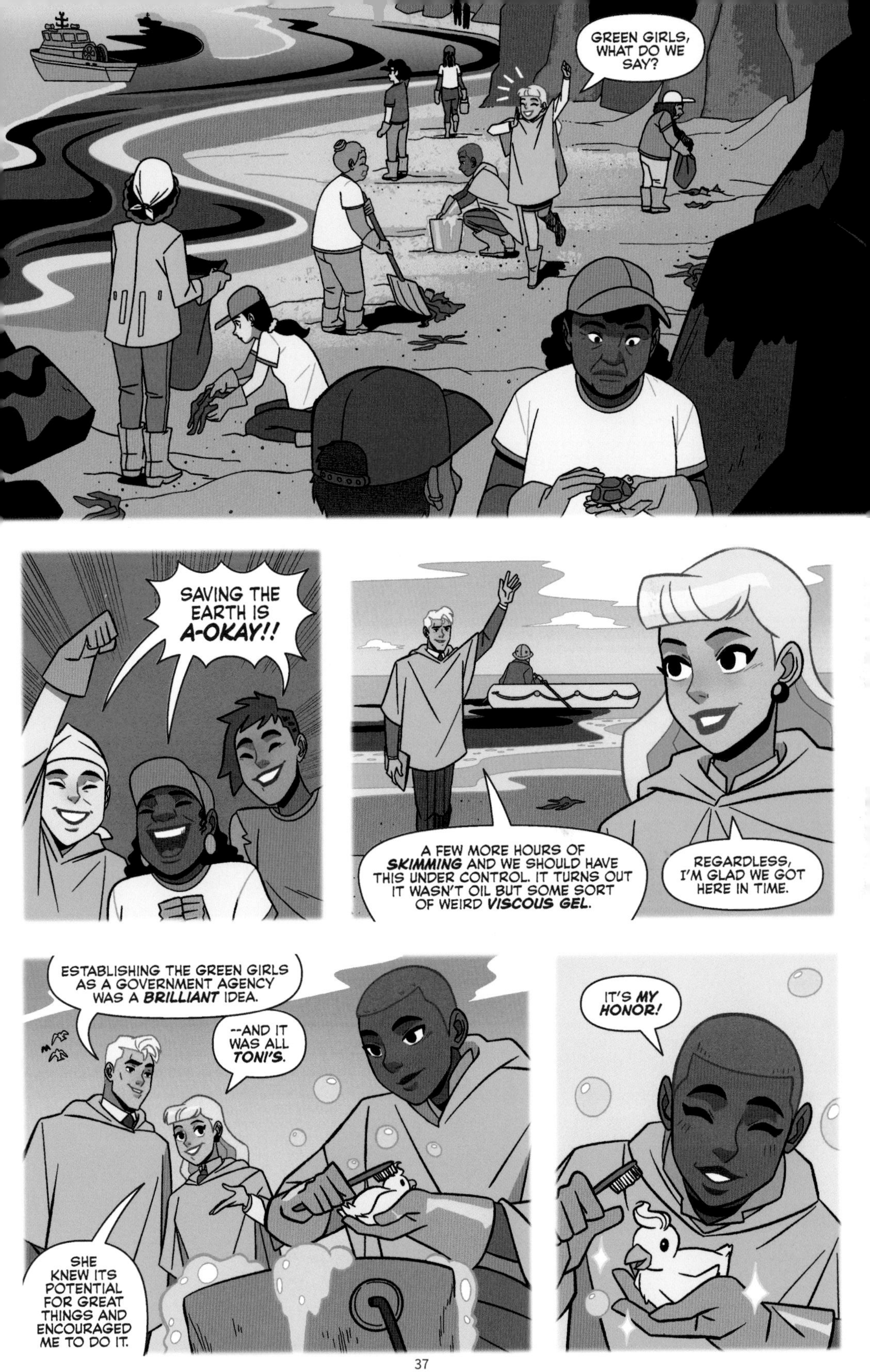

GREEN GIRLS, WHAT DO WE SAY?
SAVING THE EARTH IS **A-OKAY!!**
A FEW MORE HOURS OF **SKIMMING** AND WE SHOULD HAVE THIS UNDER CONTROL. IT TURNS OUT IT WASN'T OIL BUT SOME SORT OF WEIRD **VISCOUS GEL**.
REGARDLESS, I'M GLAD WE GOT HERE IN TIME.
ESTABLISHING THE GREEN GIRLS AS A GOVERNMENT AGENCY WAS A **BRILLIANT** IDEA.
--AND IT WAS ALL **TONI'S**.
SHE KNEW ITS POTENTIAL FOR GREAT THINGS AND ENCOURAGED ME TO DO IT.
IT'S **MY HONOR!**

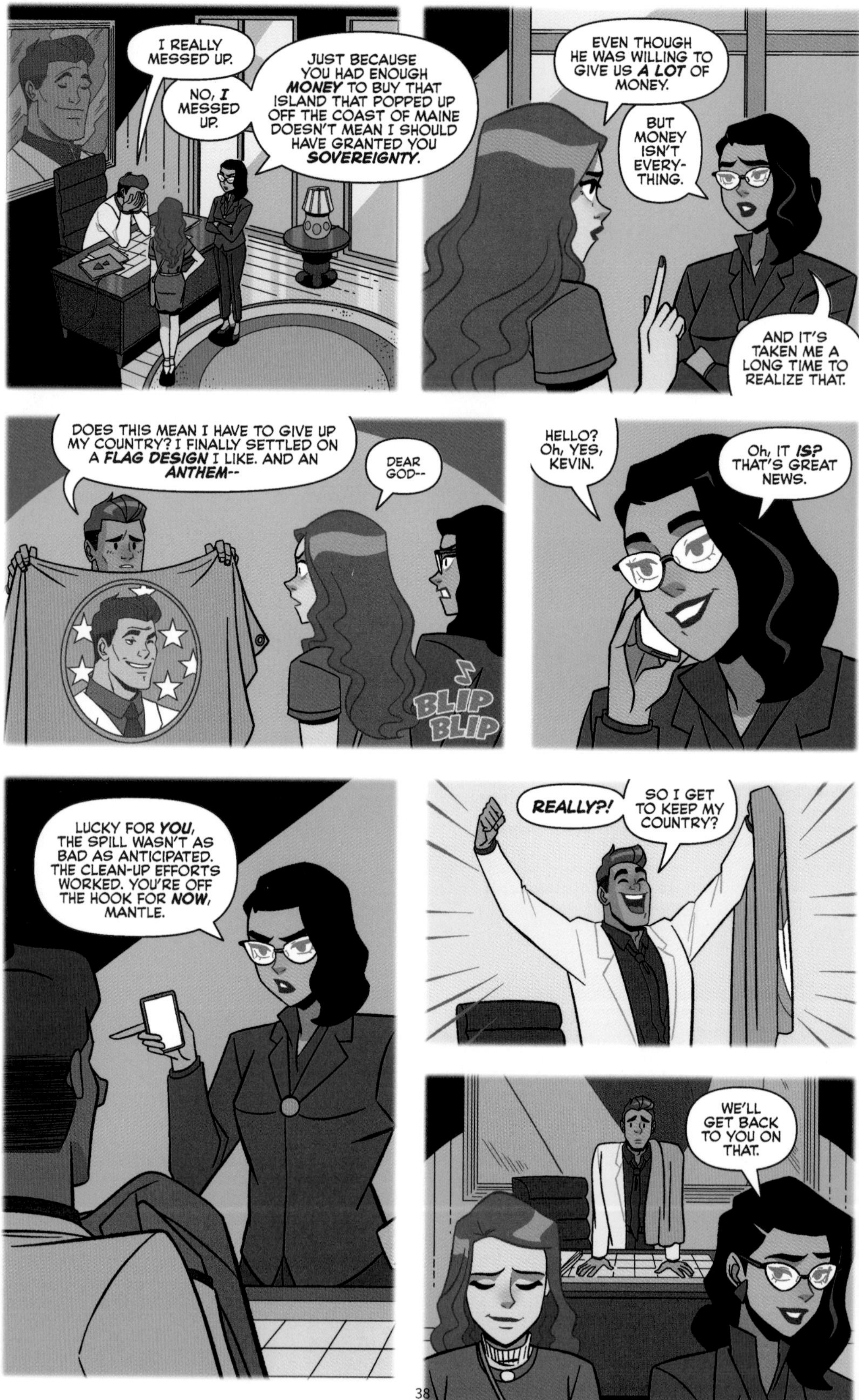
I REALLY MESSED UP.
NO, *I* MESSED UP.
JUST BECAUSE YOU HAD ENOUGH **MONEY** TO BUY THAT ISLAND THAT POPPED UP OFF THE COAST OF MAINE DOESN'T MEAN I SHOULD HAVE GRANTED YOU **SOVEREIGNTY**.
EVEN THOUGH HE WAS WILLING TO GIVE US *A LOT* OF MONEY.
BUT MONEY ISN'T EVERY-THING.
AND IT'S TAKEN ME A LONG TIME TO REALIZE THAT.
DOES THIS MEAN I HAVE TO GIVE UP MY COUNTRY? I FINALLY SETTLED ON A *FLAG DESIGN* I LIKE. AND AN *ANTHEM*--
DEAR GOD--
BLIP BLIP
HELLO? Oh, YES, KEVIN.
Oh, IT *IS?* THAT'S GREAT NEWS.
LUCKY FOR *YOU*, THE SPILL WASN'T AS BAD AS ANTICIPATED. THE CLEAN-UP EFFORTS WORKED. YOU'RE OFF THE HOOK FOR *NOW*, MANTLE.
REALLY?!
SO I GET TO KEEP MY COUNTRY?
WE'LL GET BACK TO YOU ON THAT.

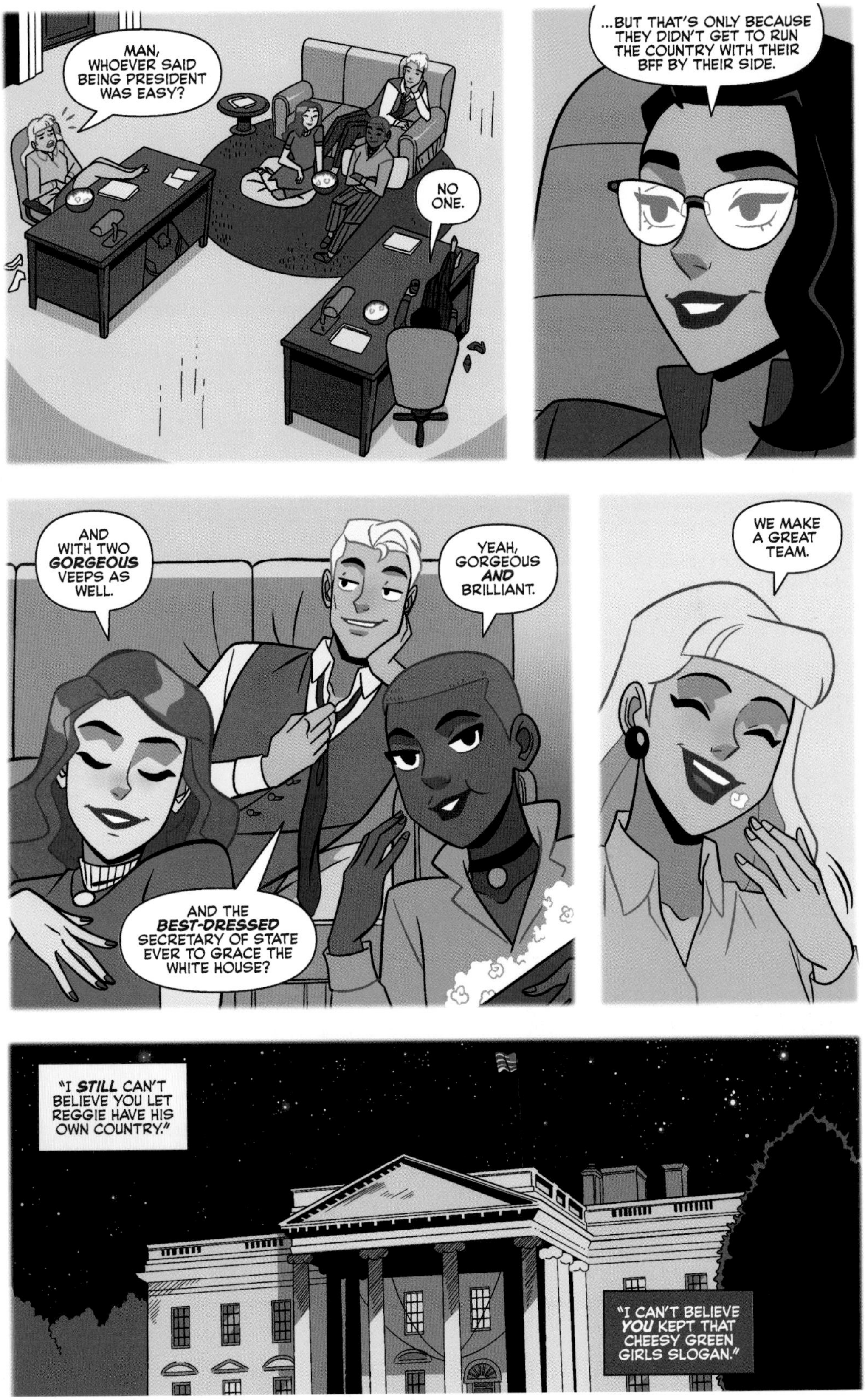
MAN, WHOEVER SAID BEING PRESIDENT WAS EASY?
NO ONE.
...BUT THAT'S ONLY BECAUSE THEY DIDN'T GET TO RUN THE COUNTRY WITH THEIR BFF BY THEIR SIDE.
AND WITH TWO **GORGEOUS** VEEPS AS WELL.
YEAH, GORGEOUS **AND** BRILLIANT.
AND THE **BEST-DRESSED** SECRETARY OF STATE EVER TO GRACE THE WHITE HOUSE?
WE MAKE A GREAT TEAM.
"I **STILL** CAN'T BELIEVE YOU LET REGGIE HAVE HIS OWN COUNTRY."
"I CAN'T BELIEVE **YOU** KEPT THAT CHEESY GREEN GIRLS SLOGAN."

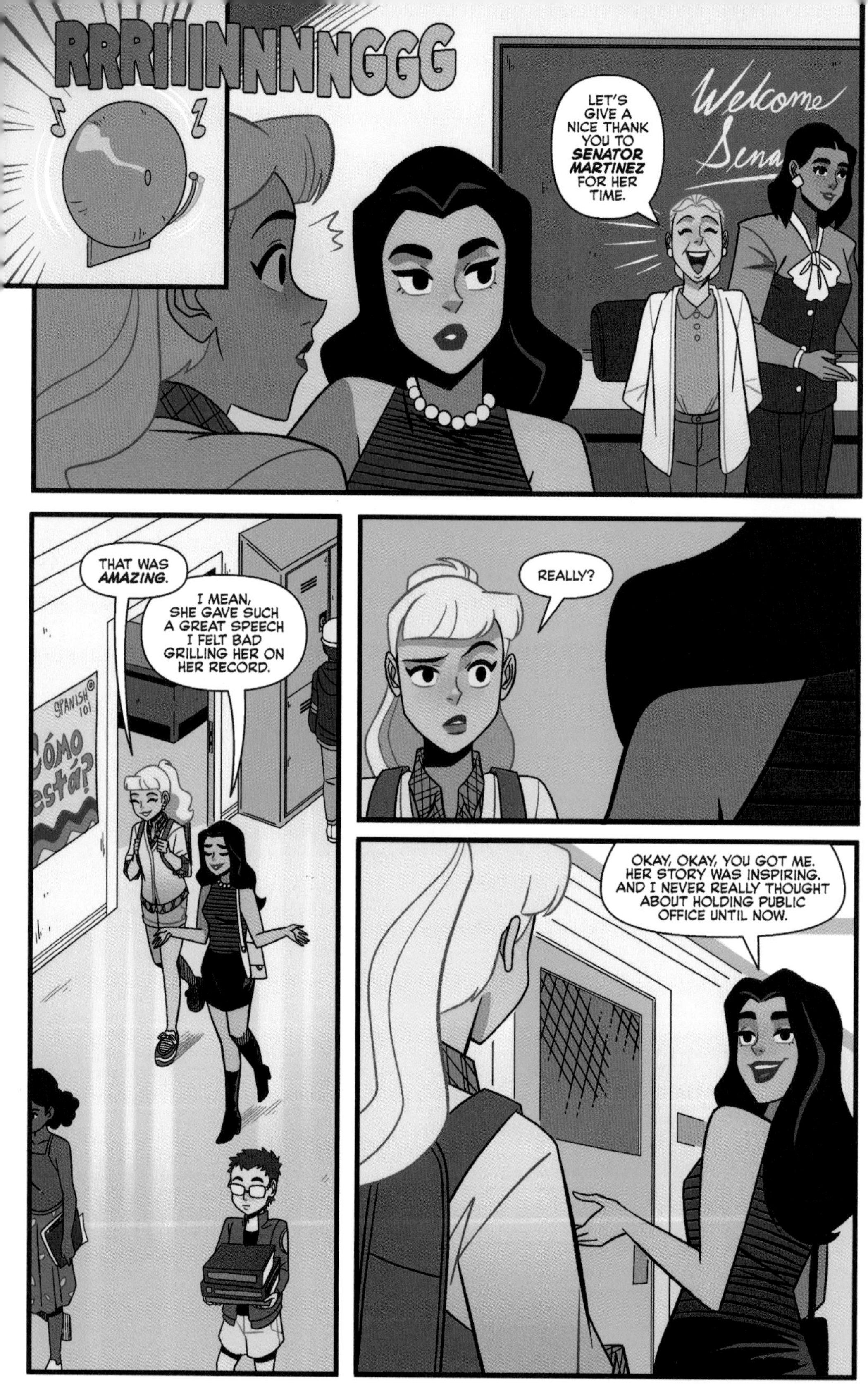
RRRIIINNNNGGG
LET'S GIVE A NICE THANK YOU TO **SENATOR MARTINEZ** FOR HER TIME.
Welcome Sena
THAT WAS **AMAZING**.
I MEAN, SHE GAVE SUCH A GREAT SPEECH I FELT BAD GRILLING HER ON HER RECORD.
SPANISH 101
¿Cómo está?
REALLY?
OKAY, OKAY, YOU GOT ME. HER STORY WAS INSPIRING. AND I NEVER REALLY THOUGHT ABOUT HOLDING PUBLIC OFFICE UNTIL NOW.

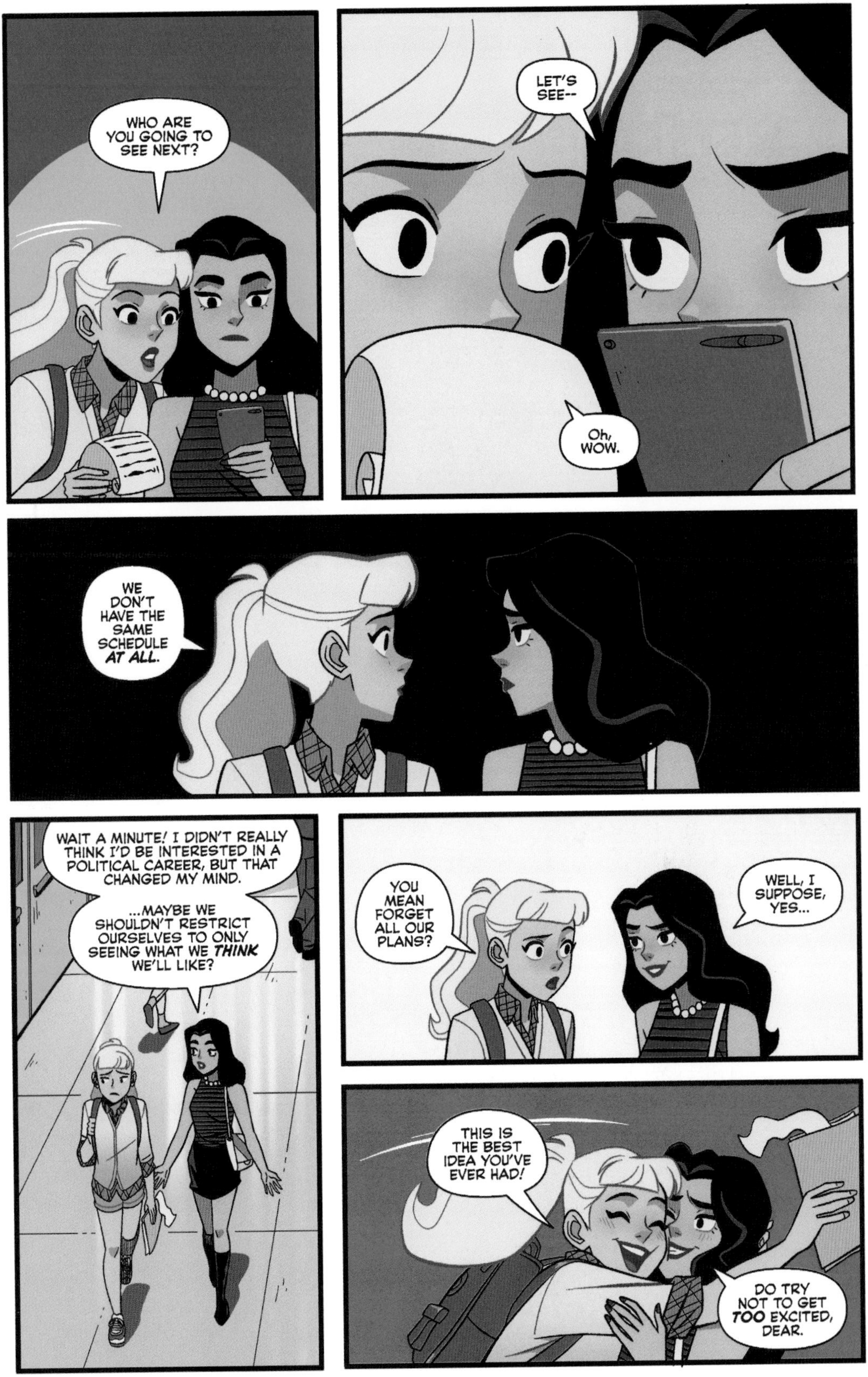
WHO ARE YOU GOING TO SEE NEXT?
LET'S SEE--
Oh, WOW.
WE DON'T HAVE THE SAME SCHEDULE *AT ALL*.
WAIT A MINUTE! I DIDN'T REALLY THINK I'D BE INTERESTED IN A POLITICAL CAREER, BUT THAT CHANGED MY MIND.
...MAYBE WE SHOULDN'T RESTRICT OURSELVES TO ONLY SEEING WHAT WE *THINK* WE'LL LIKE?
YOU MEAN FORGET ALL OUR PLANS?
WELL, I SUPPOSE, YES...
THIS IS THE BEST IDEA YOU'VE EVER HAD!
DO TRY NOT TO GET *TOO* EXCITED, DEAR.

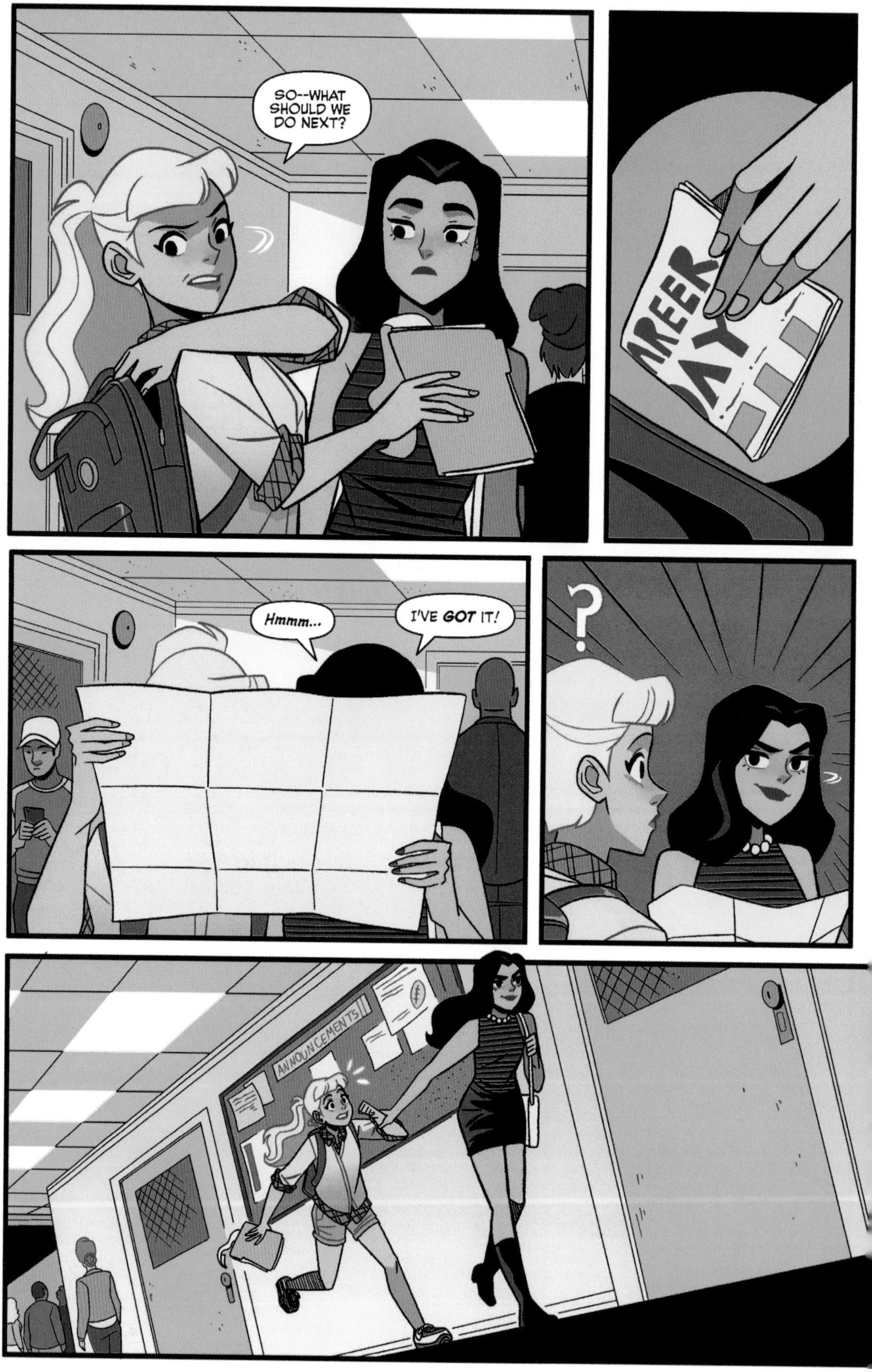
SO--WHAT SHOULD WE DO NEXT?
AREER DAY
Hmmm...
I'VE **GOT** IT!
?
ANNOUNCEMENTS

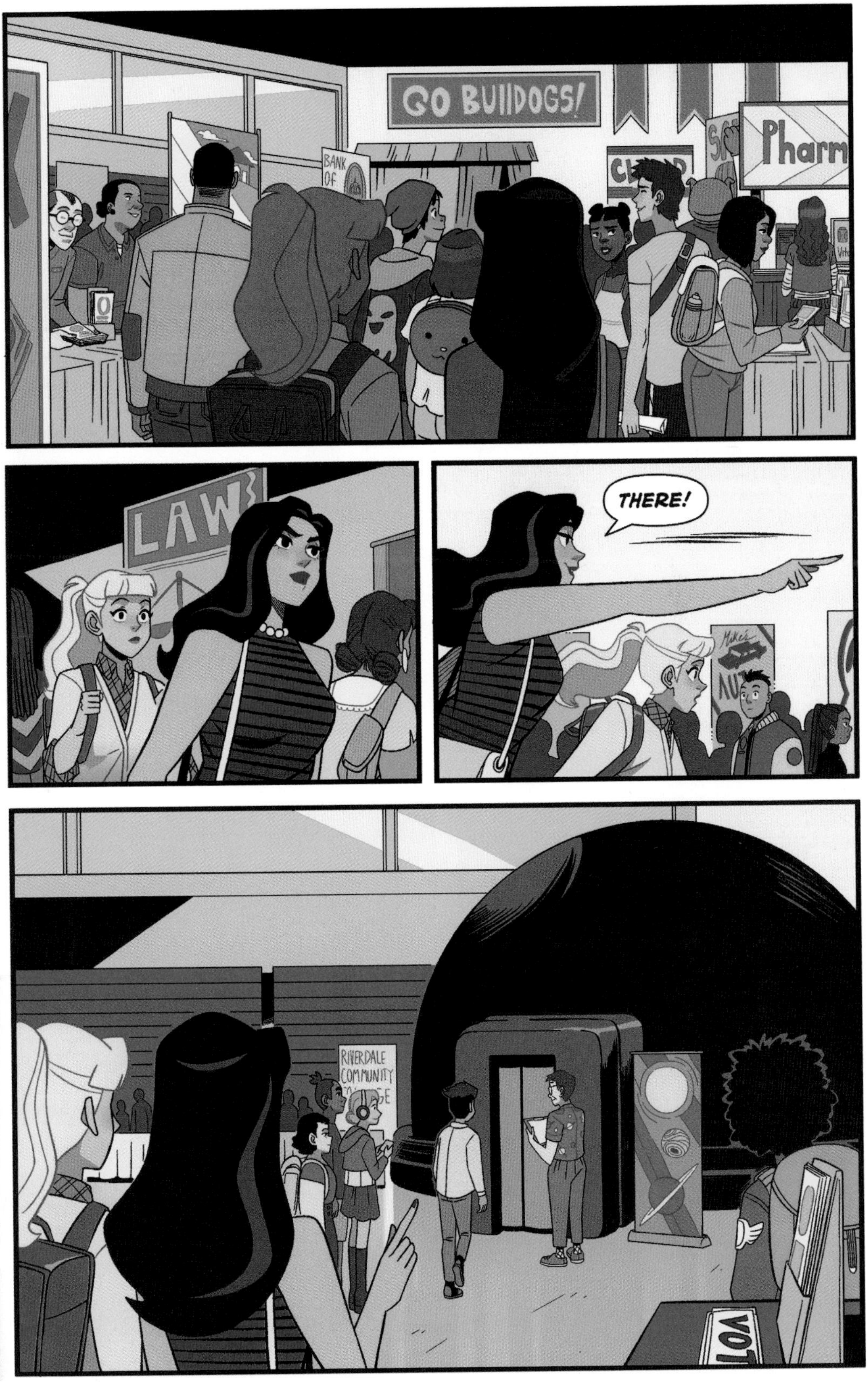
GO BULLDOGS!
BANK OF
Pharm
LAW
THERE!
Mike's
RIVERDALE COMMUNITY
VOT

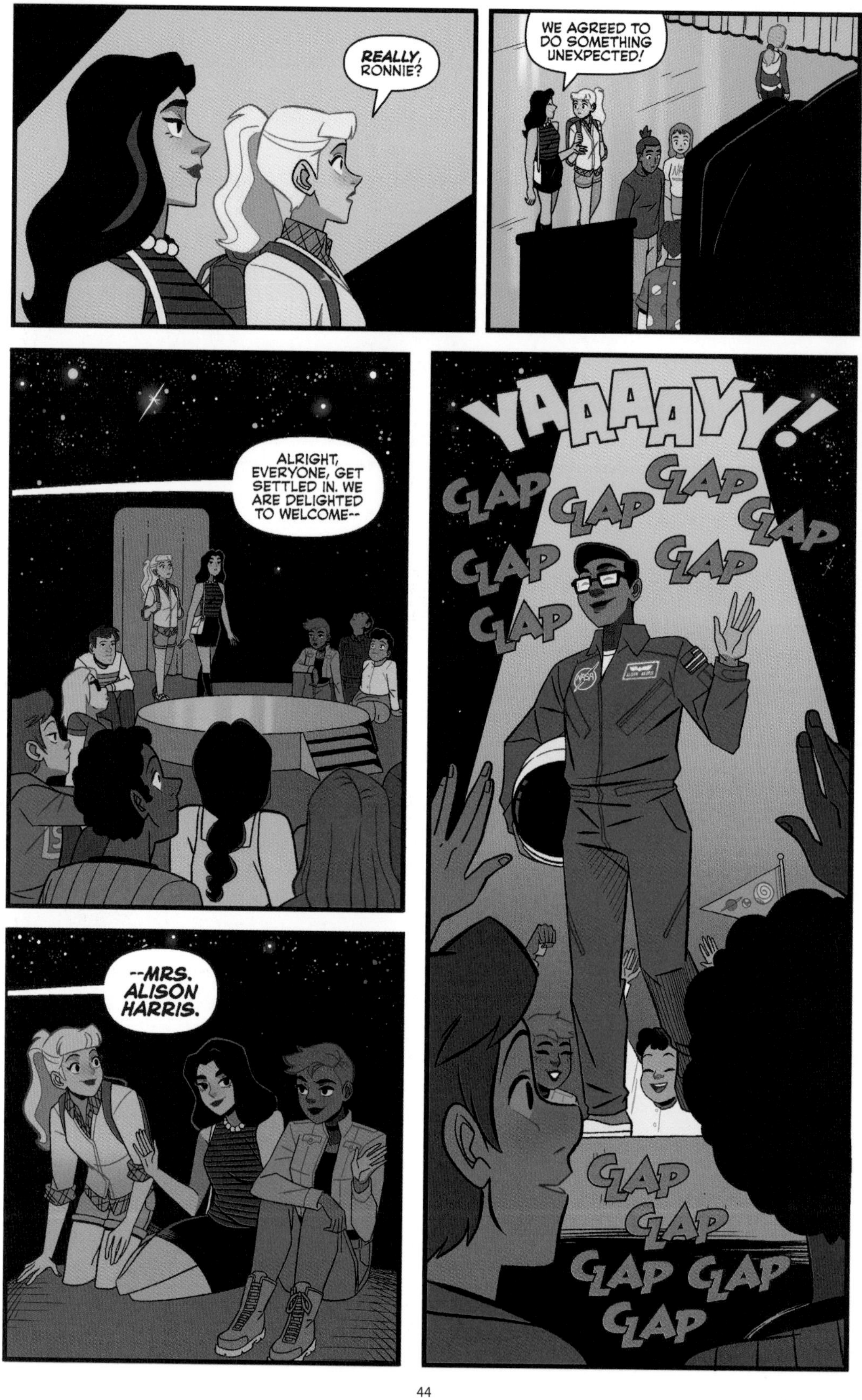
REALLY, RONNIE?
WE AGREED TO DO SOMETHING UNEXPECTED!
ALRIGHT, EVERYONE, GET SETTLED IN. WE ARE DELIGHTED TO WELCOME--
--MRS. ALISON HARRIS.
YAAAAYY!
CLAP CLAP CLAP CLAP CLAP CLAP CLAP
CLAP CLAP CLAP CLAP CLAP

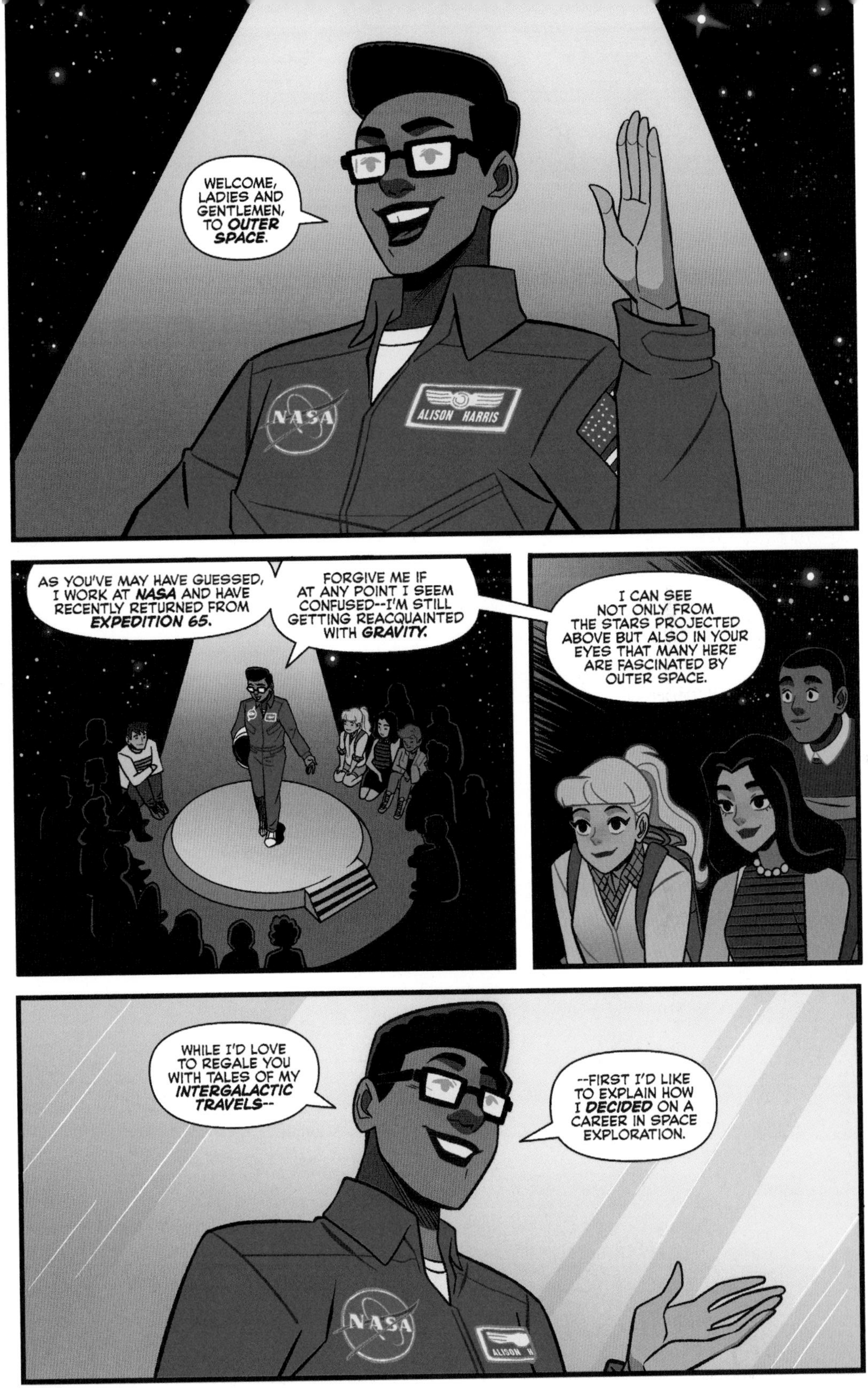
WELCOME, LADIES AND GENTLEMEN, TO OUTER SPACE.
ALISON HARRIS
NASA
AS YOU'VE MAY HAVE GUESSED, I WORK AT NASA AND HAVE RECENTLY RETURNED FROM EXPEDITION 65.
FORGIVE ME IF AT ANY POINT I SEEM CONFUSED--I'M STILL GETTING REACQUAINTED WITH GRAVITY.
I CAN SEE NOT ONLY FROM THE STARS PROJECTED ABOVE BUT ALSO IN YOUR EYES THAT MANY HERE ARE FASCINATED BY OUTER SPACE.
WHILE I'D LOVE TO REGALE YOU WITH TALES OF MY INTERGALACTIC TRAVELS--
--FIRST I'D LIKE TO EXPLAIN HOW I DECIDED ON A CAREER IN SPACE EXPLORATION.

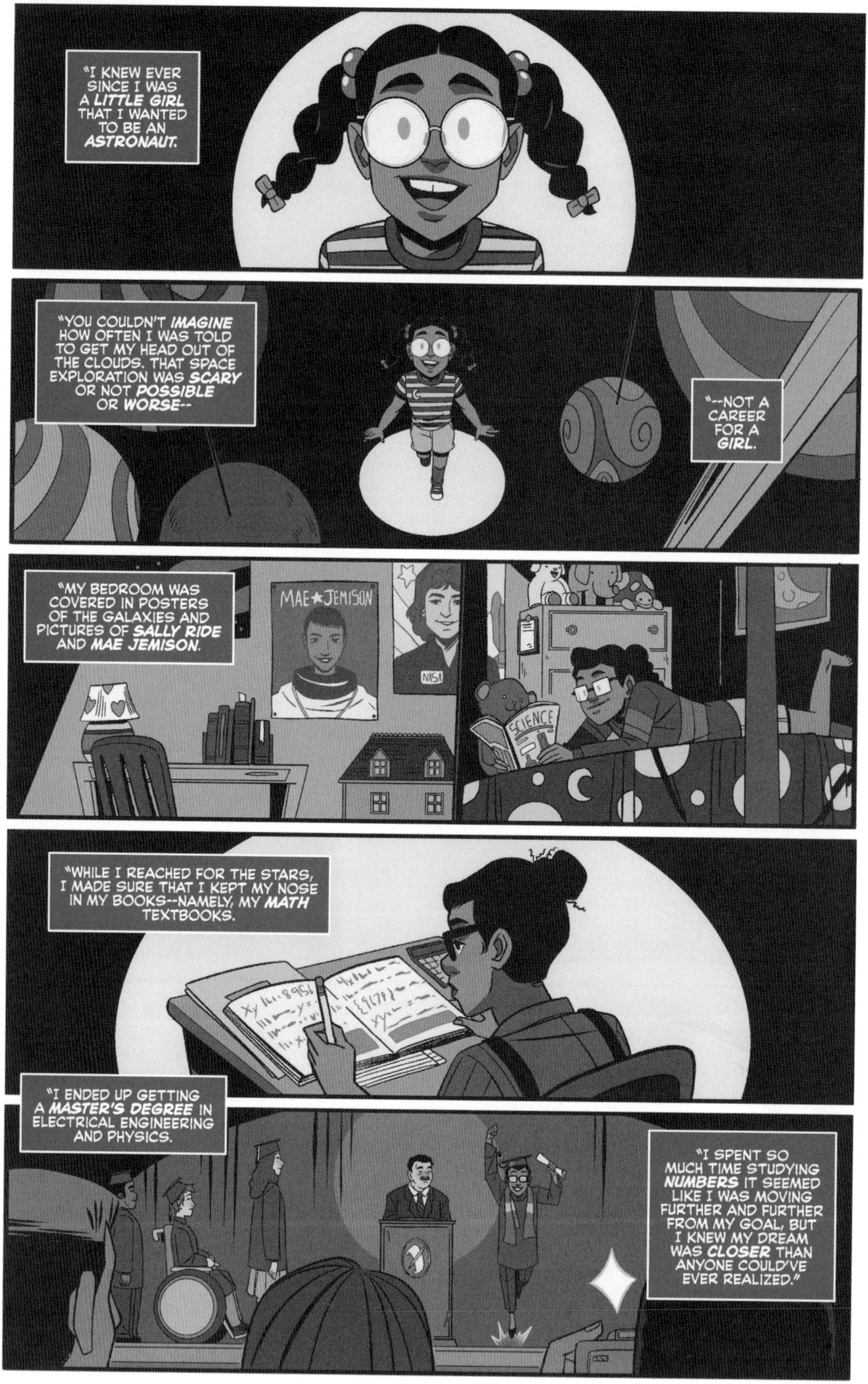
"I KNEW EVER SINCE I WAS A LITTLE GIRL THAT I WANTED TO BE AN ASTRONAUT.
"YOU COULDN'T IMAGINE HOW OFTEN I WAS TOLD TO GET MY HEAD OUT OF THE CLOUDS. THAT SPACE EXPLORATION WAS SCARY OR NOT POSSIBLE OR WORSE--
"--NOT A CAREER FOR A GIRL.
"MY BEDROOM WAS COVERED IN POSTERS OF THE GALAXIES AND PICTURES OF SALLY RIDE AND MAE JEMISON.
MAE★JEMISON
NASA
SCIENCE
"WHILE I REACHED FOR THE STARS, I MADE SURE THAT I KEPT MY NOSE IN MY BOOKS--NAMELY, MY MATH TEXTBOOKS.
"I ENDED UP GETTING A MASTER'S DEGREE IN ELECTRICAL ENGINEERING AND PHYSICS.
"I SPENT SO MUCH TIME STUDYING NUMBERS IT SEEMED LIKE I WAS MOVING FURTHER AND FURTHER FROM MY GOAL, BUT I KNEW MY DREAM WAS CLOSER THAN ANYONE COULD'VE EVER REALIZED."

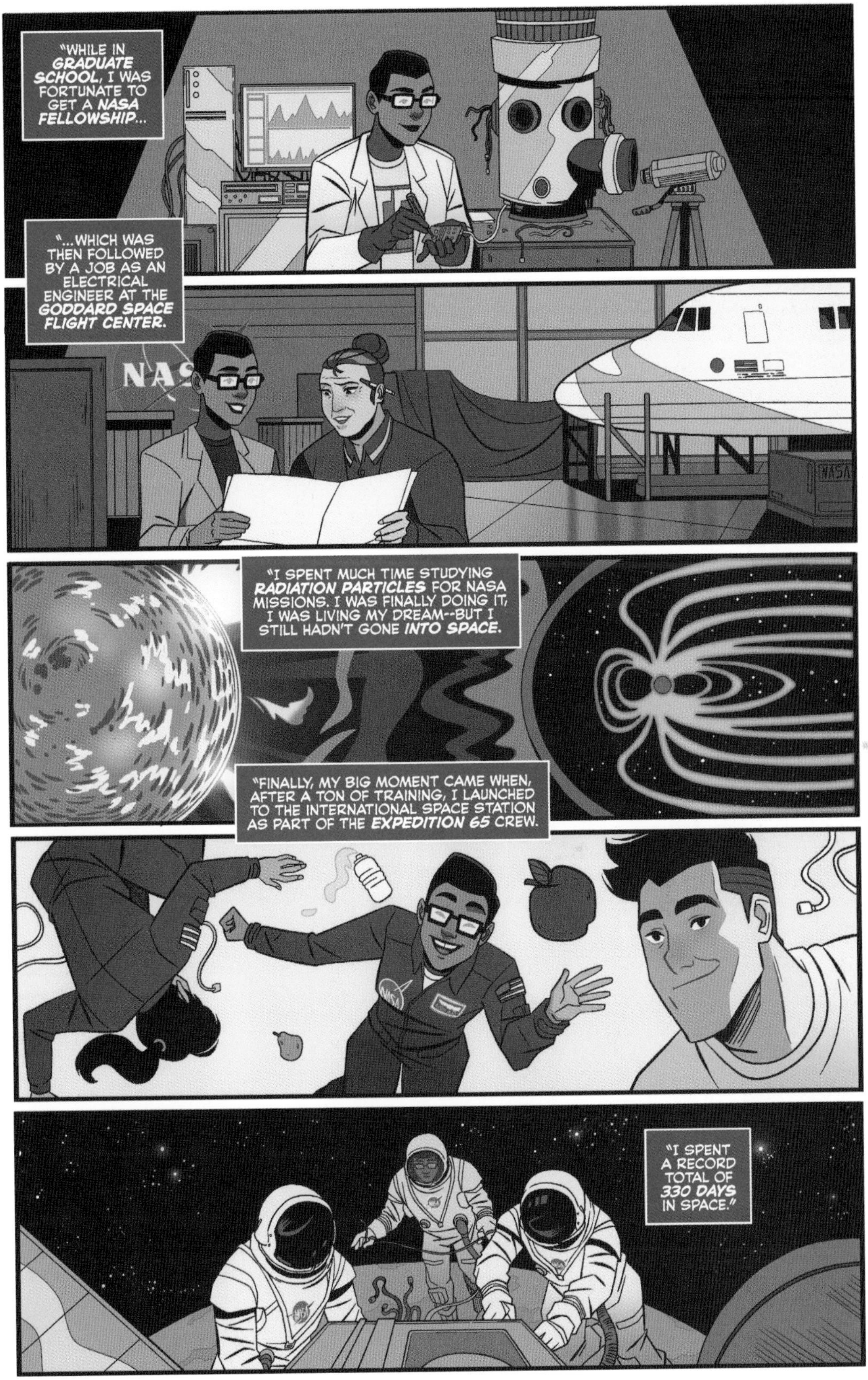
"WHILE IN GRADUATE SCHOOL, I WAS FORTUNATE TO GET A NASA FELLOWSHIP...
"...WHICH WAS THEN FOLLOWED BY A JOB AS AN ELECTRICAL ENGINEER AT THE GODDARD SPACE FLIGHT CENTER.
NASA
NASA
"I SPENT MUCH TIME STUDYING RADIATION PARTICLES FOR NASA MISSIONS. I WAS FINALLY DOING IT, I WAS LIVING MY DREAM--BUT I STILL HADN'T GONE INTO SPACE.
"FINALLY, MY BIG MOMENT CAME WHEN, AFTER A TON OF TRAINING, I LAUNCHED TO THE INTERNATIONAL SPACE STATION AS PART OF THE EXPEDITION 65 CREW.
NASA
"I SPENT A RECORD TOTAL OF 330 DAYS IN SPACE."

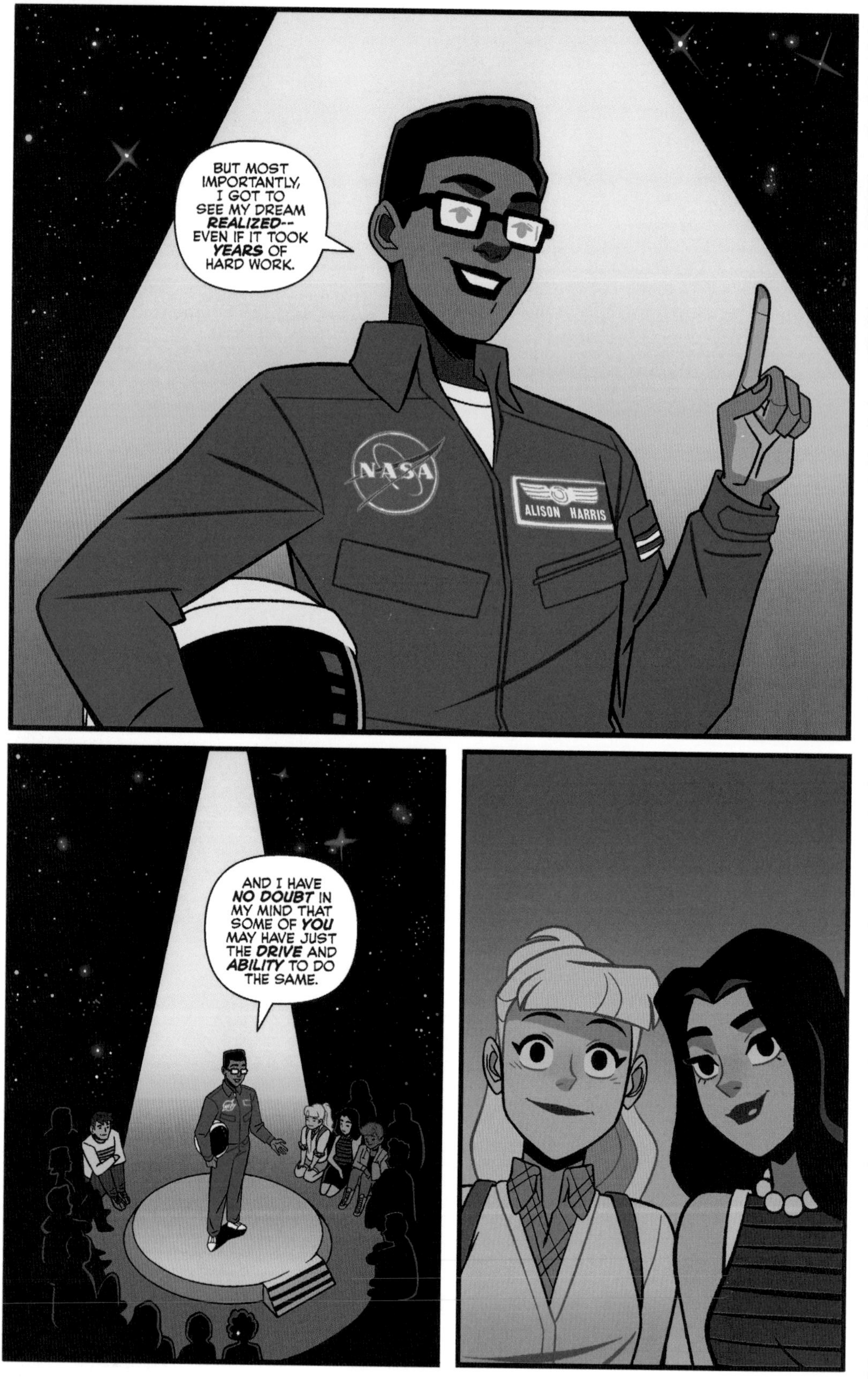
BUT MOST IMPORTANTLY, I GOT TO SEE MY DREAM **REALIZED**-- EVEN IF IT TOOK **YEARS** OF HARD WORK.
NASA
ALISON HARRIS
AND I HAVE **NO DOUBT** IN MY MIND THAT SOME OF **YOU** MAY HAVE JUST THE **DRIVE** AND **ABILITY** TO DO THE SAME.

CHAPTER TWO

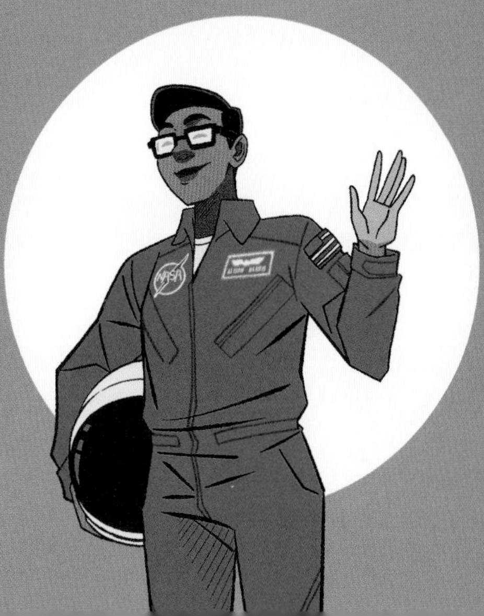
NASA

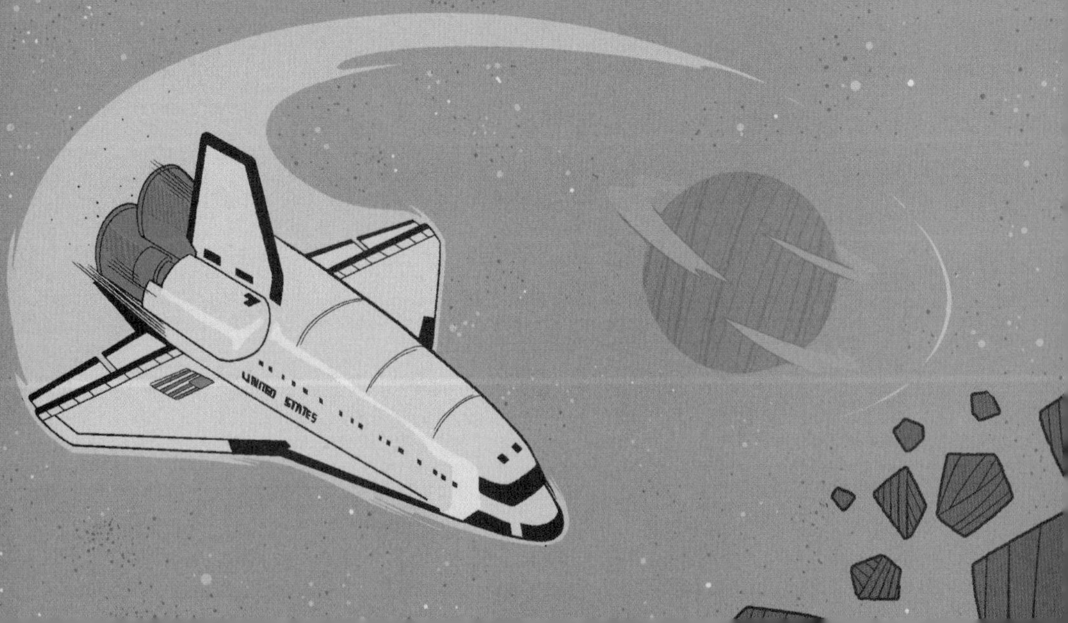
UNITED STATES

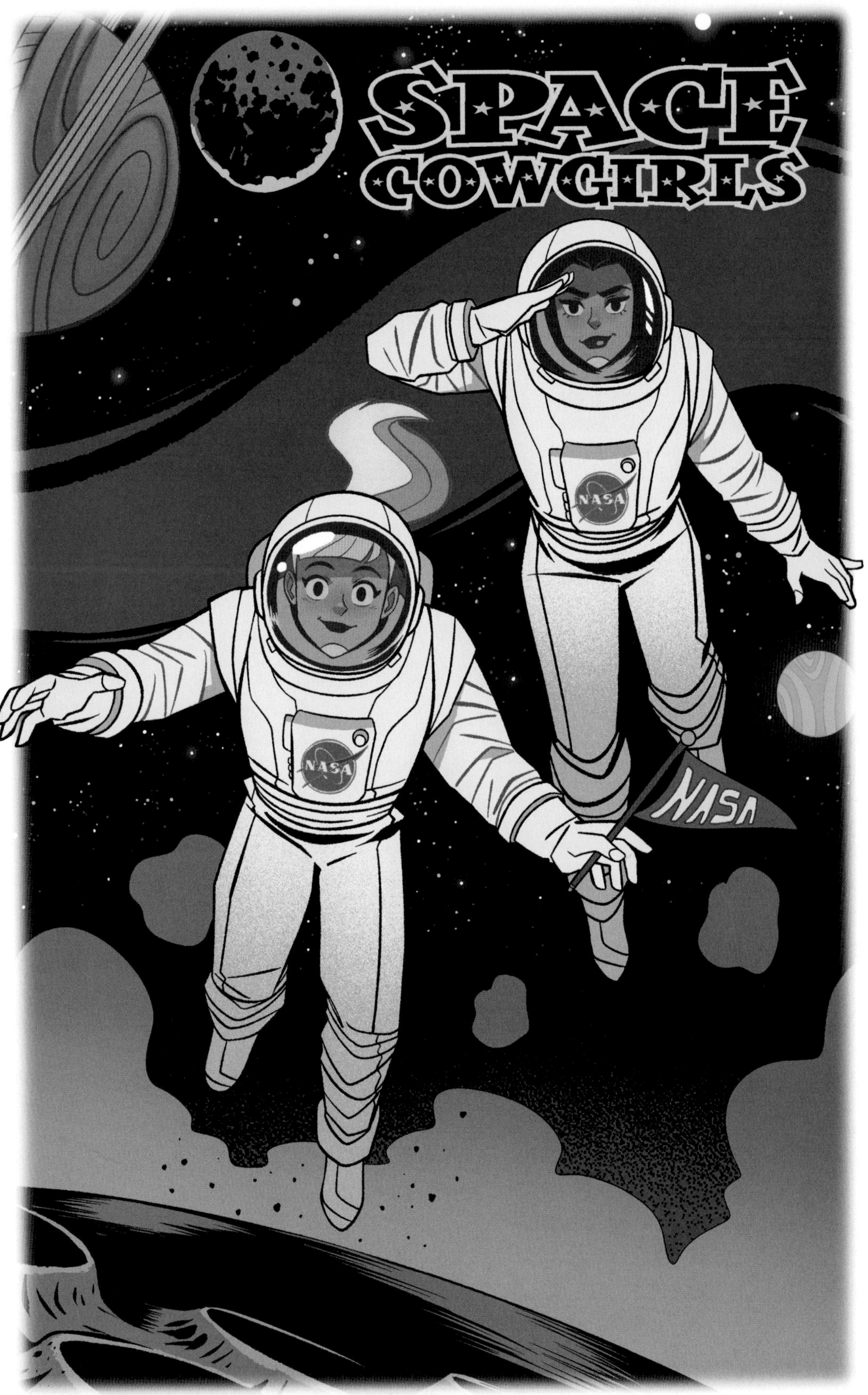
SPACE COWGIRLS
NASA
NASA
NASA

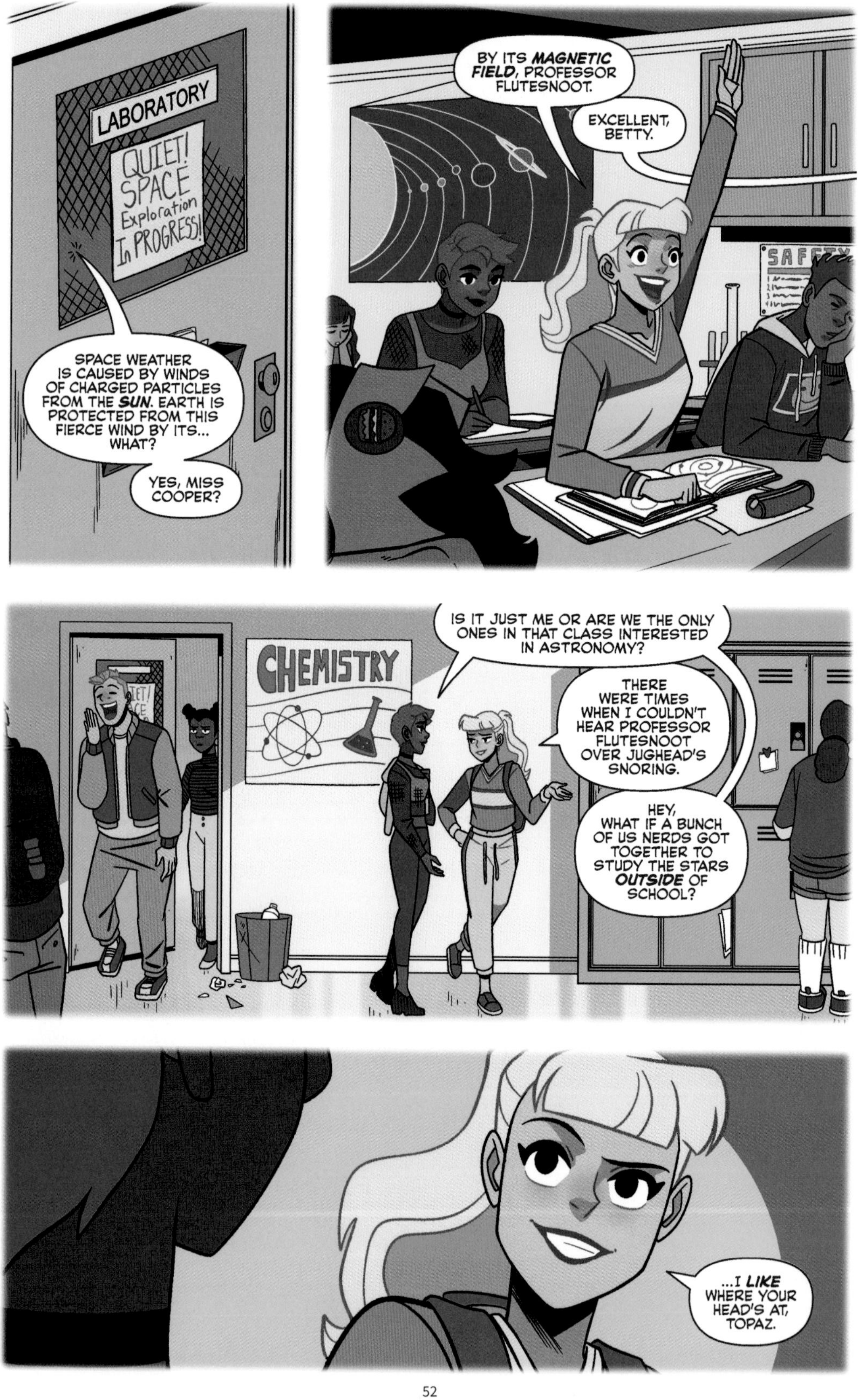
LABORATORY
QUIET! SPACE Exploration In PROGRESS!
SPACE WEATHER IS CAUSED BY WINDS OF CHARGED PARTICLES FROM THE **SUN**. EARTH IS PROTECTED FROM THIS FIERCE WIND BY ITS... WHAT?
YES, MISS COOPER?
BY ITS ***MAGNETIC FIELD***, PROFESSOR FLUTESNOOT.
EXCELLENT, BETTY.
CHEMISTRY
IS IT JUST ME OR ARE WE THE ONLY ONES IN THAT CLASS INTERESTED IN ASTRONOMY?
THERE WERE TIMES WHEN I COULDN'T HEAR PROFESSOR FLUTESNOOT OVER JUGHEAD'S SNORING.
HEY, WHAT IF A BUNCH OF US NERDS GOT TOGETHER TO STUDY THE STARS ***OUTSIDE*** OF SCHOOL?
...I ***LIKE*** WHERE YOUR HEAD'S AT, TOPAZ.

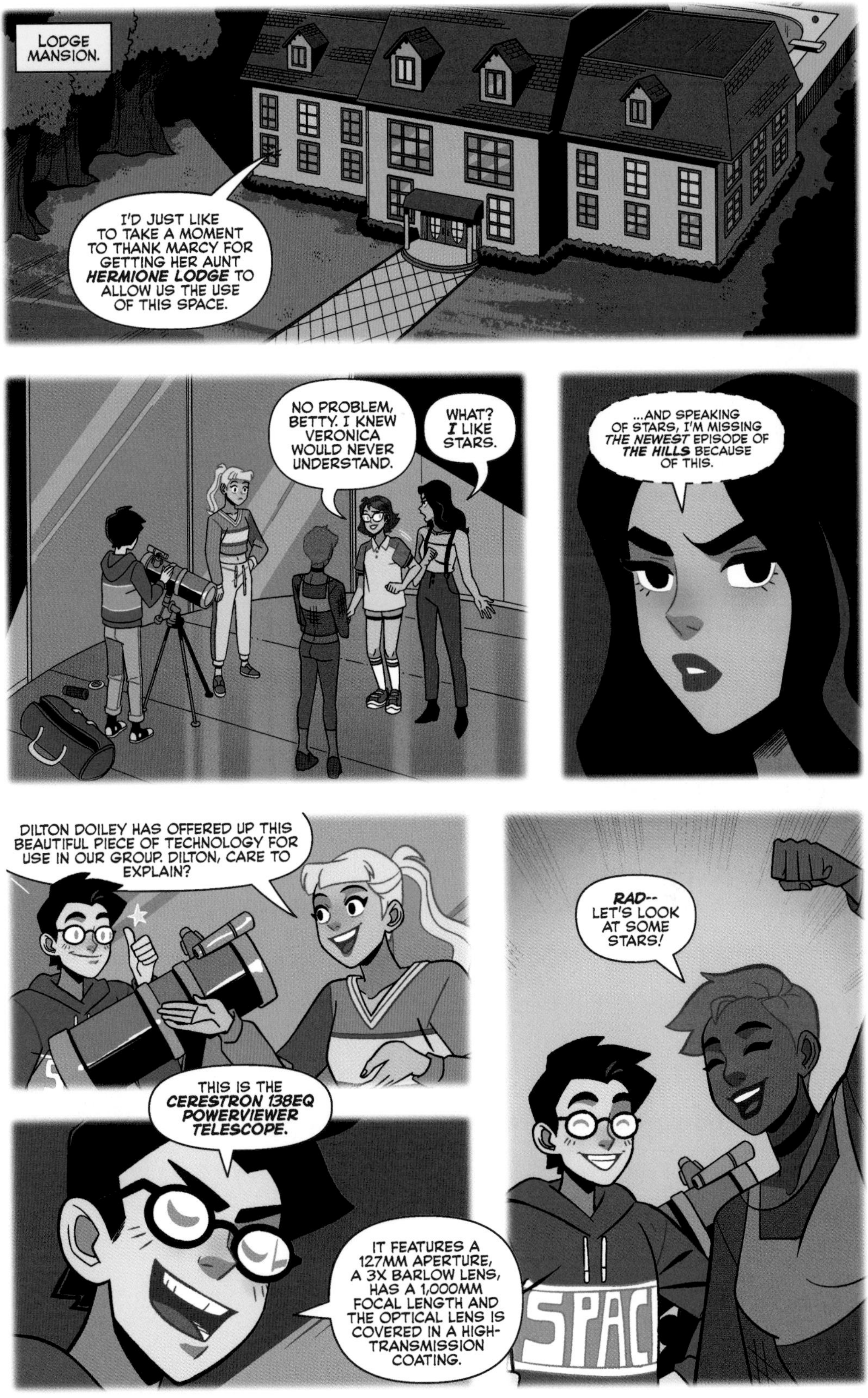
LODGE MANSION.
I'D JUST LIKE TO TAKE A MOMENT TO THANK MARCY FOR GETTING HER AUNT HERMIONE LODGE TO ALLOW US THE USE OF THIS SPACE.
NO PROBLEM, BETTY. I KNEW VERONICA WOULD NEVER UNDERSTAND.
WHAT? I LIKE STARS.
...AND SPEAKING OF STARS, I'M MISSING THE NEWEST EPISODE OF THE HILLS BECAUSE OF THIS.
DILTON DOILEY HAS OFFERED UP THIS BEAUTIFUL PIECE OF TECHNOLOGY FOR USE IN OUR GROUP. DILTON, CARE TO EXPLAIN?
THIS IS THE CERESTRON 138EQ POWERVIEWER TELESCOPE.
IT FEATURES A 127MM APERTURE, A 3X BARLOW LENS, HAS A 1,000MM FOCAL LENGTH AND THE OPTICAL LENS IS COVERED IN A HIGH-TRANSMISSION COATING.
RAD-- LET'S LOOK AT SOME STARS!
SPAC

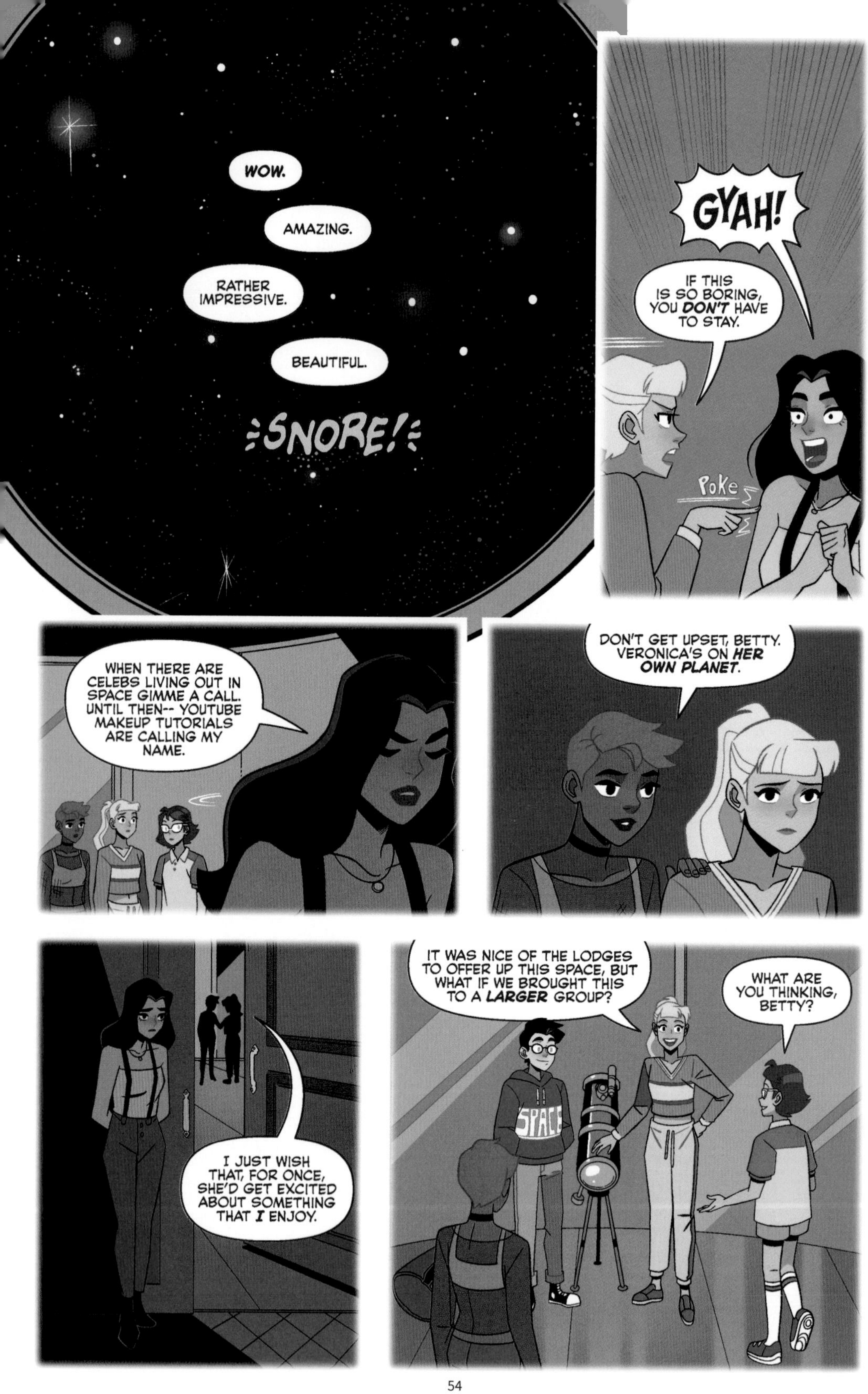
WOW.
AMAZING.
RATHER IMPRESSIVE.
BEAUTIFUL.
SNORE!
GYAH!
IF THIS IS SO BORING, YOU DON'T HAVE TO STAY.
POKE
WHEN THERE ARE CELEBS LIVING OUT IN SPACE GIMME A CALL. UNTIL THEN-- YOUTUBE MAKEUP TUTORIALS ARE CALLING MY NAME.
DON'T GET UPSET, BETTY. VERONICA'S ON HER OWN PLANET.
I JUST WISH THAT, FOR ONCE, SHE'D GET EXCITED ABOUT SOMETHING THAT I ENJOY.
IT WAS NICE OF THE LODGES TO OFFER UP THIS SPACE, BUT WHAT IF WE BROUGHT THIS TO A LARGER GROUP?
WHAT ARE YOU THINKING, BETTY?
SPACE

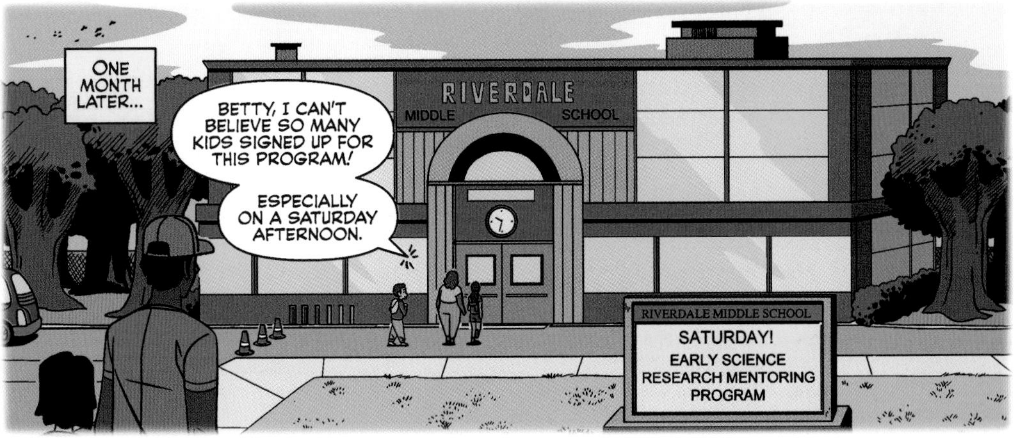

ONE MONTH LATER...
RIVERDALE MIDDLE SCHOOL
BETTY, I CAN'T BELIEVE SO MANY KIDS SIGNED UP FOR THIS PROGRAM!
ESPECIALLY ON A SATURDAY AFTERNOON.
RIVERDALE MIDDLE SCHOOL
SATURDAY!
EARLY SCIENCE RESEARCH MENTORING PROGRAM

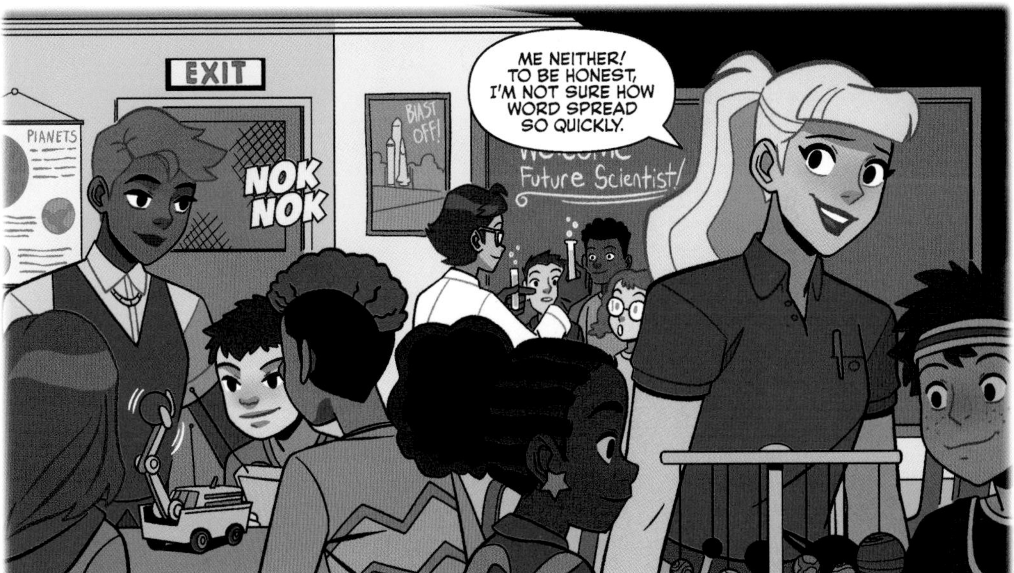

EXIT
PLANETS
BLAST OFF!
NOK NOK
ME NEITHER! TO BE HONEST, I'M NOT SURE HOW WORD SPREAD SO QUICKLY.
Welcome Future Scientist!

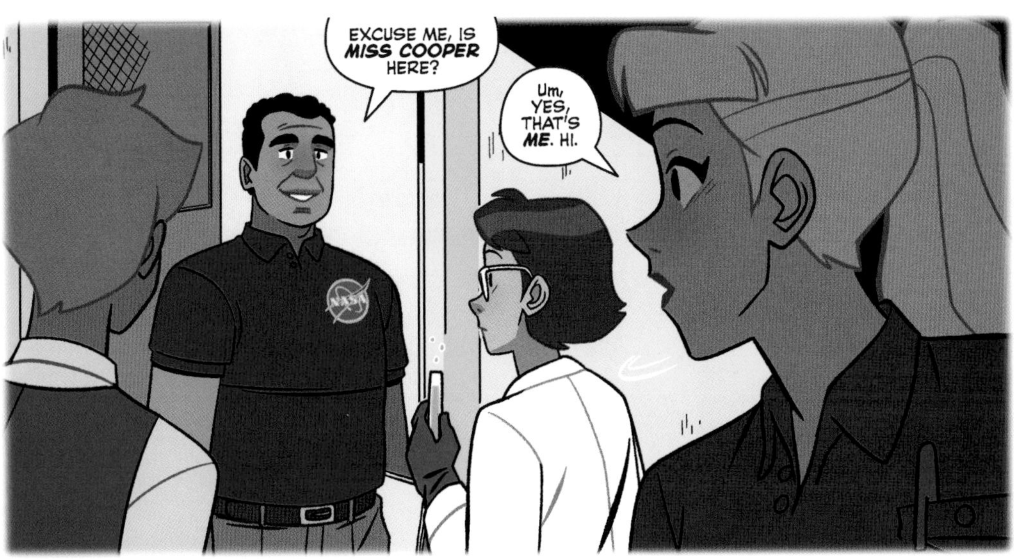

EXCUSE ME, IS ***MISS COOPER*** HERE?
Um, YES, THAT'S ***ME***. HI.
NASA

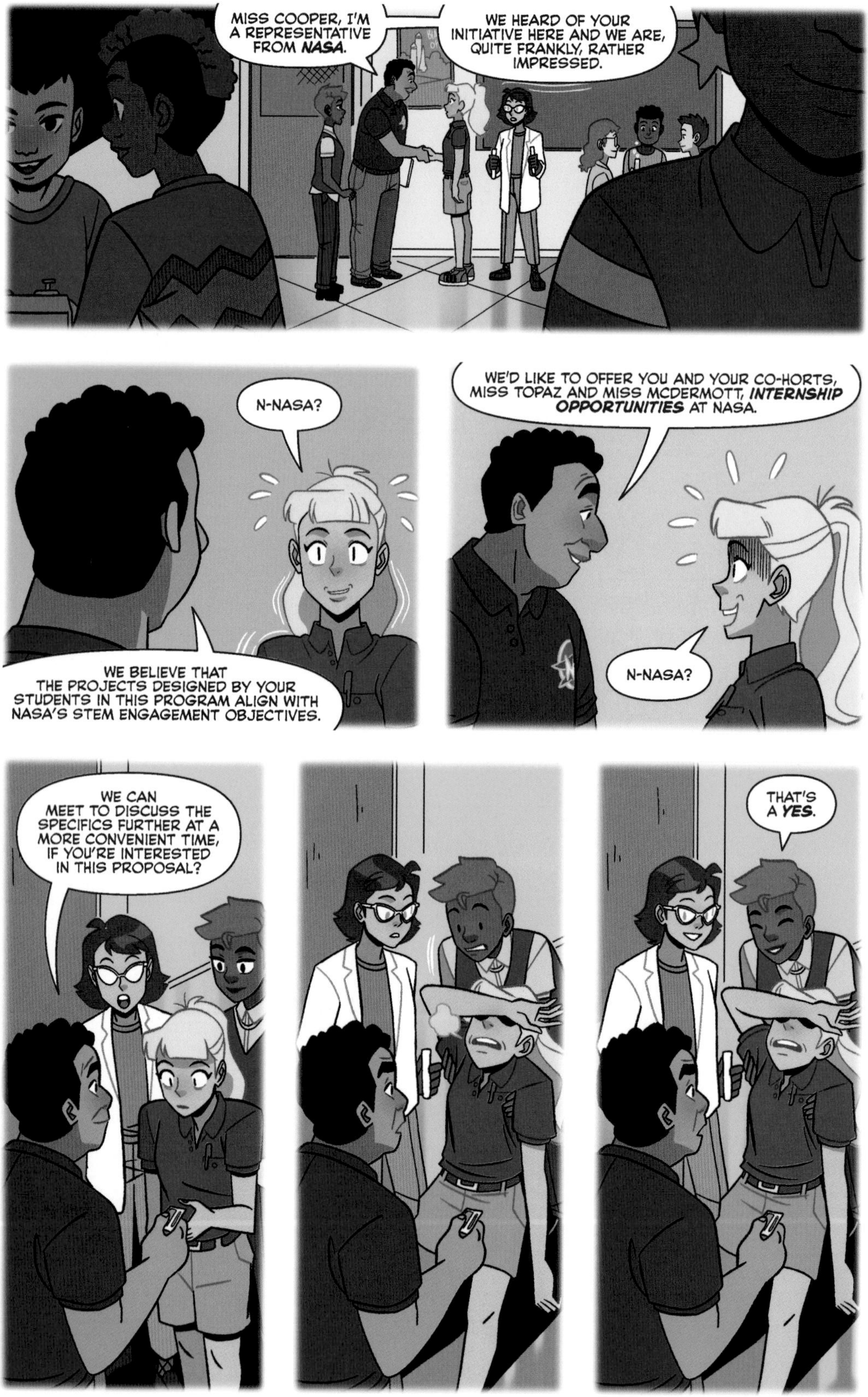
MISS COOPER, I'M A REPRESENTATIVE FROM NASA.
WE HEARD OF YOUR INITIATIVE HERE AND WE ARE, QUITE FRANKLY, RATHER IMPRESSED.
N-NASA?
WE BELIEVE THAT THE PROJECTS DESIGNED BY YOUR STUDENTS IN THIS PROGRAM ALIGN WITH NASA'S STEM ENGAGEMENT OBJECTIVES.
WE'D LIKE TO OFFER YOU AND YOUR CO-HORTS, MISS TOPAZ AND MISS MCDERMOTT, INTERNSHIP OPPORTUNITIES AT NASA.
N-NASA?
WE CAN MEET TO DISCUSS THE SPECIFICS FURTHER AT A MORE CONVENIENT TIME, IF YOU'RE INTERESTED IN THIS PROPOSAL?
THAT'S A YES.

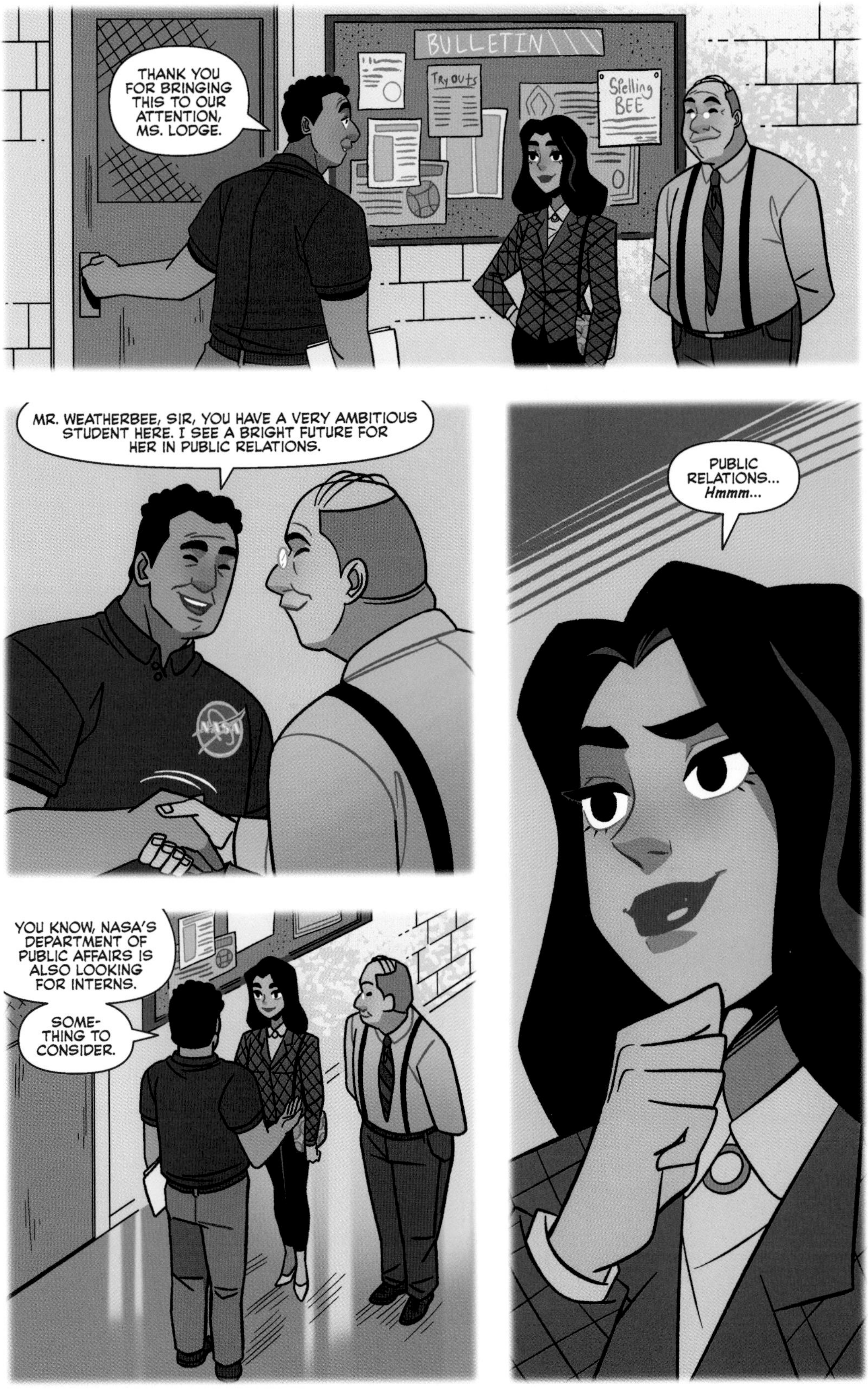
THANK YOU FOR BRINGING THIS TO OUR ATTENTION, MS. LODGE.
BULLETIN
Try Outs
Spelling BEE
MR. WEATHERBEE, SIR, YOU HAVE A VERY AMBITIOUS STUDENT HERE. I SEE A BRIGHT FUTURE FOR HER IN PUBLIC RELATIONS.
NASA
PUBLIC RELATIONS... *Hmmm...*
YOU KNOW, NASA'S DEPARTMENT OF PUBLIC AFFAIRS IS ALSO LOOKING FOR INTERNS.
SOME-THING TO CONSIDER.

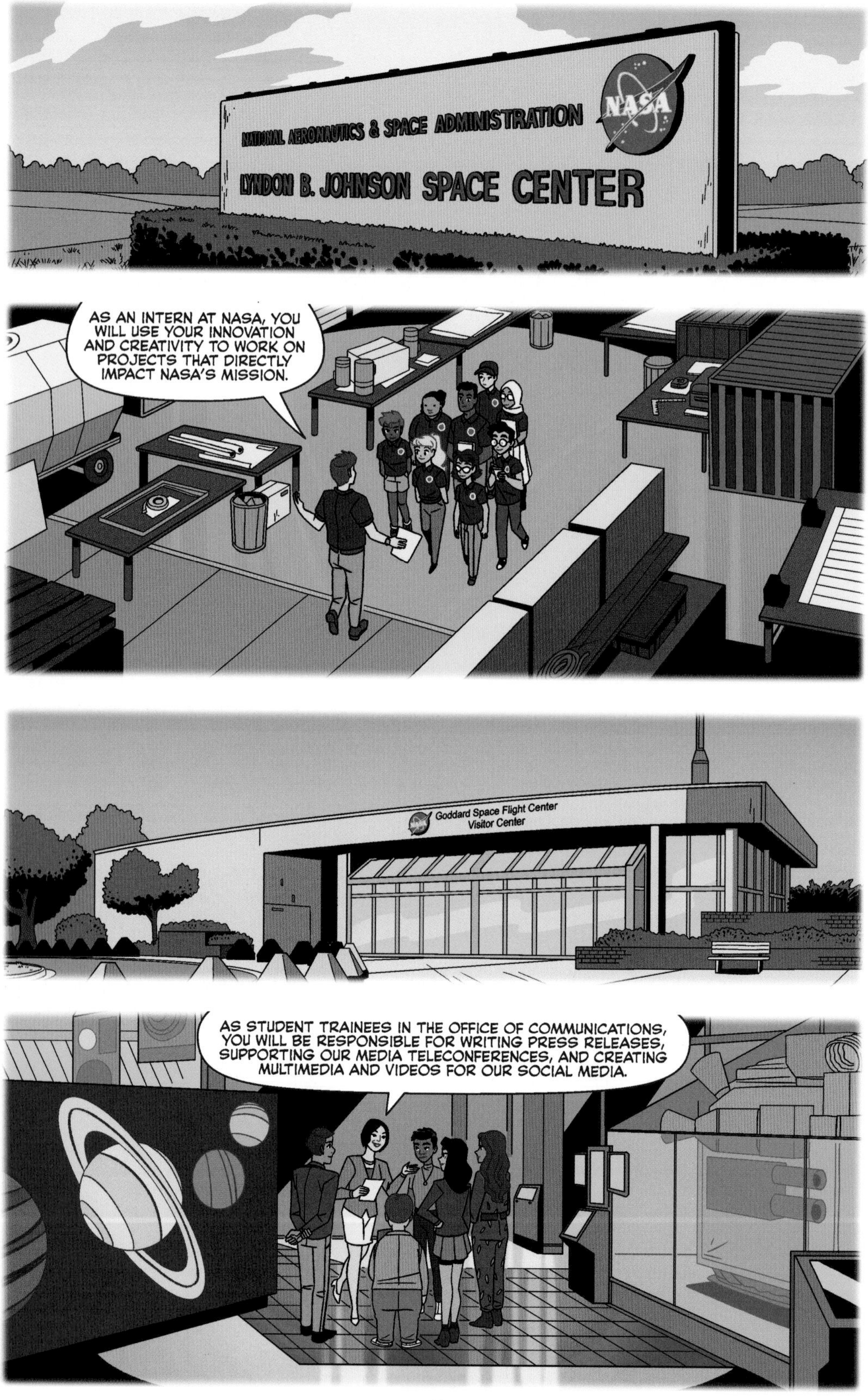
NATIONAL AERONAUTICS & SPACE ADMINISTRATION
NASA
LYNDON B. JOHNSON SPACE CENTER
AS AN INTERN AT NASA, YOU WILL USE YOUR INNOVATION AND CREATIVITY TO WORK ON PROJECTS THAT DIRECTLY IMPACT NASA'S MISSION.
Goddard Space Flight Center Visitor Center
AS STUDENT TRAINEES IN THE OFFICE OF COMMUNICATIONS, YOU WILL BE RESPONSIBLE FOR WRITING PRESS RELEASES, SUPPORTING OUR MEDIA TELECONFERENCES, AND CREATING MULTIMEDIA AND VIDEOS FOR OUR SOCIAL MEDIA.

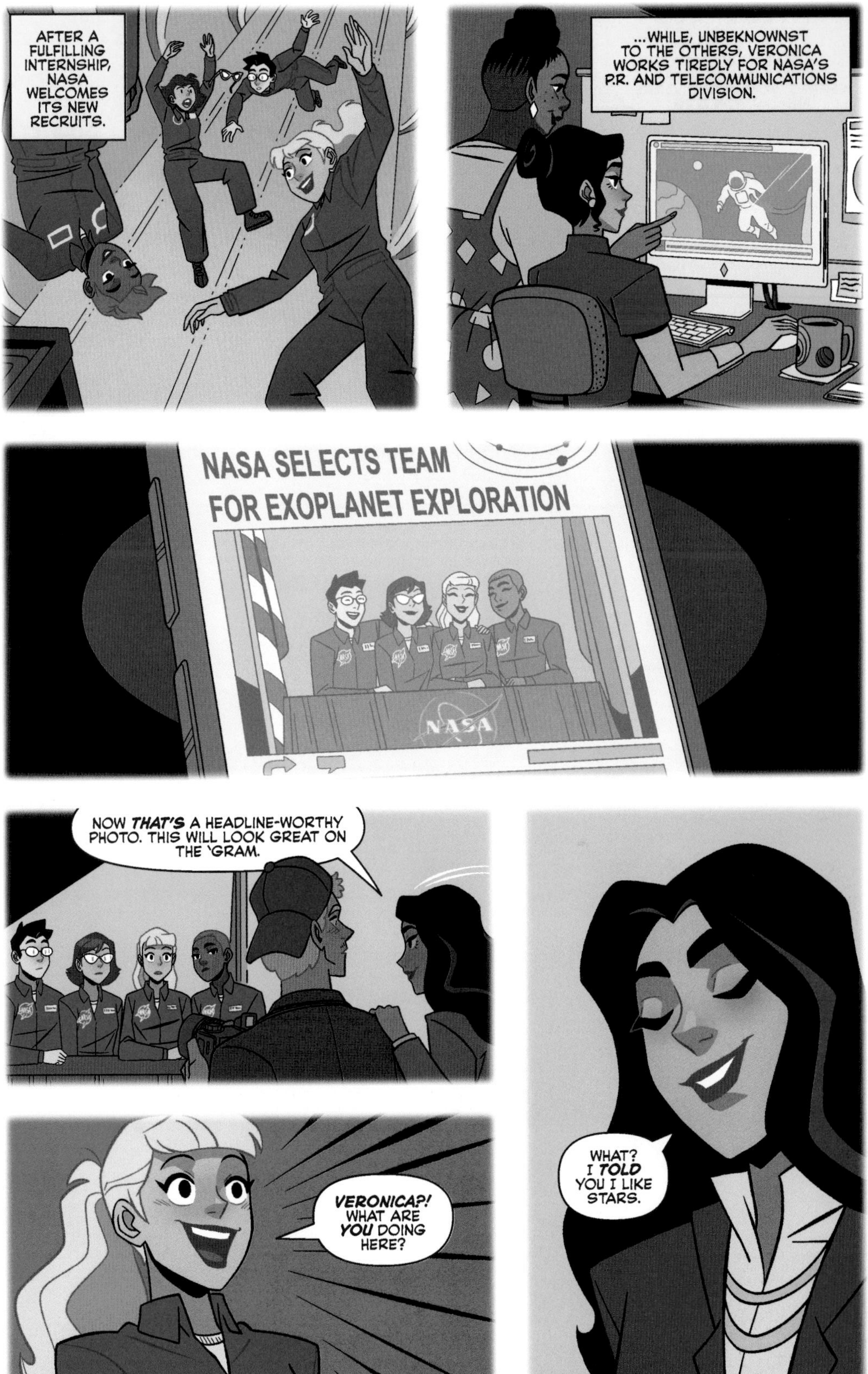

AFTER A FULFILLING INTERNSHIP, NASA WELCOMES ITS NEW RECRUITS.
...WHILE, UNBEKNOWNST TO THE OTHERS, VERONICA WORKS TIREDLY FOR NASA'S P.R. AND TELECOMMUNICATIONS DIVISION.
NASA SELECTS TEAM FOR EXOPLANET EXPLORATION
NASA
NOW *THAT'S* A HEADLINE-WORTHY PHOTO. THIS WILL LOOK GREAT ON THE 'GRAM.
VERONICA?! WHAT ARE *YOU* DOING HERE?
WHAT? I *TOLD* YOU I LIKE STARS.

YOU'VE ALL BEEN CHOSEN FOR THIS MISSION BECAUSE YOU'VE DEMONSTRATED THE GREATEST UNDERSTANDING OF OUR PURPOSE AND A RESPECT FOR OUR UNIVERSE AND ITS WONDERS.

THANKS TO THE FUNDING OF LODGE INDUSTRIES AND THE WORK OF P.R. GURU VERONICA LODGE, WE CAN LIVESTREAM THE WHOLE TRIP--EVEN FROM THE DEPTHS OF SPACE.

OUR DIGITAL EDITING AND SOCIAL MEDIA TEAM WILL BE WORKING AROUND THE CLOCK TO COORDINATE THE MESSAGING AND FOOTAGE.

SO MANY BUTTONS.

SCIENCE IS WILD. THANK GOD I'M A PEOPLE-PERSON AND NOT A MARTIAN-PERSON.

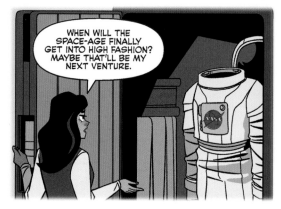

WHEN WILL THE SPACE-AGE FINALLY GET INTO HIGH FASHION? MAYBE THAT'LL BE MY NEXT VENTURE.

THAT BEING SAID, I'VE *ALWAYS* WANTED TO TRY ONE OF THESE ON...

SLAM

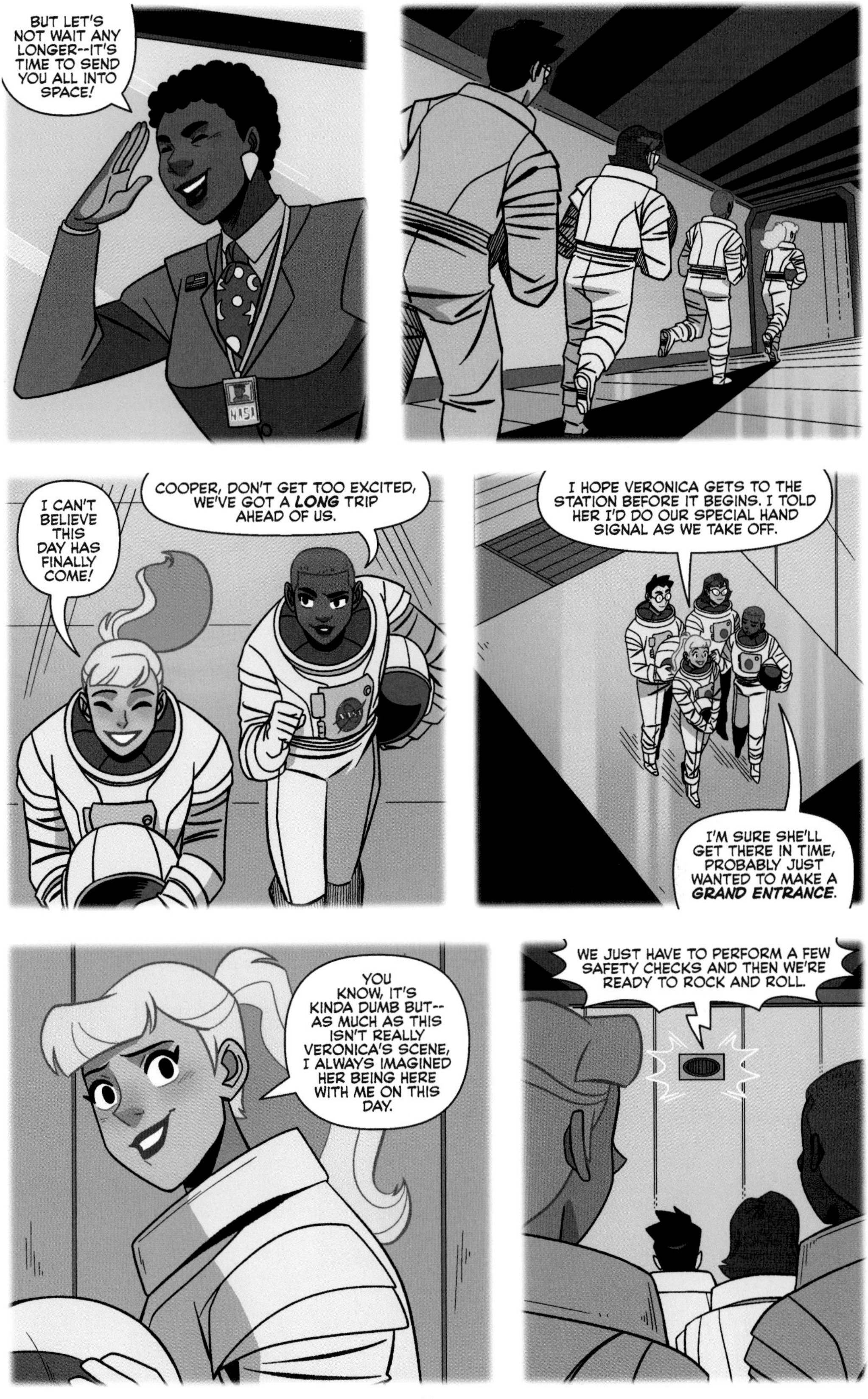

BUT LET'S NOT WAIT ANY LONGER--IT'S TIME TO SEND YOU ALL INTO SPACE!
NASA
I CAN'T BELIEVE THIS DAY HAS FINALLY COME!
COOPER, DON'T GET TOO EXCITED, WE'VE GOT A **LONG** TRIP AHEAD OF US.
I HOPE VERONICA GETS TO THE STATION BEFORE IT BEGINS. I TOLD HER I'D DO OUR SPECIAL HAND SIGNAL AS WE TAKE OFF.
I'M SURE SHE'LL GET THERE IN TIME, PROBABLY JUST WANTED TO MAKE A ***GRAND ENTRANCE***.
YOU KNOW, IT'S KINDA DUMB BUT--AS MUCH AS THIS ISN'T REALLY VERONICA'S SCENE, I ALWAYS IMAGINED HER BEING HERE WITH ME ON THIS DAY.
WE JUST HAVE TO PERFORM A FEW SAFETY CHECKS AND THEN WE'RE READY TO ROCK AND ROLL.

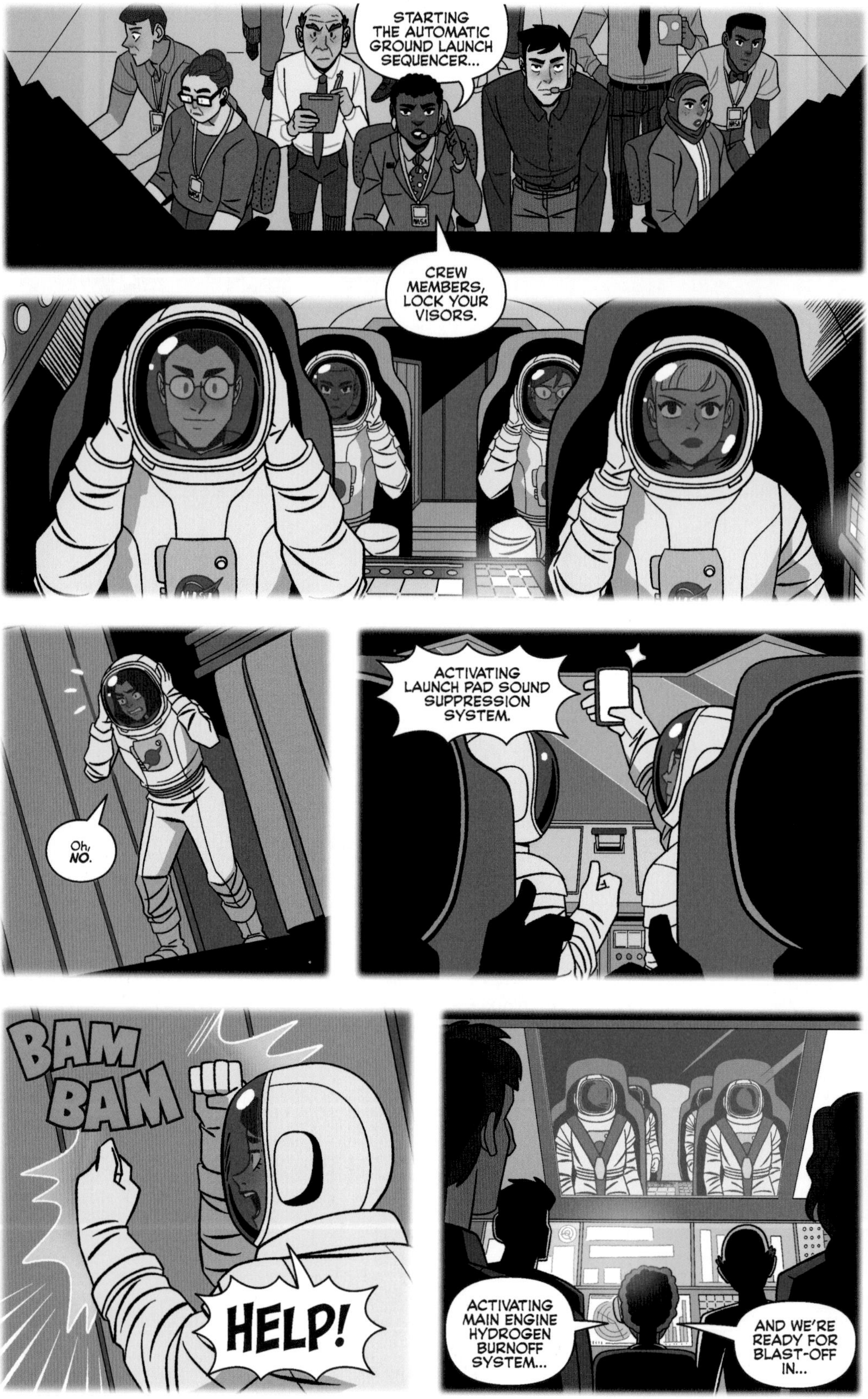
STARTING THE AUTOMATIC GROUND LAUNCH SEQUENCER...
CREW MEMBERS, LOCK YOUR VISORS.
Oh, NO.
ACTIVATING LAUNCH PAD SOUND SUPPRESSION SYSTEM.
BAM BAM
HELP!
ACTIVATING MAIN ENGINE HYDROGEN BURNOFF SYSTEM...
AND WE'RE READY FOR BLAST-OFF IN...

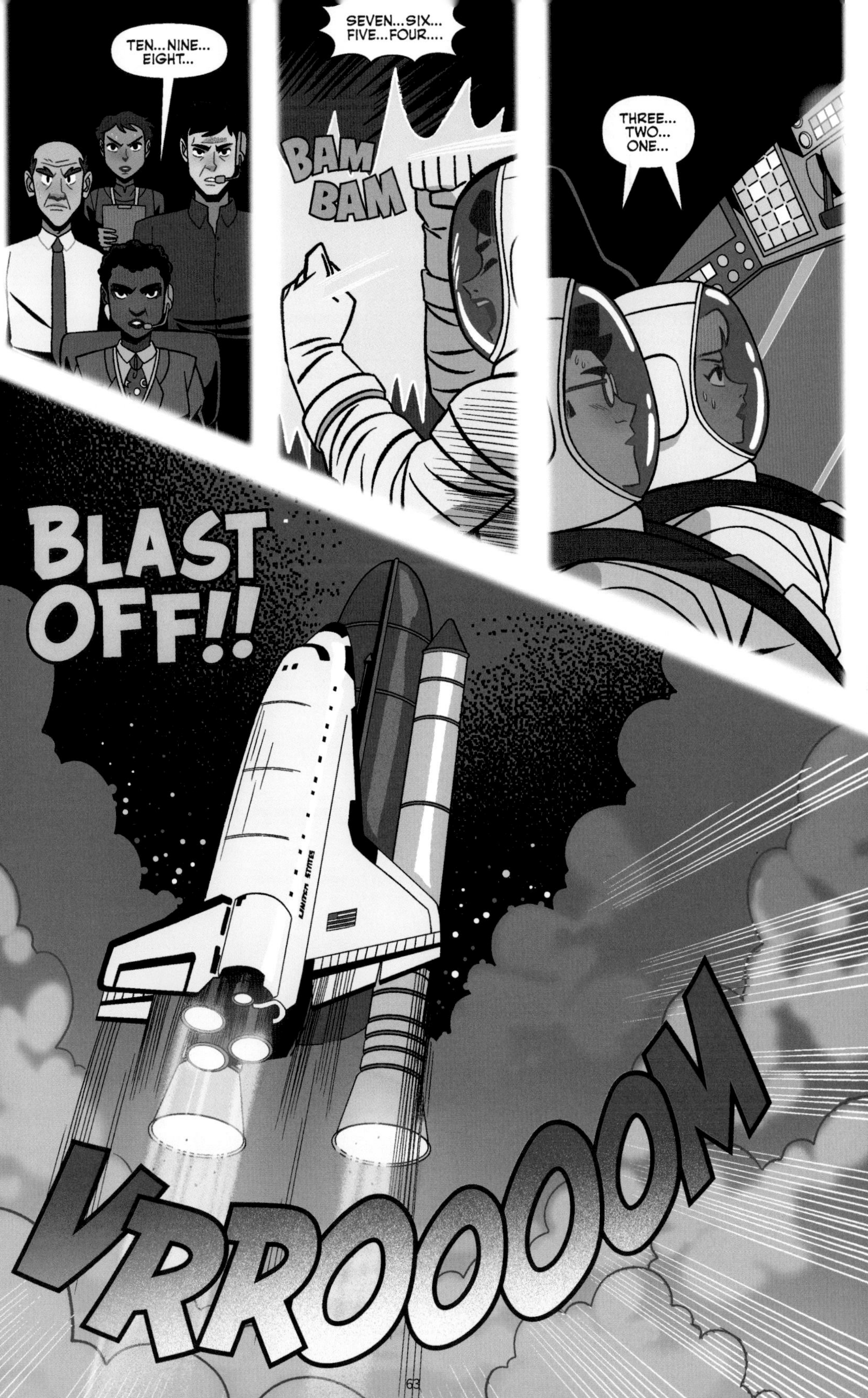

TEN...NINE...
EIGHT...
SEVEN...SIX...
FIVE...FOUR....
BAM
BAM
THREE...
TWO...
ONE...
BLAST
OFF!!
UNITED STATES
VRROOOOOM

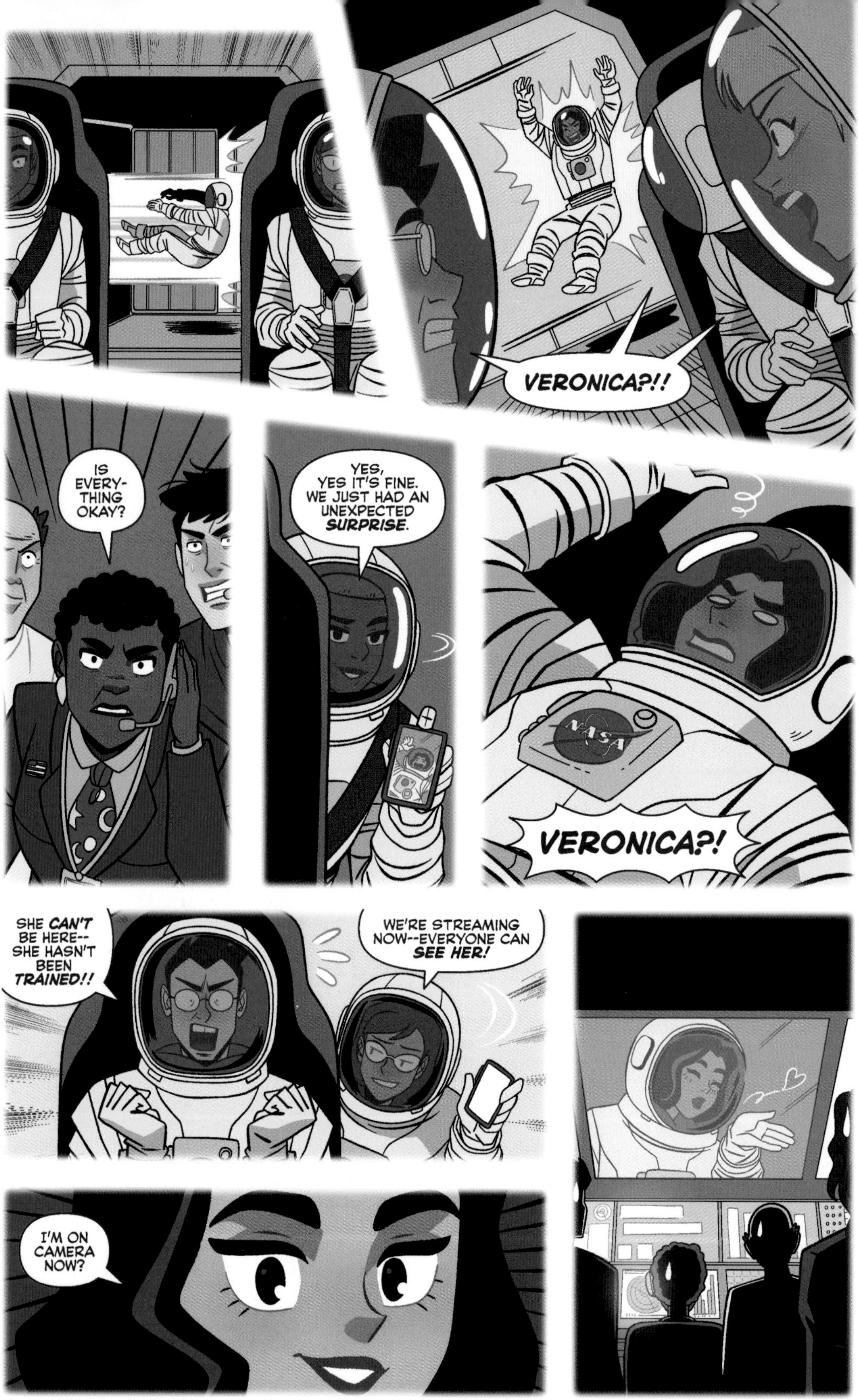
VERONICA?!!
IS EVERY-THING OKAY?
YES, YES IT'S FINE. WE JUST HAD AN UNEXPECTED SURPRISE.
VERONICA?!
SHE CAN'T BE HERE-- SHE HASN'T BEEN TRAINED!!
WE'RE STREAMING NOW--EVERYONE CAN SEE HER!
I'M ON CAMERA NOW?

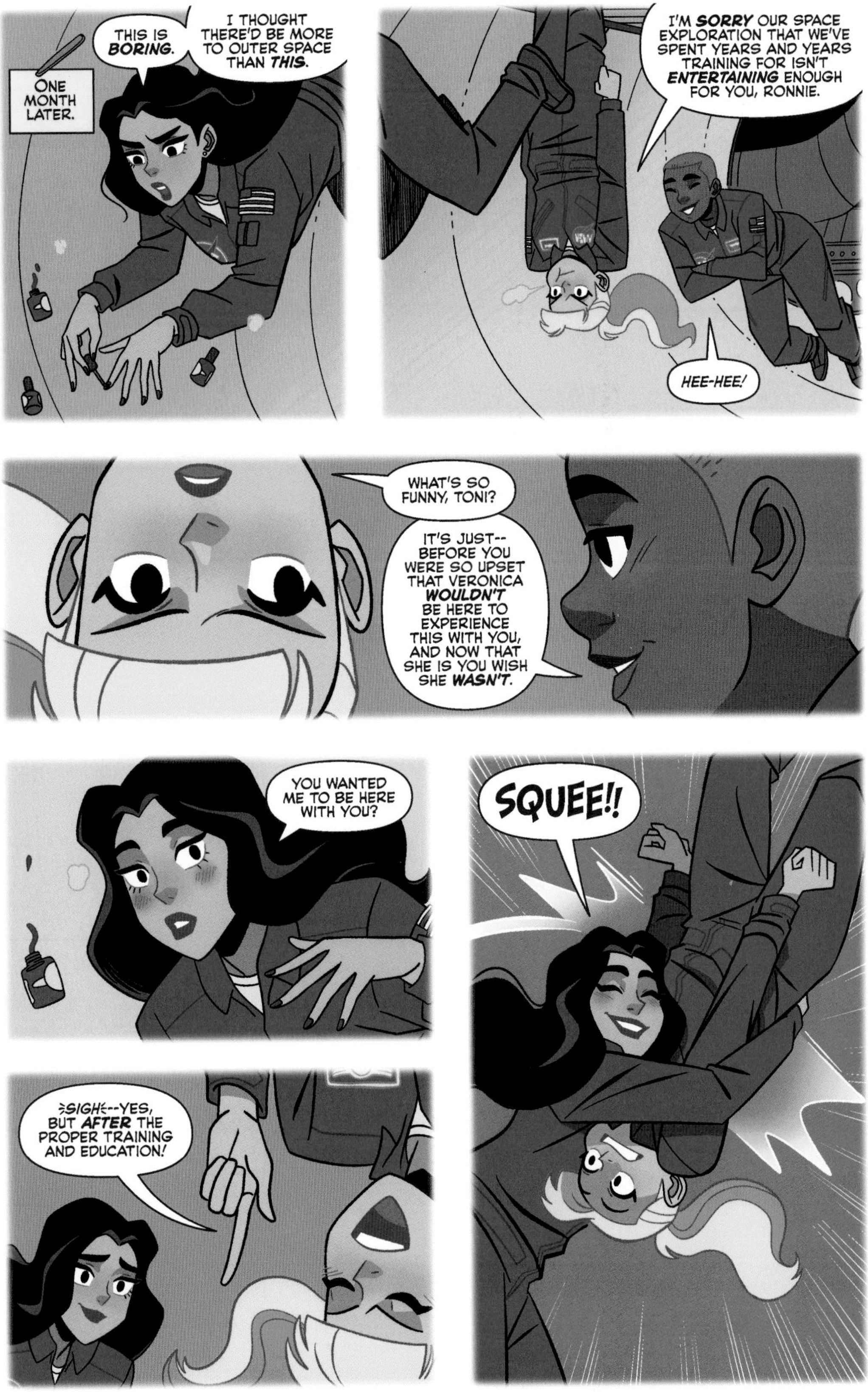
ONE MONTH LATER.
THIS IS BORING.
I THOUGHT THERE'D BE MORE TO OUTER SPACE THAN THIS.
I'M SORRY OUR SPACE EXPLORATION THAT WE'VE SPENT YEARS AND YEARS TRAINING FOR ISN'T ENTERTAINING ENOUGH FOR YOU, RONNIE.
HEE-HEE!
WHAT'S SO FUNNY, TONI?
IT'S JUST-- BEFORE YOU WERE SO UPSET THAT VERONICA WOULDN'T BE HERE TO EXPERIENCE THIS WITH YOU, AND NOW THAT SHE IS YOU WISH SHE WASN'T.
YOU WANTED ME TO BE HERE WITH YOU?
SIGH--YES, BUT AFTER THE PROPER TRAINING AND EDUCATION!
SQUEE!!

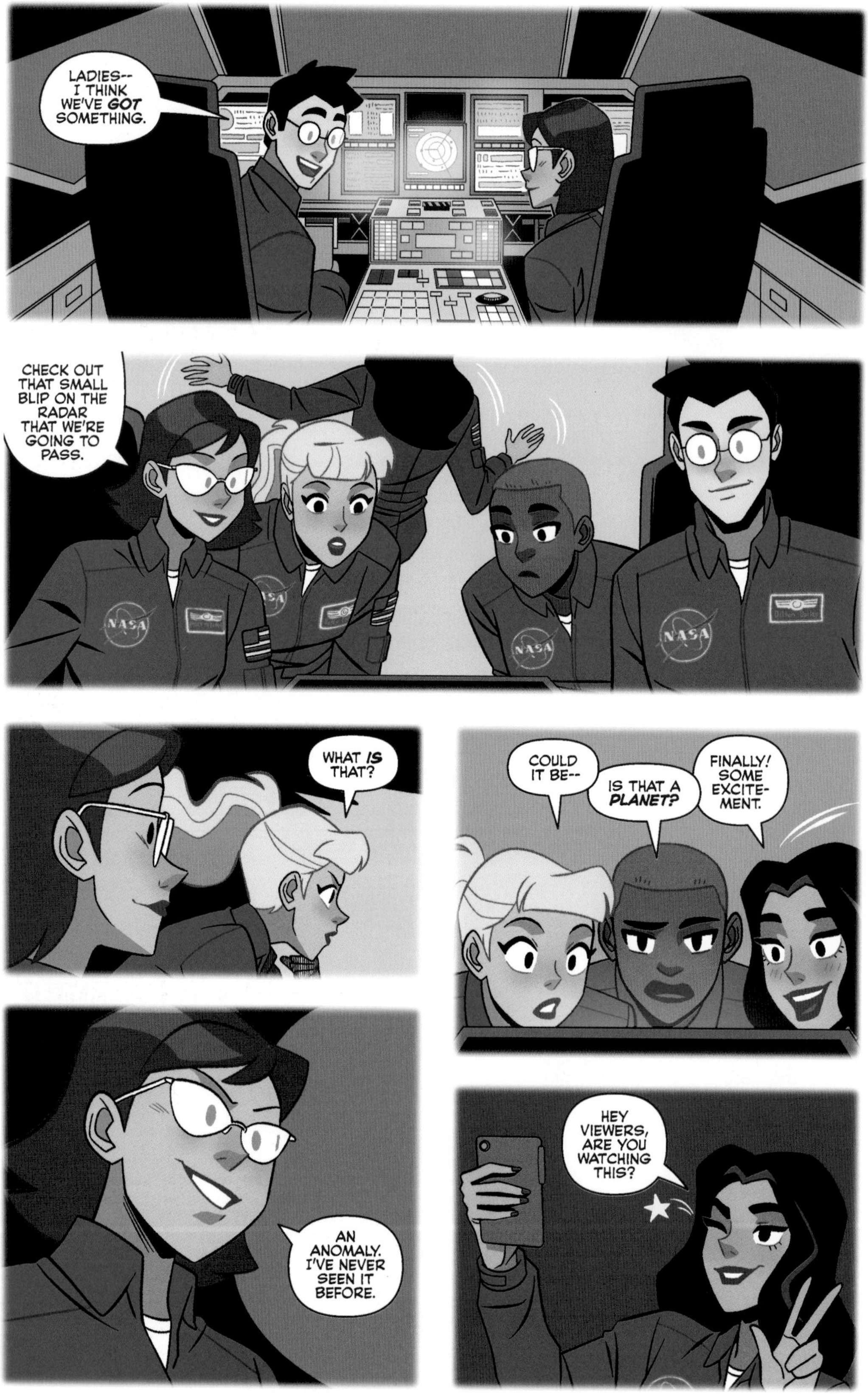
LADIES-- I THINK WE'VE **GOT** SOMETHING.
CHECK OUT THAT SMALL BLIP ON THE RADAR THAT WE'RE GOING TO PASS.
WHAT **IS** THAT?
AN ANOMALY. I'VE NEVER SEEN IT BEFORE.
COULD IT BE--
IS THAT A **PLANET?**
FINALLY! SOME EXCITE-MENT.
HEY VIEWERS, ARE YOU WATCHING THIS?

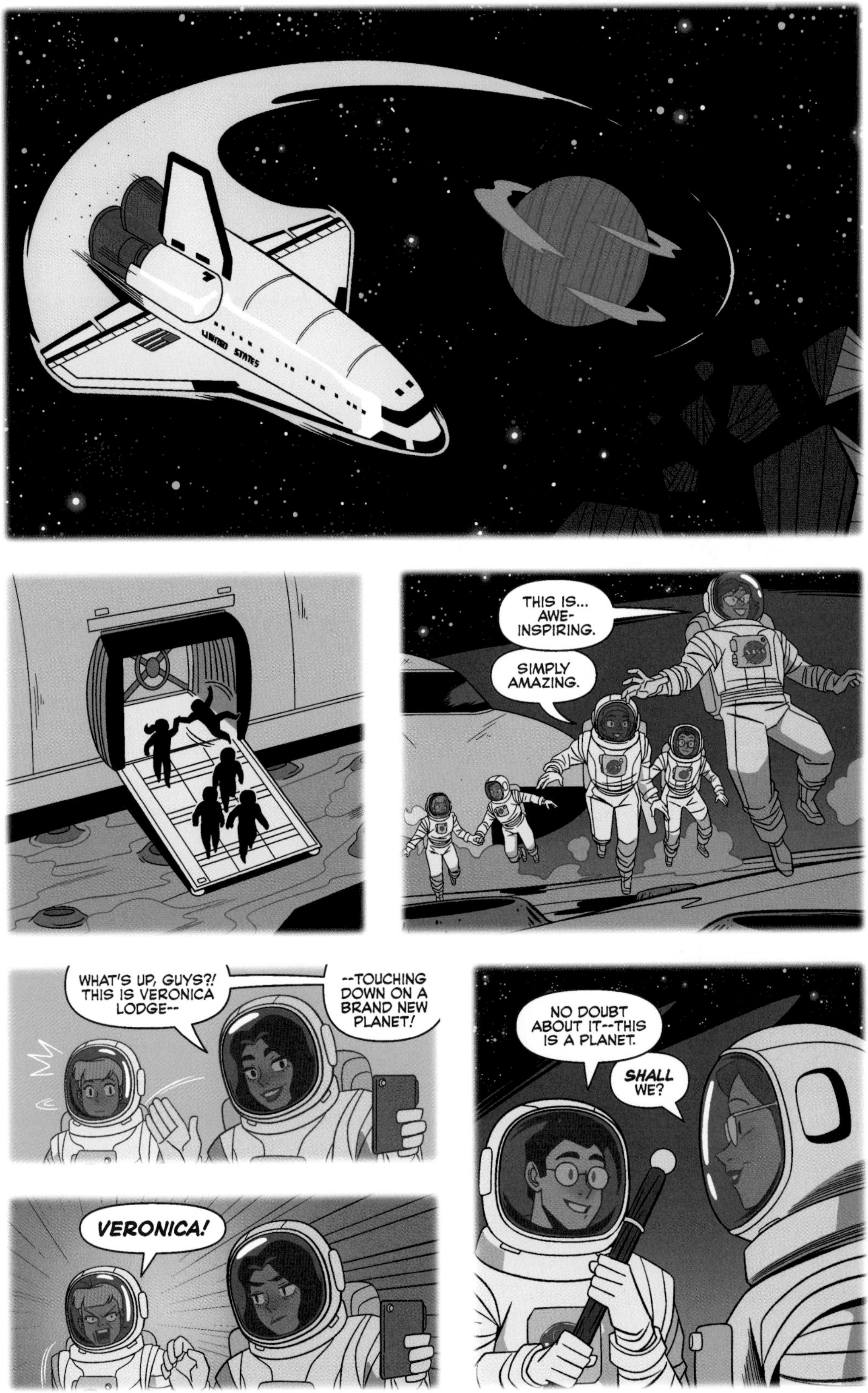
UNITED STATES
THIS IS... AWE-INSPIRING.
SIMPLY AMAZING.
WHAT'S UP, GUYS?! THIS IS VERONICA LODGE--
--TOUCHING DOWN ON A BRAND NEW PLANET!
VERONICA!
NO DOUBT ABOUT IT--THIS IS A PLANET.
SHALL WE?

SHOULD WE EXPLORE FOR ANY SIGNS OF LIFE?

Uh, MARCY-- I THINK *LIFE* HAS FOUND *US.*

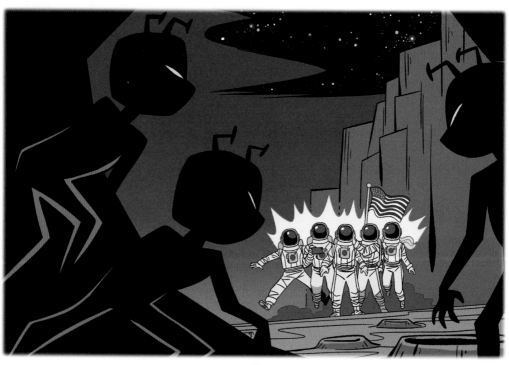

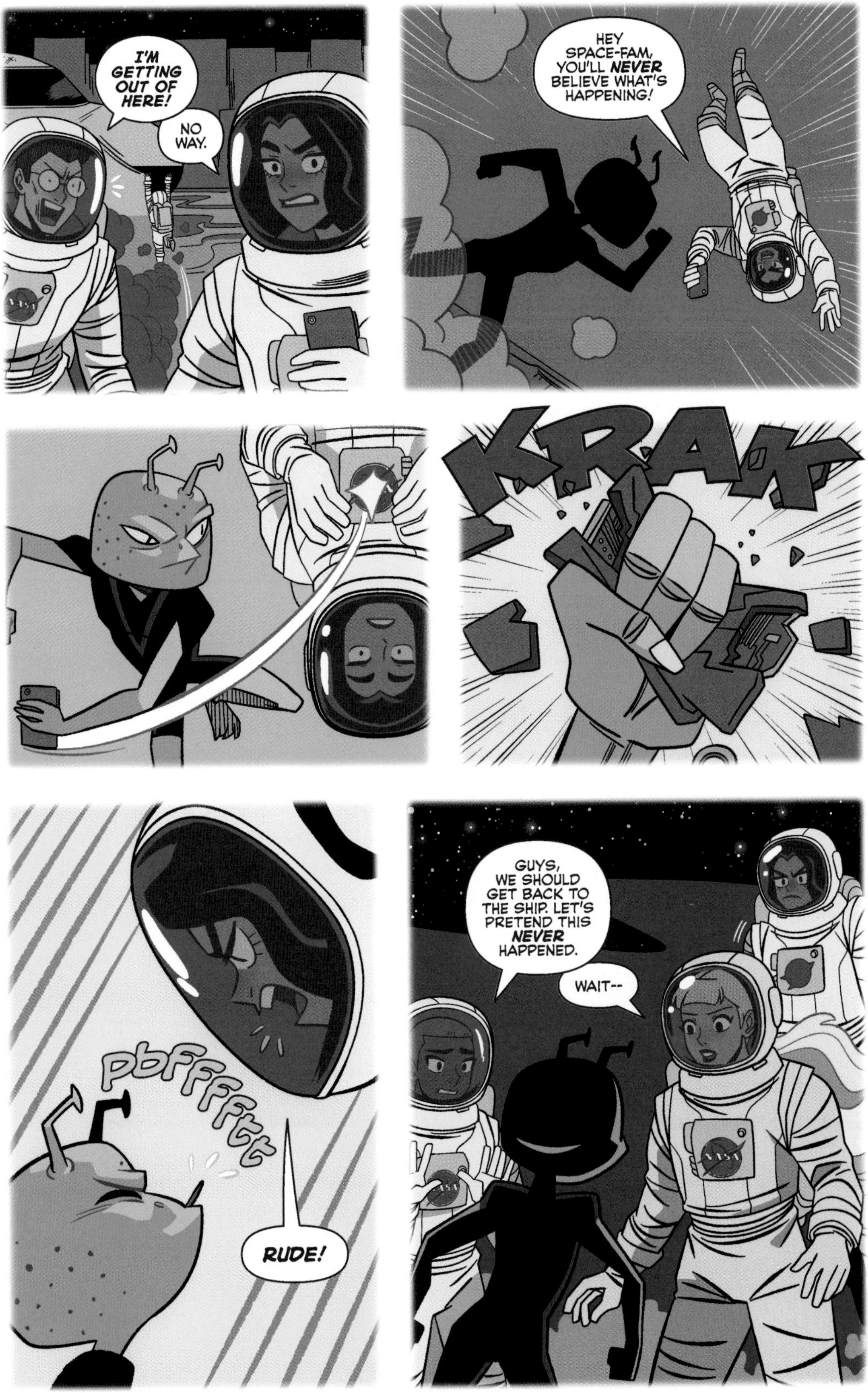
I'M GETTING OUT OF HERE!
NO WAY.
HEY SPACE-FAM, YOU'LL NEVER BELIEVE WHAT'S HAPPENING!
KRAK
pbffffttt
RUDE!
GUYS, WE SHOULD GET BACK TO THE SHIP. LET'S PRETEND THIS NEVER HAPPENED.
WAIT--

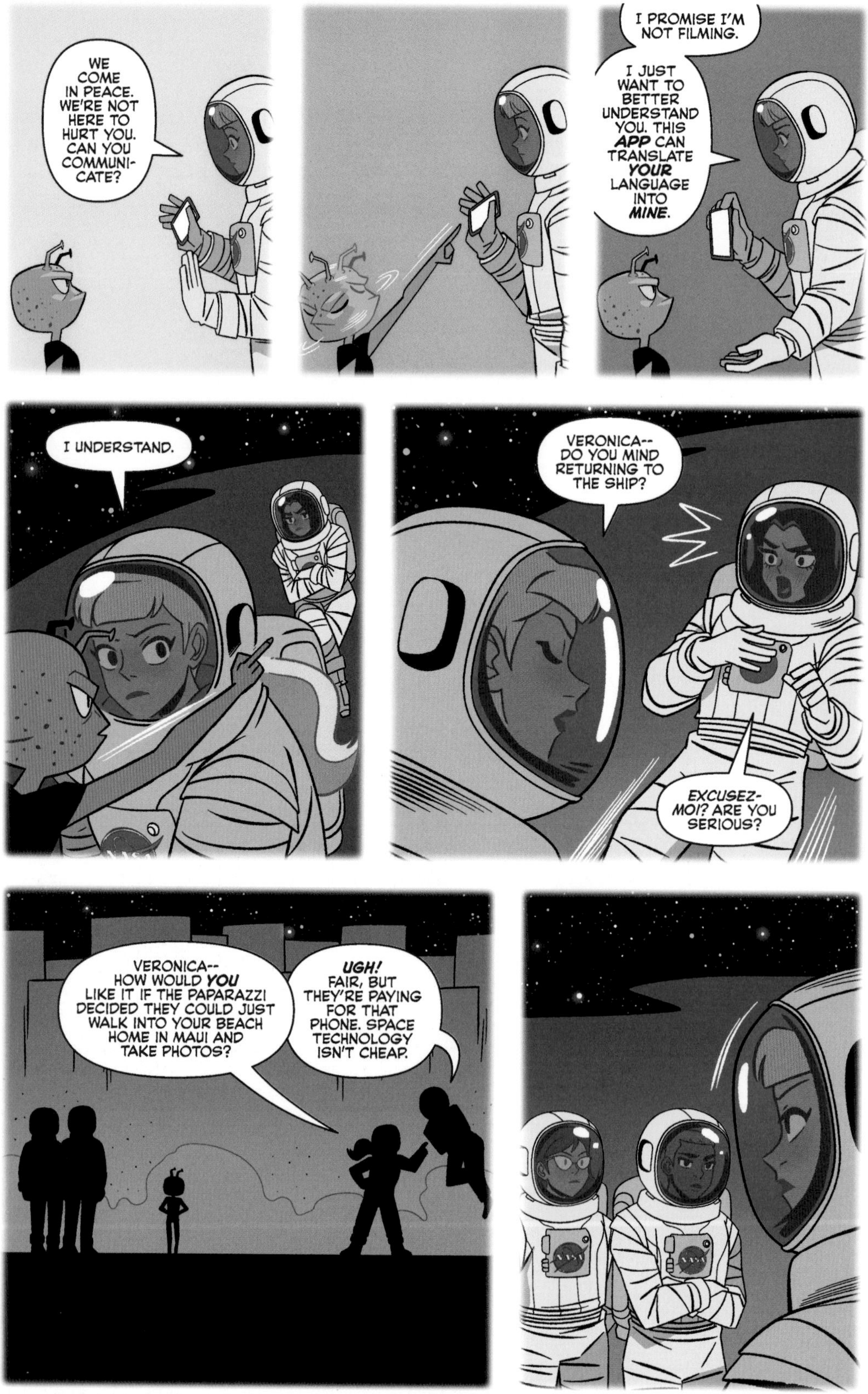
WE COME IN PEACE. WE'RE NOT HERE TO HURT YOU. CAN YOU COMMUNI-CATE?
I PROMISE I'M NOT FILMING.
I JUST WANT TO BETTER UNDERSTAND YOU. THIS APP CAN TRANSLATE YOUR LANGUAGE INTO MINE.
I UNDERSTAND.
VERONICA-- DO YOU MIND RETURNING TO THE SHIP?
EXCUSEZ-MOI? ARE YOU SERIOUS?
VERONICA-- HOW WOULD YOU LIKE IT IF THE PAPARAZZI DECIDED THEY COULD JUST WALK INTO YOUR BEACH HOME IN MAUI AND TAKE PHOTOS?
UGH! FAIR, BUT THEY'RE PAYING FOR THAT PHONE. SPACE TECHNOLOGY ISN'T CHEAP.

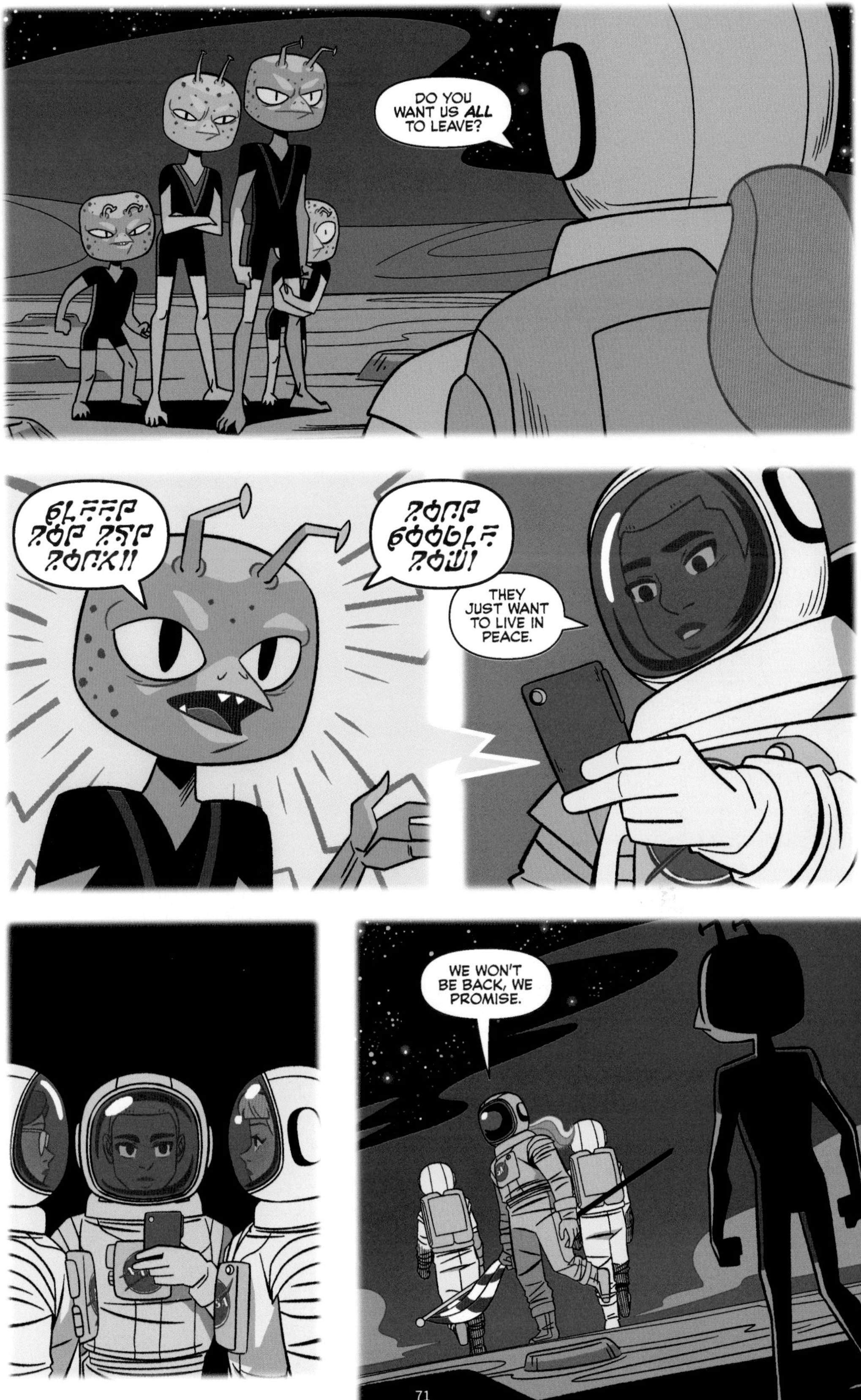
DO YOU WANT US ALL TO LEAVE?
THEY JUST WANT TO LIVE IN PEACE.
WE WON'T BE BACK, WE PROMISE.

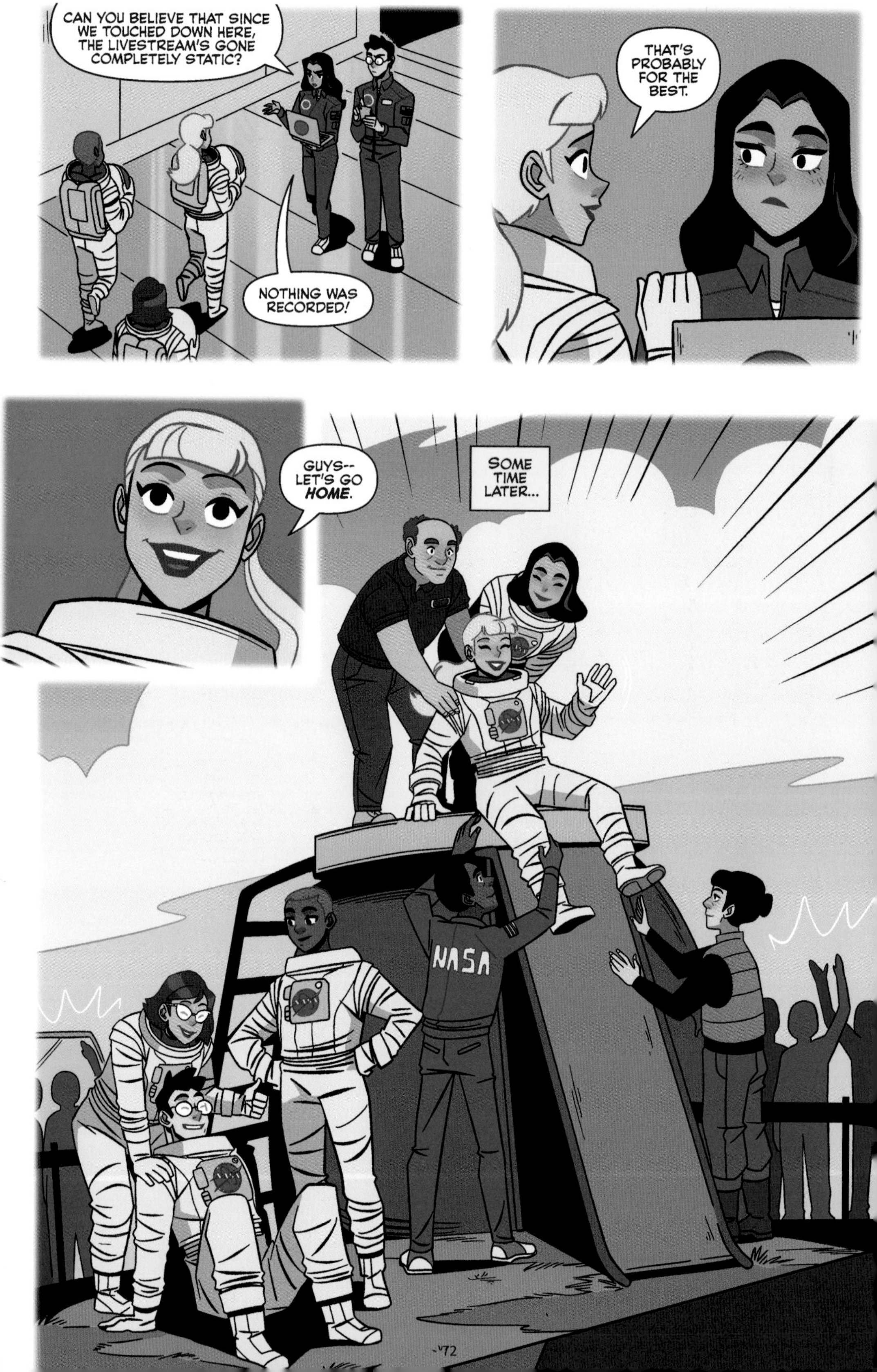
CAN YOU BELIEVE THAT SINCE WE TOUCHED DOWN HERE, THE LIVESTREAM'S GONE COMPLETELY STATIC?
NOTHING WAS RECORDED!
THAT'S PROBABLY FOR THE BEST.
GUYS-- LET'S GO HOME.
SOME TIME LATER...
NASA

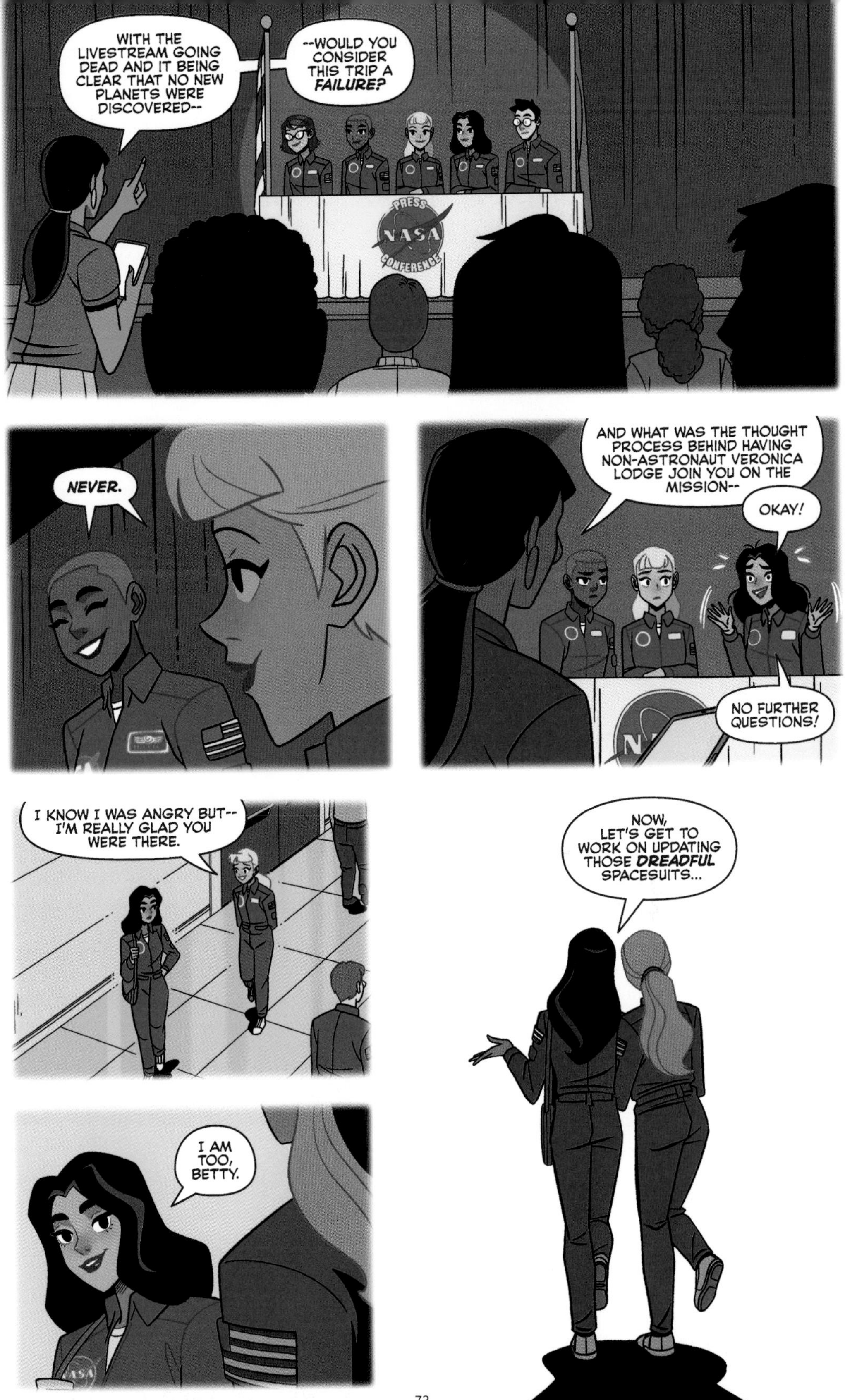
WITH THE LIVESTREAM GOING DEAD AND IT BEING CLEAR THAT NO NEW PLANETS WERE DISCOVERED--
--WOULD YOU CONSIDER THIS TRIP A FAILURE?
PRESS NASA CONFERENCE
NEVER.
AND WHAT WAS THE THOUGHT PROCESS BEHIND HAVING NON-ASTRONAUT VERONICA LODGE JOIN YOU ON THE MISSION--
OKAY!
NO FURTHER QUESTIONS!
I KNOW I WAS ANGRY BUT-- I'M REALLY GLAD YOU WERE THERE.
I AM TOO, BETTY.
NOW, LET'S GET TO WORK ON UPDATING THOSE DREADFUL SPACESUITS...

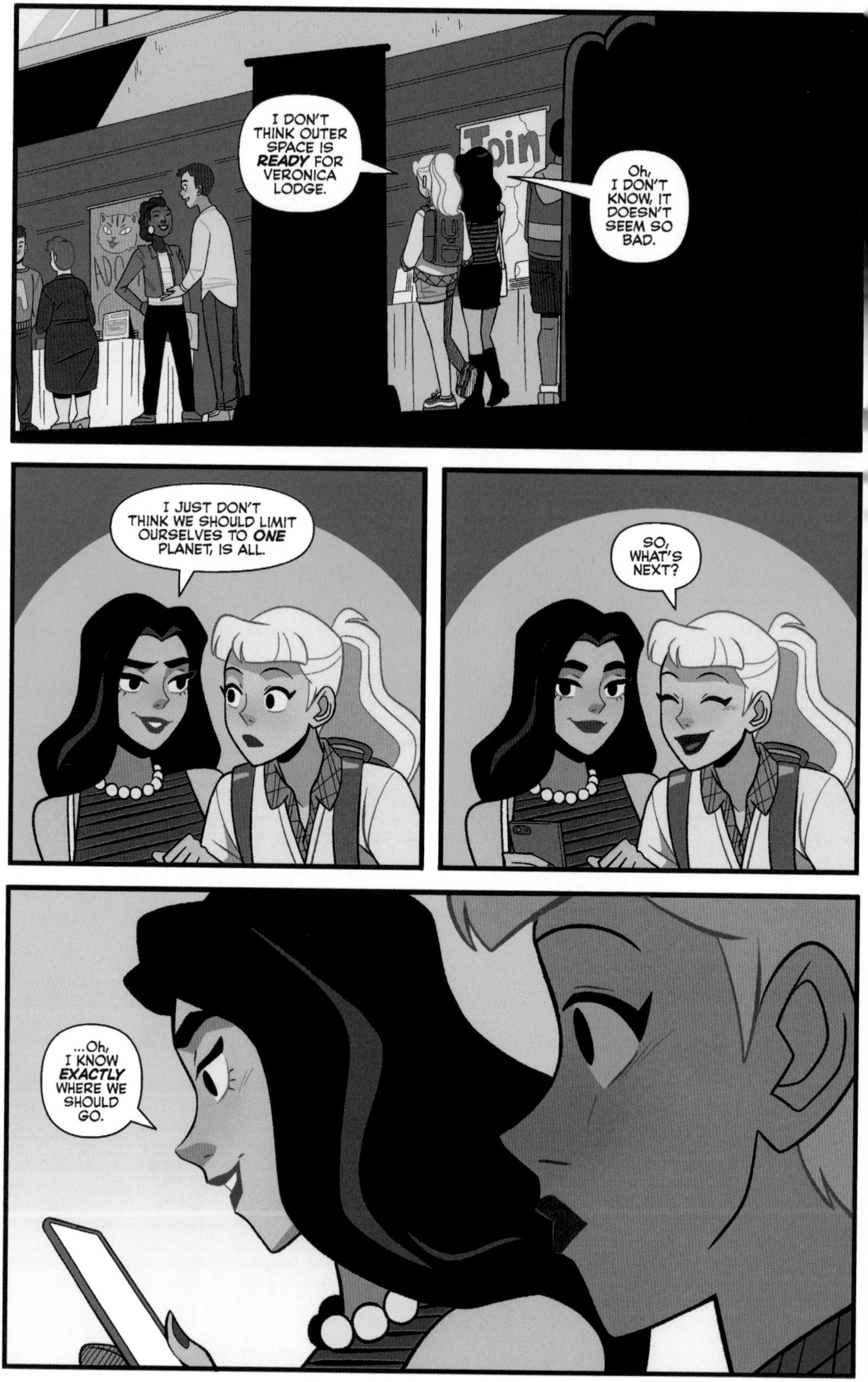
I DON'T THINK OUTER SPACE IS READY FOR VERONICA LODGE.
Oh, I DON'T KNOW, IT DOESN'T SEEM SO BAD.
I JUST DON'T THINK WE SHOULD LIMIT OURSELVES TO ONE PLANET, IS ALL.
SO, WHAT'S NEXT?
...Oh, I KNOW EXACTLY WHERE WE SHOULD GO.

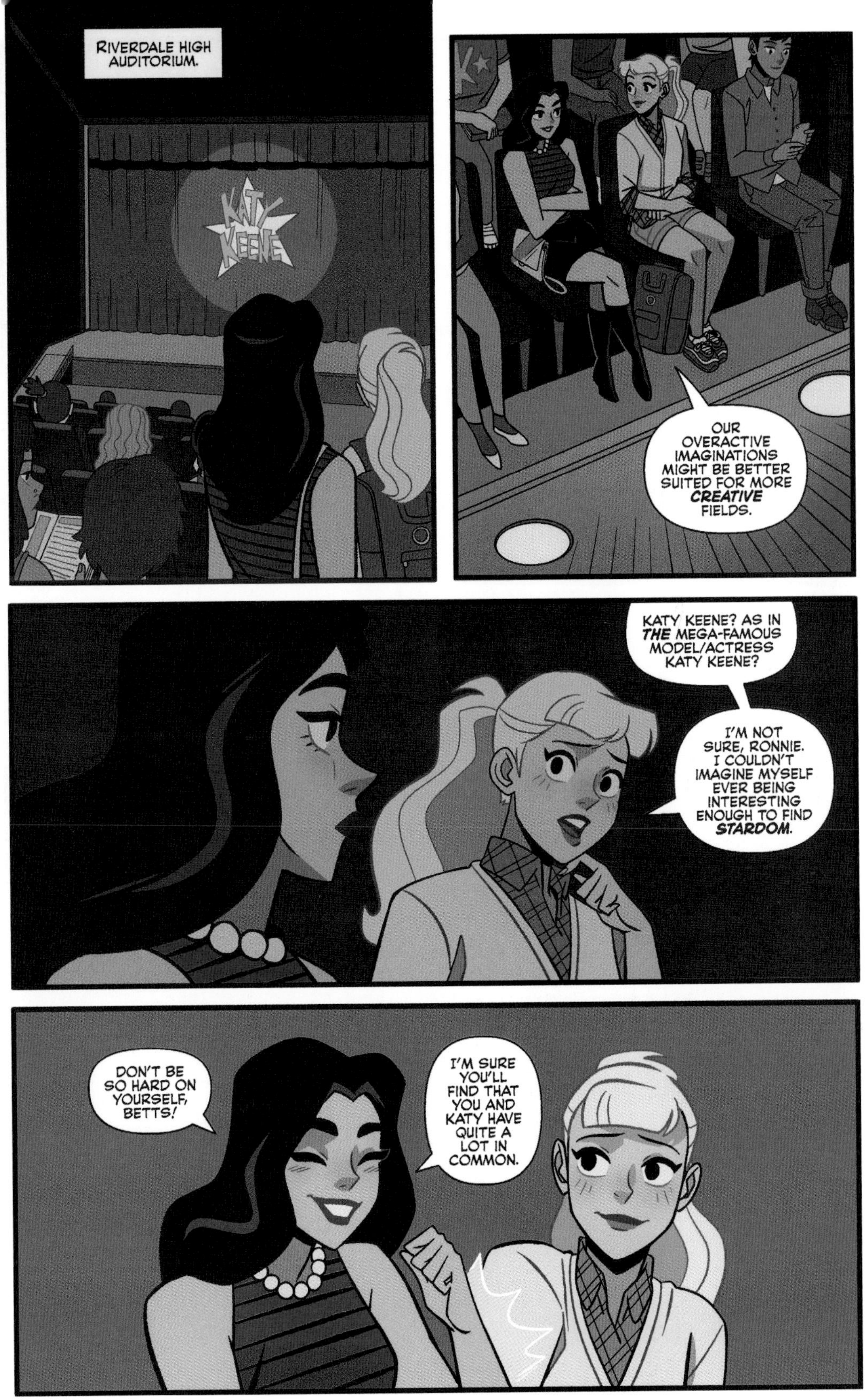
RIVERDALE HIGH AUDITORIUM.
KATY KEENE
OUR OVERACTIVE IMAGINATIONS MIGHT BE BETTER SUITED FOR MORE *CREATIVE* FIELDS.
KATY KEENE? AS IN *THE* MEGA-FAMOUS MODEL/ACTRESS KATY KEENE?
I'M NOT SURE, RONNIE. I COULDN'T IMAGINE MYSELF EVER BEING INTERESTING ENOUGH TO FIND *STARDOM*.
DON'T BE SO HARD ON YOURSELF, BETTS!
I'M SURE YOU'LL FIND THAT YOU AND KATY HAVE QUITE A LOT IN COMMON.

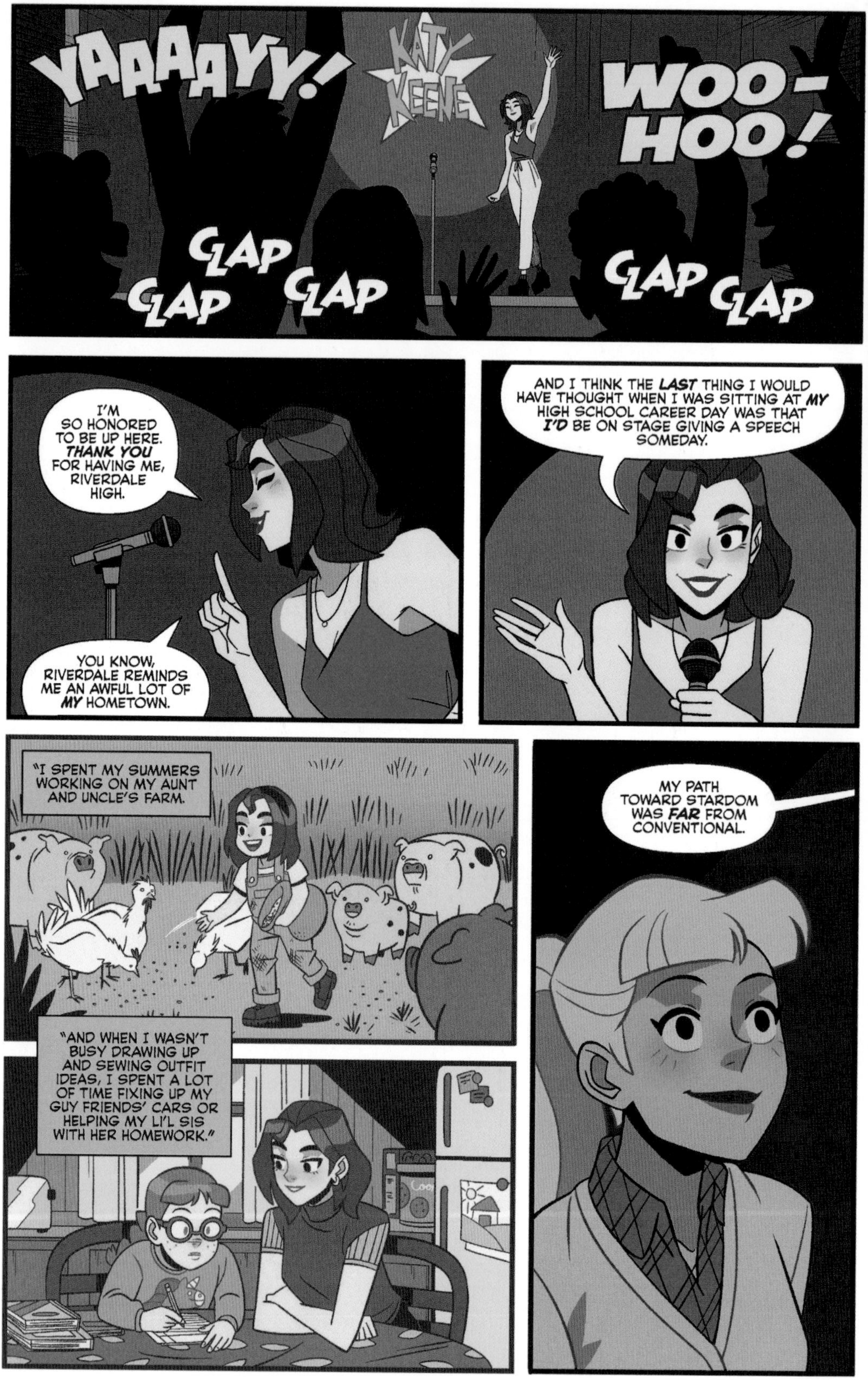
YAAAAYY!
KATY KEENE
WOO-HOO!
CLAP CLAP CLAP
CLAP CLAP
I'M SO HONORED TO BE UP HERE. THANK YOU FOR HAVING ME, RIVERDALE HIGH.
YOU KNOW, RIVERDALE REMINDS ME AN AWFUL LOT OF MY HOMETOWN.
AND I THINK THE LAST THING I WOULD HAVE THOUGHT WHEN I WAS SITTING AT MY HIGH SCHOOL CAREER DAY WAS THAT I'D BE ON STAGE GIVING A SPEECH SOMEDAY.
"I SPENT MY SUMMERS WORKING ON MY AUNT AND UNCLE'S FARM.
"AND WHEN I WASN'T BUSY DRAWING UP AND SEWING OUTFIT IDEAS, I SPENT A LOT OF TIME FIXING UP MY GUY FRIENDS' CARS OR HELPING MY LI'L SIS WITH HER HOMEWORK."
MY PATH TOWARD STARDOM WAS FAR FROM CONVENTIONAL.

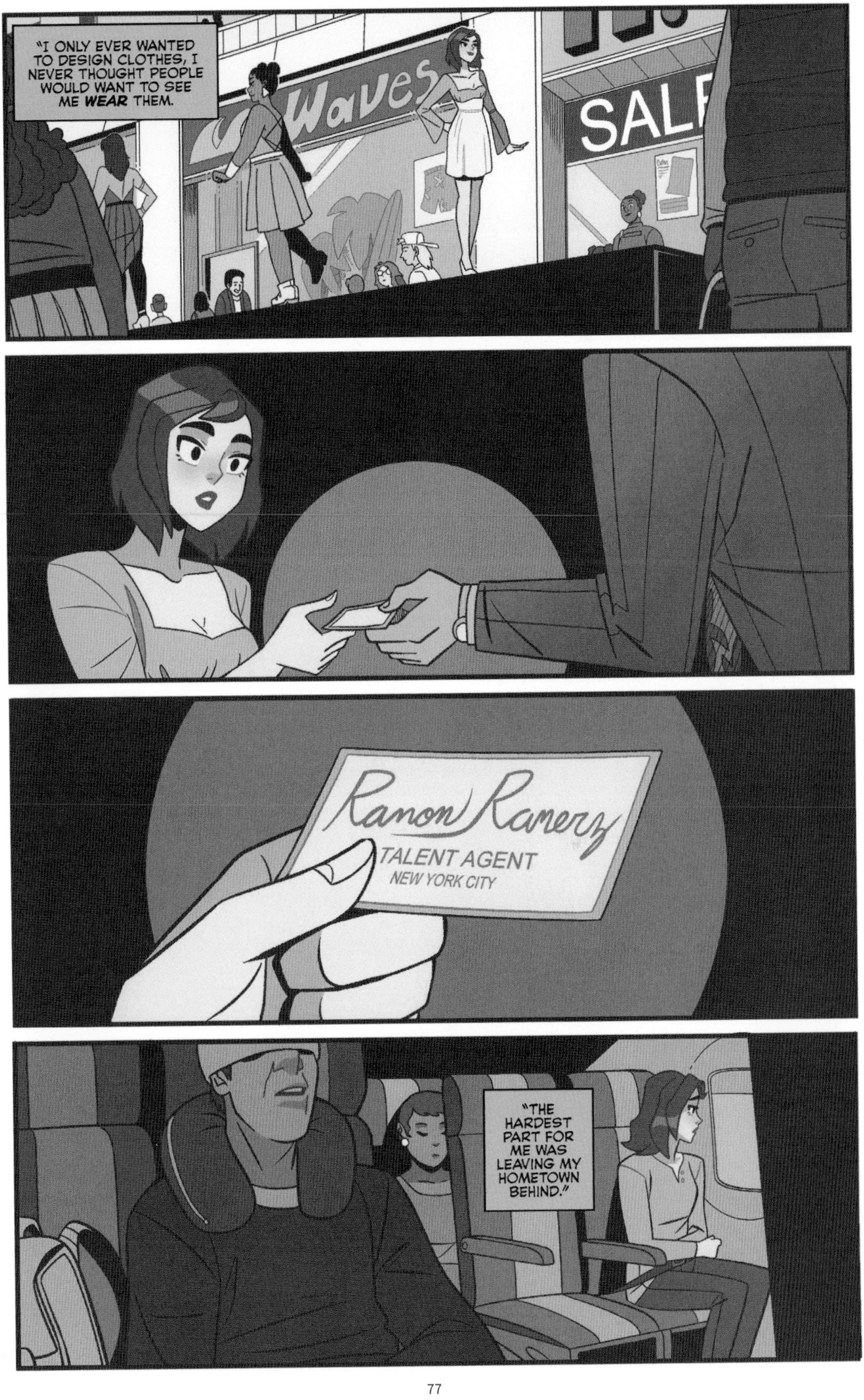
"I ONLY EVER WANTED TO DESIGN CLOTHES, I NEVER THOUGHT PEOPLE WOULD WANT TO SEE ME WEAR THEM.
Waves
SAL
Ranon Ranerz
TALENT AGENT
NEW YORK CITY
"THE HARDEST PART FOR ME WAS LEAVING MY HOMETOWN BEHIND."

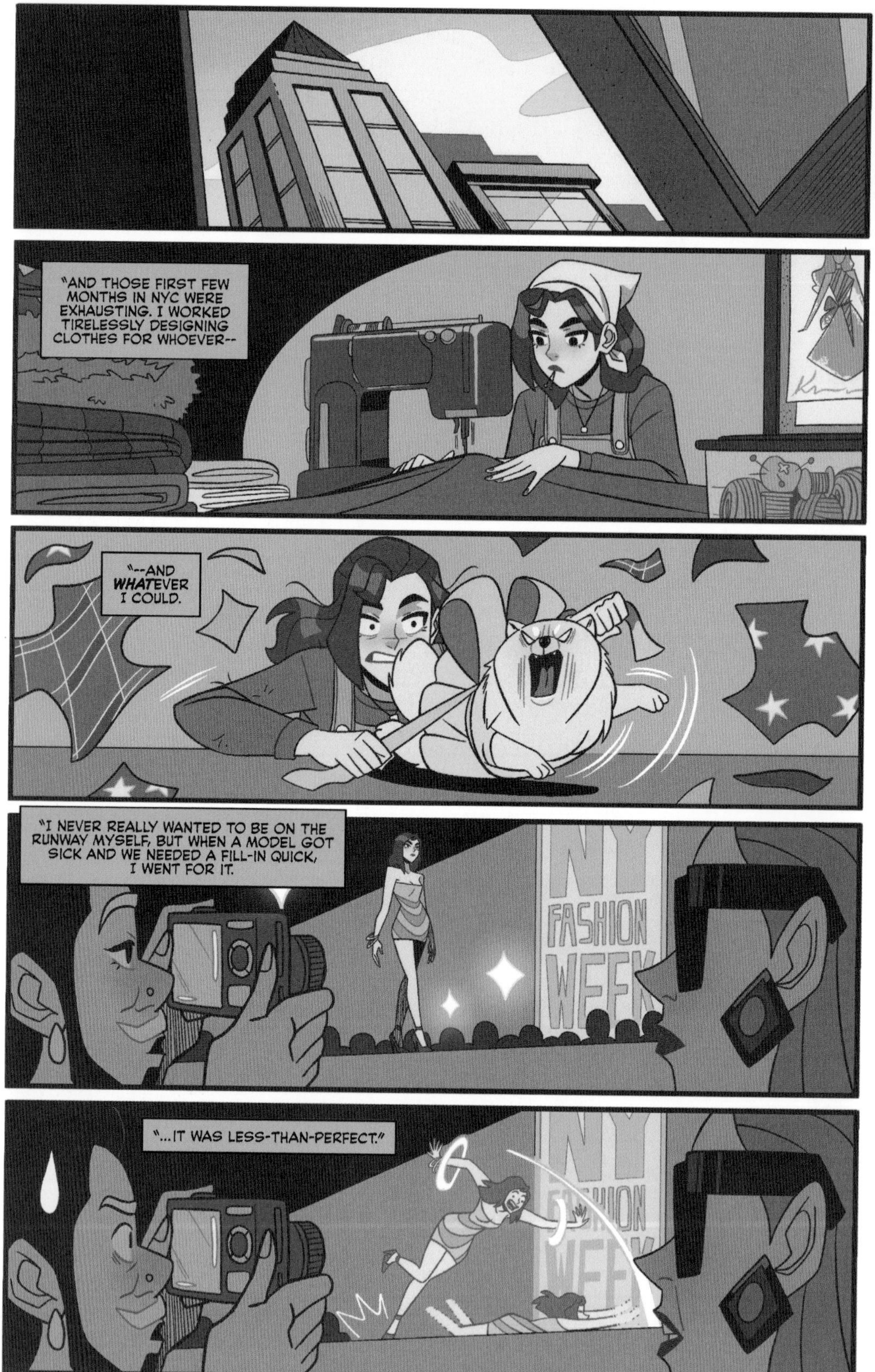
"AND THOSE FIRST FEW MONTHS IN NYC WERE EXHAUSTING. I WORKED TIRELESSLY DESIGNING CLOTHES FOR WHOEVER--
"--AND WHATEVER I COULD.
"I NEVER REALLY WANTED TO BE ON THE RUNWAY MYSELF, BUT WHEN A MODEL GOT SICK AND WE NEEDED A FILL-IN QUICK, I WENT FOR IT.
NY FASHION WEEK
"...IT WAS LESS-THAN-PERFECT."

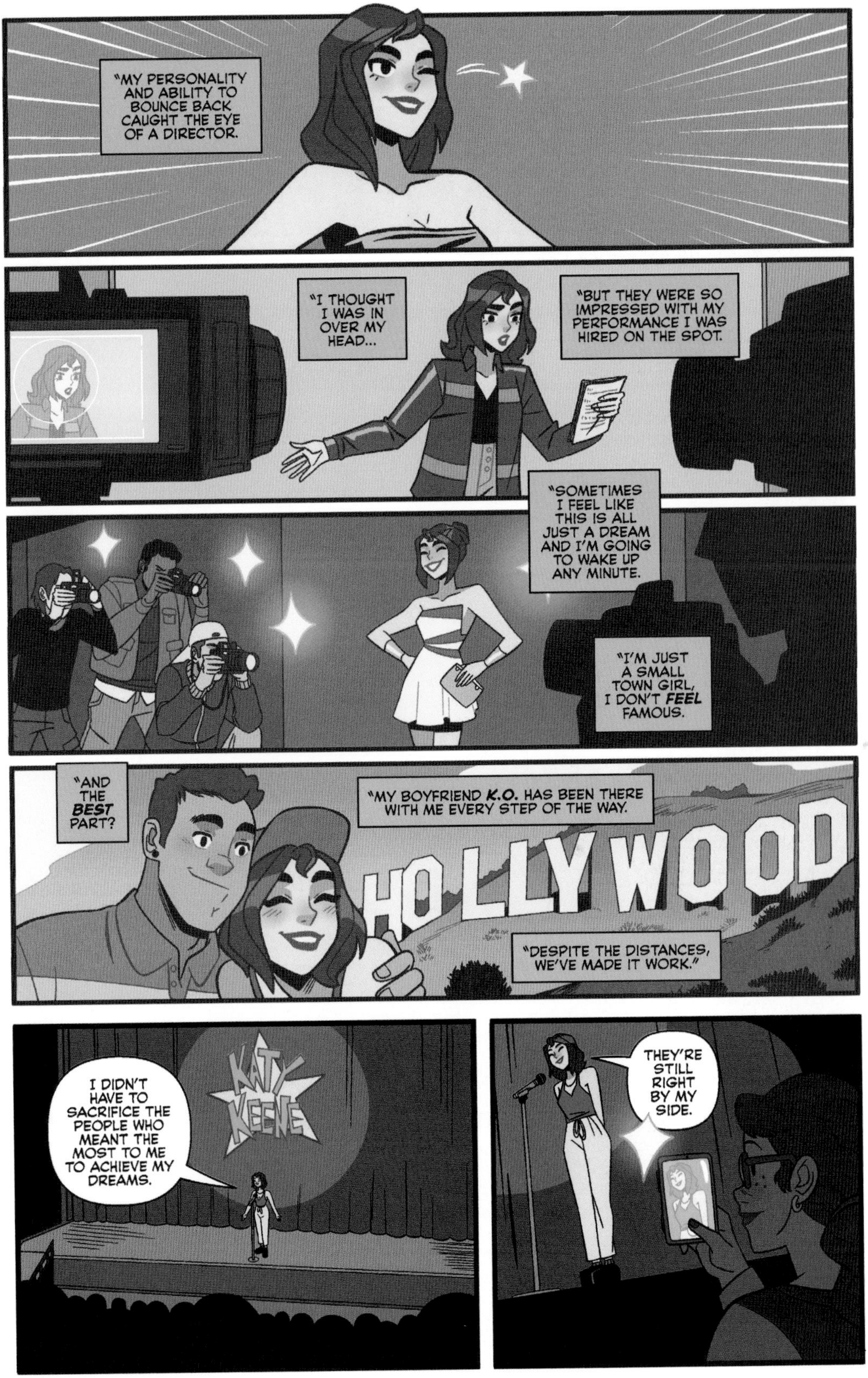
"MY PERSONALITY AND ABILITY TO BOUNCE BACK CAUGHT THE EYE OF A DIRECTOR.
"I THOUGHT I WAS IN OVER MY HEAD...
"BUT THEY WERE SO IMPRESSED WITH MY PERFORMANCE I WAS HIRED ON THE SPOT.
"SOMETIMES I FEEL LIKE THIS IS ALL JUST A DREAM AND I'M GOING TO WAKE UP ANY MINUTE.
"I'M JUST A SMALL TOWN GIRL, I DON'T *FEEL* FAMOUS.
"AND THE *BEST* PART?
"MY BOYFRIEND *K.O.* HAS BEEN THERE WITH ME EVERY STEP OF THE WAY.
HOLLYWOOD
"DESPITE THE DISTANCES, WE'VE MADE IT WORK."
KATY KEENE
I DIDN'T HAVE TO SACRIFICE THE PEOPLE WHO MEANT THE MOST TO ME TO ACHIEVE MY DREAMS.
THEY'RE STILL RIGHT BY MY SIDE.

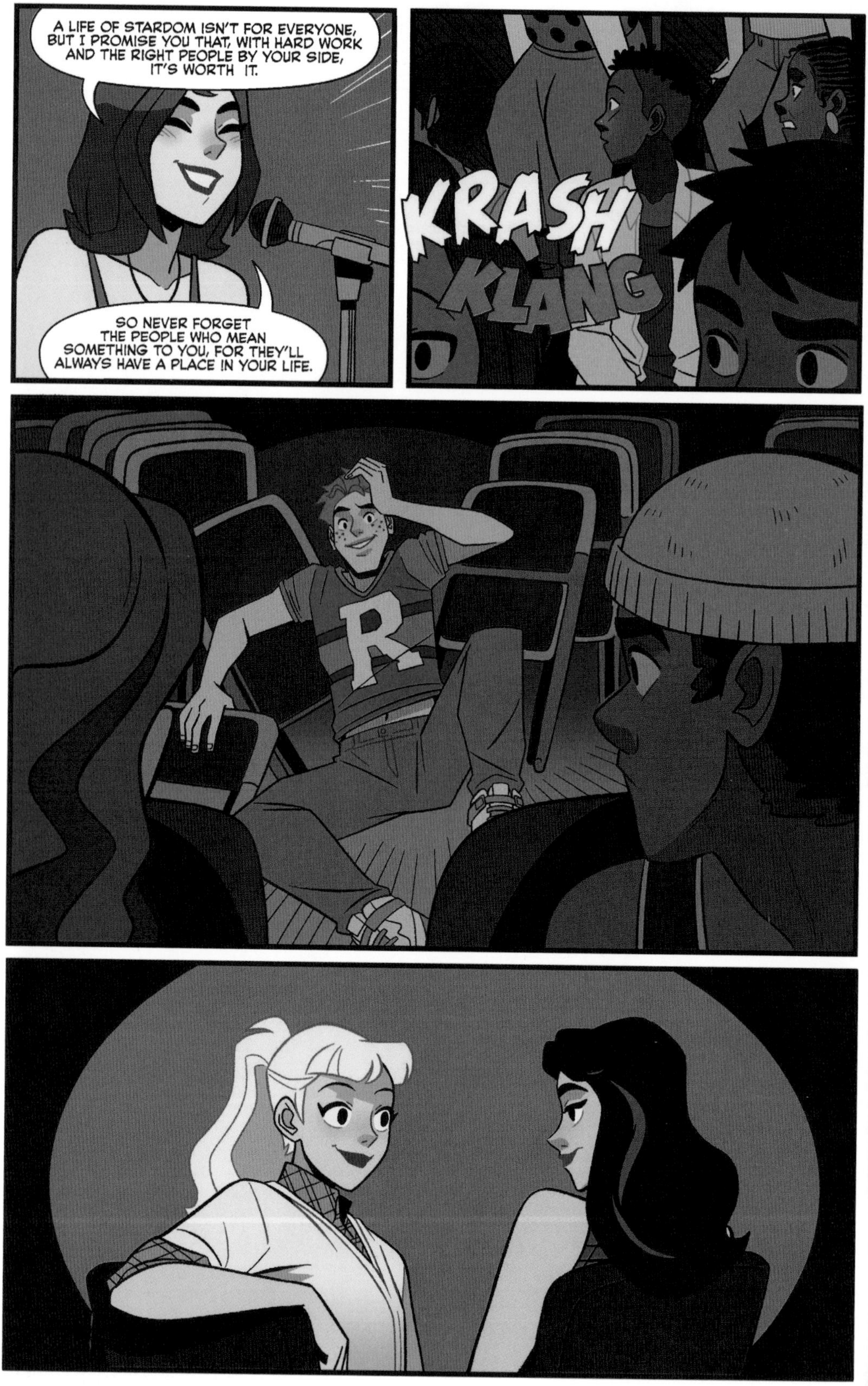
A LIFE OF STARDOM ISN'T FOR EVERYONE, BUT I PROMISE YOU THAT, WITH HARD WORK AND THE RIGHT PEOPLE BY YOUR SIDE, IT'S WORTH IT.
SO NEVER FORGET THE PEOPLE WHO MEAN SOMETHING TO YOU, FOR THEY'LL ALWAYS HAVE A PLACE IN YOUR LIFE.
KRASH
KLANG

CHAPTER THREE

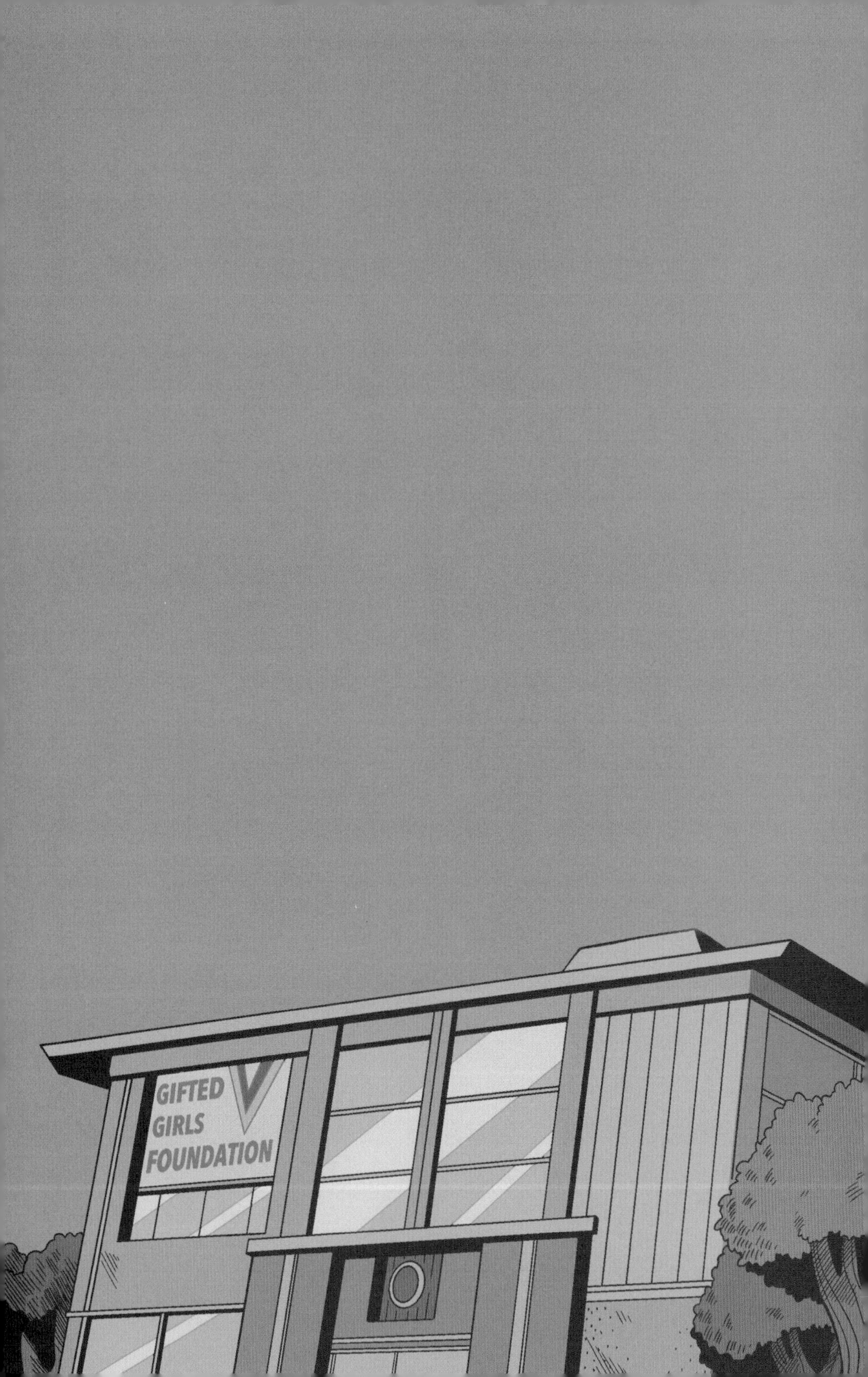
GIFTED
GIRLS
FOUNDATION

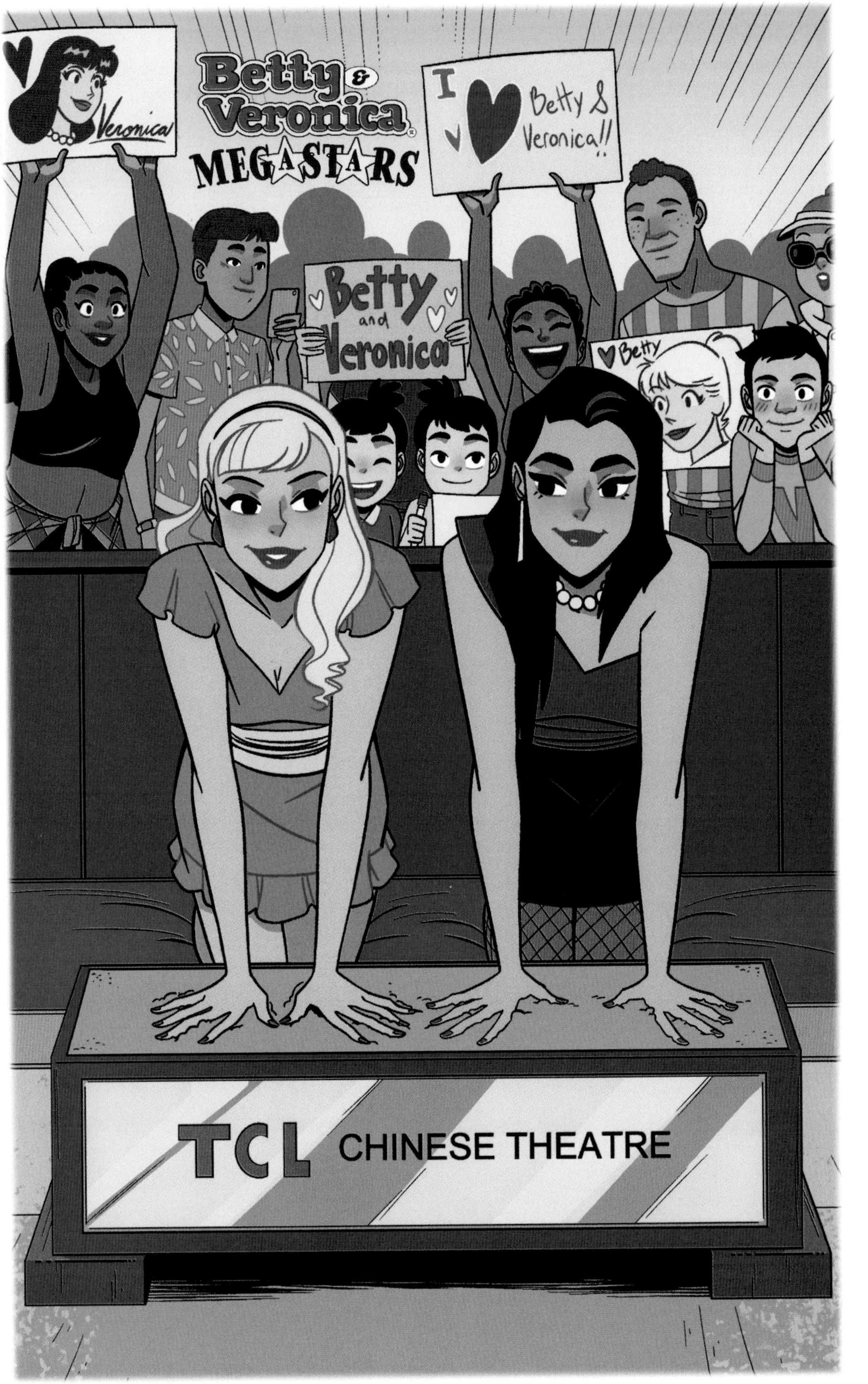
Veronica
Betty & Veronica MEGASTARS
I Betty & Veronica!!
Betty and Veronica
Betty
TCL CHINESE THEATRE

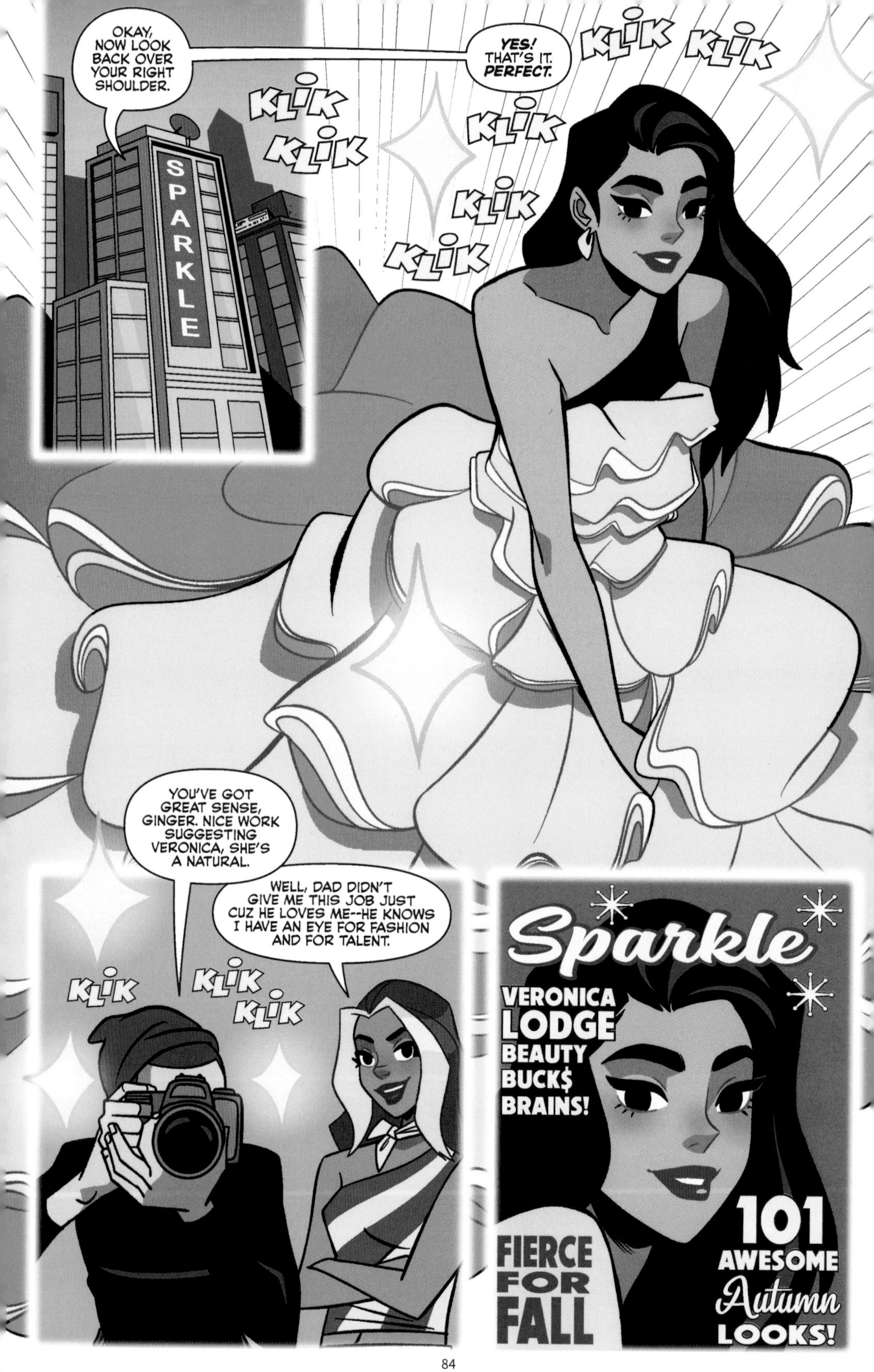
OKAY, NOW LOOK BACK OVER YOUR RIGHT SHOULDER.
SPARKLE
YES! THAT'S IT. PERFECT.
KLIK KLIK
KLIK
KLIK
KLIK
KLIK
KLIK
YOU'VE GOT GREAT SENSE, GINGER. NICE WORK SUGGESTING VERONICA, SHE'S A NATURAL.
WELL, DAD DIDN'T GIVE ME THIS JOB JUST CUZ HE LOVES ME--HE KNOWS I HAVE AN EYE FOR FASHION AND FOR TALENT.
KLIK
KLIK
KLIK
Sparkle
VERONICA LODGE
BEAUTY
BUCK$
BRAINS!
FIERCE FOR FALL
101 AWESOME Autumn LOOKS!

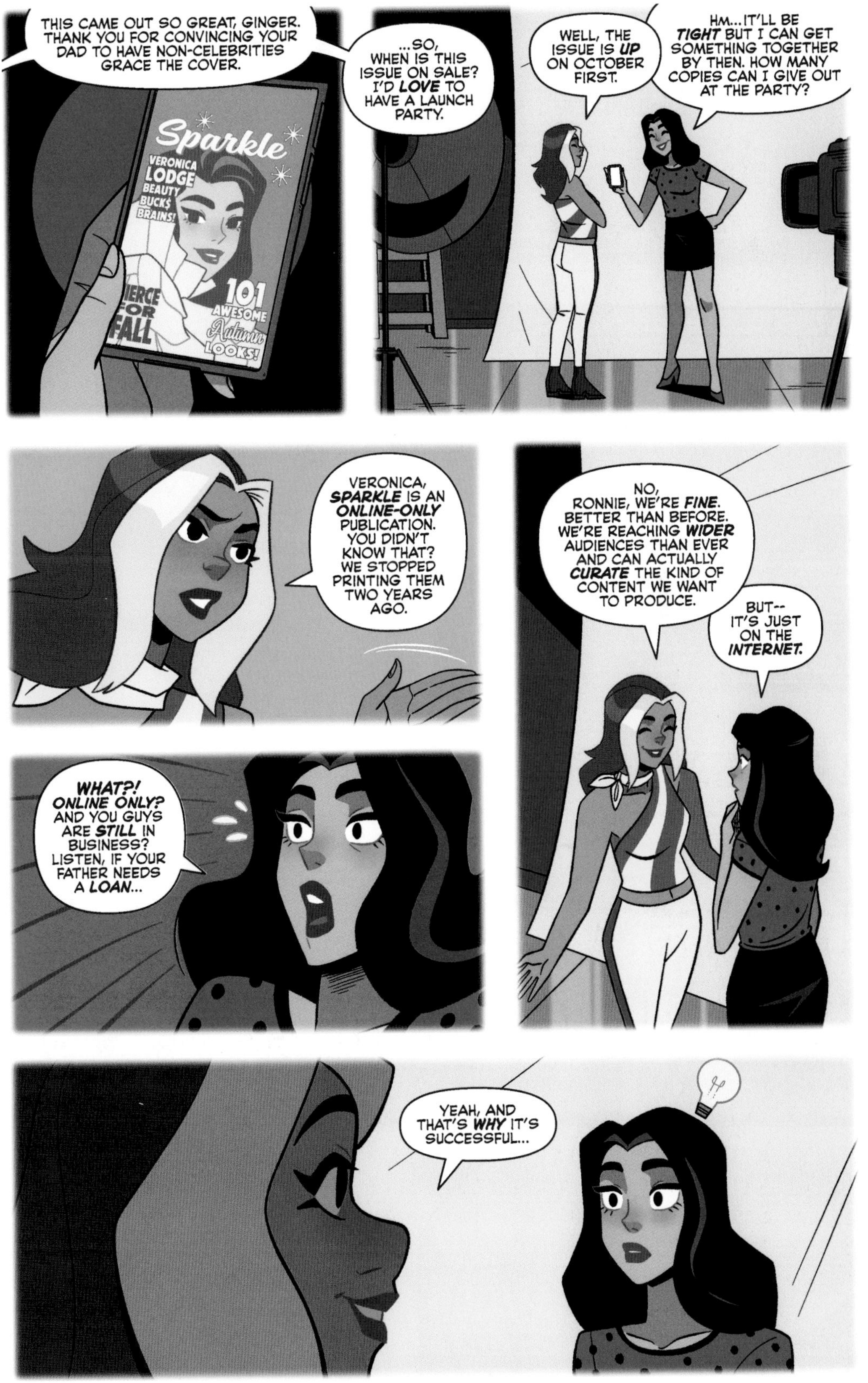
THIS CAME OUT SO GREAT, GINGER. THANK YOU FOR CONVINCING YOUR DAD TO HAVE NON-CELEBRITIES GRACE THE COVER.
Sparkle
VERONICA LODGE BEAUTY BUCK$ BRAINS!
IERCE FOR FALL
101 AWESOME Autumn LOOKS!
...SO, WHEN IS THIS ISSUE ON SALE? I'D **LOVE** TO HAVE A LAUNCH PARTY.
WELL, THE ISSUE IS **UP** ON OCTOBER FIRST.
HM...IT'LL BE **TIGHT** BUT I CAN GET SOMETHING TOGETHER BY THEN. HOW MANY COPIES CAN I GIVE OUT AT THE PARTY?
VERONICA, **SPARKLE** IS AN **ONLINE-ONLY** PUBLICATION. YOU DIDN'T KNOW THAT? WE STOPPED PRINTING THEM TWO YEARS AGO.
WHAT?! ONLINE ONLY? AND YOU GUYS ARE **STILL** IN BUSINESS? LISTEN, IF YOUR FATHER NEEDS A **LOAN**...
NO, RONNIE, WE'RE **FINE**. BETTER THAN BEFORE. WE'RE REACHING **WIDER** AUDIENCES THAN EVER AND CAN ACTUALLY **CURATE** THE KIND OF CONTENT WE WANT TO PRODUCE.
BUT-- IT'S JUST ON THE **INTERNET**.
YEAH, AND THAT'S **WHY** IT'S SUCCESSFUL...

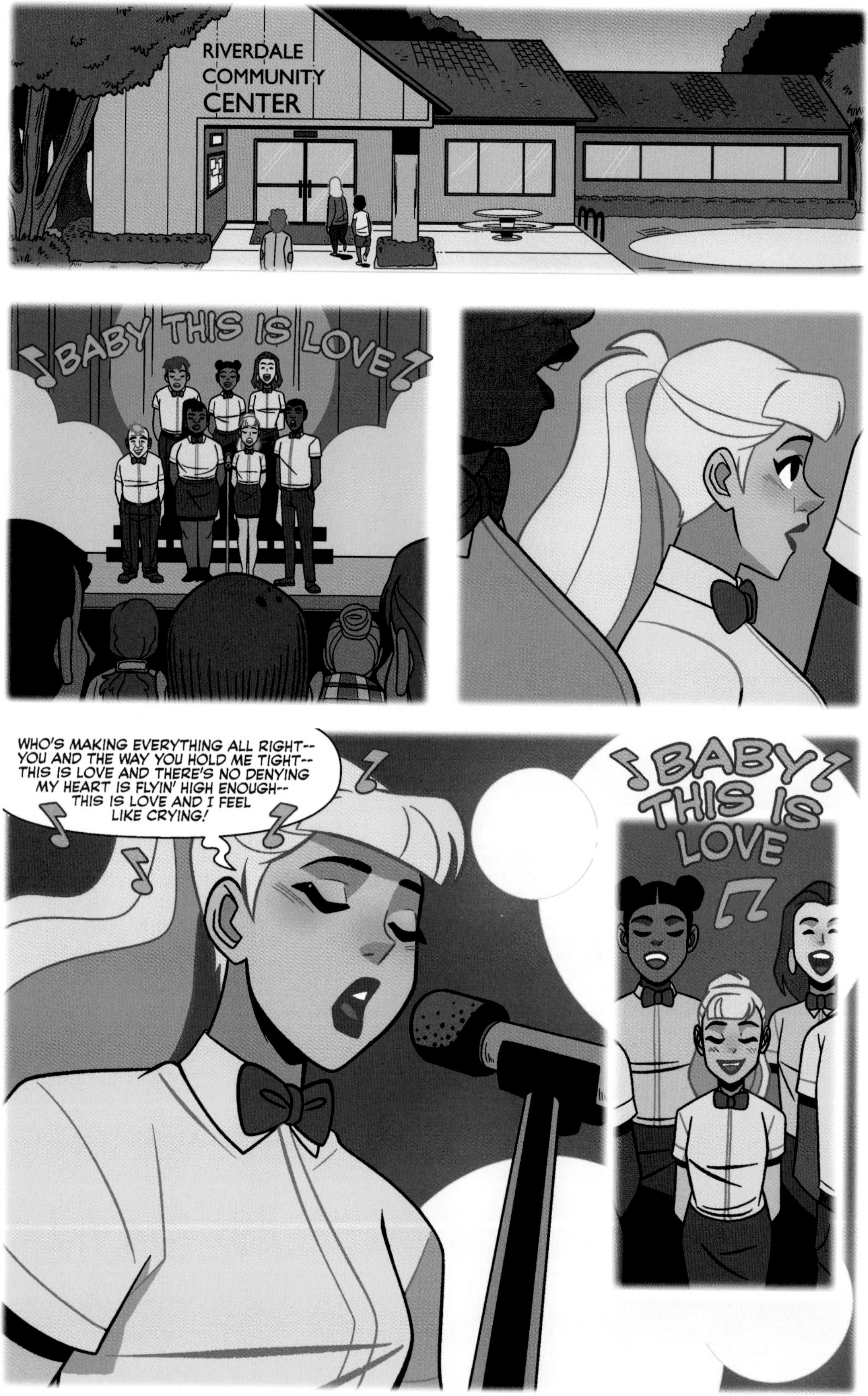
RIVERDALE
COMMUNITY
CENTER
BABY THIS IS LOVE
WHO'S MAKING EVERYTHING ALL RIGHT--
YOU AND THE WAY YOU HOLD ME TIGHT--
THIS IS LOVE AND THERE'S NO DENYING
MY HEART IS FLYIN' HIGH ENOUGH--
THIS IS LOVE AND I FEEL
LIKE CRYING!
BABY
THIS IS
LOVE

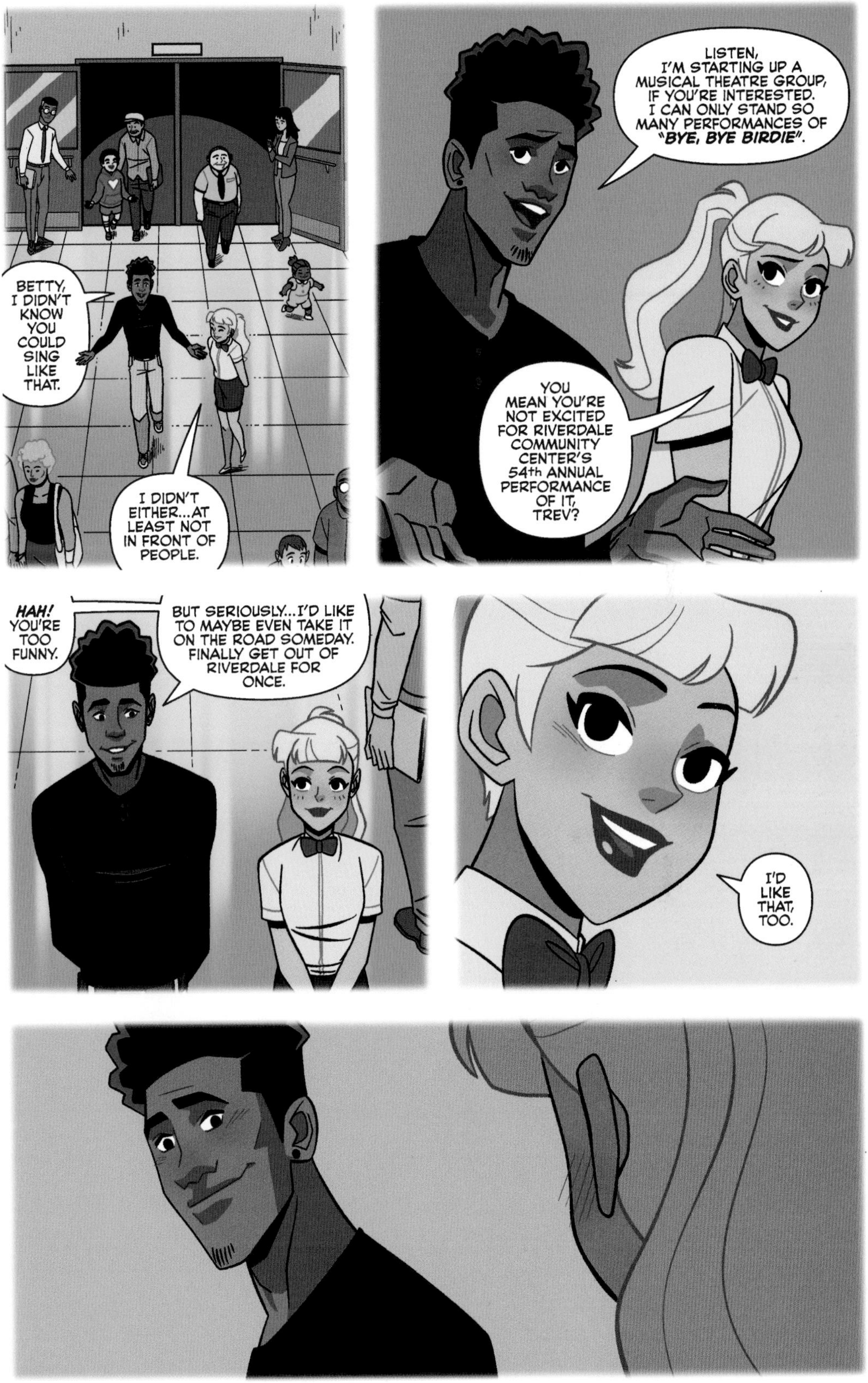
BETTY, I DIDN'T KNOW YOU COULD SING LIKE THAT.
I DIDN'T EITHER...AT LEAST NOT IN FRONT OF PEOPLE.
LISTEN, I'M STARTING UP A MUSICAL THEATRE GROUP, IF YOU'RE INTERESTED. I CAN ONLY STAND SO MANY PERFORMANCES OF *"BYE, BYE BIRDIE"*.
YOU MEAN YOU'RE NOT EXCITED FOR RIVERDALE COMMUNITY CENTER'S 54th ANNUAL PERFORMANCE OF IT, TREV?
HAH! YOU'RE TOO FUNNY.
BUT SERIOUSLY...I'D LIKE TO MAYBE EVEN TAKE IT ON THE ROAD SOMEDAY. FINALLY GET OUT OF RIVERDALE FOR ONCE.
I'D LIKE THAT, TOO.

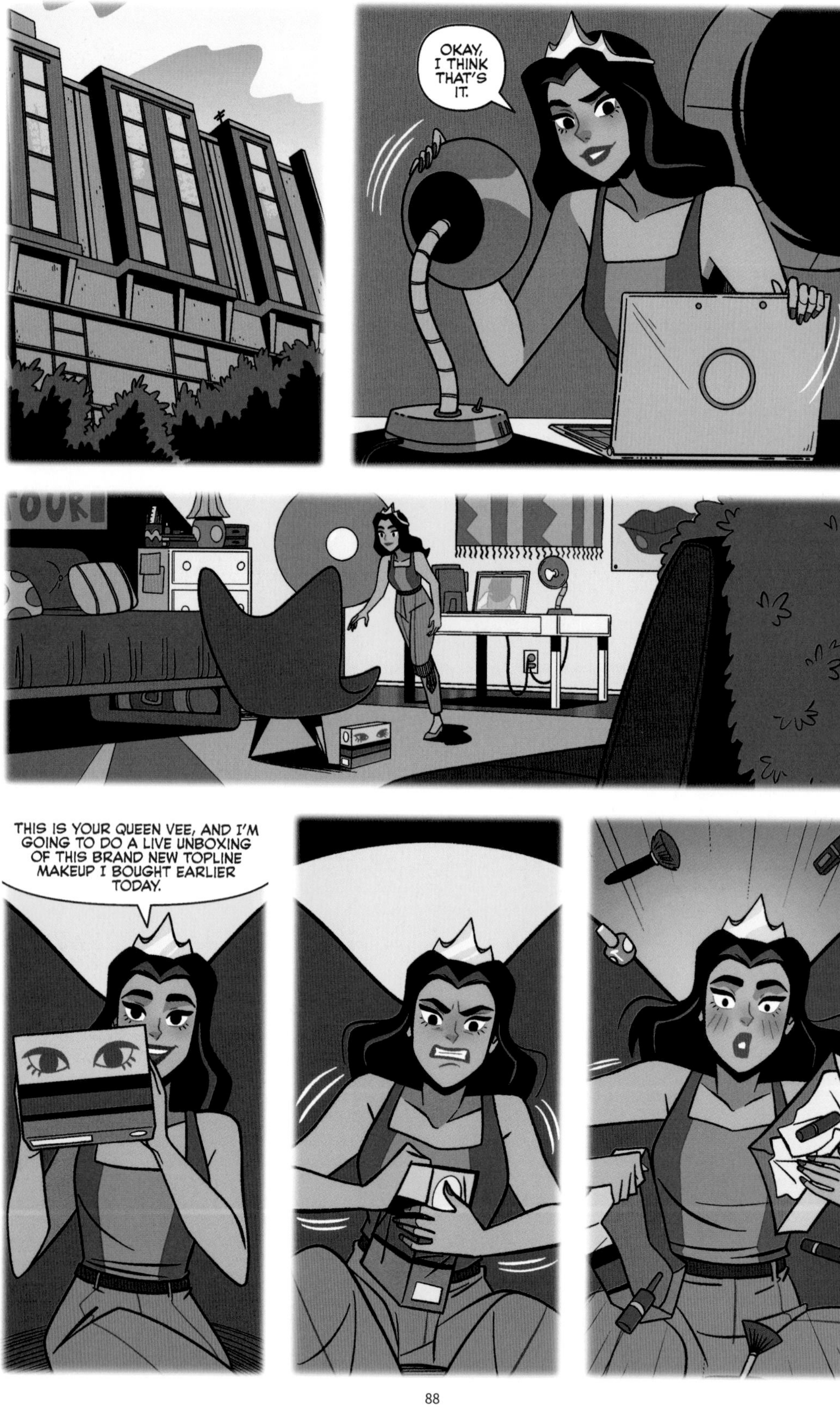
OKAY, I THINK THAT'S IT.
THIS IS YOUR QUEEN VEE, AND I'M GOING TO DO A LIVE UNBOXING OF THIS BRAND NEW TOPLINE MAKEUP I BOUGHT EARLIER TODAY.

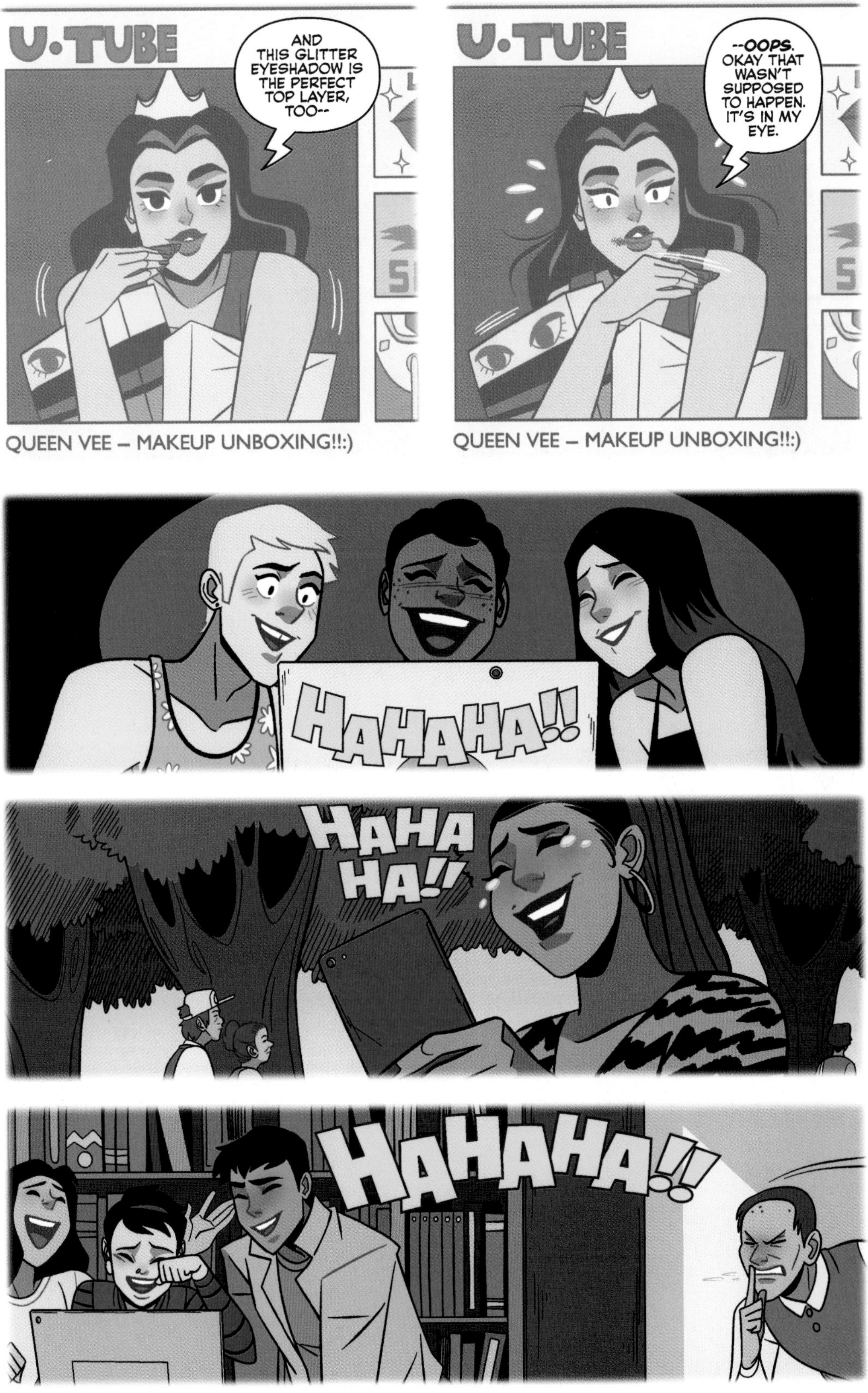
U-TUBE
AND THIS GLITTER EYESHADOW IS THE PERFECT TOP LAYER, TOO--
QUEEN VEE – MAKEUP UNBOXING!!:)
U-TUBE
--OOPS. OKAY THAT WASN'T SUPPOSED TO HAPPEN. IT'S IN MY EYE.
QUEEN VEE – MAKEUP UNBOXING!!:)
HAHAHA!!
HAHA HA!!
HAHAHA!!

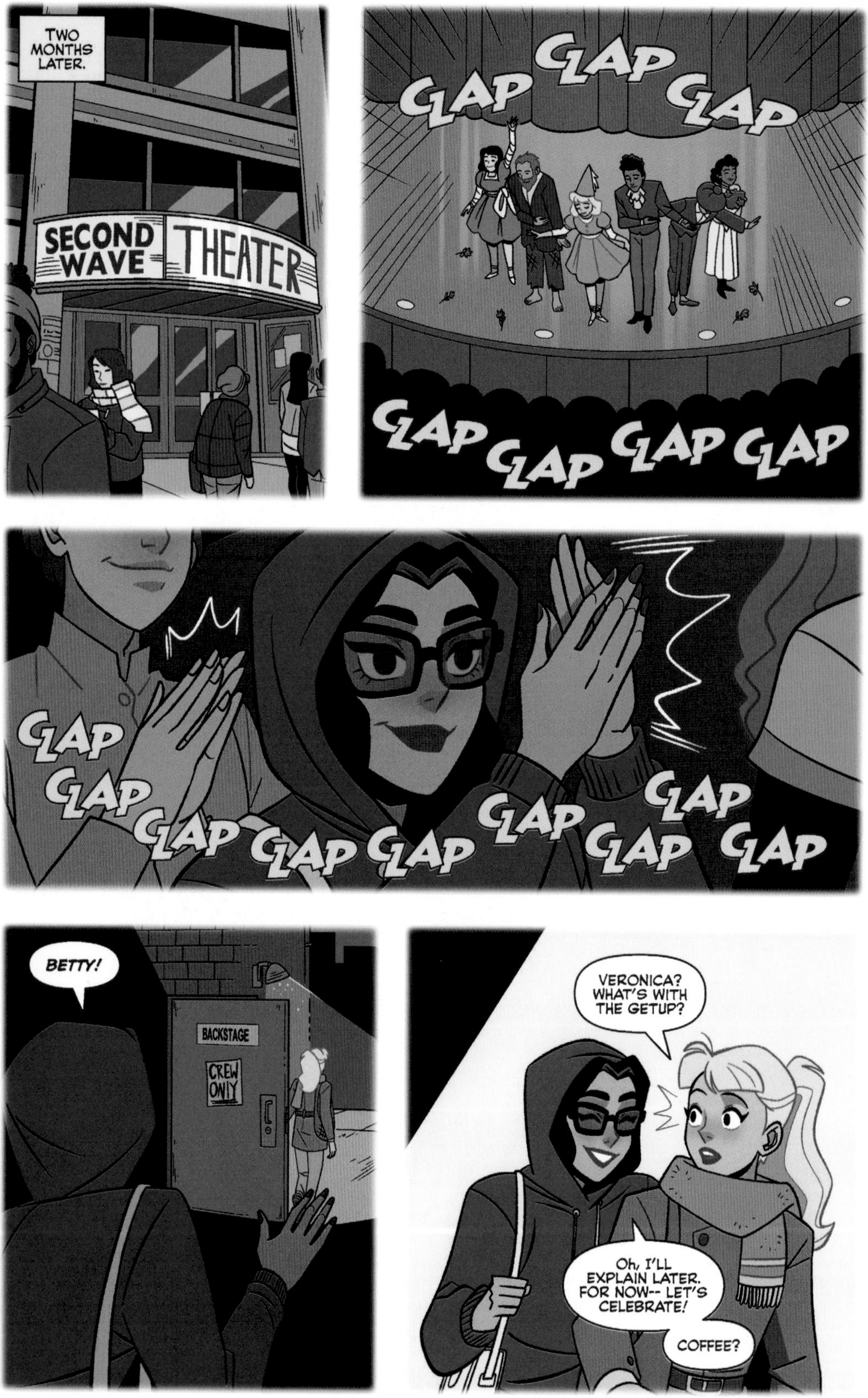
TWO MONTHS LATER.
SECOND WAVE THEATER
CLAP CLAP CLAP CLAP
CLAP CLAP CLAP CLAP
CLAP CLAP CLAP CLAP CLAP CLAP CLAP CLAP CLAP
BETTY!
BACKSTAGE
CREW ONLY
VERONICA? WHAT'S WITH THE GETUP?
Oh, I'LL EXPLAIN LATER. FOR NOW-- LET'S CELEBRATE!
COFFEE?

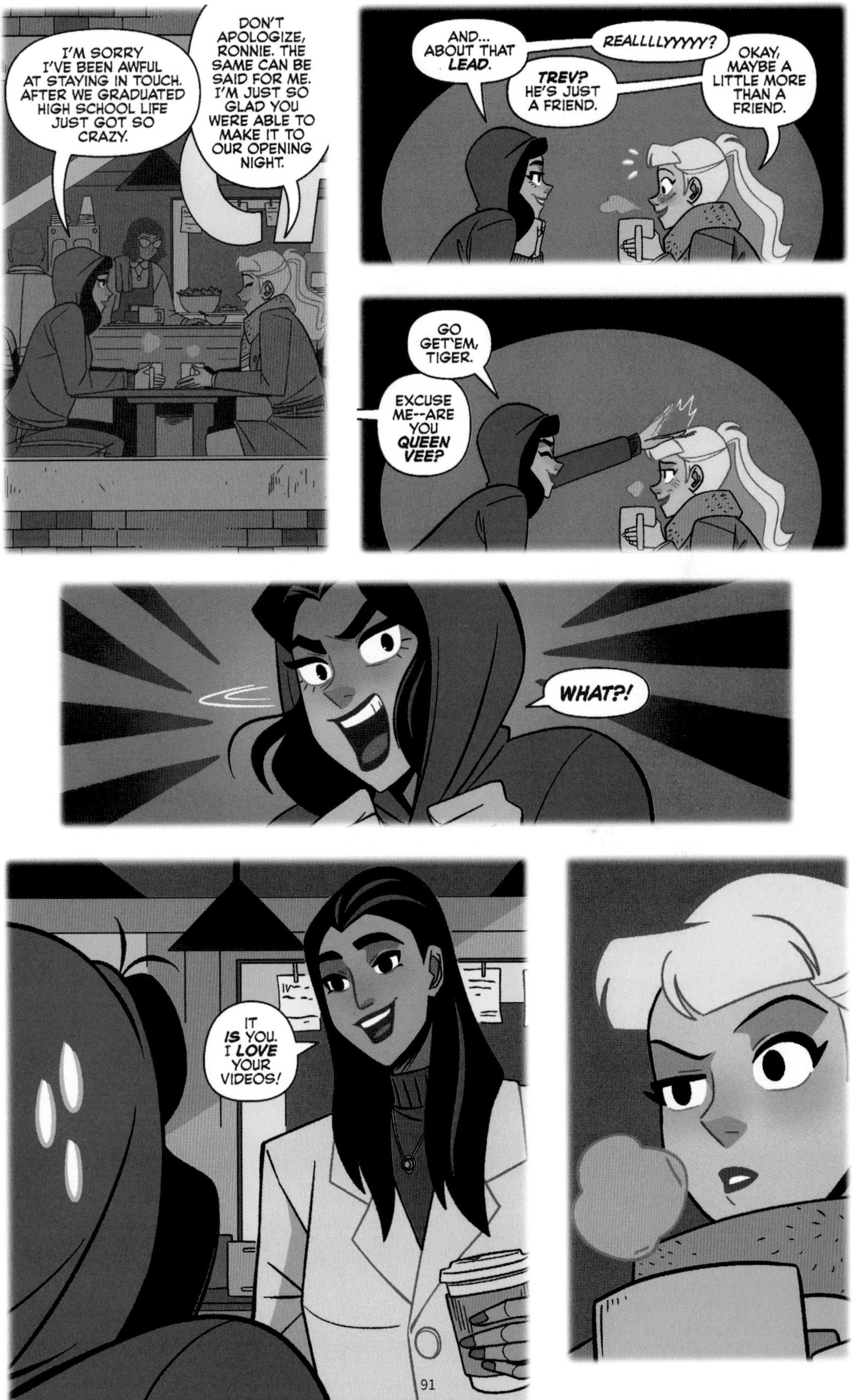

I'M SORRY I'VE BEEN AWFUL AT STAYING IN TOUCH. AFTER WE GRADUATED HIGH SCHOOL LIFE JUST GOT SO CRAZY.
DON'T APOLOGIZE, RONNIE. THE SAME CAN BE SAID FOR ME. I'M JUST SO GLAD YOU WERE ABLE TO MAKE IT TO OUR OPENING NIGHT.
AND... ABOUT THAT LEAD.
TREV? HE'S JUST A FRIEND.
REALLLLYYYYY?
OKAY, MAYBE A LITTLE MORE THAN A FRIEND.
GO GET'EM, TIGER.
EXCUSE ME--ARE YOU QUEEN VEE?
WHAT?!
IT IS YOU. I LOVE YOUR VIDEOS!

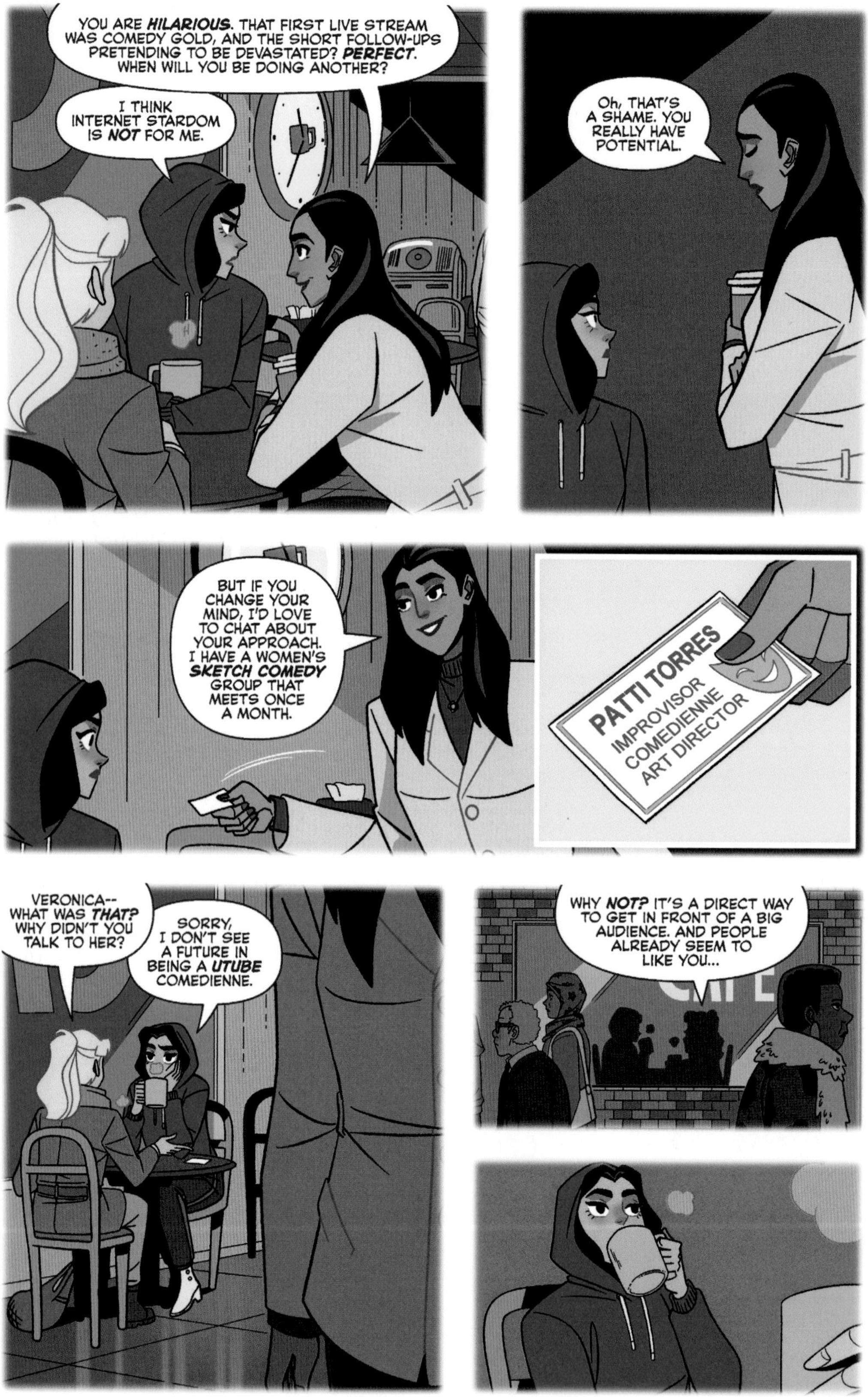

YOU ARE HILARIOUS. THAT FIRST LIVE STREAM WAS COMEDY GOLD, AND THE SHORT FOLLOW-UPS PRETENDING TO BE DEVASTATED? PERFECT. WHEN WILL YOU BE DOING ANOTHER?
I THINK INTERNET STARDOM IS NOT FOR ME.
Oh, THAT'S A SHAME. YOU REALLY HAVE POTENTIAL.
BUT IF YOU CHANGE YOUR MIND, I'D LOVE TO CHAT ABOUT YOUR APPROACH. I HAVE A WOMEN'S SKETCH COMEDY GROUP THAT MEETS ONCE A MONTH.
PATTI TORRES
IMPROVISOR
COMEDIENNE
ART DIRECTOR
VERONICA-- WHAT WAS THAT? WHY DIDN'T YOU TALK TO HER?
SORRY, I DON'T SEE A FUTURE IN BEING A UTUBE COMEDIENNE.
WHY NOT? IT'S A DIRECT WAY TO GET IN FRONT OF A BIG AUDIENCE. AND PEOPLE ALREADY SEEM TO LIKE YOU...

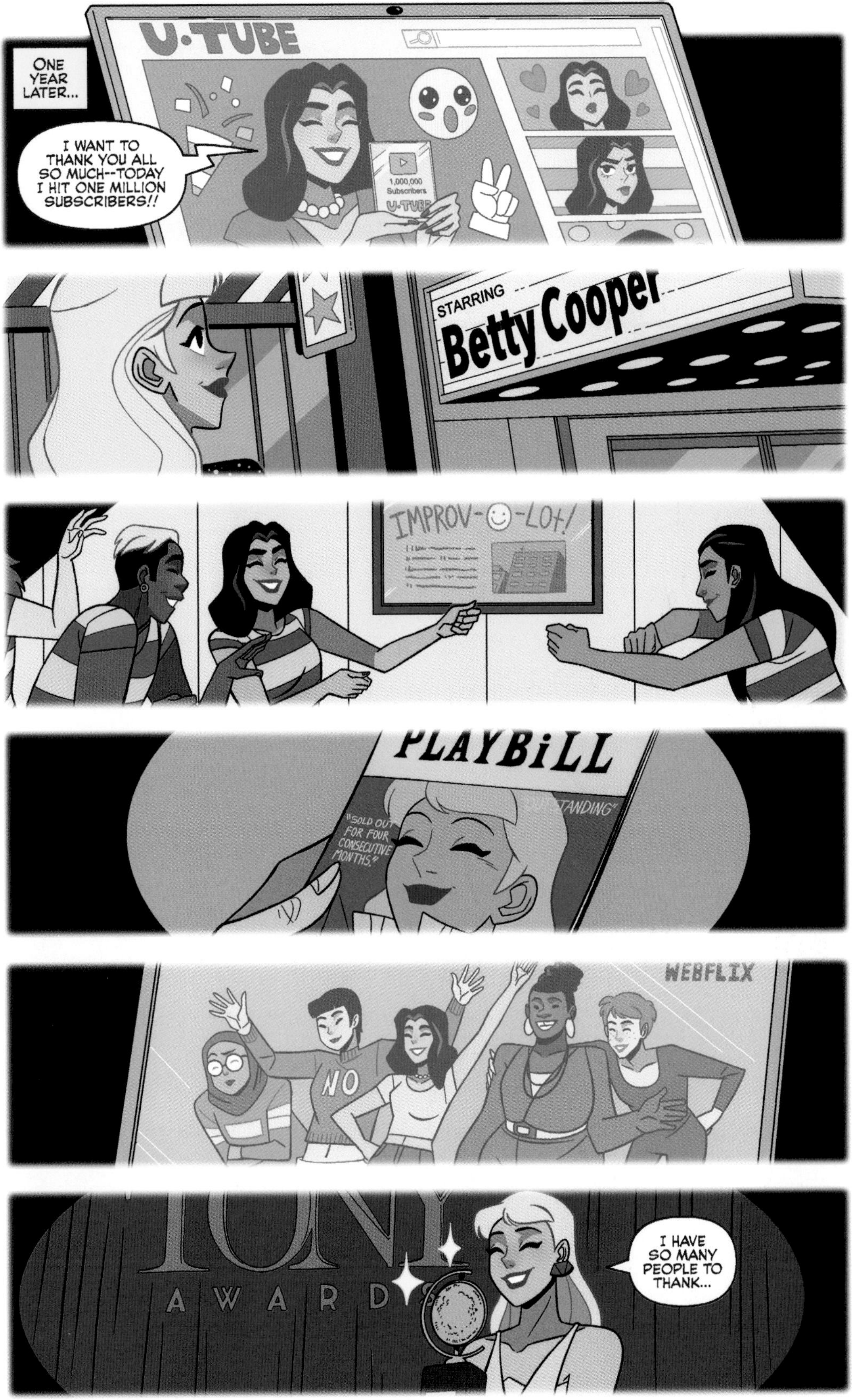

ONE YEAR LATER...
U-TUBE
1,000,000 Subscribers
U-TUBE
I WANT TO THANK YOU ALL SO MUCH--TODAY I HIT ONE MILLION SUBSCRIBERS!!
STARRING
Betty Cooper
IMPROV-☺-LOT!
PLAYBILL
"SOLD OUT FOR FOUR CONSECUTIVE MONTHS."
"OUTSTANDING"
WEBFLIX
NO
TONY AWARDS
I HAVE SO MANY PEOPLE TO THANK...

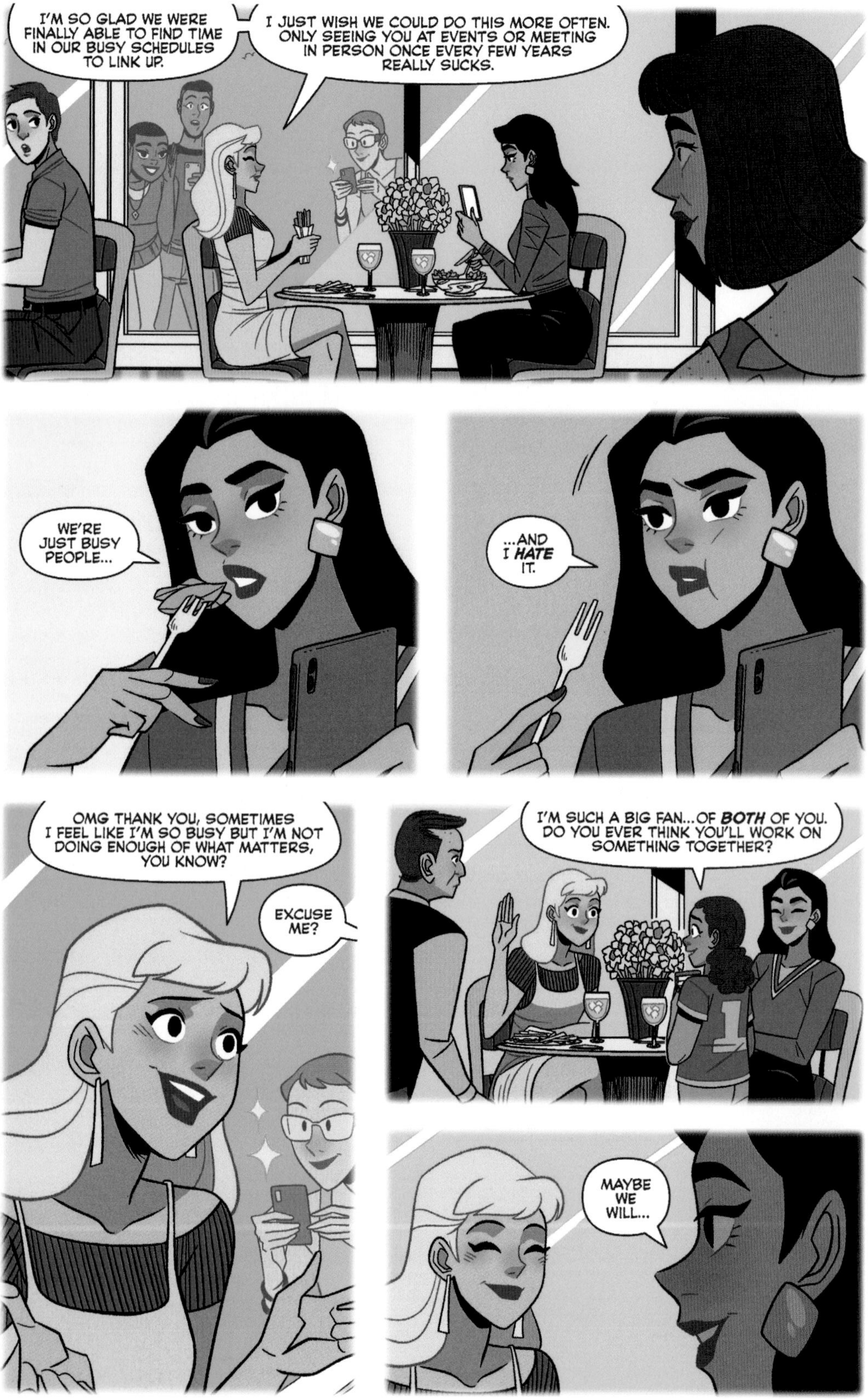
I'M SO GLAD WE WERE FINALLY ABLE TO FIND TIME IN OUR BUSY SCHEDULES TO LINK UP.
I JUST WISH WE COULD DO THIS MORE OFTEN. ONLY SEEING YOU AT EVENTS OR MEETING IN PERSON ONCE EVERY FEW YEARS REALLY SUCKS.
WE'RE JUST BUSY PEOPLE...
...AND I *HATE* IT.
OMG THANK YOU, SOMETIMES I FEEL LIKE I'M SO BUSY BUT I'M NOT DOING ENOUGH OF WHAT MATTERS, YOU KNOW?
EXCUSE ME?
I'M SUCH A BIG FAN...OF *BOTH* OF YOU. DO YOU EVER THINK YOU'LL WORK ON SOMETHING TOGETHER?
MAYBE WE WILL...

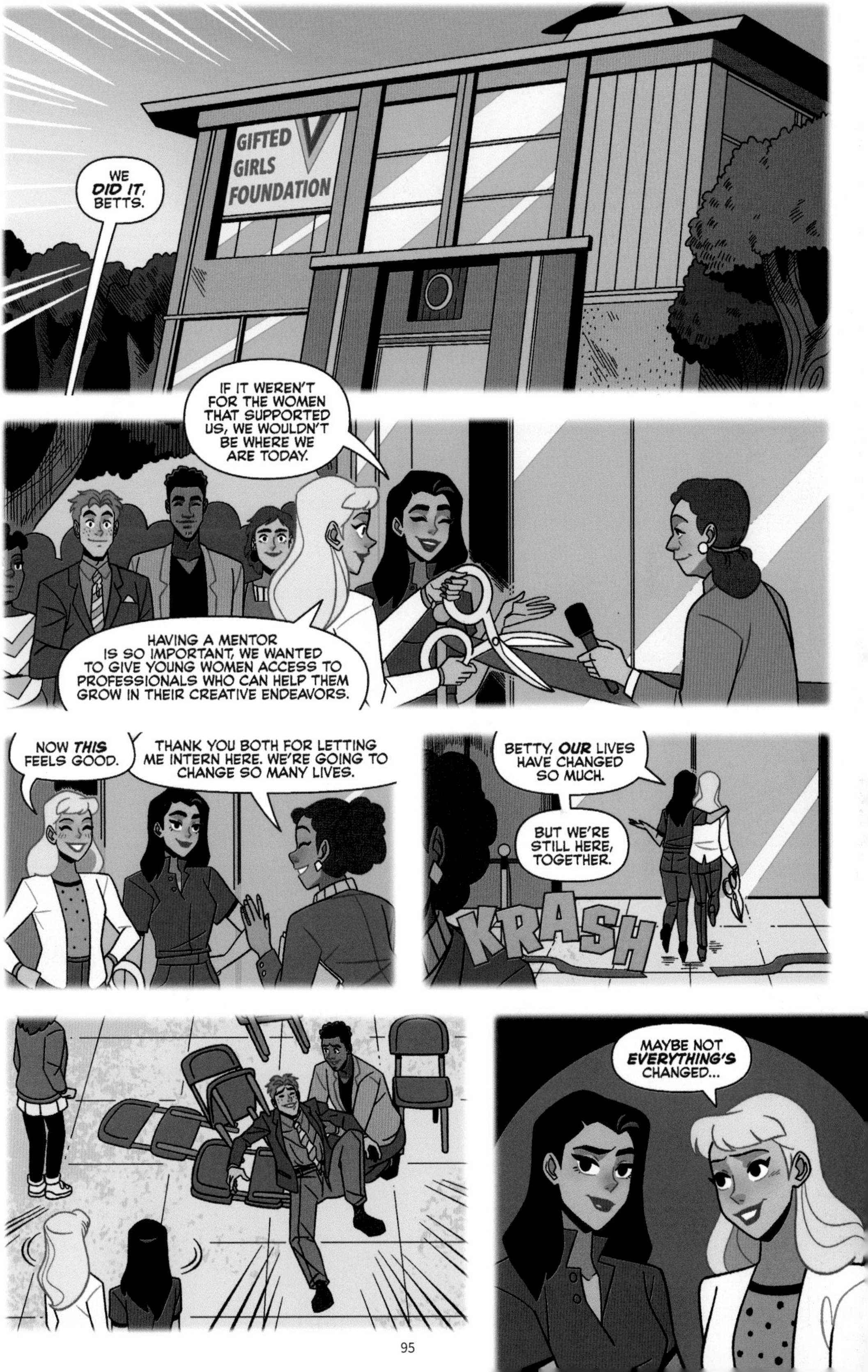
GIFTED GIRLS FOUNDATION
WE DID IT, BETTS.
IF IT WEREN'T FOR THE WOMEN THAT SUPPORTED US, WE WOULDN'T BE WHERE WE ARE TODAY.
HAVING A MENTOR IS SO IMPORTANT, WE WANTED TO GIVE YOUNG WOMEN ACCESS TO PROFESSIONALS WHO CAN HELP THEM GROW IN THEIR CREATIVE ENDEAVORS.
NOW THIS FEELS GOOD.
THANK YOU BOTH FOR LETTING ME INTERN HERE. WE'RE GOING TO CHANGE SO MANY LIVES.
BETTY, OUR LIVES HAVE CHANGED SO MUCH.
BUT WE'RE STILL HERE, TOGETHER.
KRASH
MAYBE NOT EVERYTHING'S CHANGED...

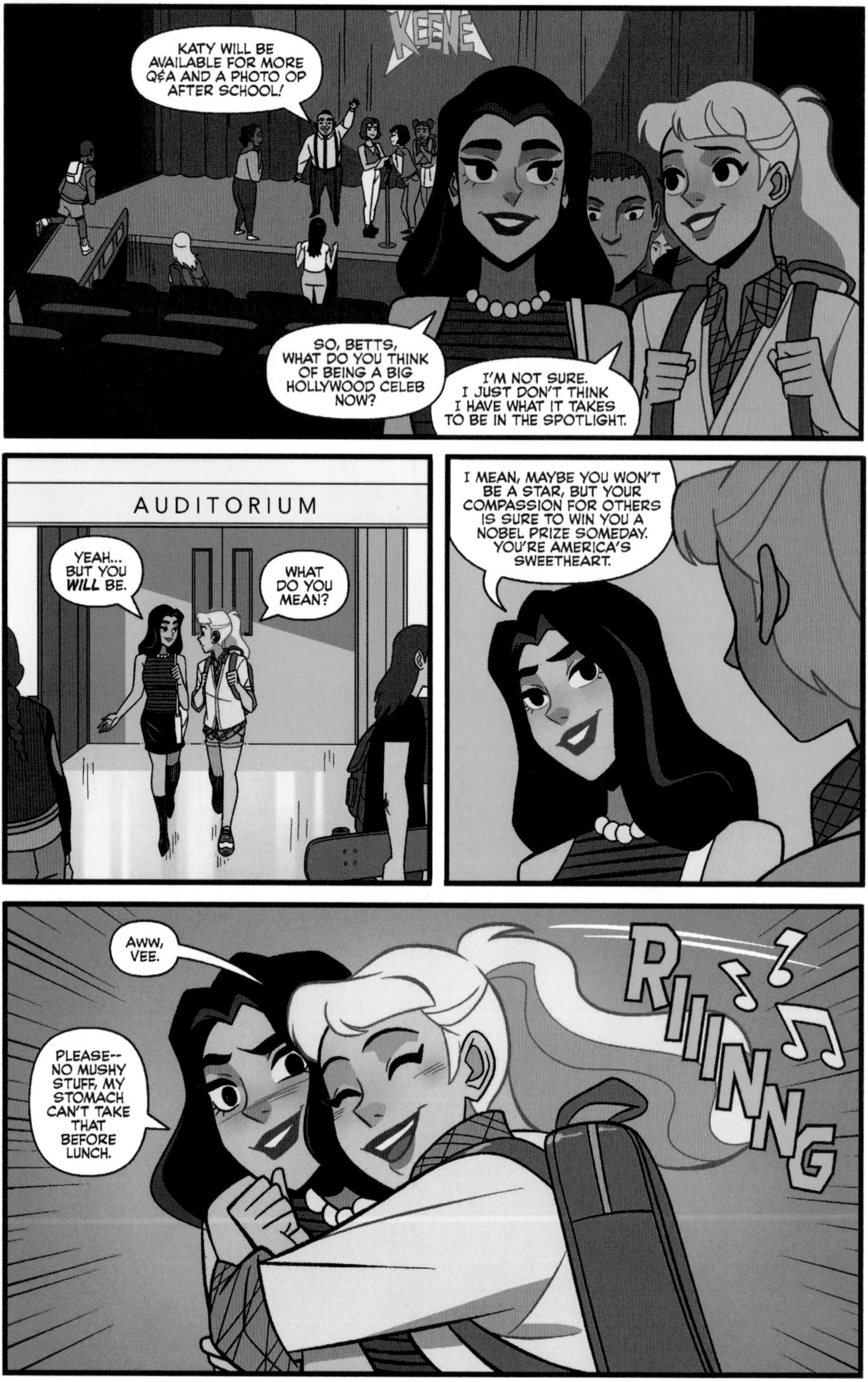
KEENE
KATY WILL BE AVAILABLE FOR MORE Q&A AND A PHOTO OP AFTER SCHOOL!
SO, BETTS, WHAT DO YOU THINK OF BEING A BIG HOLLYWOOD CELEB NOW?
I'M NOT SURE. I JUST DON'T THINK I HAVE WHAT IT TAKES TO BE IN THE SPOTLIGHT.
AUDITORIUM
YEAH... BUT YOU WILL BE.
WHAT DO YOU MEAN?
I MEAN, MAYBE YOU WON'T BE A STAR, BUT YOUR COMPASSION FOR OTHERS IS SURE TO WIN YOU A NOBEL PRIZE SOMEDAY. YOU'RE AMERICA'S SWEETHEART.
AWW, VEE.
PLEASE-- NO MUSHY STUFF, MY STOMACH CAN'T TAKE THAT BEFORE LUNCH.
RIIINNG

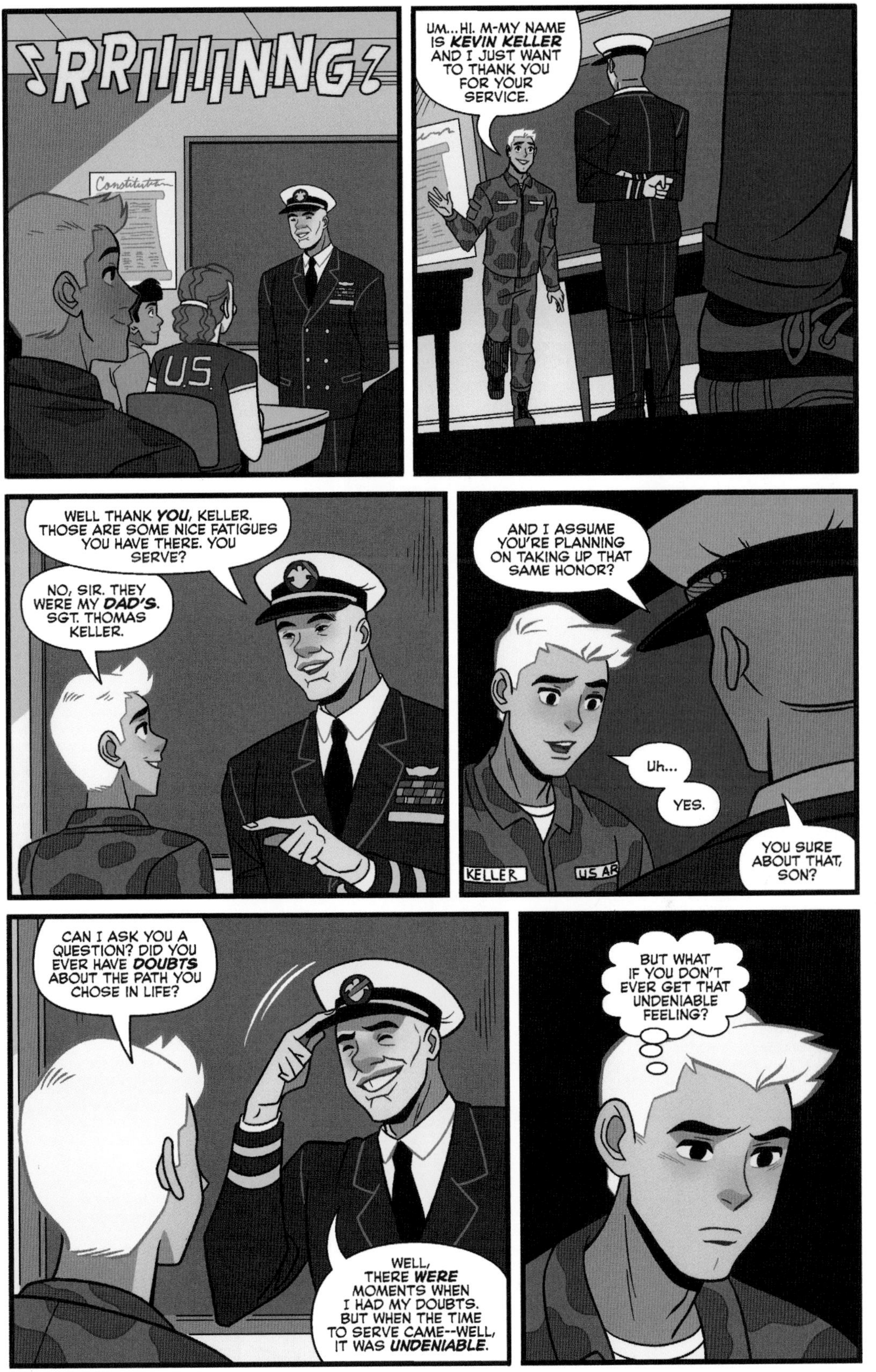
RRIIIIINNG
UM...HI. M-MY NAME IS KEVIN KELLER AND I JUST WANT TO THANK YOU FOR YOUR SERVICE.
WELL THANK YOU, KELLER. THOSE ARE SOME NICE FATIGUES YOU HAVE THERE. YOU SERVE?
NO, SIR. THEY WERE MY DAD'S. SGT. THOMAS KELLER.
AND I ASSUME YOU'RE PLANNING ON TAKING UP THAT SAME HONOR?
Uh...
YES.
KELLER
US AR
YOU SURE ABOUT THAT, SON?
CAN I ASK YOU A QUESTION? DID YOU EVER HAVE DOUBTS ABOUT THE PATH YOU CHOSE IN LIFE?
WELL, THERE WERE MOMENTS WHEN I HAD MY DOUBTS. BUT WHEN THE TIME TO SERVE CAME--WELL, IT WAS UNDENIABLE.
BUT WHAT IF YOU DON'T EVER GET THAT UNDENIABLE FEELING?

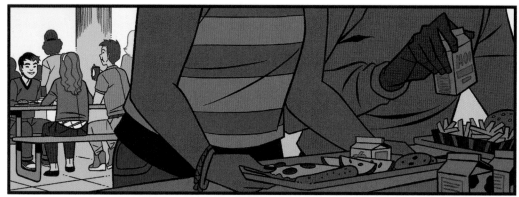

MAN, IF I THOUGHT CHOOSING A CAREER WAS DIFFICULT BEFORE, IT'S WAY *WORSE* NOW. THERE ARE JUST TOO MANY OPTIONS!

...THE PROBLEM IS PROFESSIONAL TASTE-TESTER *ISN'T* ONE OF THEM.

SERIOUSLY, JUG? THAT'S ALL YOU'VE GOTTEN OUT OF TODAY?

...ACTUALLY DR. TWYST GAVE A FASCINATING TALK ON BEING A THERAPIST. THE HUMAN MIND IS SO INTERESTING AND THE LACK OF MENTAL HEALTH AWARENESS OUT THERE IS ALARMING.

...OR I'LL BE A *FAST FOOD MASCOT.* HAVEN'T MADE MY MIND UP YET.

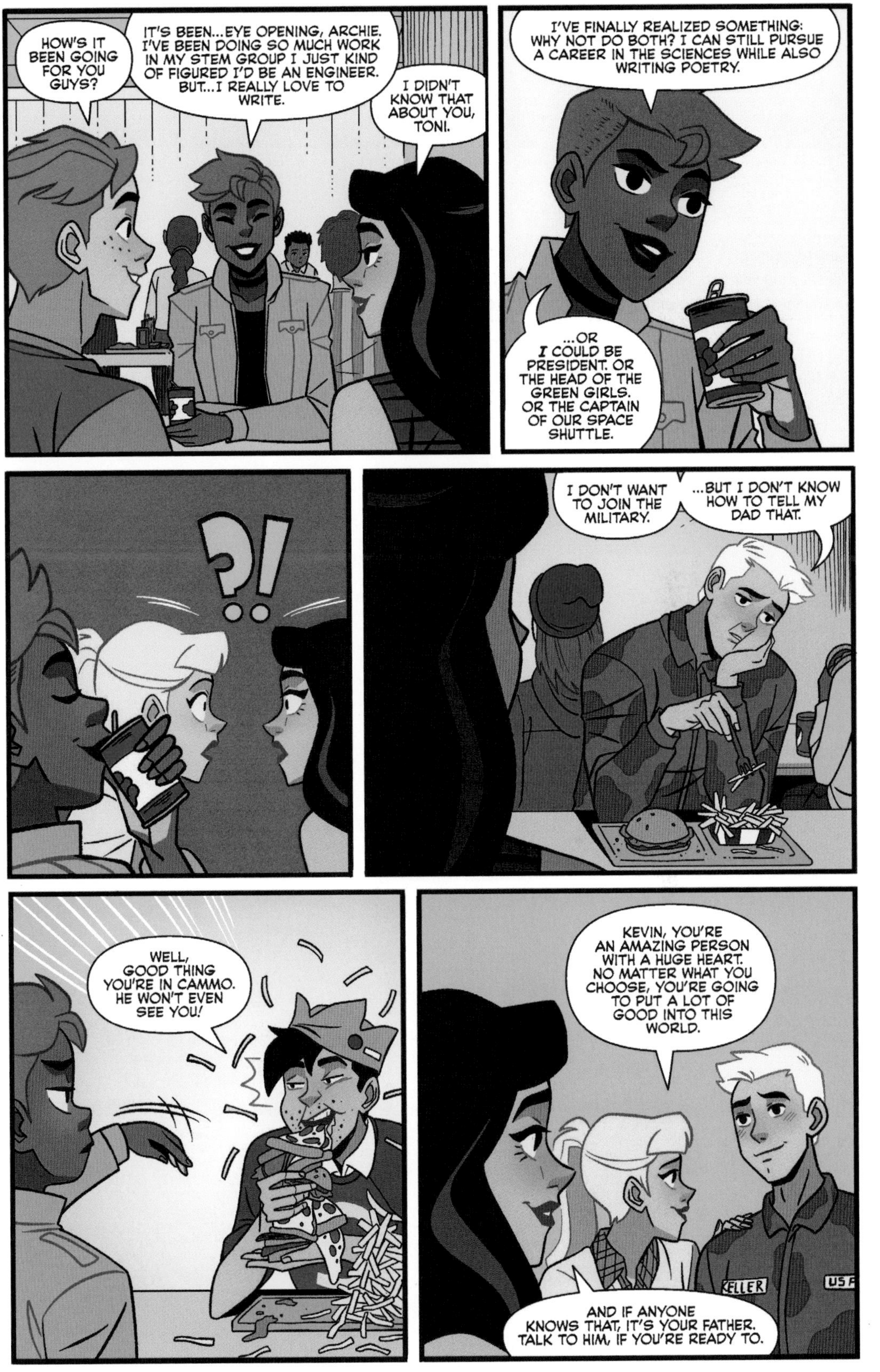
HOW'S IT BEEN GOING FOR YOU GUYS?
IT'S BEEN...EYE OPENING, ARCHIE. I'VE BEEN DOING SO MUCH WORK IN MY STEM GROUP I JUST KIND OF FIGURED I'D BE AN ENGINEER. BUT...I REALLY LOVE TO WRITE.
I DIDN'T KNOW THAT ABOUT YOU, TONI.
I'VE FINALLY REALIZED SOMETHING: WHY NOT DO BOTH? I CAN STILL PURSUE A CAREER IN THE SCIENCES WHILE ALSO WRITING POETRY.
...OR *I* COULD BE PRESIDENT. OR THE HEAD OF THE GREEN GIRLS. OR THE CAPTAIN OF OUR SPACE SHUTTLE.
?!
I DON'T WANT TO JOIN THE MILITARY.
...BUT I DON'T KNOW HOW TO TELL MY DAD THAT.
WELL, GOOD THING YOU'RE IN CAMMO. HE WON'T EVEN SEE YOU!
KEVIN, YOU'RE AN AMAZING PERSON WITH A HUGE HEART. NO MATTER WHAT YOU CHOOSE, YOU'RE GOING TO PUT A LOT OF GOOD INTO THIS WORLD.
KELLER
USA
AND IF ANYONE KNOWS THAT, IT'S YOUR FATHER. TALK TO HIM, IF YOU'RE READY TO.

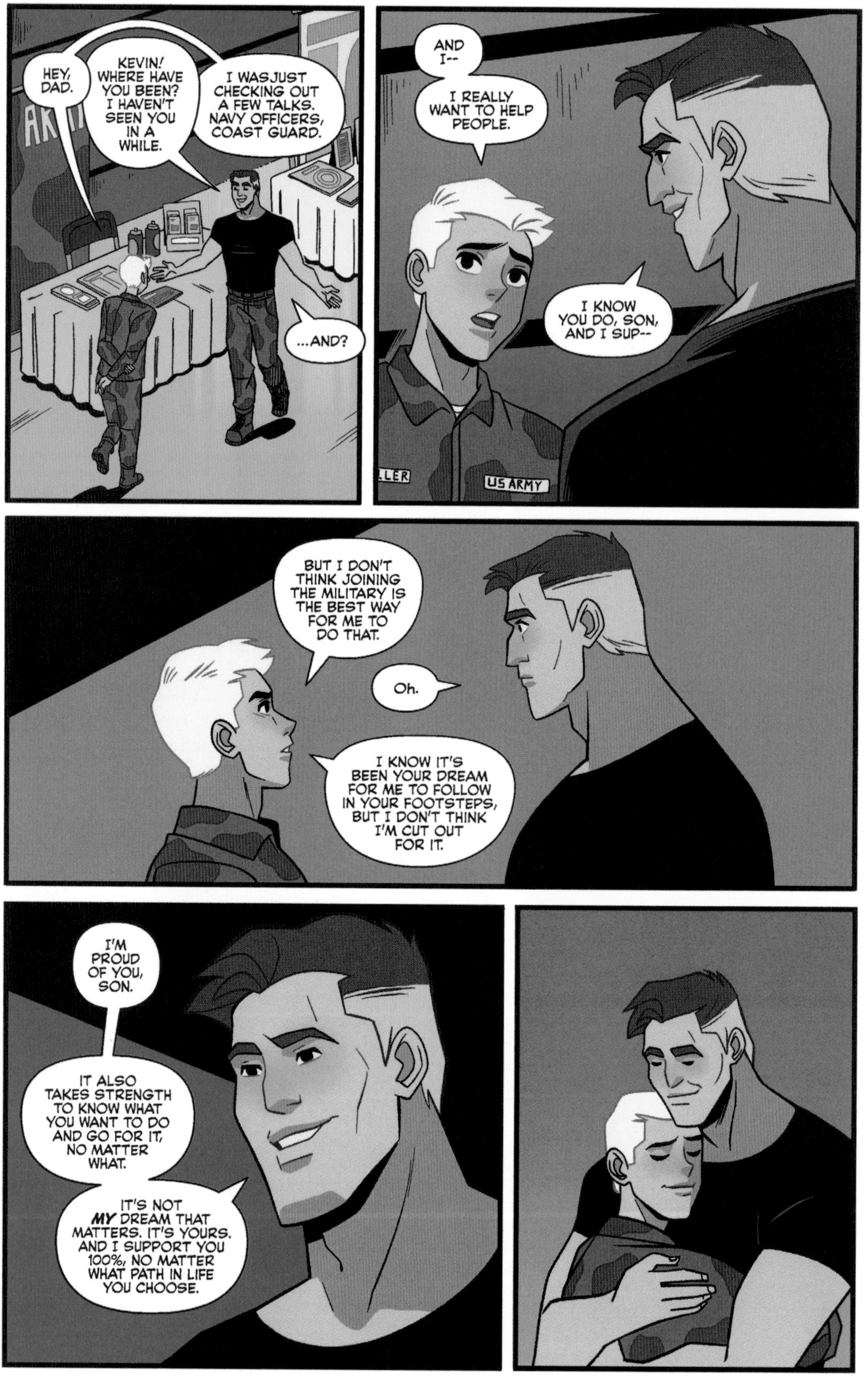
HEY, DAD.
KEVIN! WHERE HAVE YOU BEEN? I HAVEN'T SEEN YOU IN A WHILE.
I WASJUST CHECKING OUT A FEW TALKS. NAVY OFFICERS, COAST GUARD.
...AND?
AND I--
I REALLY WANT TO HELP PEOPLE.
I KNOW YOU DO, SON, AND I SUP--
LLER
US ARMY
BUT I DON'T THINK JOINING THE MILITARY IS THE BEST WAY FOR ME TO DO THAT.
Oh.
I KNOW IT'S BEEN YOUR DREAM FOR ME TO FOLLOW IN YOUR FOOTSTEPS, BUT I DON'T THINK I'M CUT OUT FOR IT.
I'M PROUD OF YOU, SON.
IT ALSO TAKES STRENGTH TO KNOW WHAT YOU WANT TO DO AND GO FOR IT, NO MATTER WHAT.
IT'S NOT MY DREAM THAT MATTERS. IT'S YOURS. AND I SUPPORT YOU 100%, NO MATTER WHAT PATH IN LIFE YOU CHOOSE.

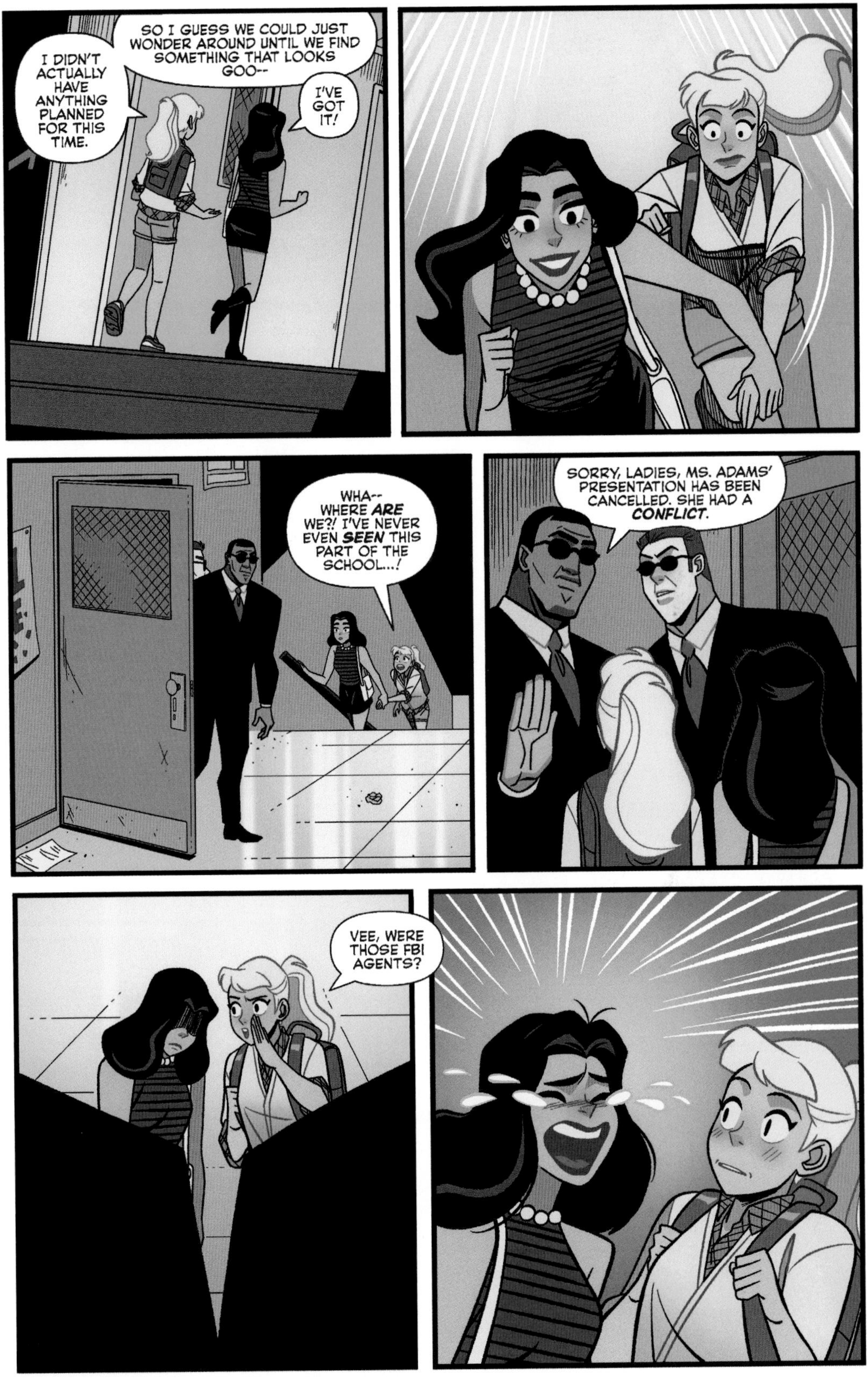
SO I GUESS WE COULD JUST WONDER AROUND UNTIL WE FIND SOMETHING THAT LOOKS GOO--
I DIDN'T ACTUALLY HAVE ANYTHING PLANNED FOR THIS TIME.
I'VE GOT IT!
WHA-- WHERE *ARE* WE?! I'VE NEVER EVEN *SEEN* THIS PART OF THE SCHOOL...!
SORRY, LADIES, MS. ADAMS' PRESENTATION HAS BEEN CANCELLED. SHE HAD A *CONFLICT*.
VEE, WERE THOSE FBI AGENTS?

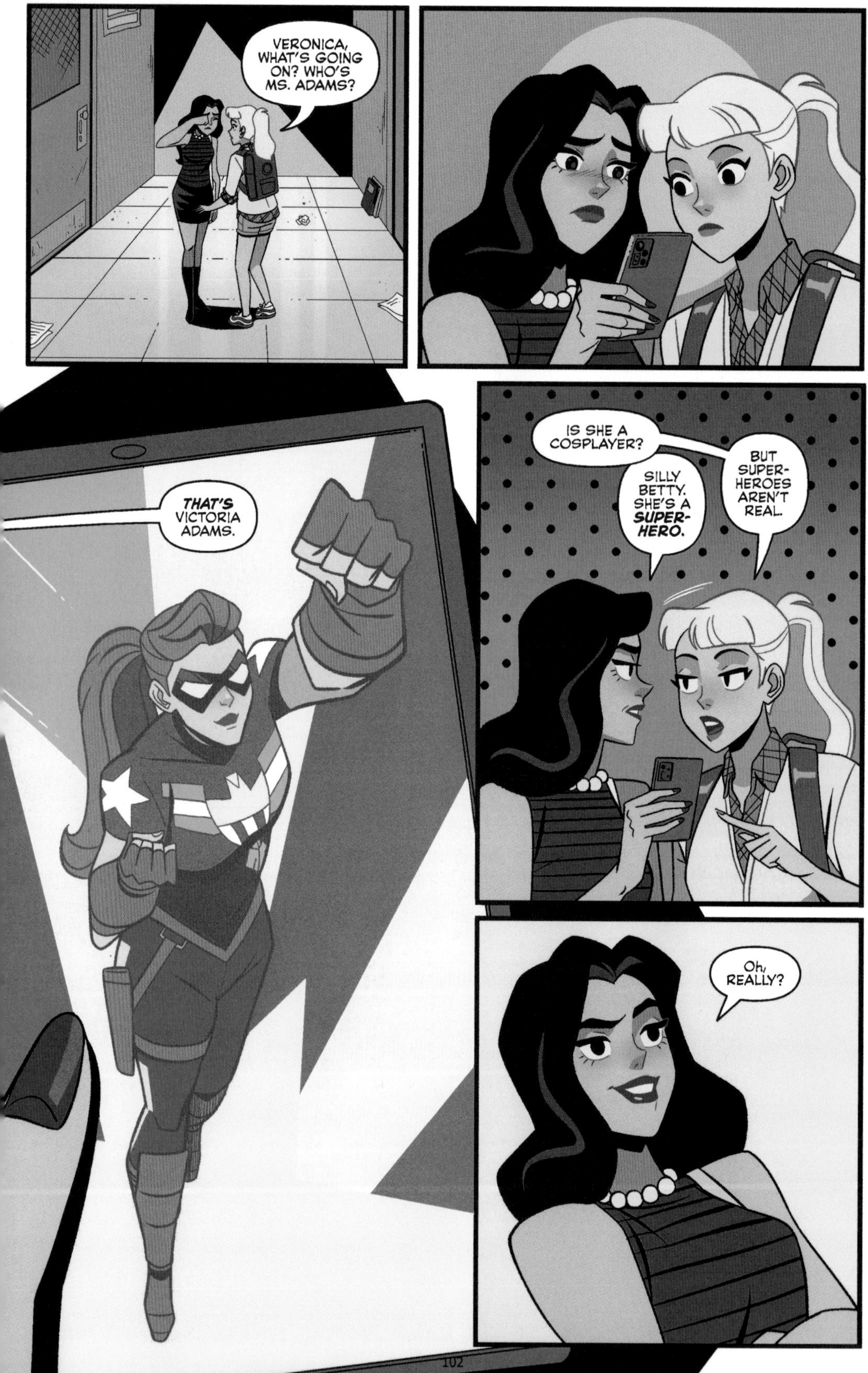
VERONICA, WHAT'S GOING ON? WHO'S MS. ADAMS?
THAT'S VICTORIA ADAMS.
IS SHE A COSPLAYER?
SILLY BETTY. SHE'S A SUPERHERO.
BUT SUPER-HEROES AREN'T REAL.
Oh, REALLY?

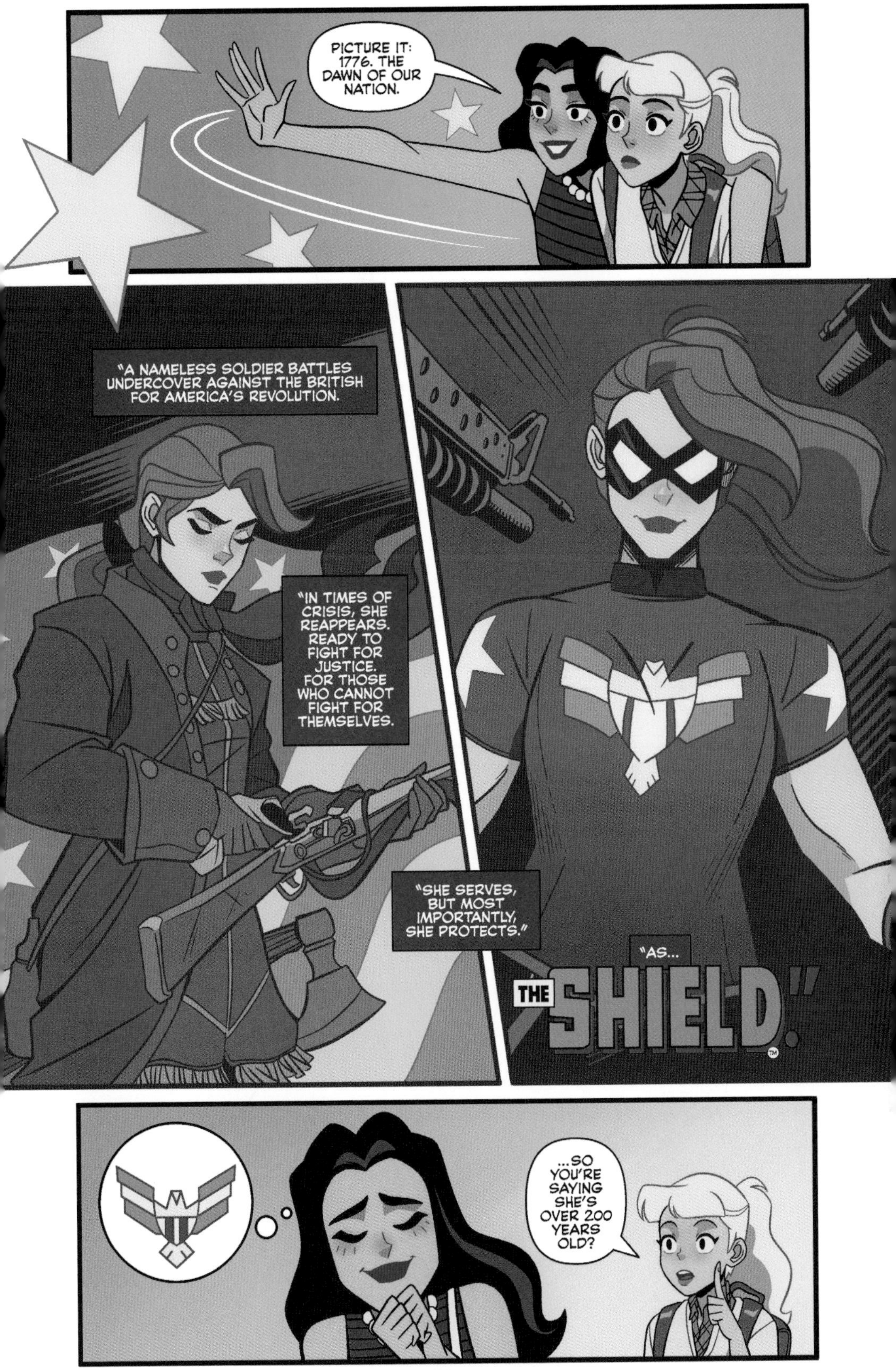
PICTURE IT: 1776. THE DAWN OF OUR NATION.
"A NAMELESS SOLDIER BATTLES UNDERCOVER AGAINST THE BRITISH FOR AMERICA'S REVOLUTION.
"IN TIMES OF CRISIS, SHE REAPPEARS. READY TO FIGHT FOR JUSTICE. FOR THOSE WHO CANNOT FIGHT FOR THEMSELVES.
"SHE SERVES, BUT MOST IMPORTANTLY, SHE PROTECTS."
"AS...
THE SHIELD."™
...SO YOU'RE SAYING SHE'S OVER 200 YEARS OLD?

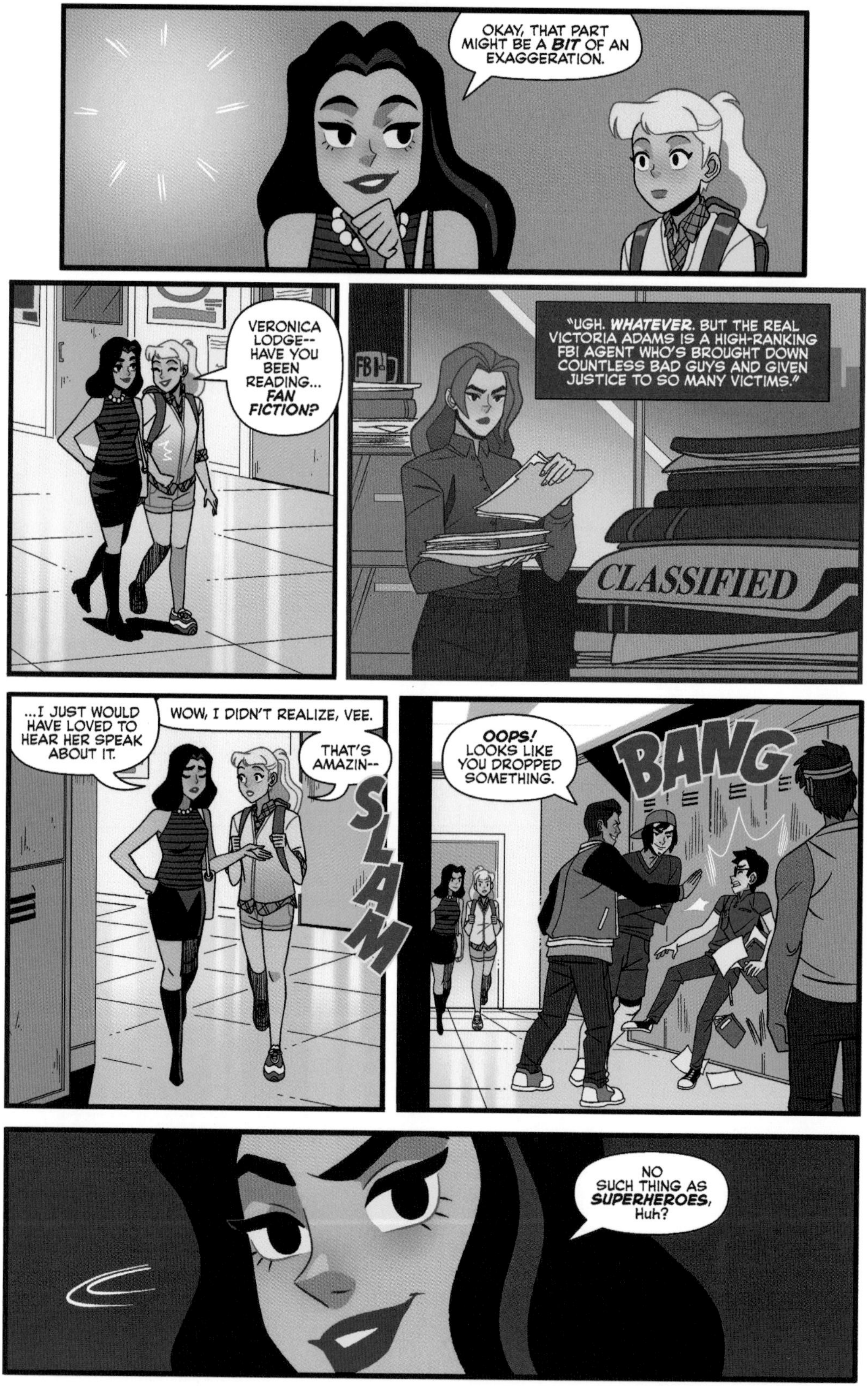
OKAY, THAT PART MIGHT BE A BIT OF AN EXAGGERATION.
VERONICA LODGE-- HAVE YOU BEEN READING... FAN FICTION?
"UGH. WHATEVER. BUT THE REAL VICTORIA ADAMS IS A HIGH-RANKING FBI AGENT WHO'S BROUGHT DOWN COUNTLESS BAD GUYS AND GIVEN JUSTICE TO SO MANY VICTIMS."
FBI
CLASSIFIED
...I JUST WOULD HAVE LOVED TO HEAR HER SPEAK ABOUT IT.
WOW, I DIDN'T REALIZE, VEE.
THAT'S AMAZIN--
SLAM
OOPS! LOOKS LIKE YOU DROPPED SOMETHING.
BANG
NO SUCH THING AS SUPERHEROES, Huh?

CHAPTER FOUR

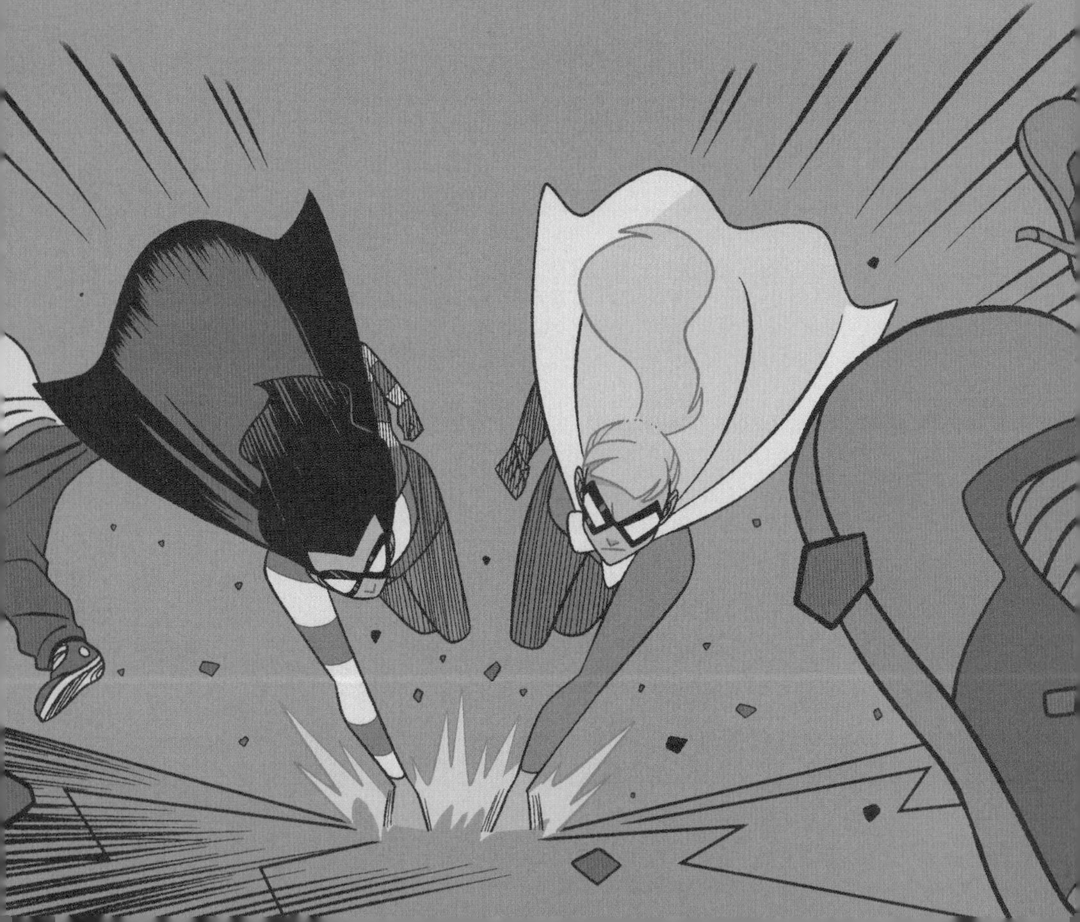

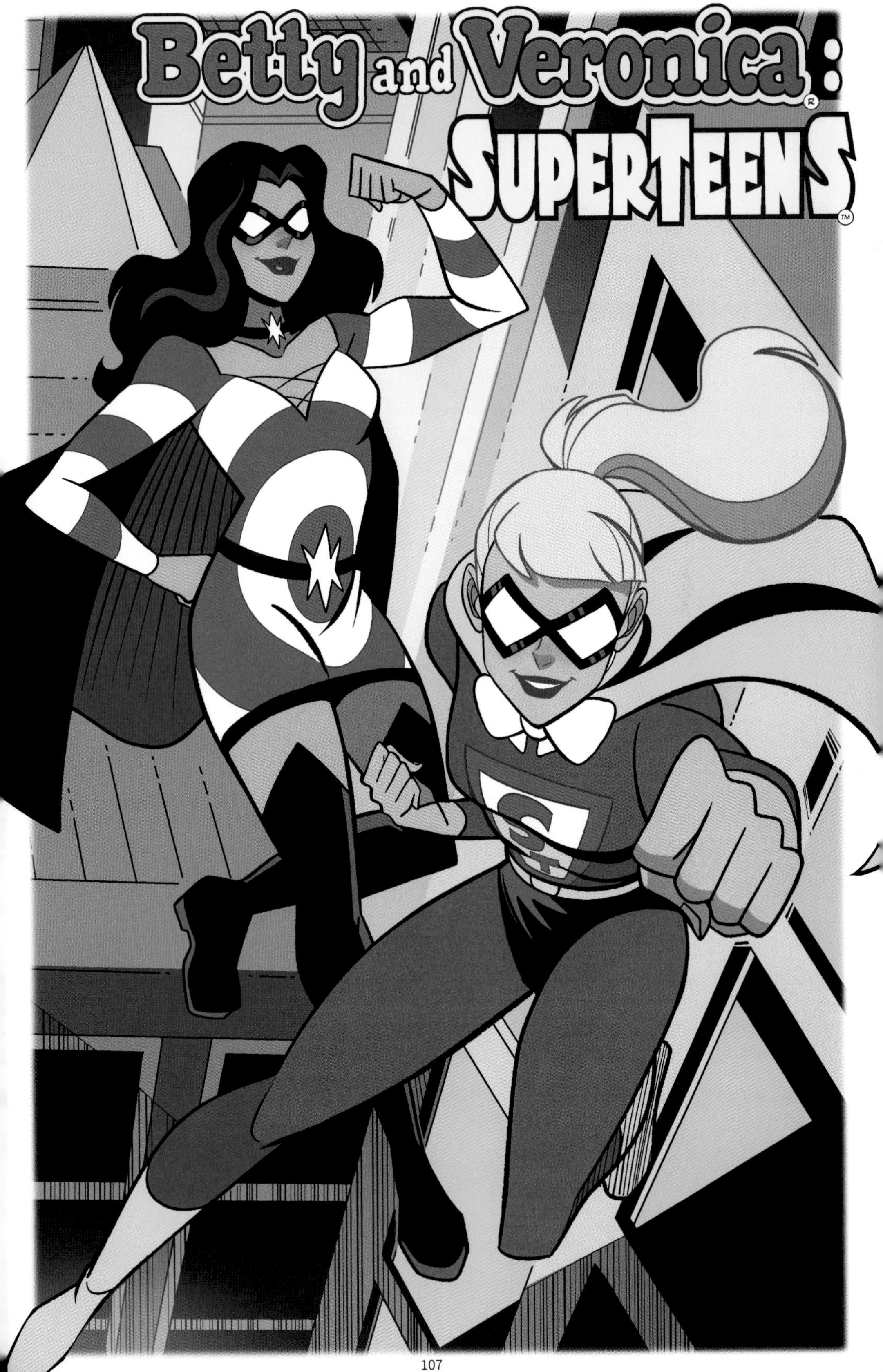
Betty and Veronica:
SUPERTEENS

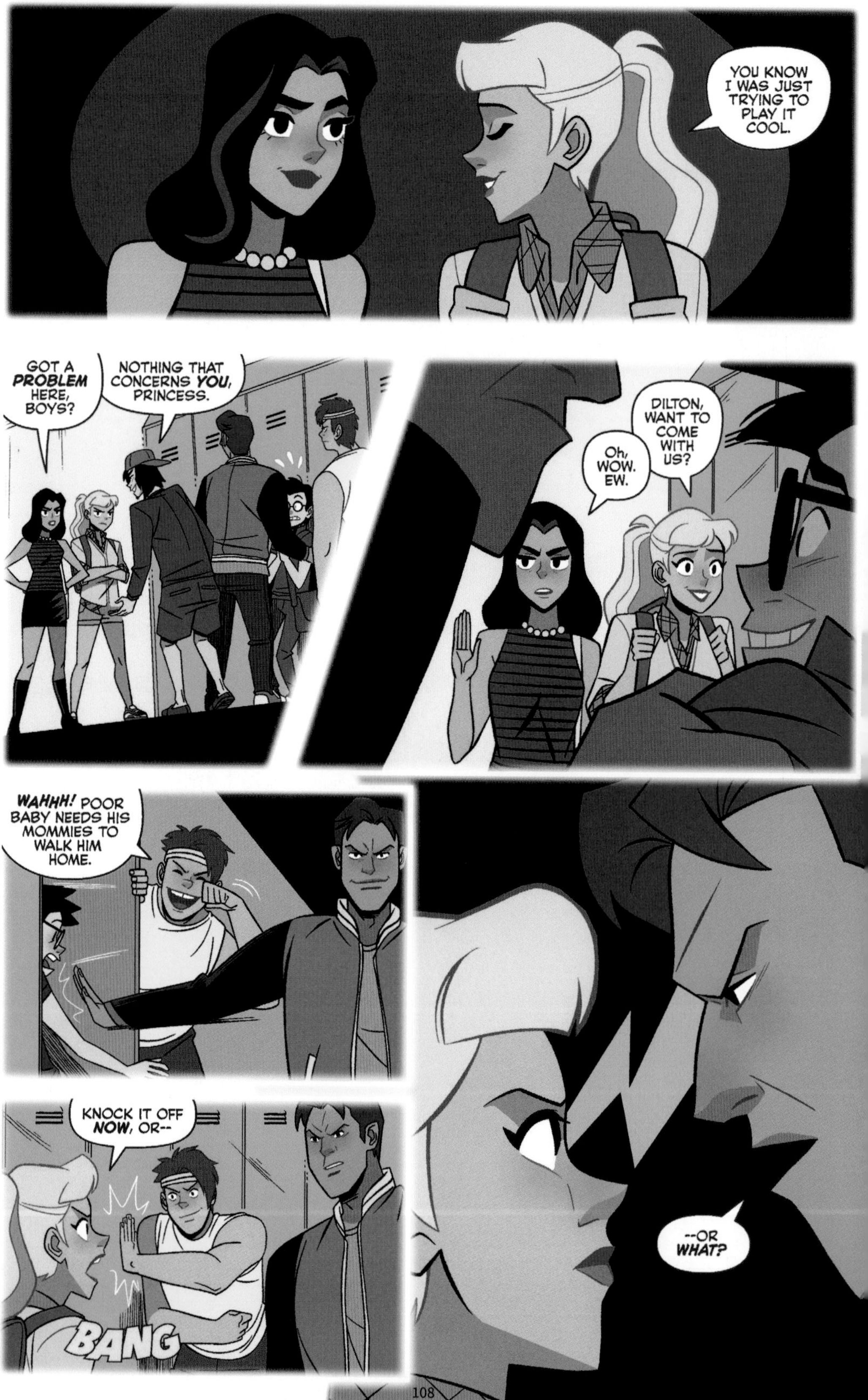

YOU KNOW I WAS JUST TRYING TO PLAY IT COOL.
GOT A PROBLEM HERE, BOYS?
NOTHING THAT CONCERNS YOU, PRINCESS.
DILTON, WANT TO COME WITH US?
Oh, WOW. EW.
WAHHH! POOR BABY NEEDS HIS MOMMIES TO WALK HIM HOME.
KNOCK IT OFF NOW, OR--
BANG
--OR WHAT?

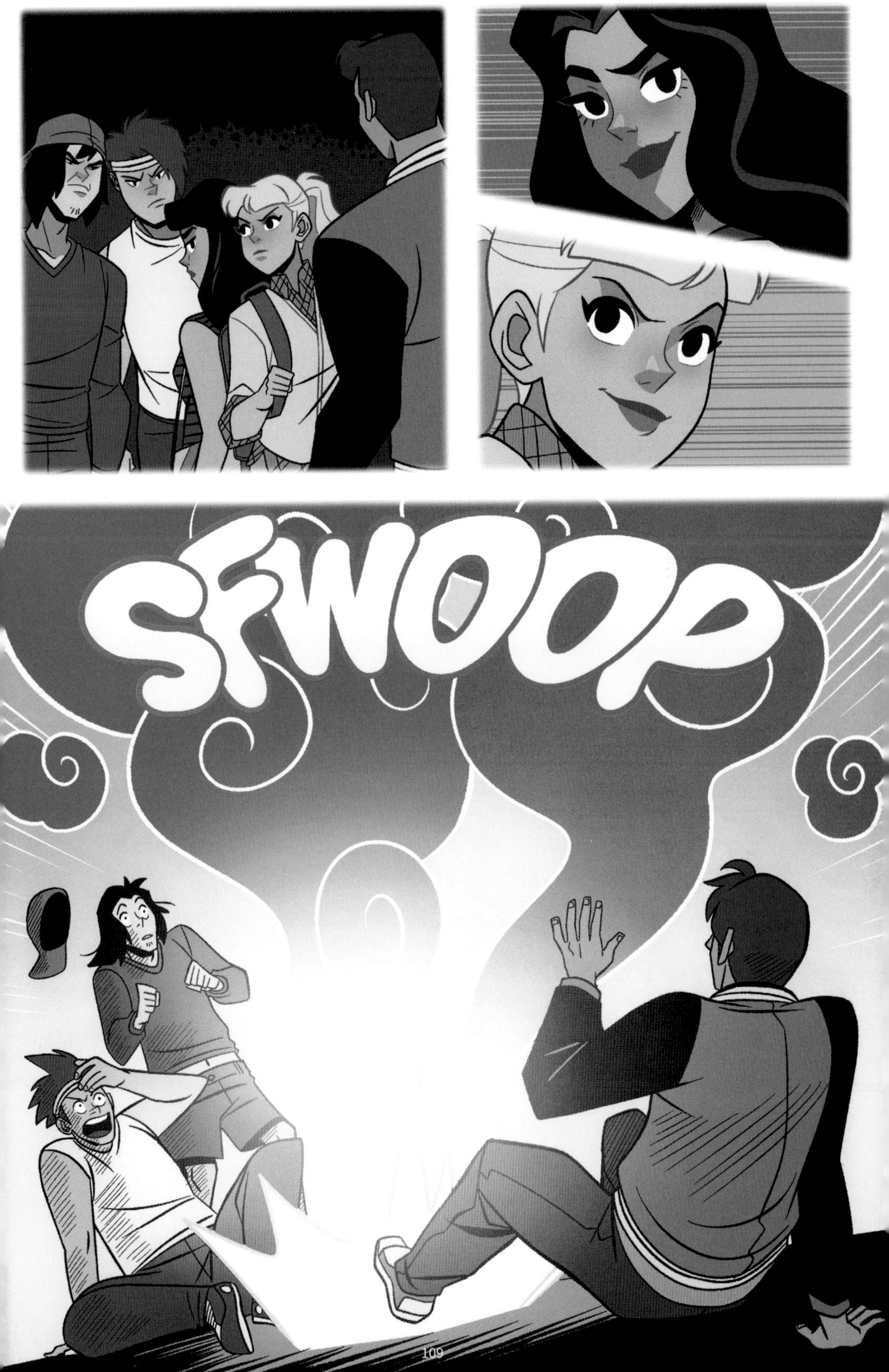
SFWOOP

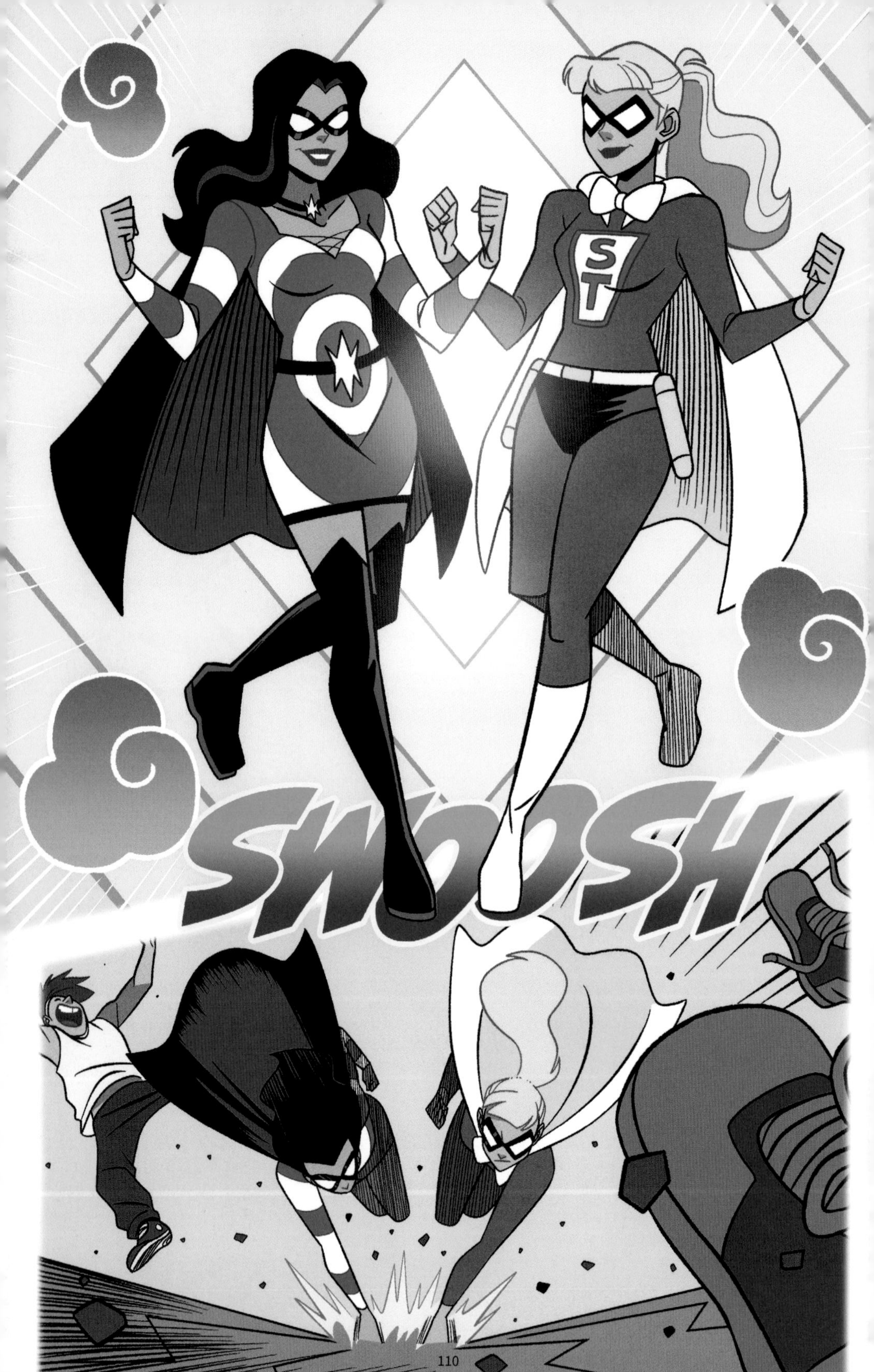
SWOOSH

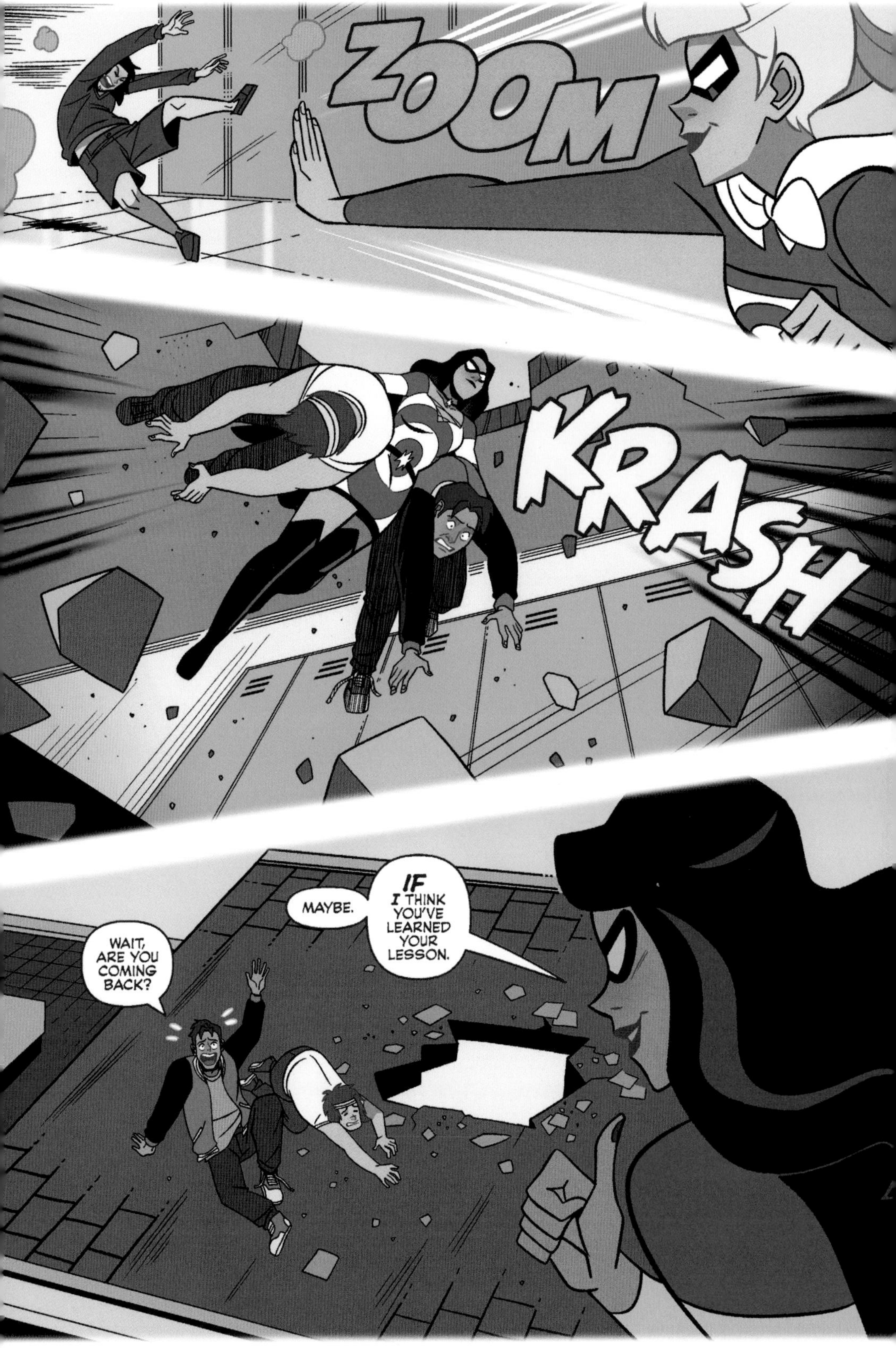
ZOOM
KRASH
WAIT, ARE YOU COMING BACK?
MAYBE.
IF I THINK YOU'VE LEARNED YOUR LESSON.

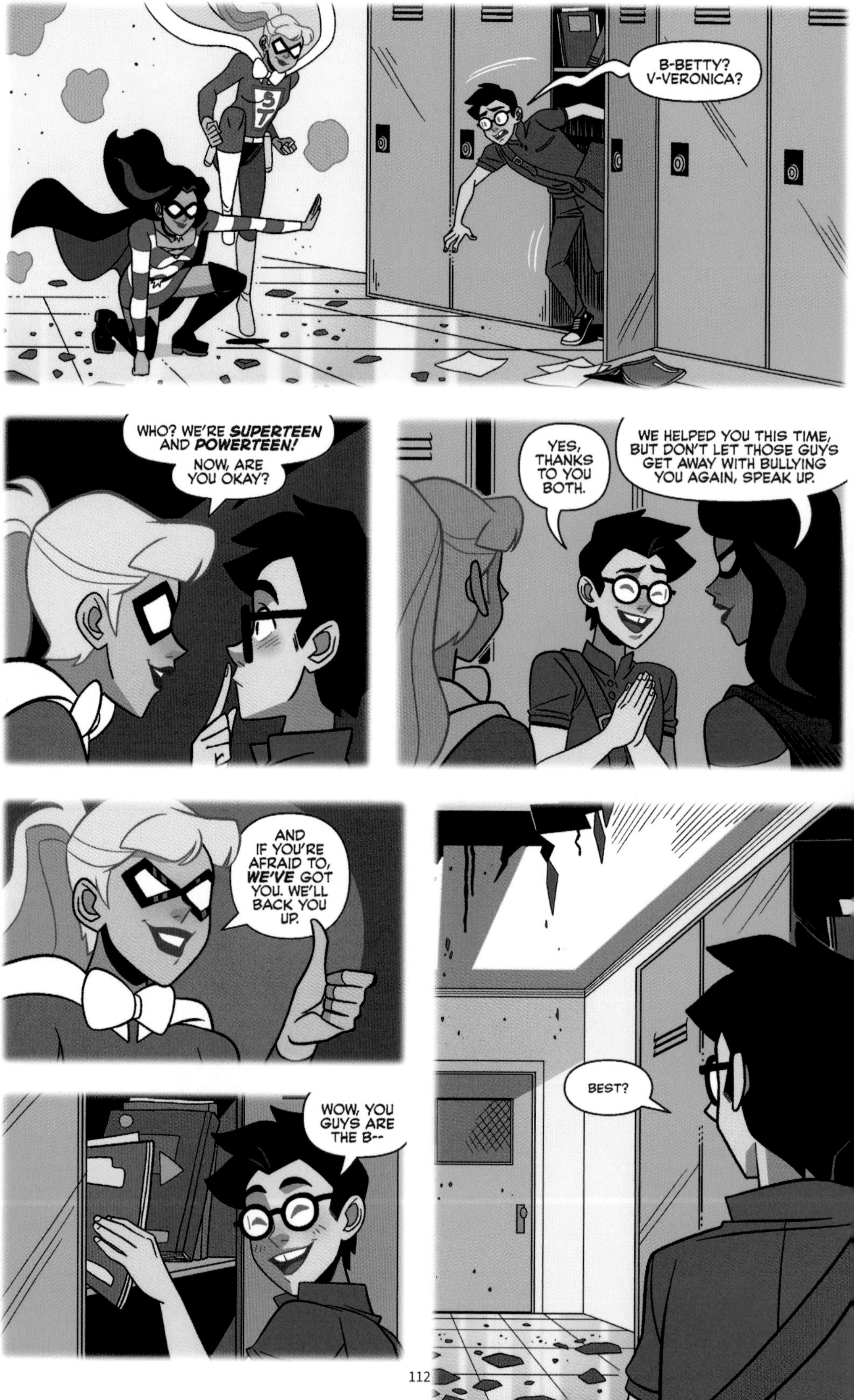
B-BETTY? V-VERONICA?
WHO? WE'RE **SUPERTEEN** AND **POWERTEEN!**
NOW, ARE YOU OKAY?
YES, THANKS TO YOU BOTH.
WE HELPED YOU THIS TIME, BUT DON'T LET THOSE GUYS GET AWAY WITH BULLYING YOU AGAIN, SPEAK UP.
AND IF YOU'RE AFRAID TO, **WE'VE** GOT YOU. WE'LL BACK YOU UP.
WOW, YOU GUYS ARE THE B--
BEST?

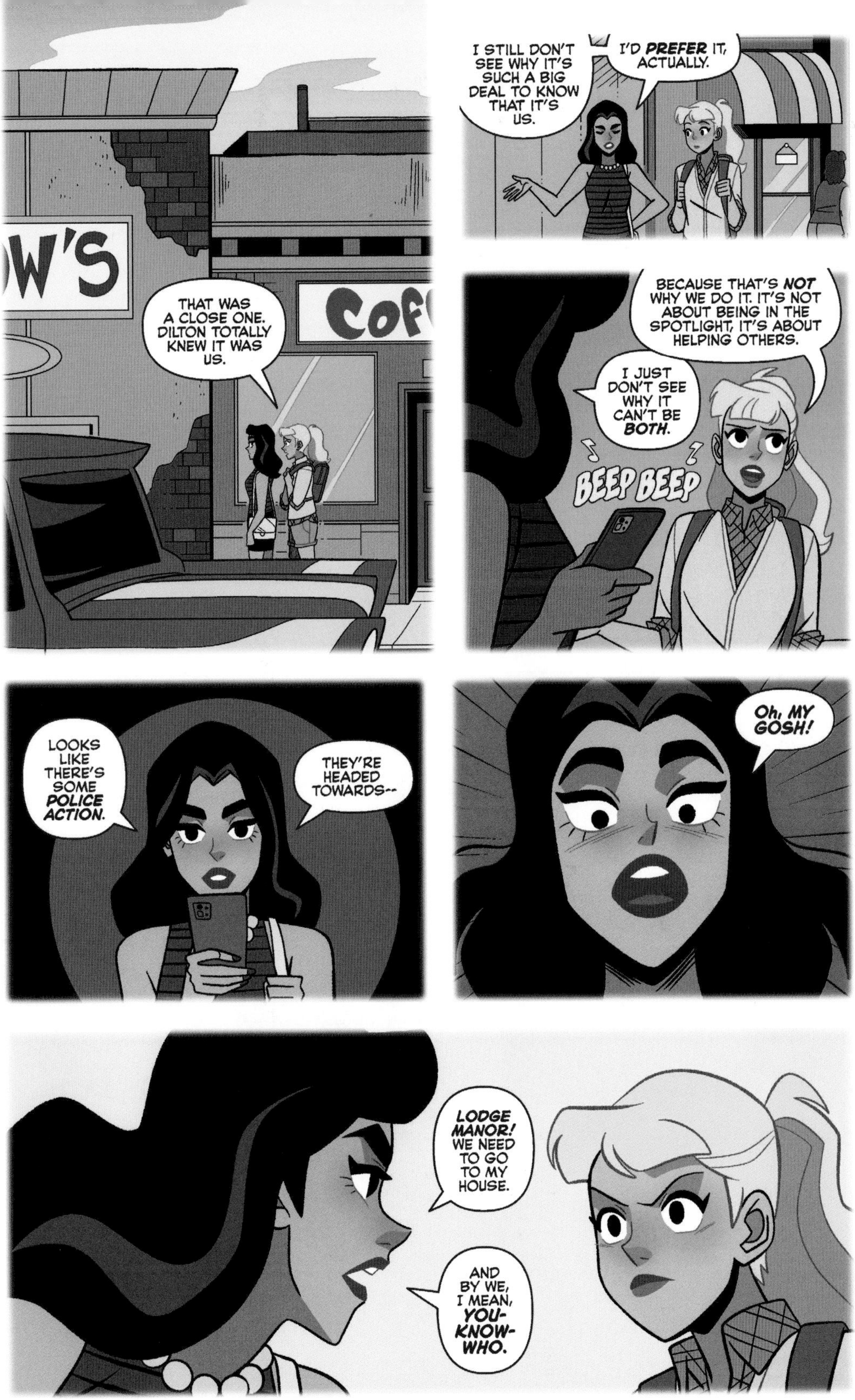
THAT WAS A CLOSE ONE. DILTON TOTALLY KNEW IT WAS US.
I STILL DON'T SEE WHY IT'S SUCH A BIG DEAL TO KNOW THAT IT'S US.
I'D PREFER IT, ACTUALLY.
BECAUSE THAT'S NOT WHY WE DO IT. IT'S NOT ABOUT BEING IN THE SPOTLIGHT, IT'S ABOUT HELPING OTHERS.
I JUST DON'T SEE WHY IT CAN'T BE BOTH.
BEEP BEEP
LOOKS LIKE THERE'S SOME POLICE ACTION.
THEY'RE HEADED TOWARDS--
Oh, MY GOSH!
LODGE MANOR! WE NEED TO GO TO MY HOUSE.
AND BY WE, I MEAN, YOU-KNOW-WHO.

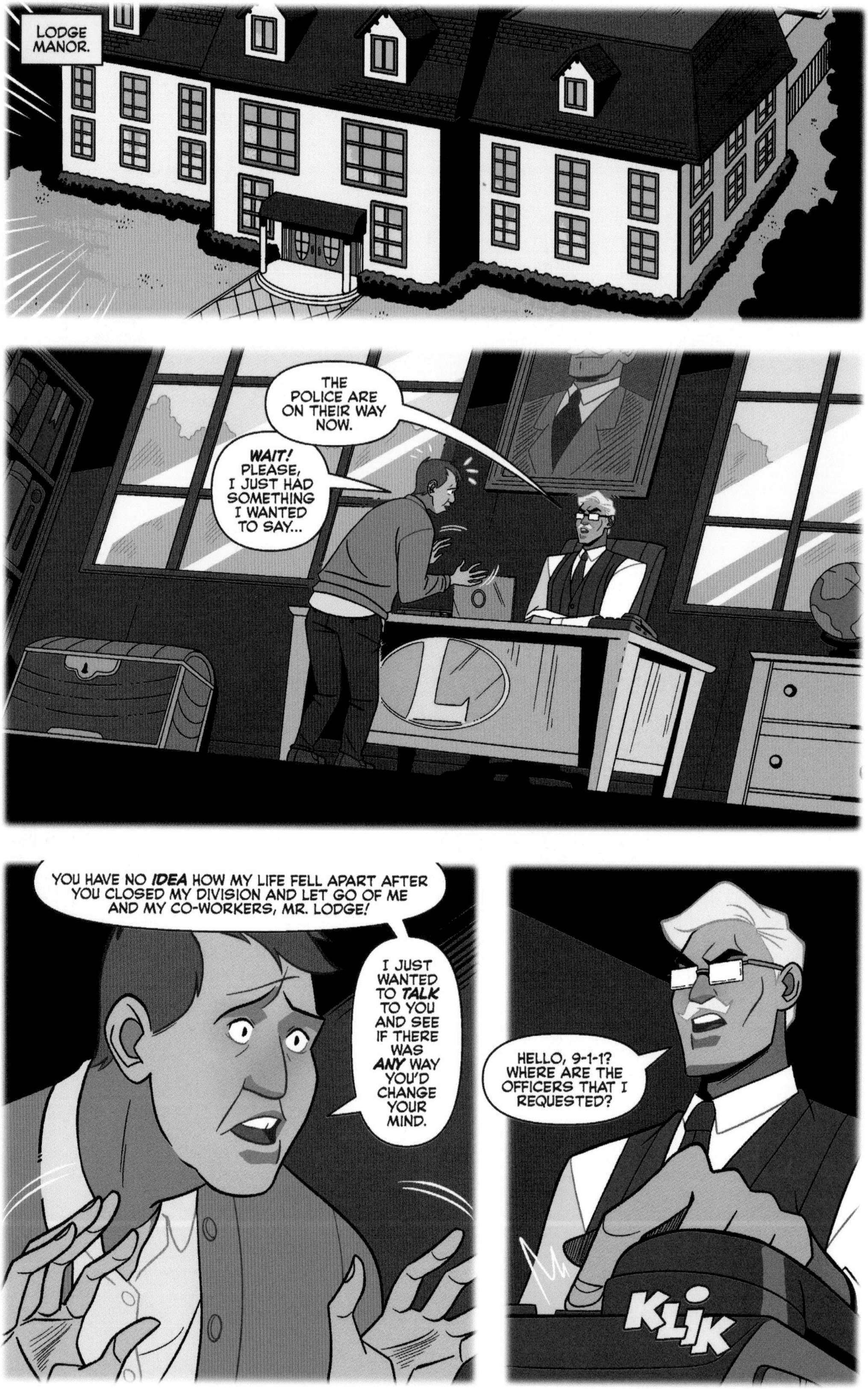
LODGE MANOR.
THE POLICE ARE ON THEIR WAY NOW.
WAIT! PLEASE, I JUST HAD SOMETHING I WANTED TO SAY...
YOU HAVE NO IDEA HOW MY LIFE FELL APART AFTER YOU CLOSED MY DIVISION AND LET GO OF ME AND MY CO-WORKERS, MR. LODGE!
I JUST WANTED TO TALK TO YOU AND SEE IF THERE WAS ANY WAY YOU'D CHANGE YOUR MIND.
HELLO, 9-1-1? WHERE ARE THE OFFICERS THAT I REQUESTED?
KLIK

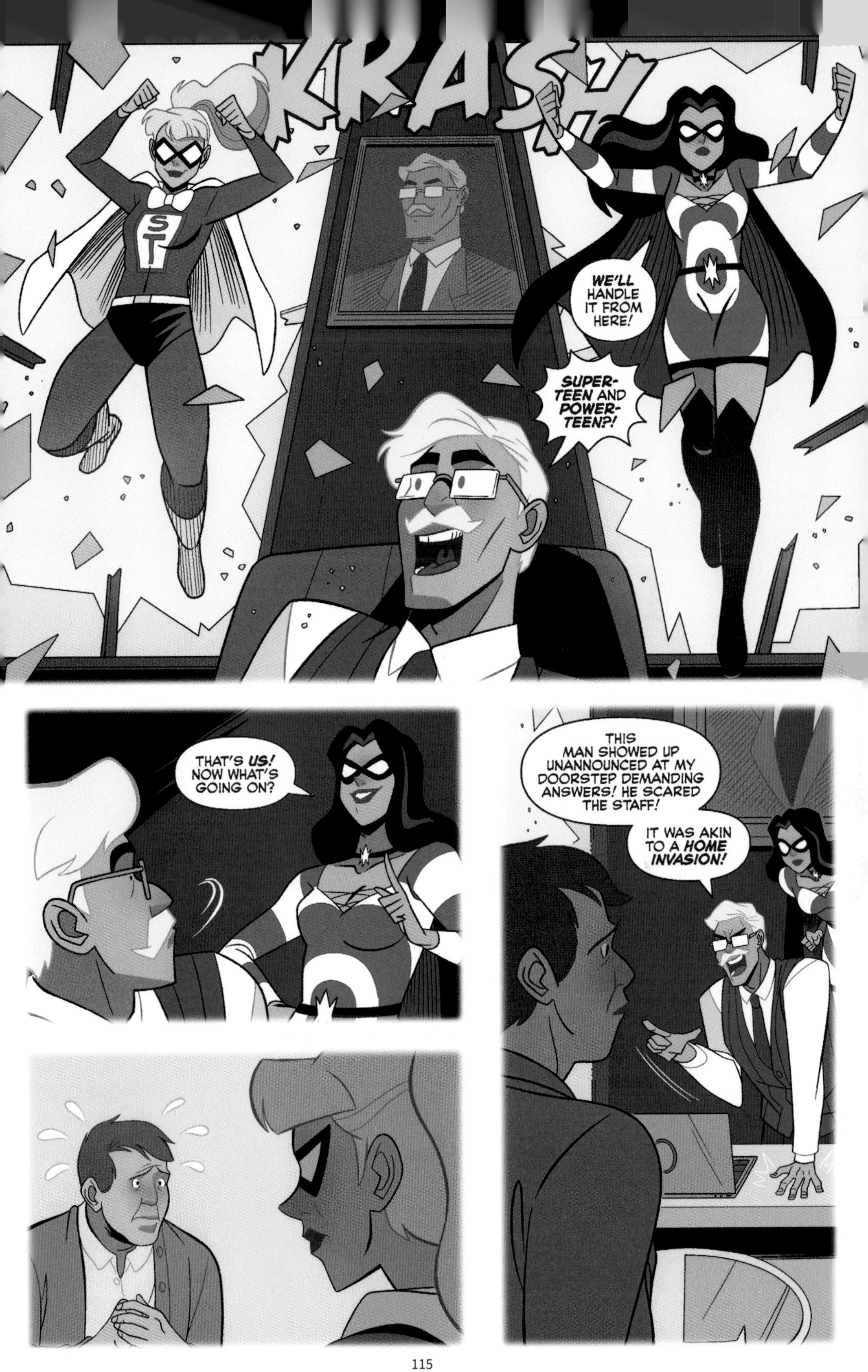
KRASH
WE'LL HANDLE IT FROM HERE!
SUPER-TEEN AND POWER-TEEN?!
THAT'S US! NOW WHAT'S GOING ON?
THIS MAN SHOWED UP UNANNOUNCED AT MY DOORSTEP DEMANDING ANSWERS! HE SCARED THE STAFF!
IT WAS AKIN TO A HOME INVASION!

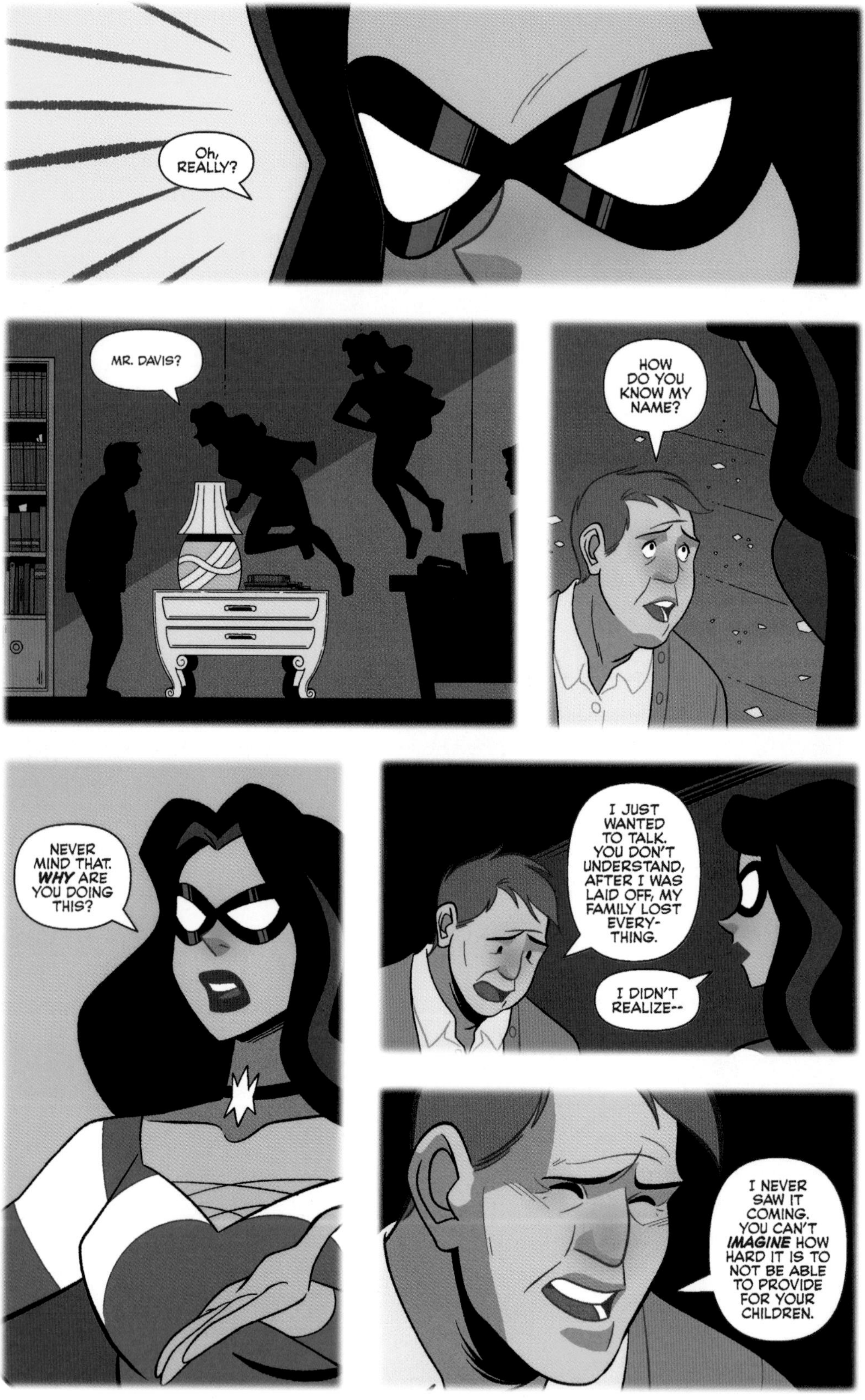
Oh, REALLY?
MR. DAVIS?
HOW DO YOU KNOW MY NAME?
NEVER MIND THAT. WHY ARE YOU DOING THIS?
I JUST WANTED TO TALK. YOU DON'T UNDERSTAND, AFTER I WAS LAID OFF, MY FAMILY LOST EVERY-THING.
I DIDN'T REALIZE--
I NEVER SAW IT COMING. YOU CAN'T IMAGINE HOW HARD IT IS TO NOT BE ABLE TO PROVIDE FOR YOUR CHILDREN.

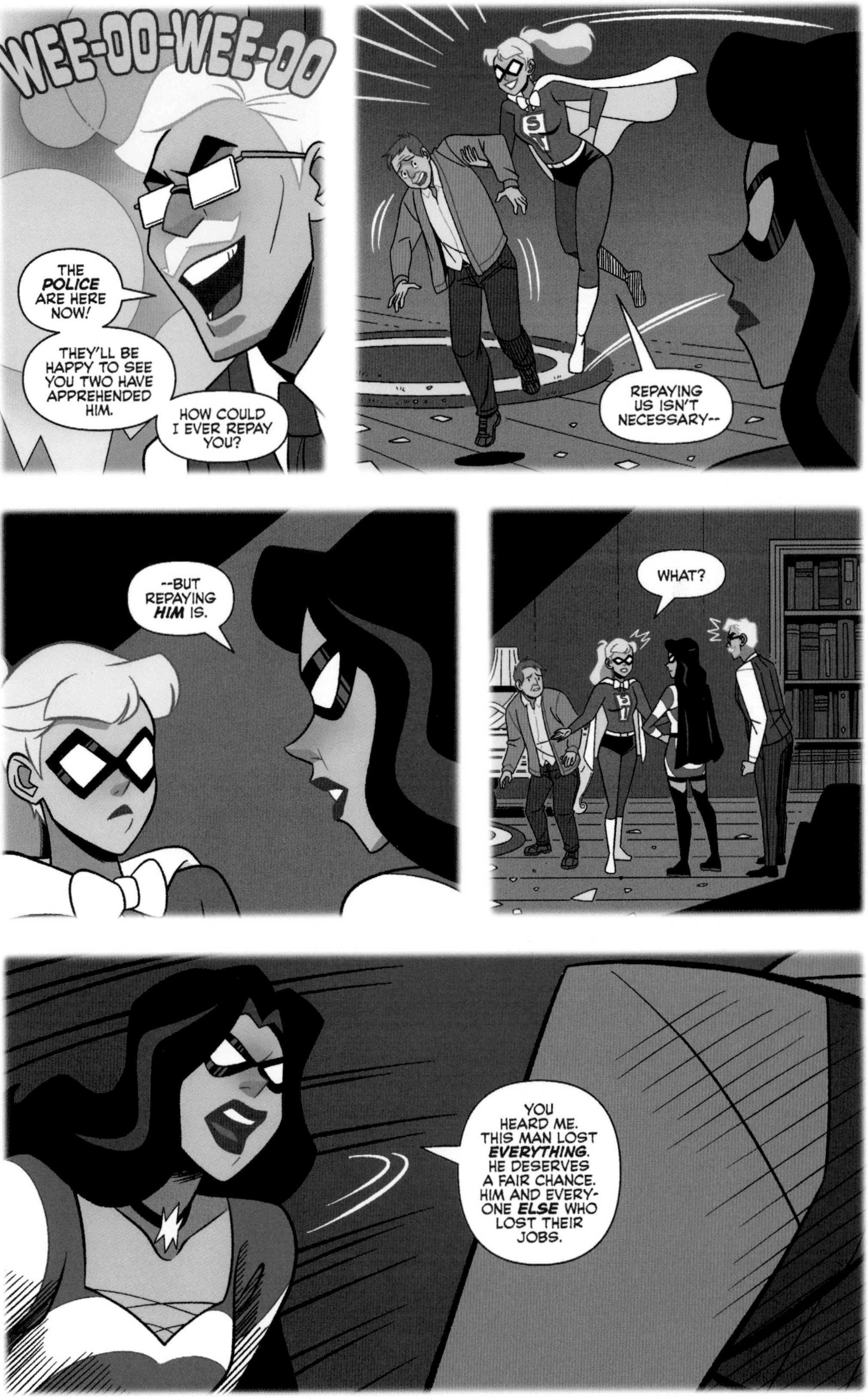
WEE-OO-WEE-OO
THE *POLICE* ARE HERE NOW!
THEY'LL BE HAPPY TO SEE YOU TWO HAVE APPREHENDED HIM.
HOW COULD I EVER REPAY YOU?
REPAYING US ISN'T NECESSARY--
--BUT REPAYING *HIM* IS.
WHAT?
YOU HEARD ME. THIS MAN LOST *EVERYTHING*. HE DESERVES A FAIR CHANCE. HIM AND EVERY-ONE *ELSE* WHO LOST THEIR JOBS.

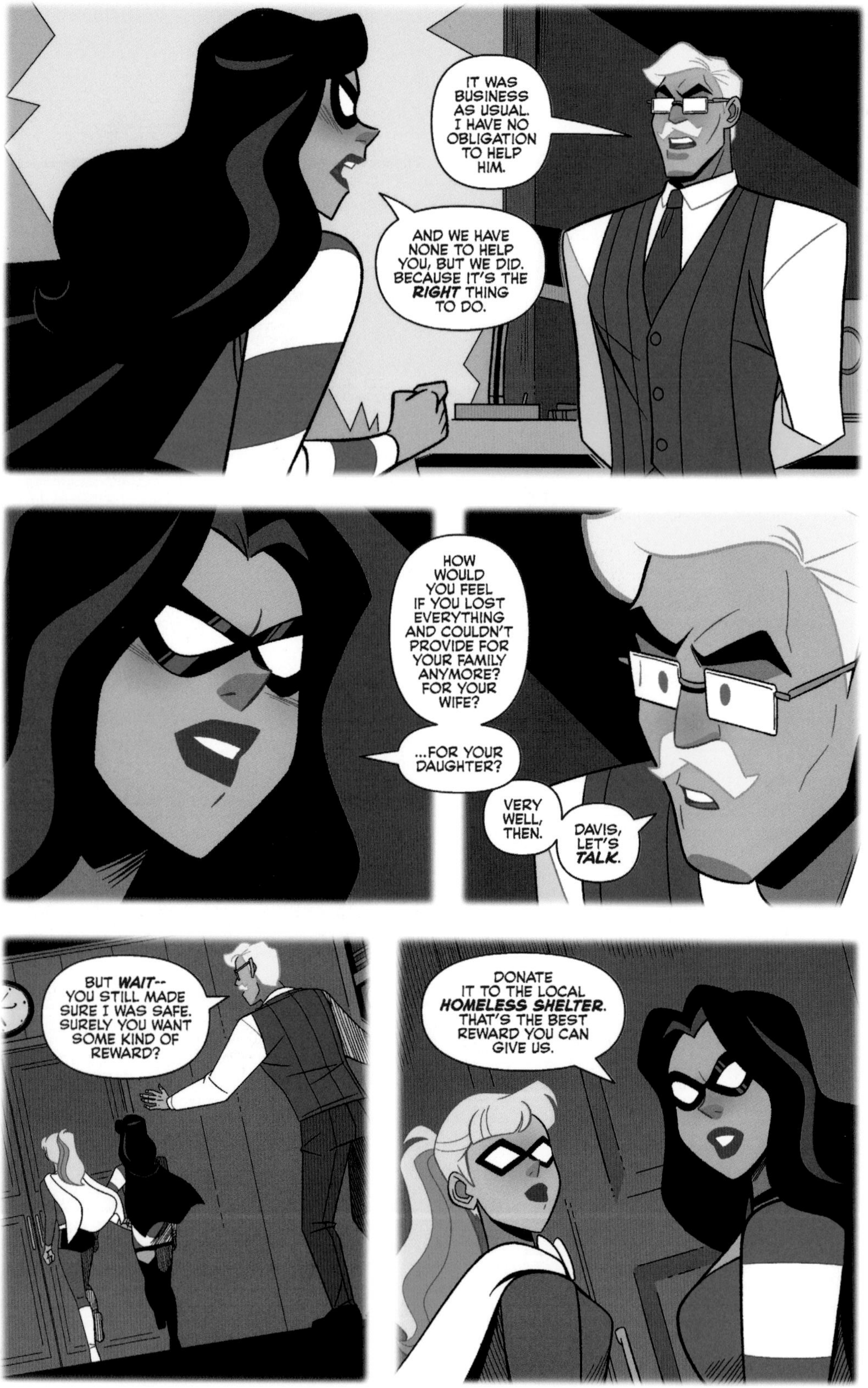
IT WAS BUSINESS AS USUAL. I HAVE NO OBLIGATION TO HELP HIM.
AND WE HAVE NONE TO HELP YOU, BUT WE DID. BECAUSE IT'S THE **RIGHT** THING TO DO.
HOW WOULD YOU FEEL IF YOU LOST EVERYTHING AND COULDN'T PROVIDE FOR YOUR FAMILY ANYMORE? FOR YOUR WIFE?
...FOR YOUR DAUGHTER?
VERY WELL, THEN.
DAVIS, LET'S **TALK**.
BUT **WAIT**-- YOU STILL MADE SURE I WAS SAFE. SURELY YOU WANT SOME KIND OF REWARD?
DONATE IT TO THE LOCAL **HOMELESS SHELTER**. THAT'S THE BEST REWARD YOU CAN GIVE US.

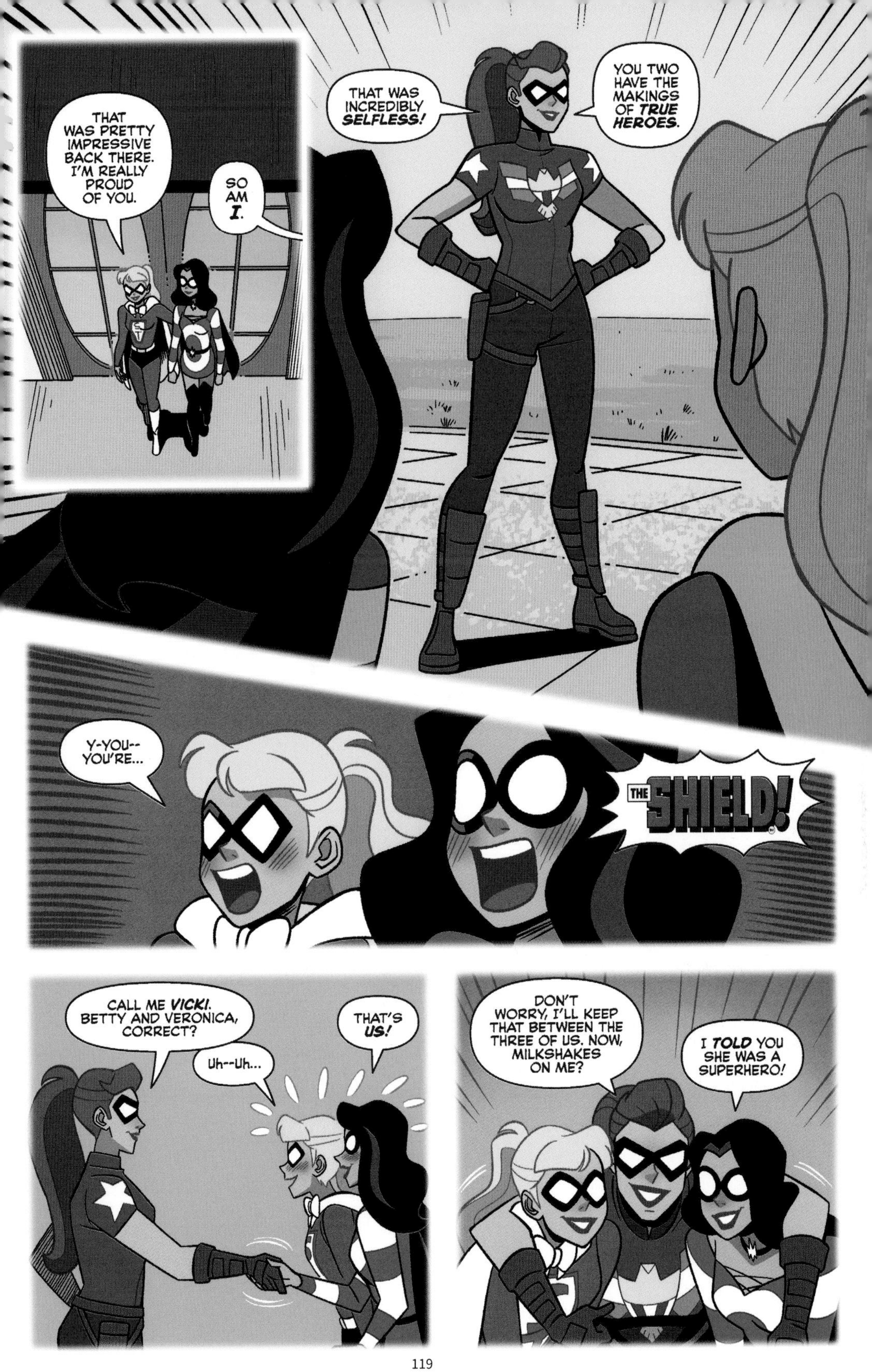
THAT WAS PRETTY IMPRESSIVE BACK THERE. I'M REALLY PROUD OF YOU.
SO AM I.
THAT WAS INCREDIBLY SELFLESS!
YOU TWO HAVE THE MAKINGS OF TRUE HEROES.
Y-YOU-- YOU'RE...
THE SHIELD!
CALL ME VICKI. BETTY AND VERONICA, CORRECT?
Uh--Uh...
THAT'S US!
DON'T WORRY, I'LL KEEP THAT BETWEEN THE THREE OF US. NOW, MILKSHAKES ON ME?
I TOLD YOU SHE WAS A SUPERHERO!

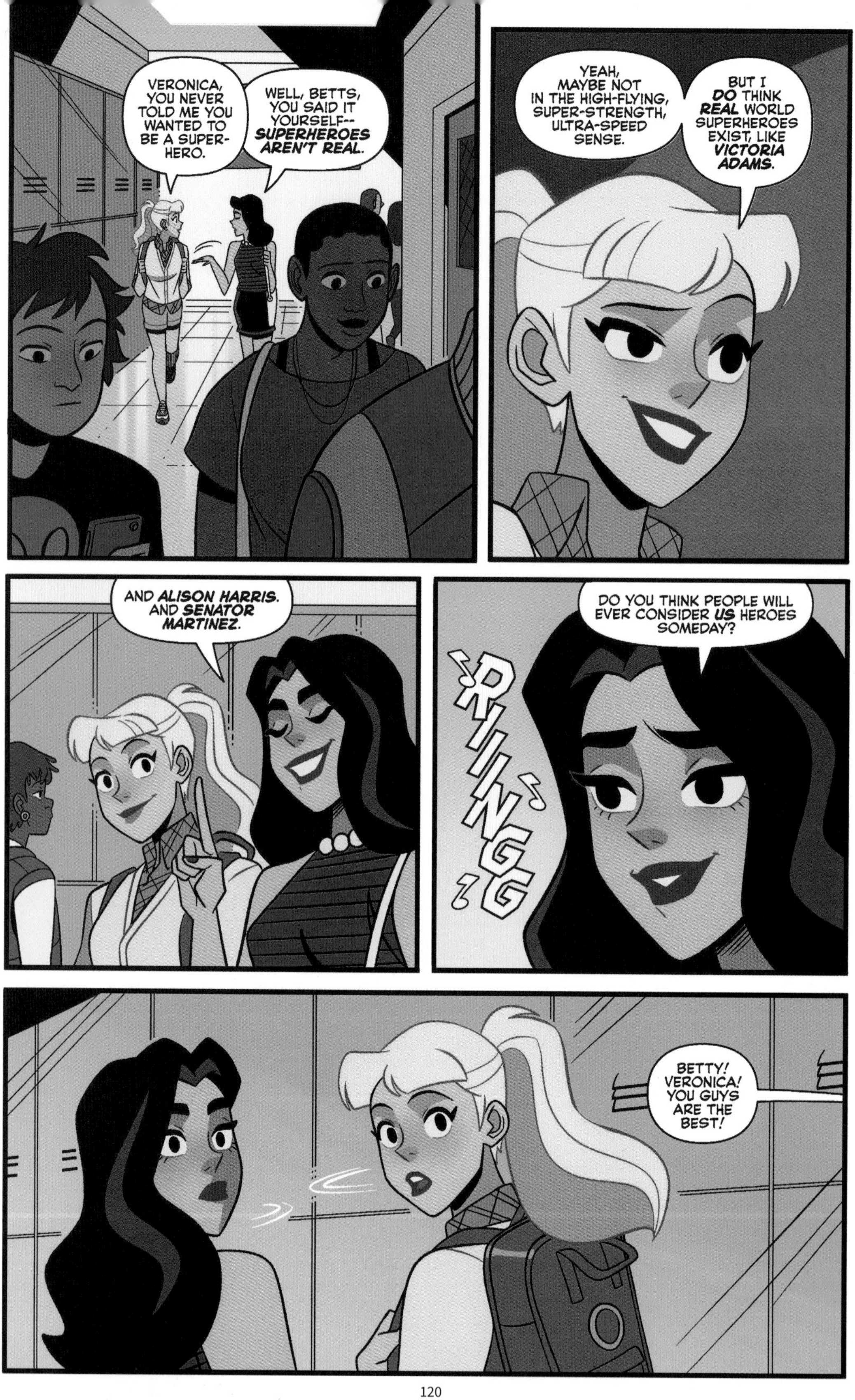
VERONICA, YOU NEVER TOLD ME YOU WANTED TO BE A SUPER-HERO.
WELL, BETTS, YOU SAID IT YOURSELF-- SUPERHEROES AREN'T REAL.
YEAH, MAYBE NOT IN THE HIGH-FLYING, SUPER-STRENGTH, ULTRA-SPEED SENSE.
BUT I DO THINK REAL WORLD SUPERHEROES EXIST, LIKE VICTORIA ADAMS.
AND ALISON HARRIS. AND SENATOR MARTINEZ.
DO YOU THINK PEOPLE WILL EVER CONSIDER US HEROES SOMEDAY?
RIIIINGG
BETTY! VERONICA! YOU GUYS ARE THE BEST!

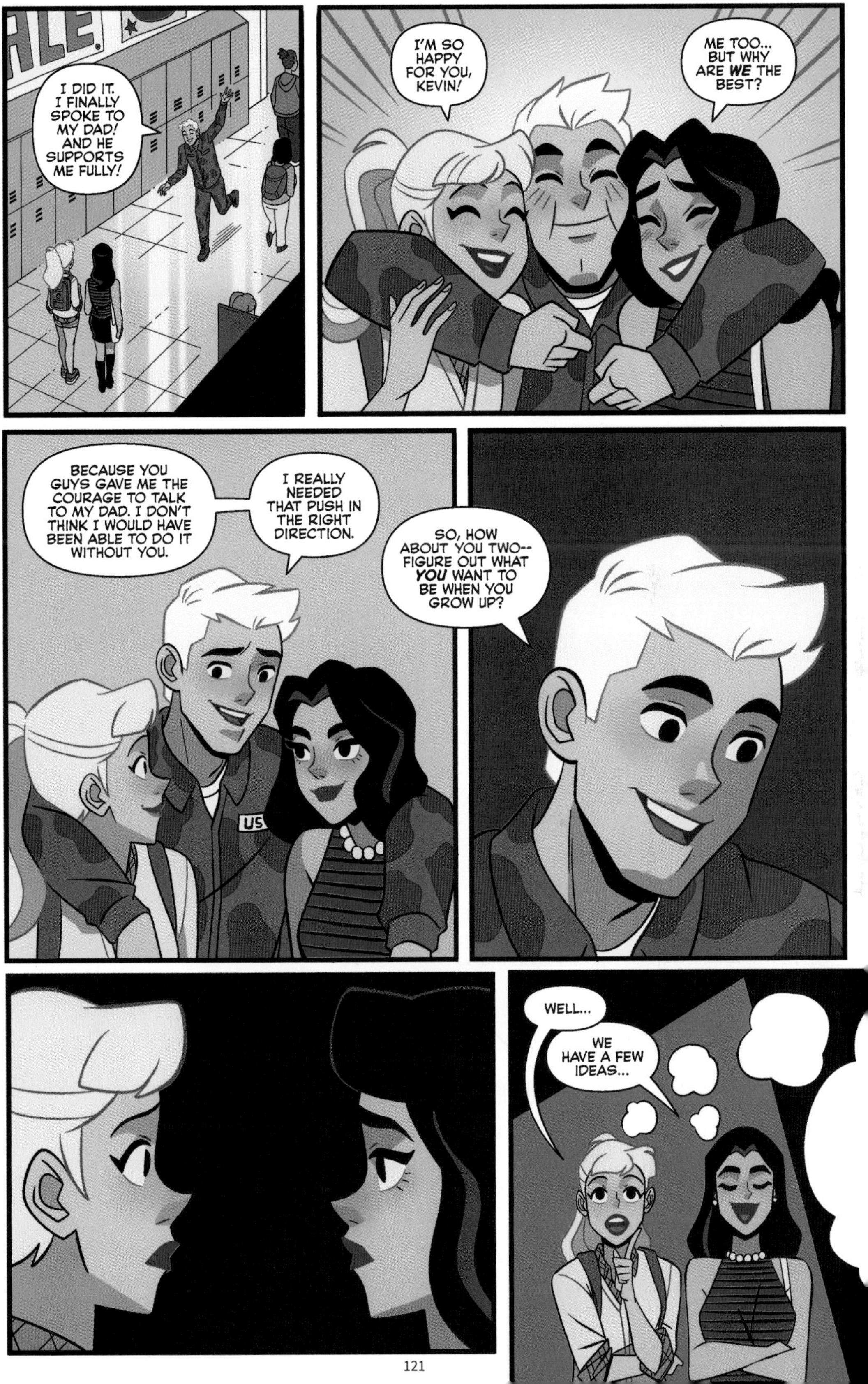
I DID IT. I FINALLY SPOKE TO MY DAD! AND HE SUPPORTS ME FULLY!
I'M SO HAPPY FOR YOU, KEVIN!
ME TOO... BUT WHY ARE *WE* THE BEST?
BECAUSE YOU GUYS GAVE ME THE COURAGE TO TALK TO MY DAD. I DON'T THINK I WOULD HAVE BEEN ABLE TO DO IT WITHOUT YOU.
I REALLY NEEDED THAT PUSH IN THE RIGHT DIRECTION.
SO, HOW ABOUT YOU TWO--FIGURE OUT WHAT *YOU* WANT TO BE WHEN YOU GROW UP?
WELL...
WE HAVE A FEW IDEAS...

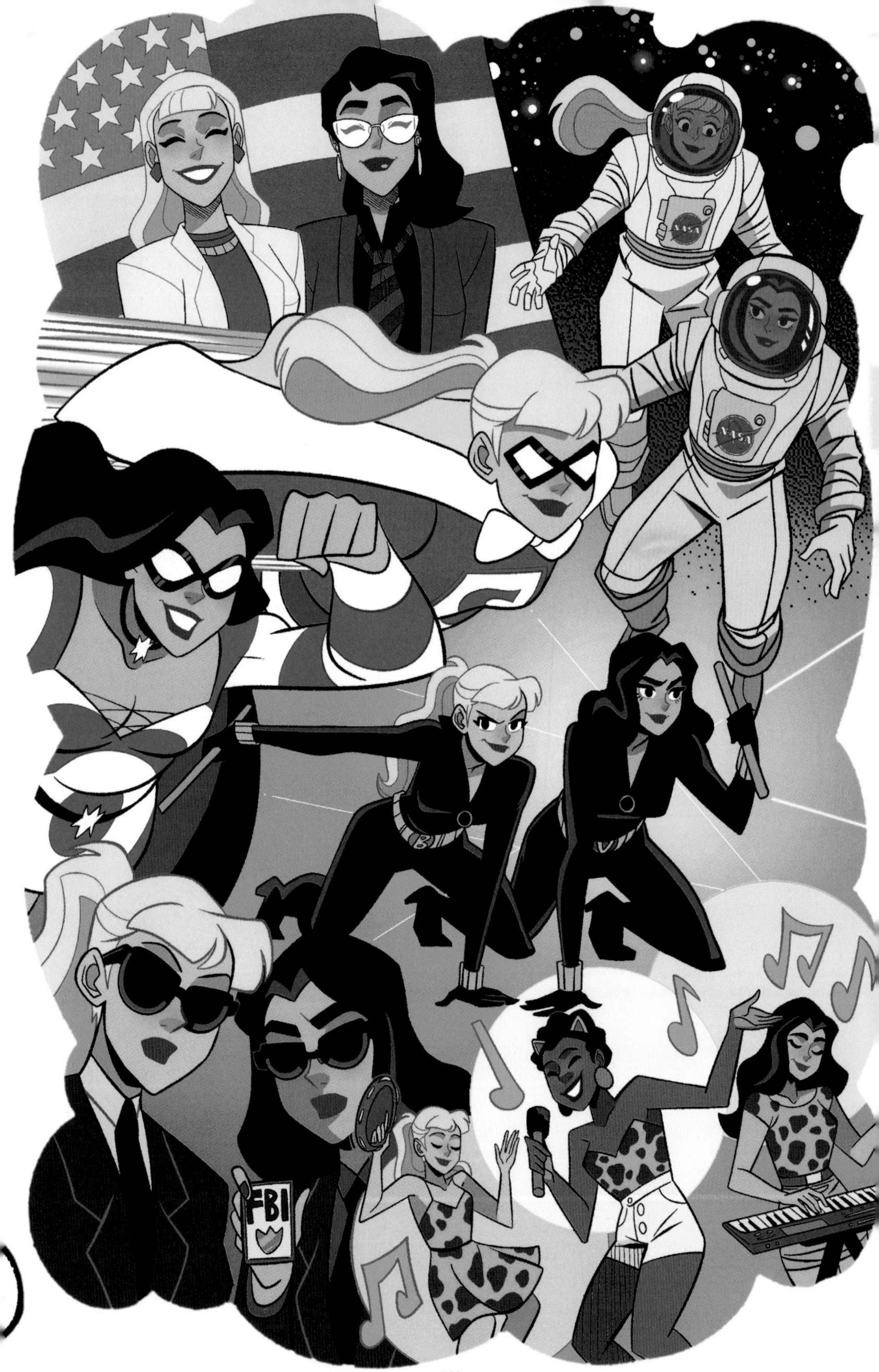
NASA
NASA
FBI

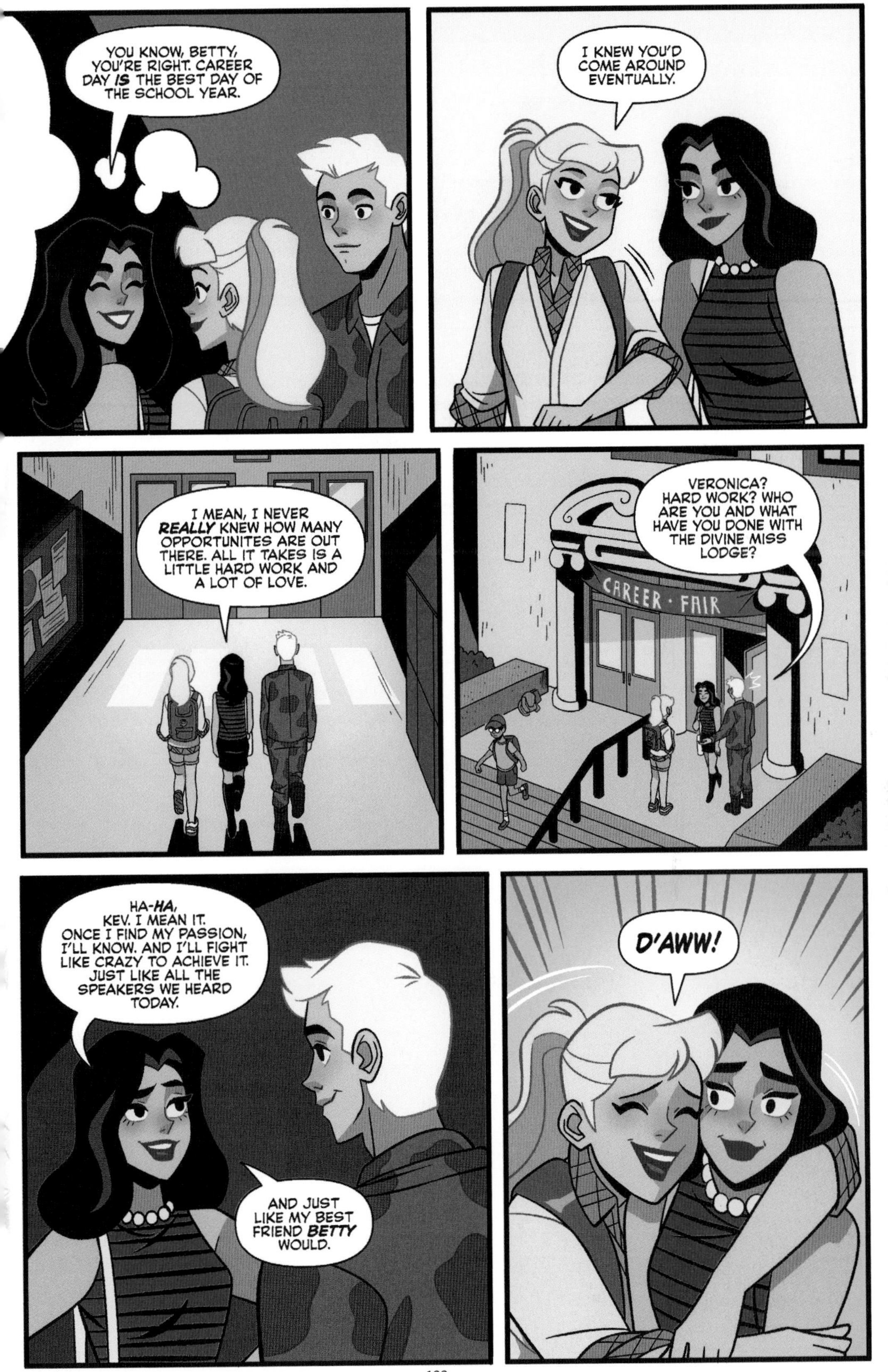
YOU KNOW, BETTY, YOU'RE RIGHT. CAREER DAY *IS* THE BEST DAY OF THE SCHOOL YEAR.
I KNEW YOU'D COME AROUND EVENTUALLY.
I MEAN, I NEVER *REALLY* KNEW HOW MANY OPPORTUNITES ARE OUT THERE. ALL IT TAKES IS A LITTLE HARD WORK AND A LOT OF LOVE.
VERONICA? HARD WORK? WHO ARE YOU AND WHAT HAVE YOU DONE WITH THE DIVINE MISS LODGE?
CAREER · FAIR
HA-*HA*, KEV. I MEAN IT. ONCE I FIND MY PASSION, I'LL KNOW. AND I'LL FIGHT LIKE CRAZY TO ACHIEVE IT. JUST LIKE ALL THE SPEAKERS WE HEARD TODAY.
AND JUST LIKE MY BEST FRIEND *BETTY* WOULD.
D'AWW!

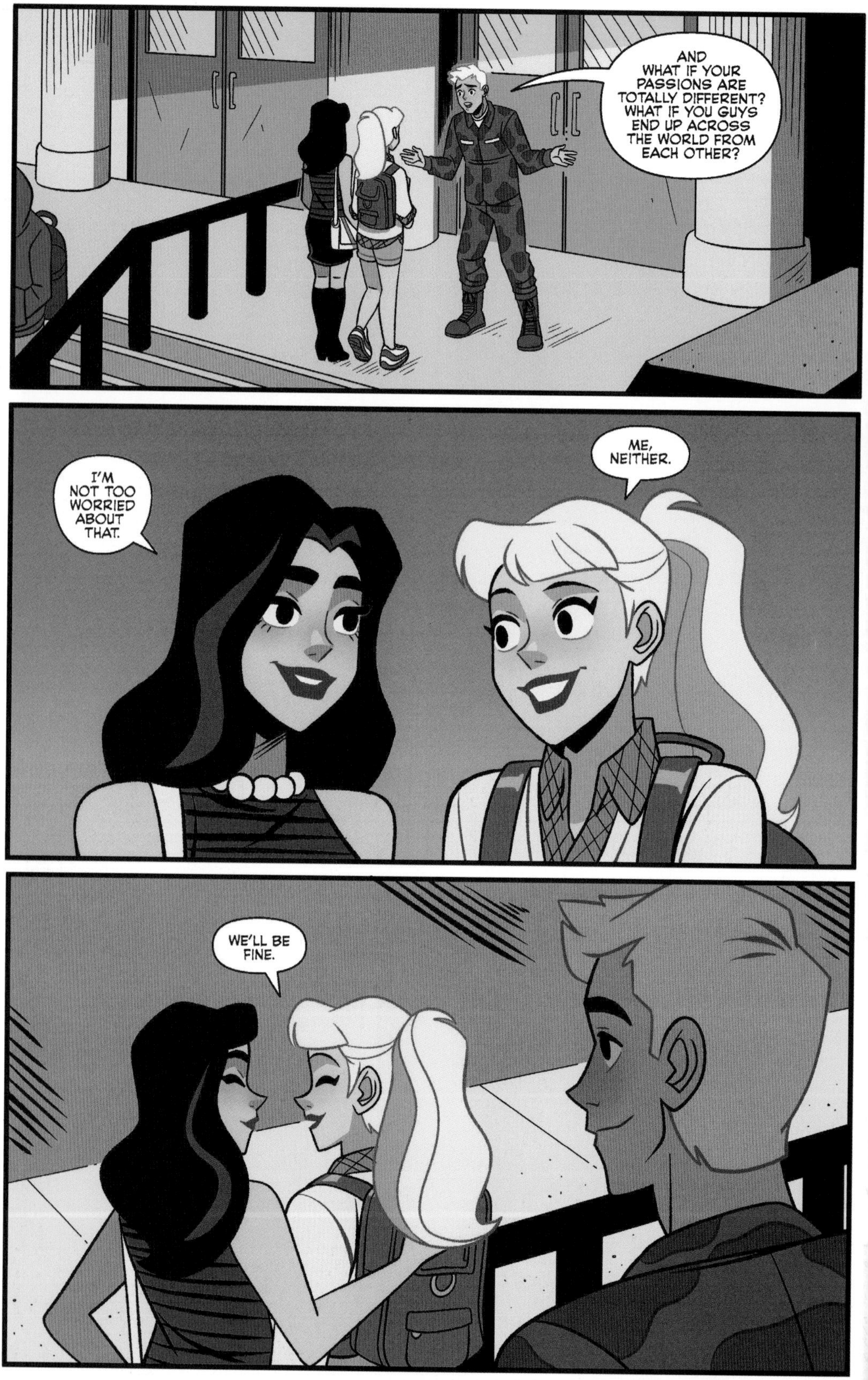
AND WHAT IF YOUR PASSIONS ARE TOTALLY DIFFERENT? WHAT IF YOU GUYS END UP ACROSS THE WORLD FROM EACH OTHER?
I'M NOT TOO WORRIED ABOUT THAT.
ME, NEITHER.
WE'LL BE FINE.

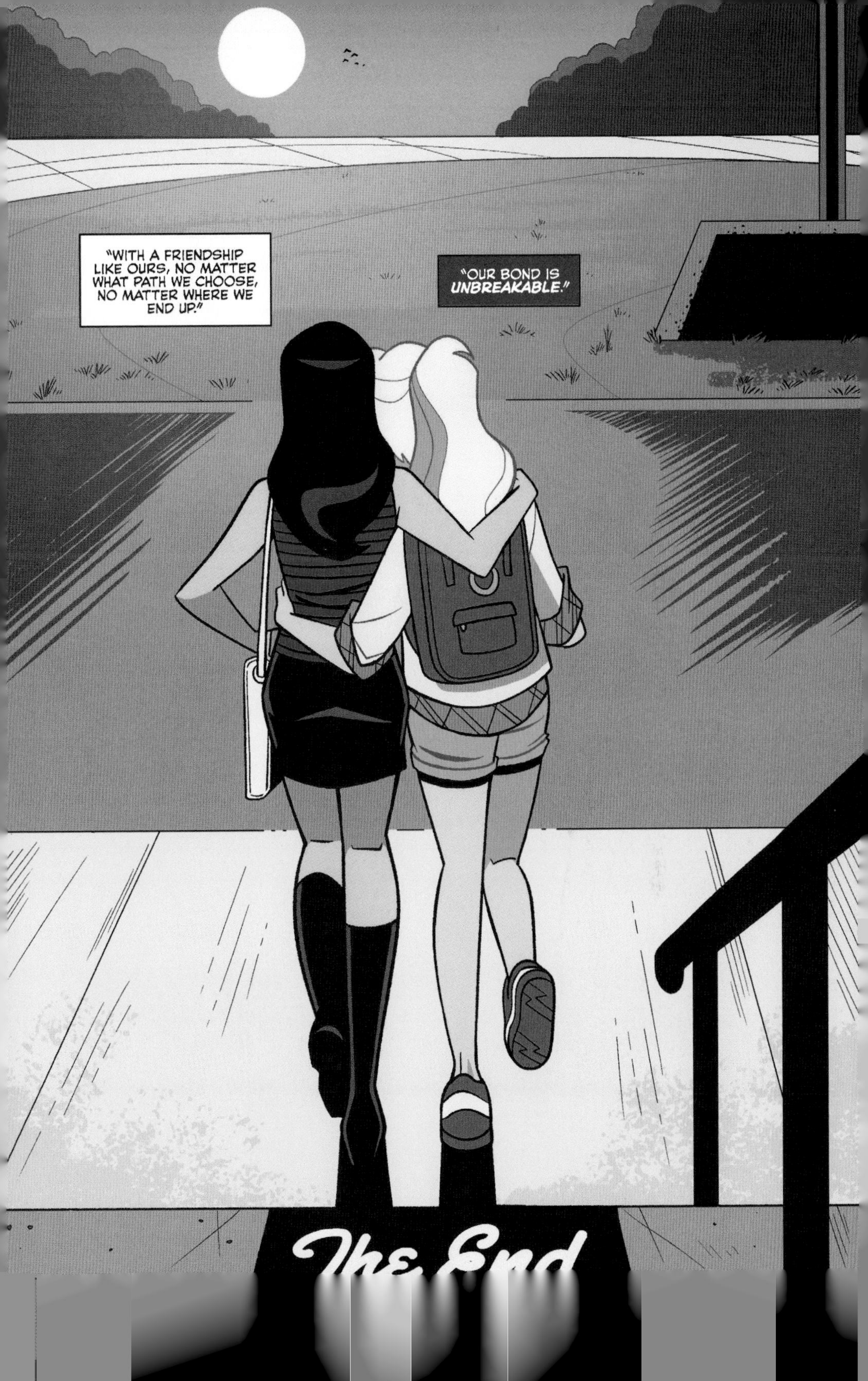
"WITH A FRIENDSHIP LIKE OURS, NO MATTER WHAT PATH WE CHOOSE, NO MATTER WHERE WE END UP."
"OUR BOND IS *UNBREAKABLE*."
The End

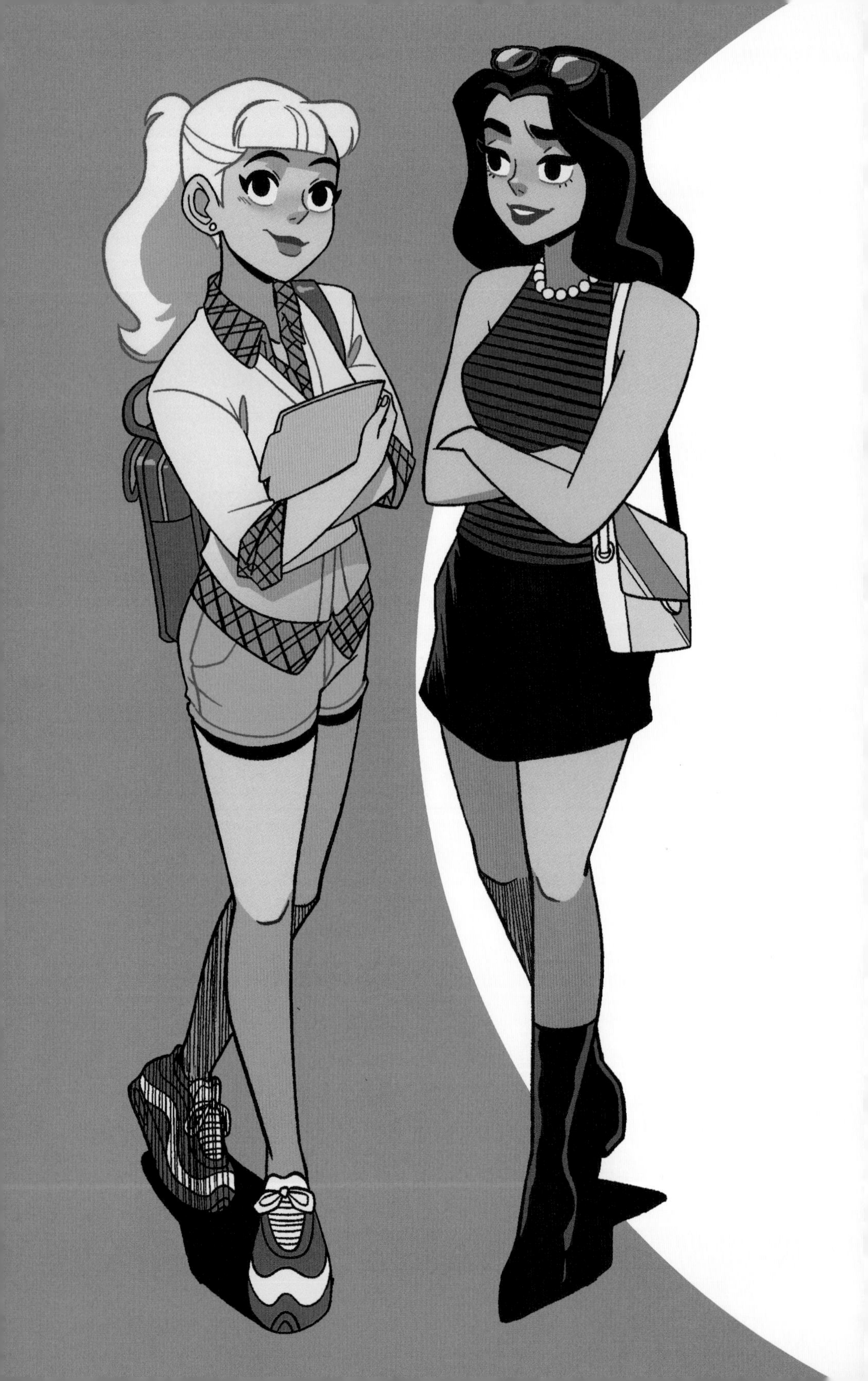

Betty and Veronica are two of my best friends.

I know that's a weird thing to say about fictional characters, but I've been writing these two characters now for three years, and reading about their adventures (both for work AND for fun) for over twenty five years. It's from this intimate knowledge of them and their character traits, personalities and quirks that I've been given the opportunity to play in their sandbox, so to speak, and push the limitations of what we've seen these characters do. From biker babes to high school grads, it's been a fun journey plopping Betty and Veronica into new, fun, and sometimes ridiculous scenarios to see how they'll not only manage, but thrive.

In this book, I got to do something a little different. I was able to both let them be "normal" high school students and also have them explore beyond the confines of the walls of Riverdale High School—like, way beyond... to infinity and beyond. But it's not just Betty and Veronica's journey that's at play here—it's anyone with a dream. As much fun as it is to write the two BFFs as Presidents of the United States of America, it was just as fun—and incredibly important—to learn how someone with a dream of holding office in politics, or joining a space exploration team, could make that a reality. The adult speakers present in this book are based off a number of real world heroes' unique and individual

journeys. And it was necessary to create a diverse landscape while portraying these characters—and all the kids at Riverdale High—because that *is* real life.

We were so fortunate to have Brittney Williams on this book for art. Britt's been one of our dream collaborators; always on our wish list of artists to work with—and never once were we disappointed. Every page that came in was so animated, so filled with excitement and expression that you could eliminate my words entirely and still get a clear sense of the story. I owe so much to Britt for not only making this story look good, but for literally breathing a life into it far beyond my wildest dreams. Couple this with Matt Herms' amazing, vibrant colors and brilliant choices when transitioning from present to fantasy and the legendary Jack Morelli's keen sense of style and always-constant fantastic lettering choices and we were able to make magic. I consider myself one lucky lady for getting the chance to work with this team.

So, could you say being a part of the creation of this book was one of my dreams come true? Absolutely. Now, go out and make YOUR dreams come true.

- Jamie L. Rotante

ABOUT THE AUTHOR

Jamie L. Rotante is a New York-based writer, editor and proofreader. She reads comic books for a living at Archie Comic Publications, Inc. and has previously written both the *Betty & Veronica: Vixens* and *Betty & Veronica: Senior Year* comic mini-series. In her free time she also writes about punk music, women's issues and being a neurotic and strives to make sure high school students have the chance to graduate and achieve their dreams.

ABOUT THE ARTIST

Brittney Williams is a storyboard and comic book artist who draws A LOT. In 2012 she interned at Walt Disney Animation Studios as a storyboard artist. Since then, she's worked for a variety of animation studios and publishers including DC Comics, Cartoon Network, Dreamworks TV, BOOM! Studios and Marvel Comics. As a two time GLAAD award nominee, she exists to create things for kids and the queer community.

RIVERDALE:
THE TIES THAT BIND

Archie's second original graphic novel features the world of CW's *Riverdale*! Four interconnected stories trap each of our main characters in a unique high-stakes conflict over the course of a few pressure-cooker hours! Will Archie and company even make it to sunrise? If they do, will they ever be the same again?

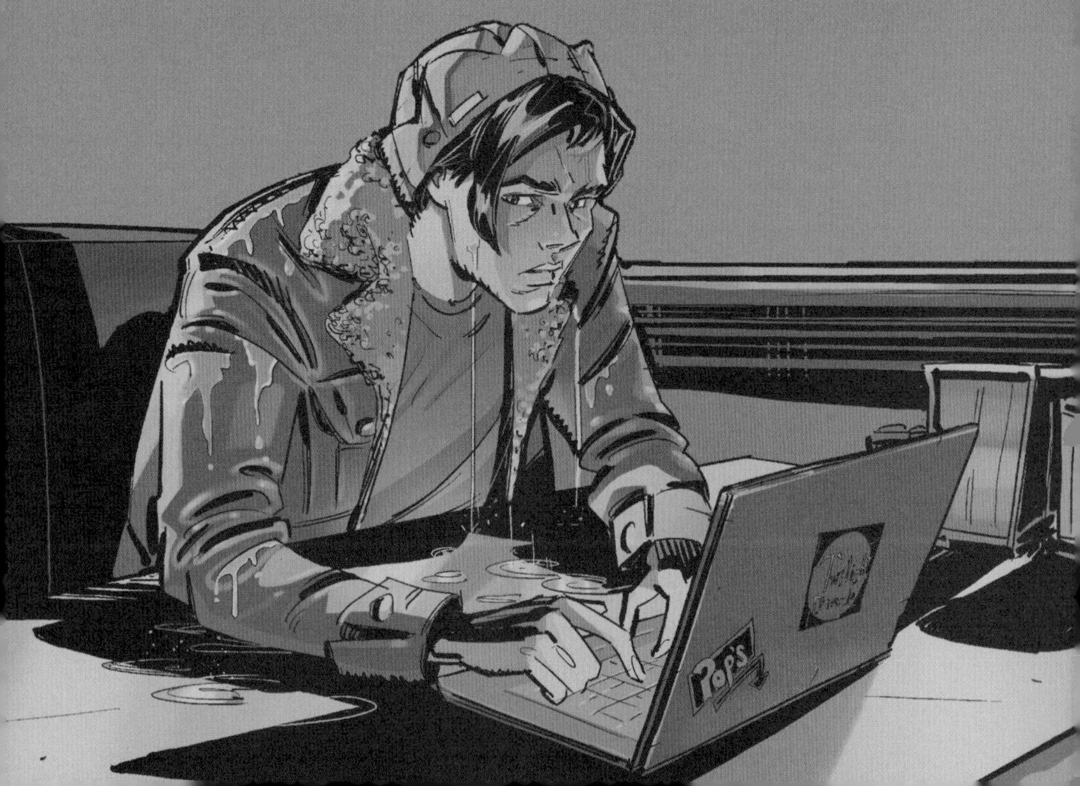
Pop's

PROLOGUE

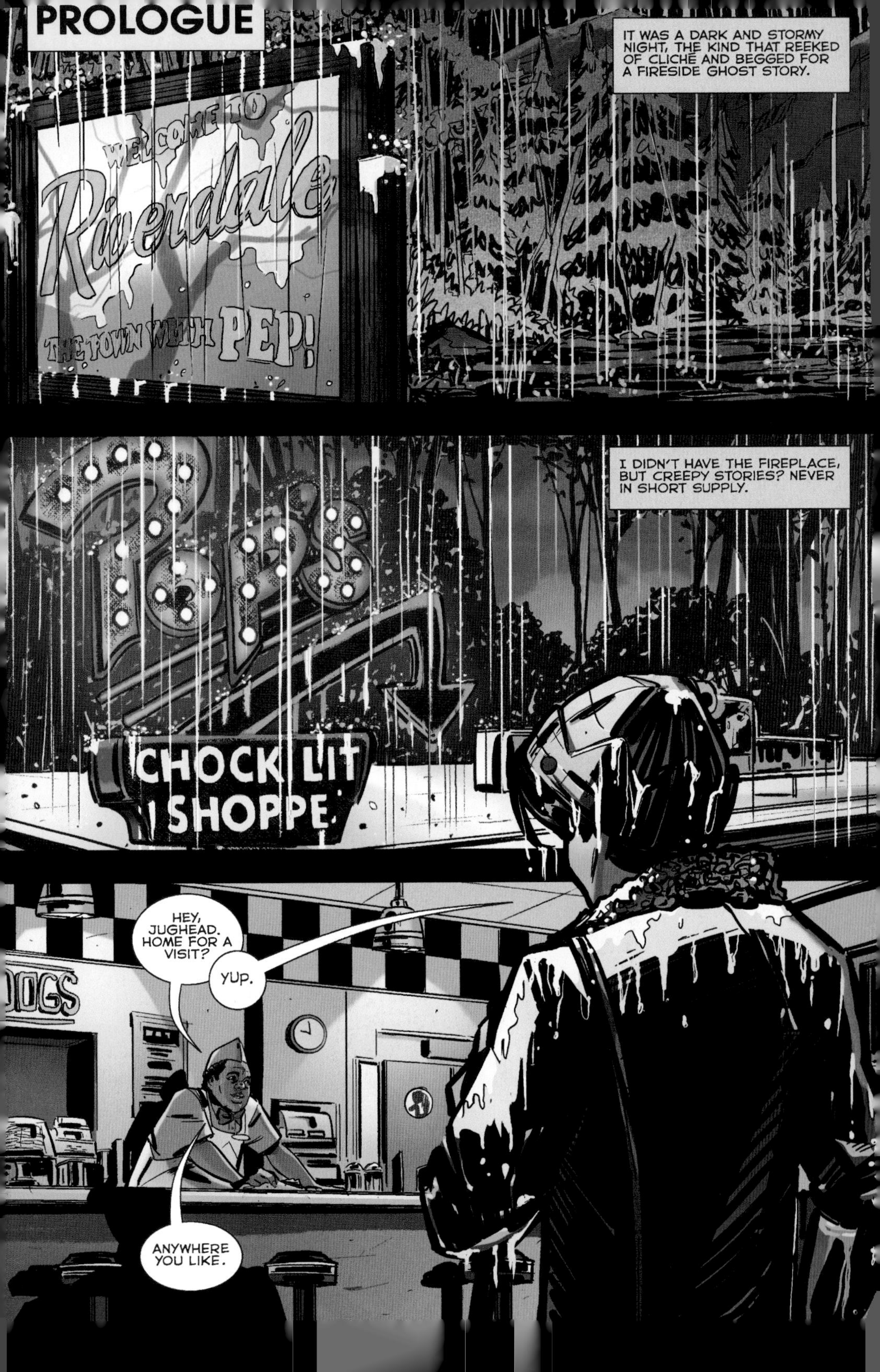
IT WAS A DARK AND STORMY NIGHT, THE KIND THAT REEKED OF CLICHÉ AND BEGGED FOR A FIRESIDE GHOST STORY.
WELCOME TO
Riverdale
THE TOWN WITH PEP!
I DIDN'T HAVE THE FIREPLACE, BUT CREEPY STORIES? NEVER IN SHORT SUPPLY.
POP'S
CHOCK LIT SHOPPE
HEY, JUGHEAD. HOME FOR A VISIT?
YUP.
ANYWHERE YOU LIKE.

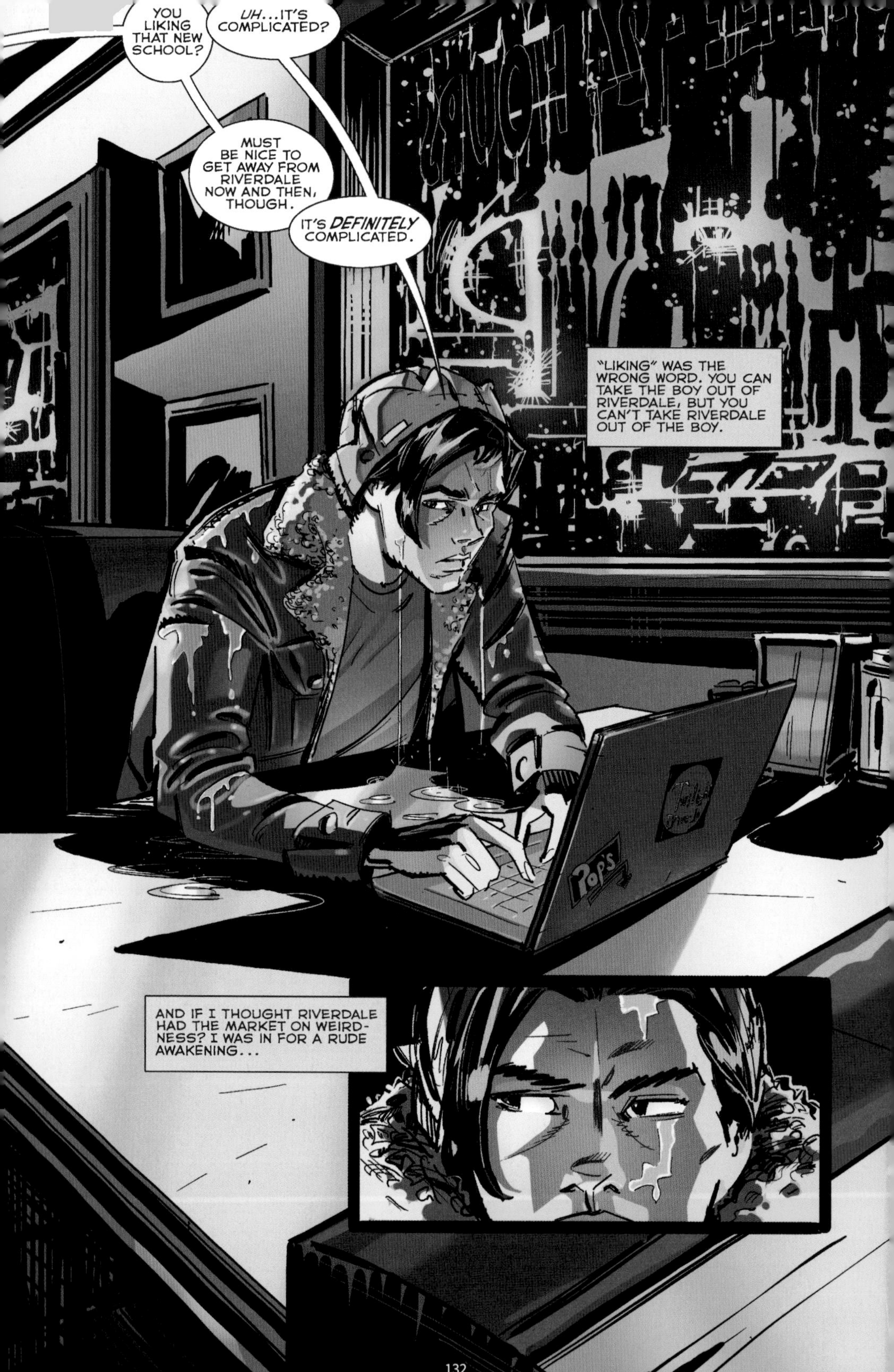
YOU LIKING THAT NEW SCHOOL?
UH...IT'S COMPLICATED?
MUST BE NICE TO GET AWAY FROM RIVERDALE NOW AND THEN, THOUGH.
IT'S DEFINITELY COMPLICATED.
"LIKING" WAS THE WRONG WORD. YOU CAN TAKE THE BOY OUT OF RIVERDALE, BUT YOU CAN'T TAKE RIVERDALE OUT OF THE BOY.
POP'S
AND IF I THOUGHT RIVERDALE HAD THE MARKET ON WEIRD-NESS? I WAS IN FOR A RUDE AWAKENING...

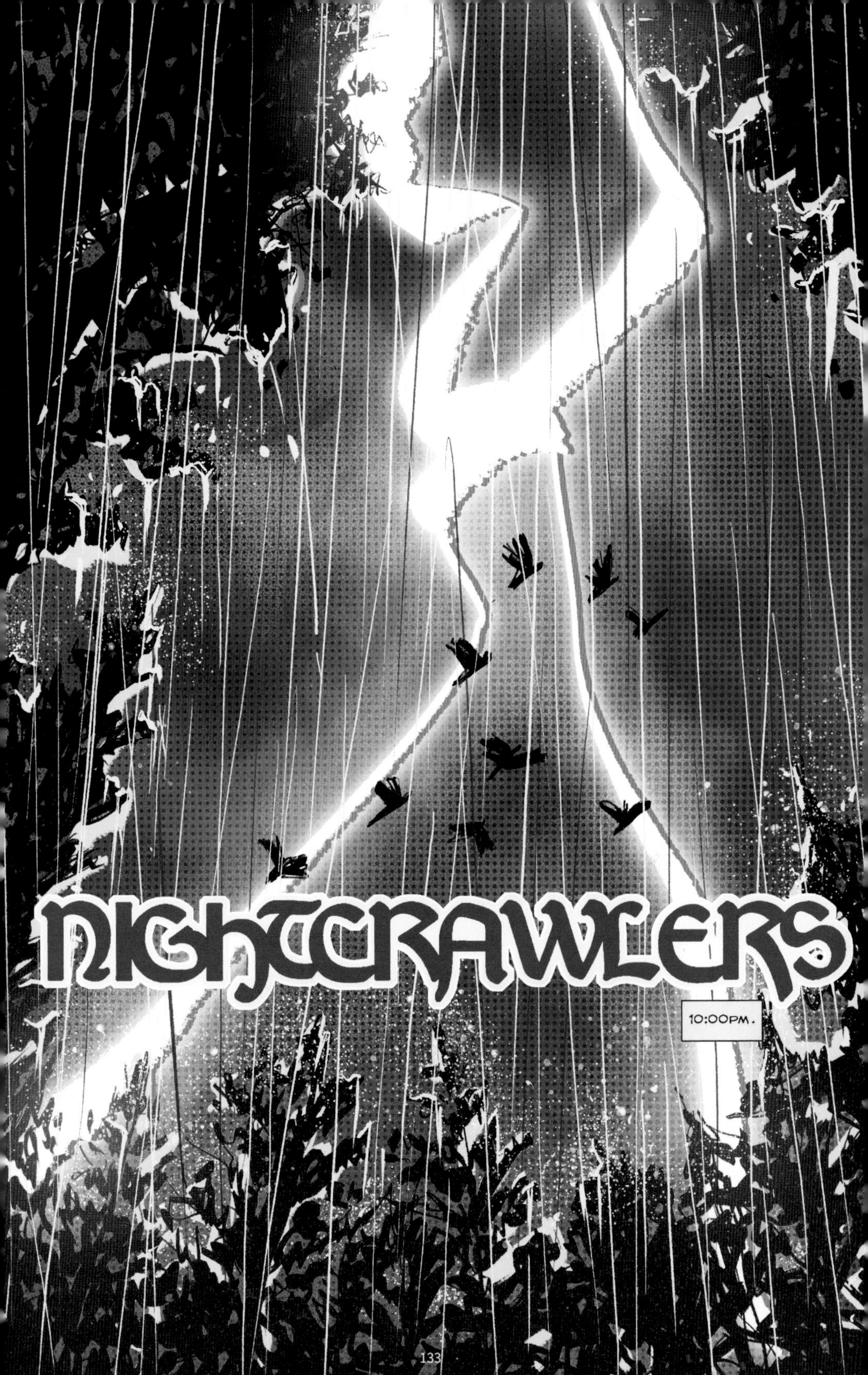
NIGHTCRAWLERS
10:00PM.

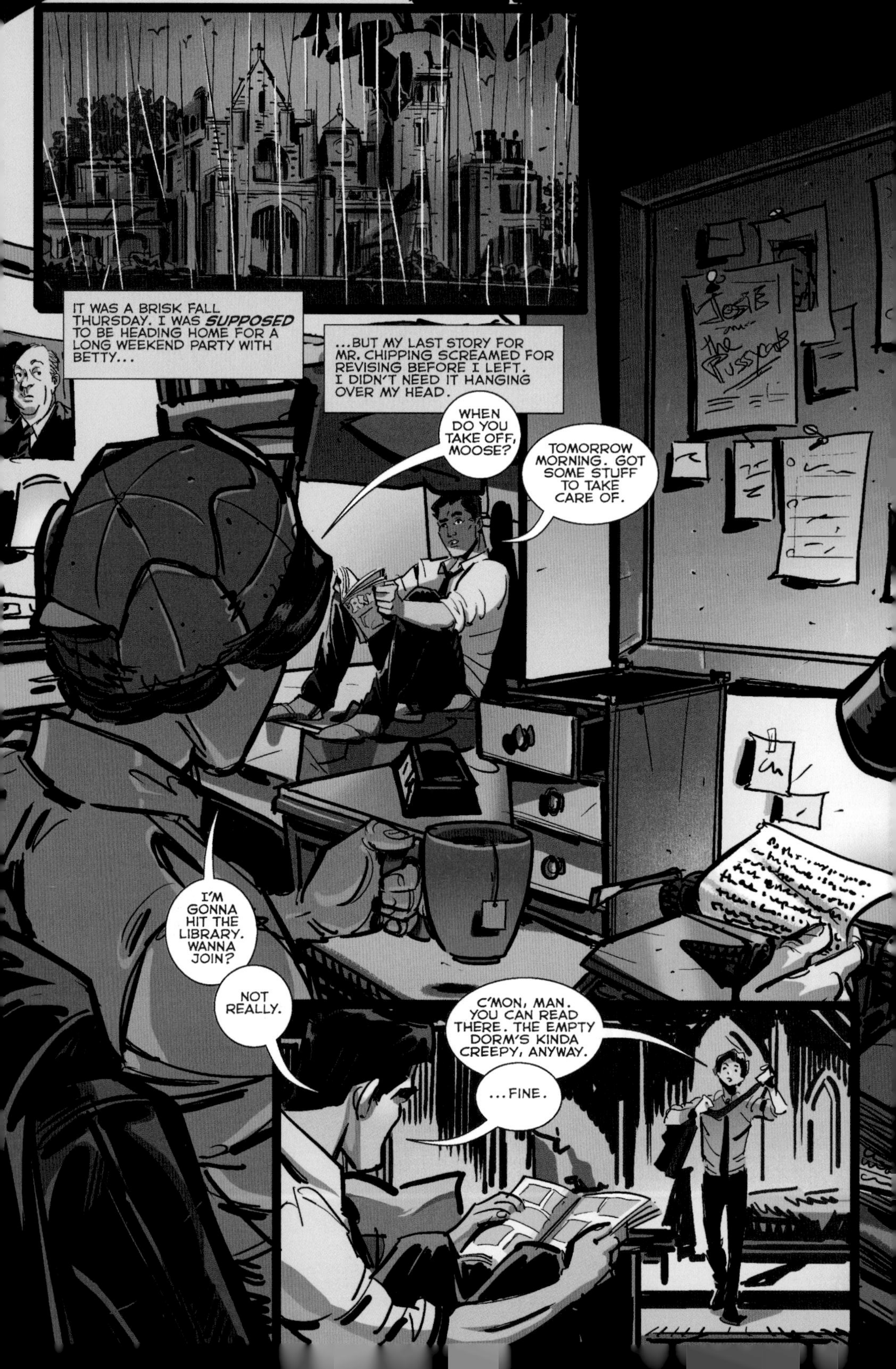
IT WAS A BRISK FALL THURSDAY. I WAS SUPPOSED TO BE HEADING HOME FOR A LONG WEEKEND PARTY WITH BETTY...
...BUT MY LAST STORY FOR MR. CHIPPING SCREAMED FOR REVISING BEFORE I LEFT. I DIDN'T NEED IT HANGING OVER MY HEAD.
WHEN DO YOU TAKE OFF, MOOSE?
TOMORROW MORNING. GOT SOME STUFF TO TAKE CARE OF.
I'M GONNA HIT THE LIBRARY. WANNA JOIN?
NOT REALLY.
C'MON, MAN. YOU CAN READ THERE. THE EMPTY DORM'S KINDA CREEPY, ANYWAY.
...FINE.
JOSIE AND THE PUSSYCATS

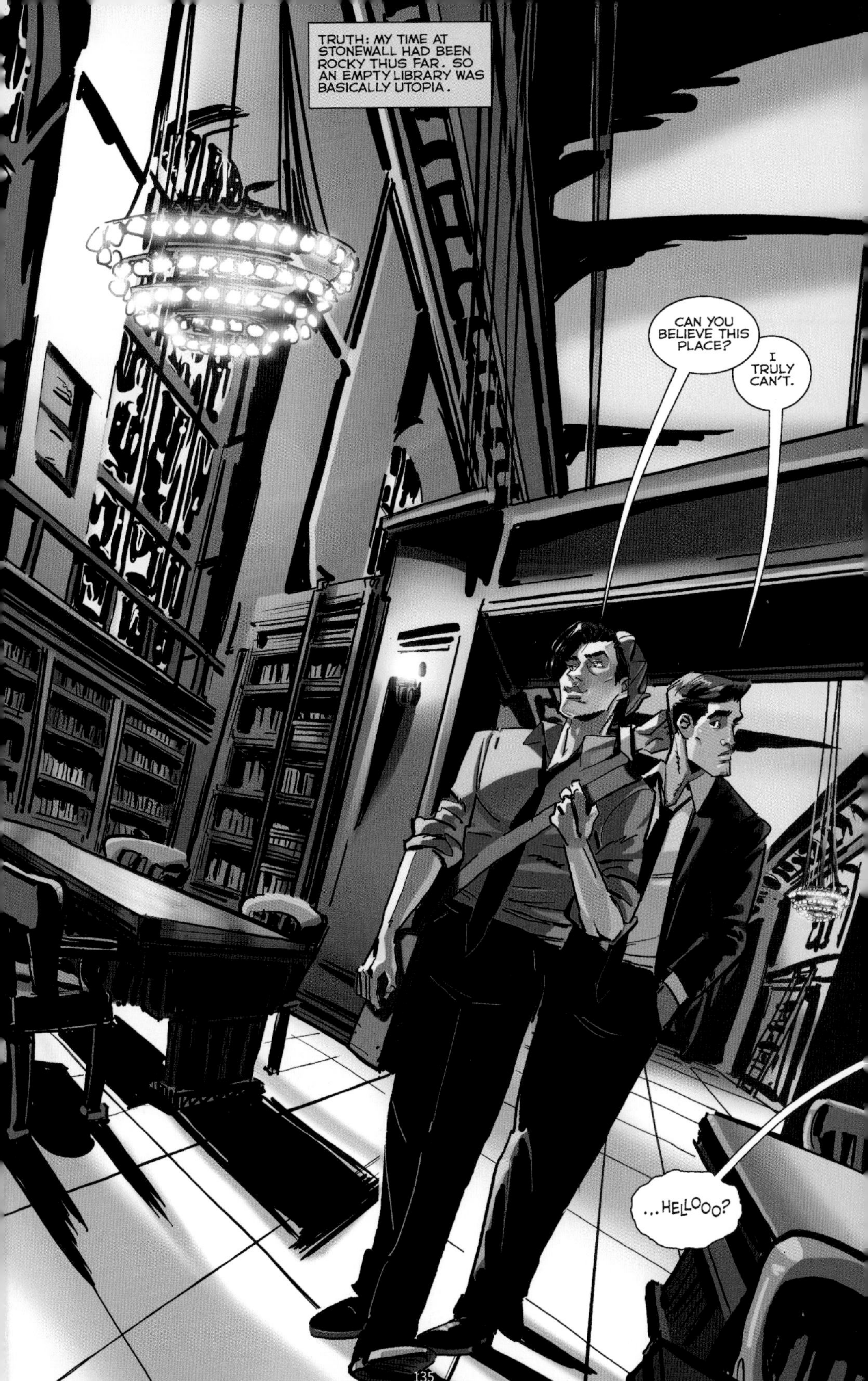
TRUTH: MY TIME AT STONEWALL HAD BEEN ROCKY THUS FAR. SO AN EMPTY LIBRARY WAS BASICALLY UTOPIA.
CAN YOU BELIEVE THIS PLACE?
I TRULY CAN'T.
...HELLOOO?

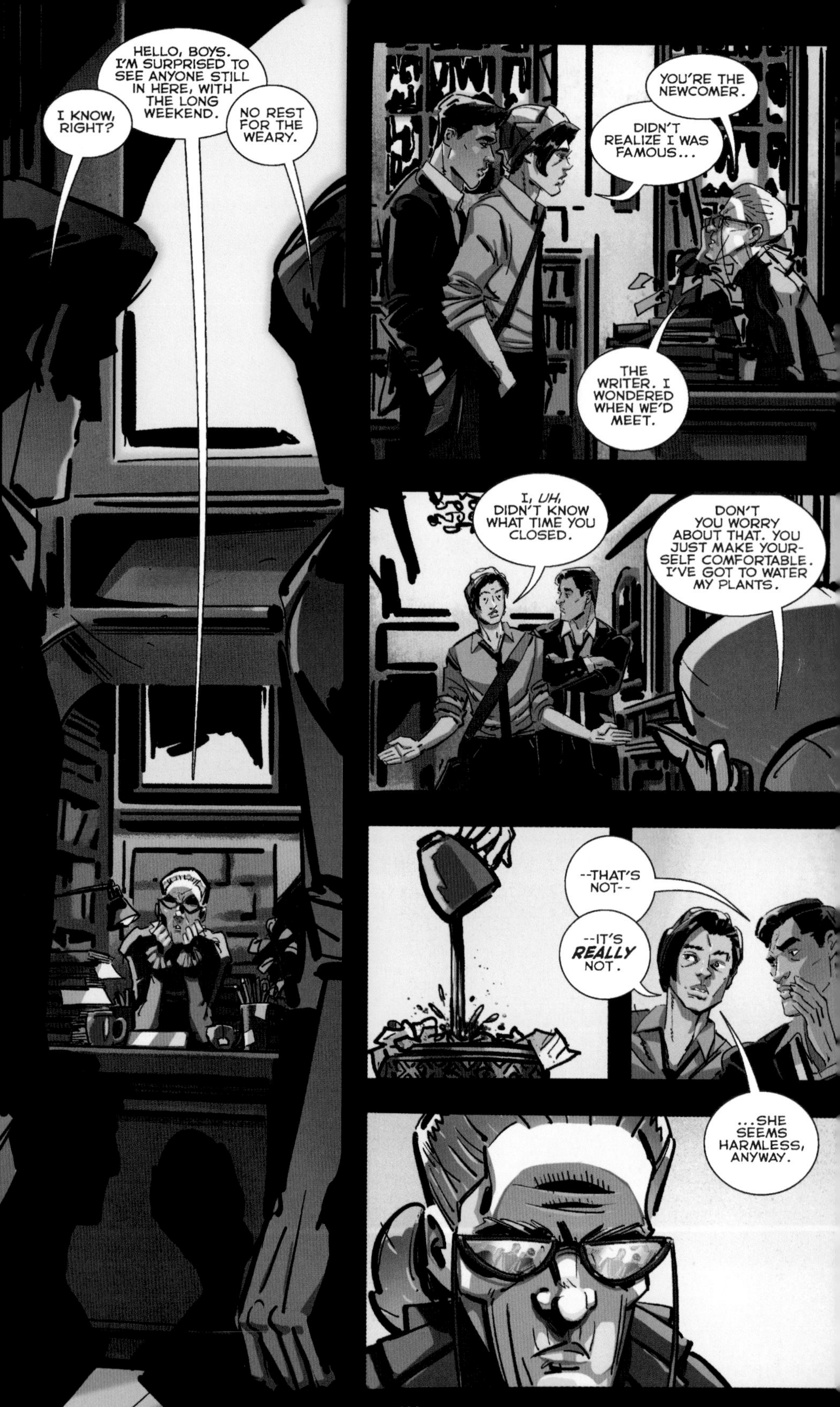
HELLO, BOYS. I'M SURPRISED TO SEE ANYONE STILL IN HERE, WITH THE LONG WEEKEND.
I KNOW, RIGHT?
NO REST FOR THE WEARY.
YOU'RE THE NEWCOMER.
DIDN'T REALIZE I WAS FAMOUS...
THE WRITER. I WONDERED WHEN WE'D MEET.
I, *UH*, DIDN'T KNOW WHAT TIME YOU CLOSED.
DON'T YOU WORRY ABOUT THAT. YOU JUST MAKE YOUR-SELF COMFORTABLE. I'VE GOT TO WATER MY PLANTS.
--THAT'S NOT--
--IT'S ***REALLY*** NOT.
...SHE SEEMS HARMLESS, ANYWAY.

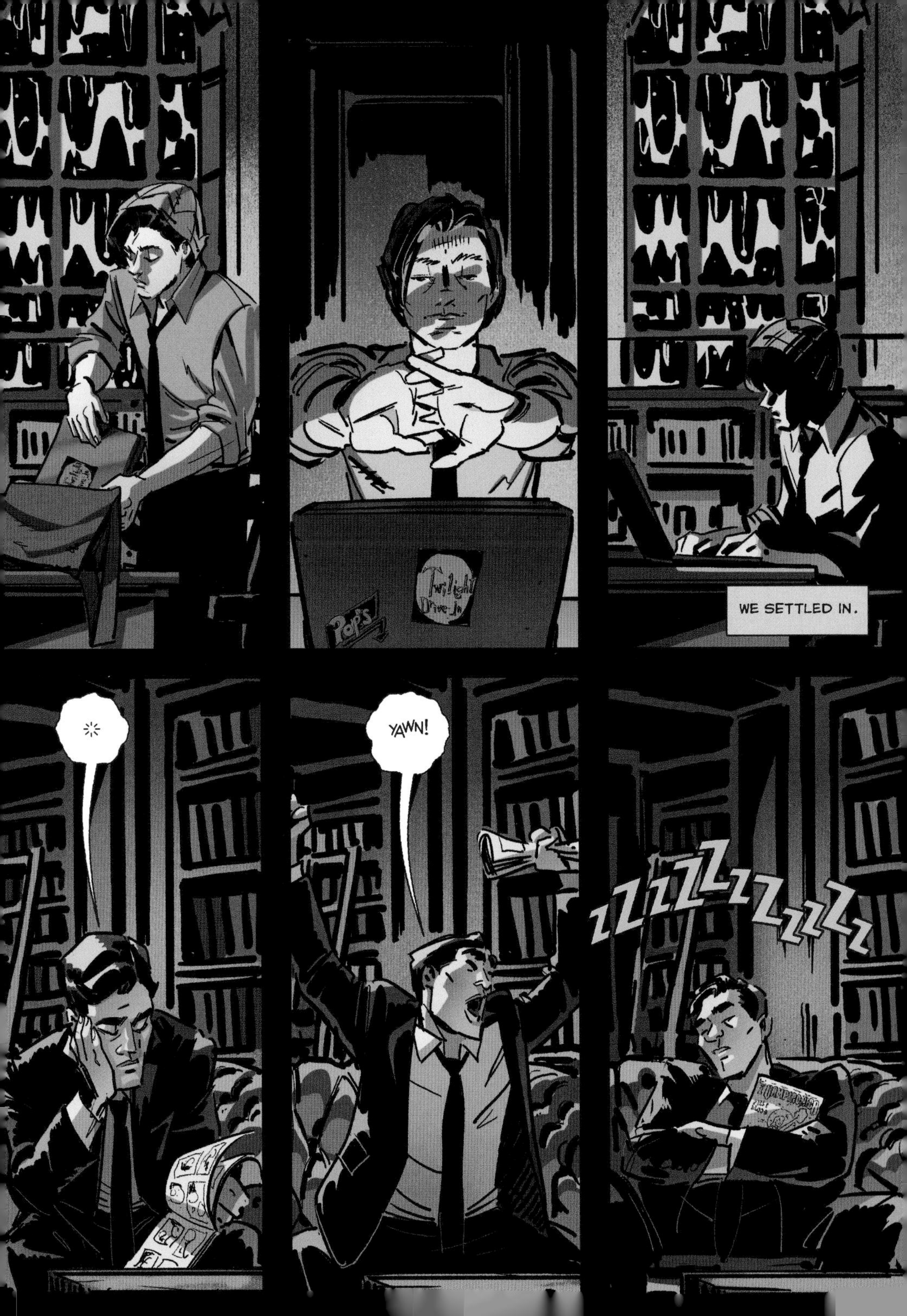

WE SETTLED IN.
YAWN!
ZZZZZZZZZZZZZZ

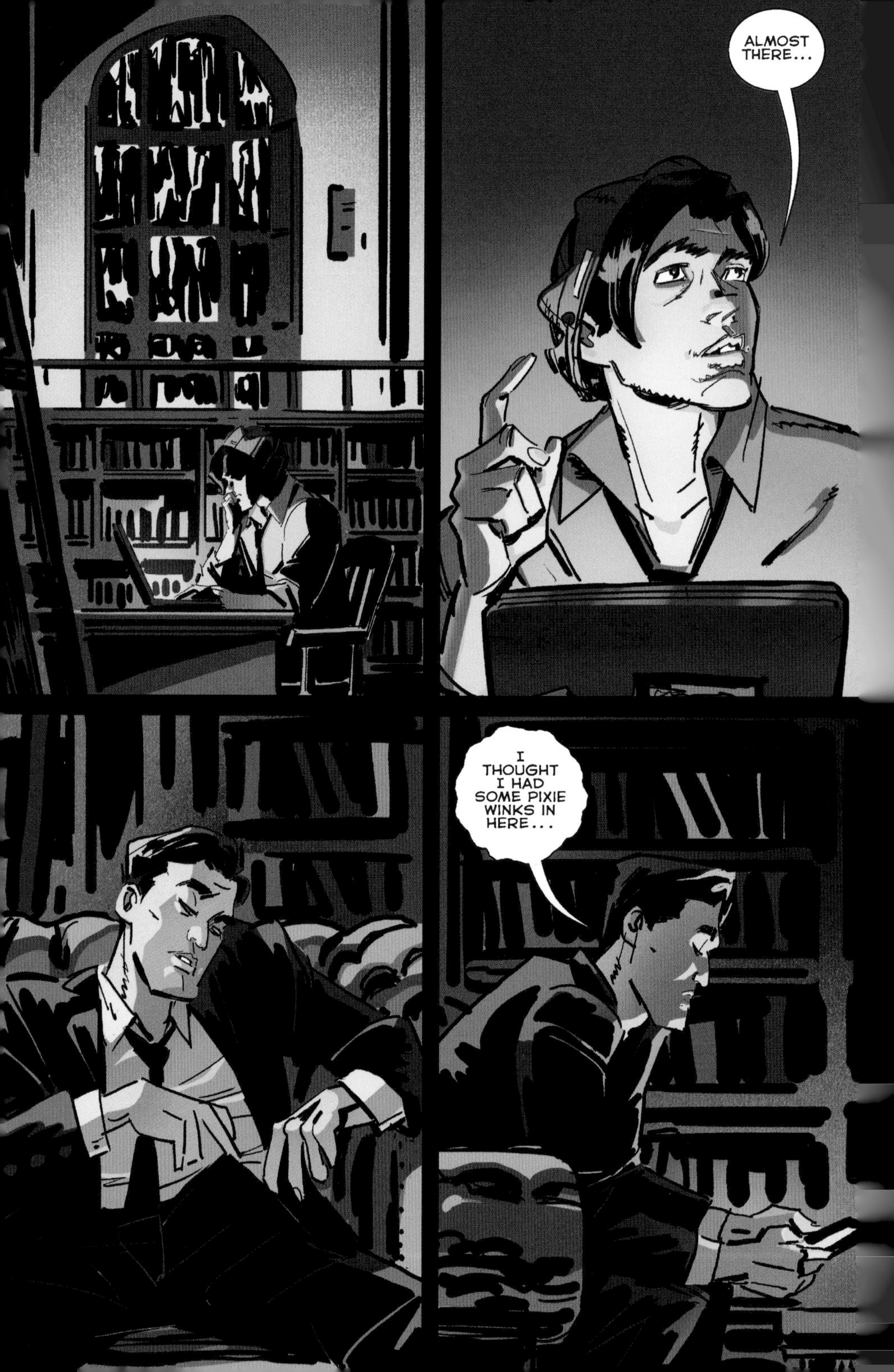
ALMOST THERE...
I THOUGHT I HAD SOME PIXIE WINKS IN HERE...

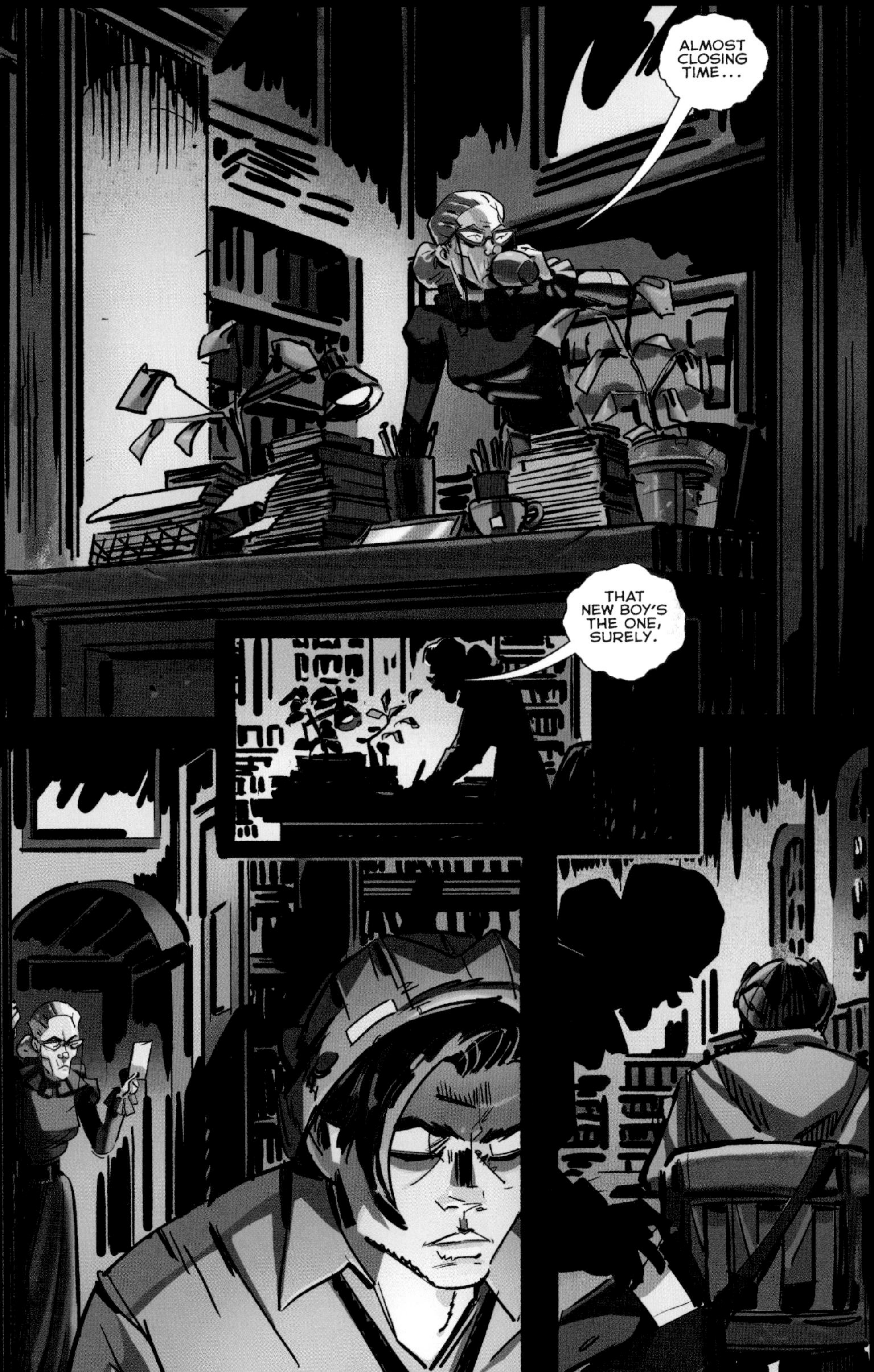
ALMOST CLOSING TIME...
THAT NEW BOY'S THE ONE, SURELY.

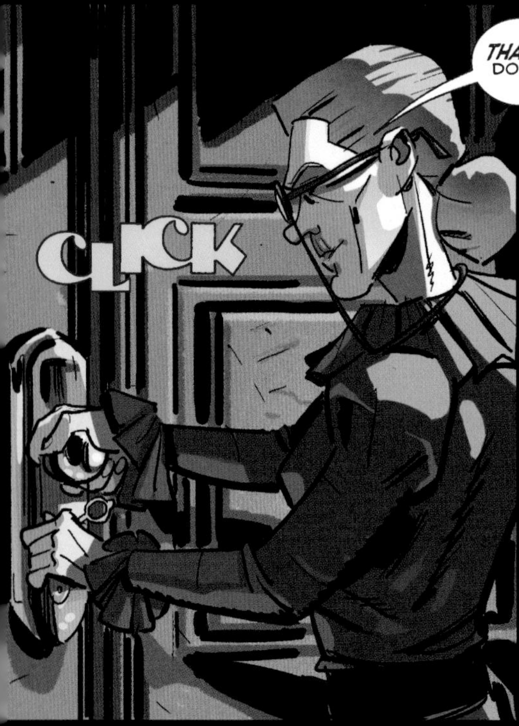
THAT'S DONE!
CLICK

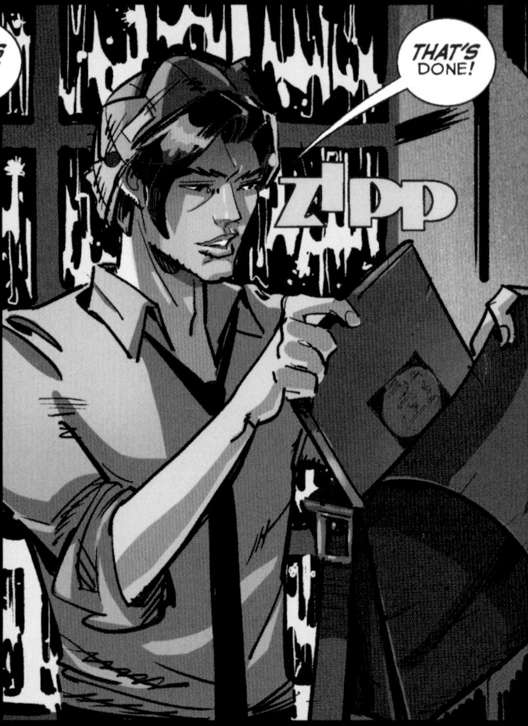
THAT'S DONE!
ZIPP

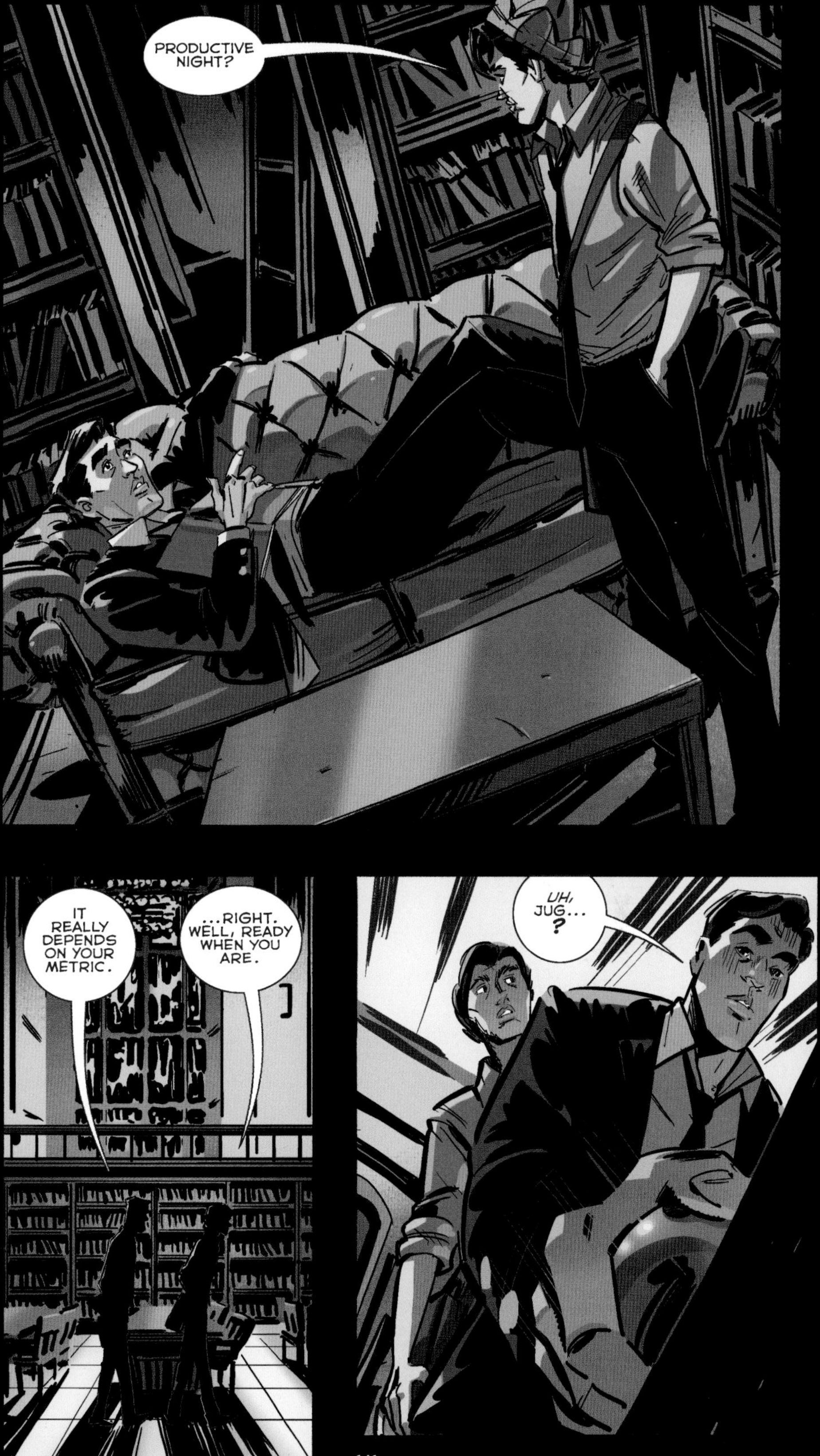
PRODUCTIVE NIGHT?
IT REALLY DEPENDS ON YOUR METRIC.
...RIGHT. WELL, READY WHEN YOU ARE.
UH, JUG...?

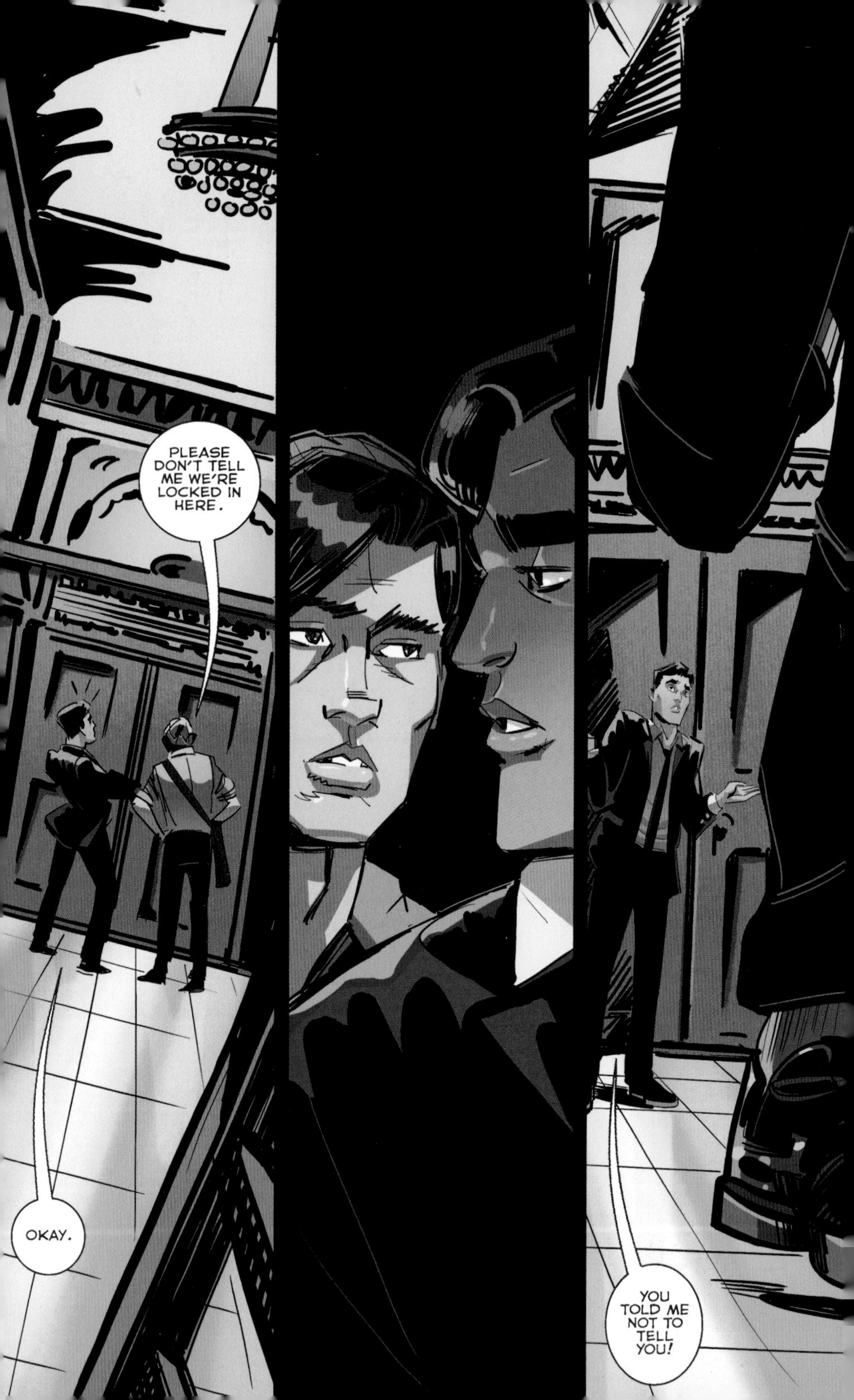
PLEASE DON'T TELL ME WE'RE LOCKED IN HERE.
OKAY.
YOU TOLD ME NOT TO TELL YOU!

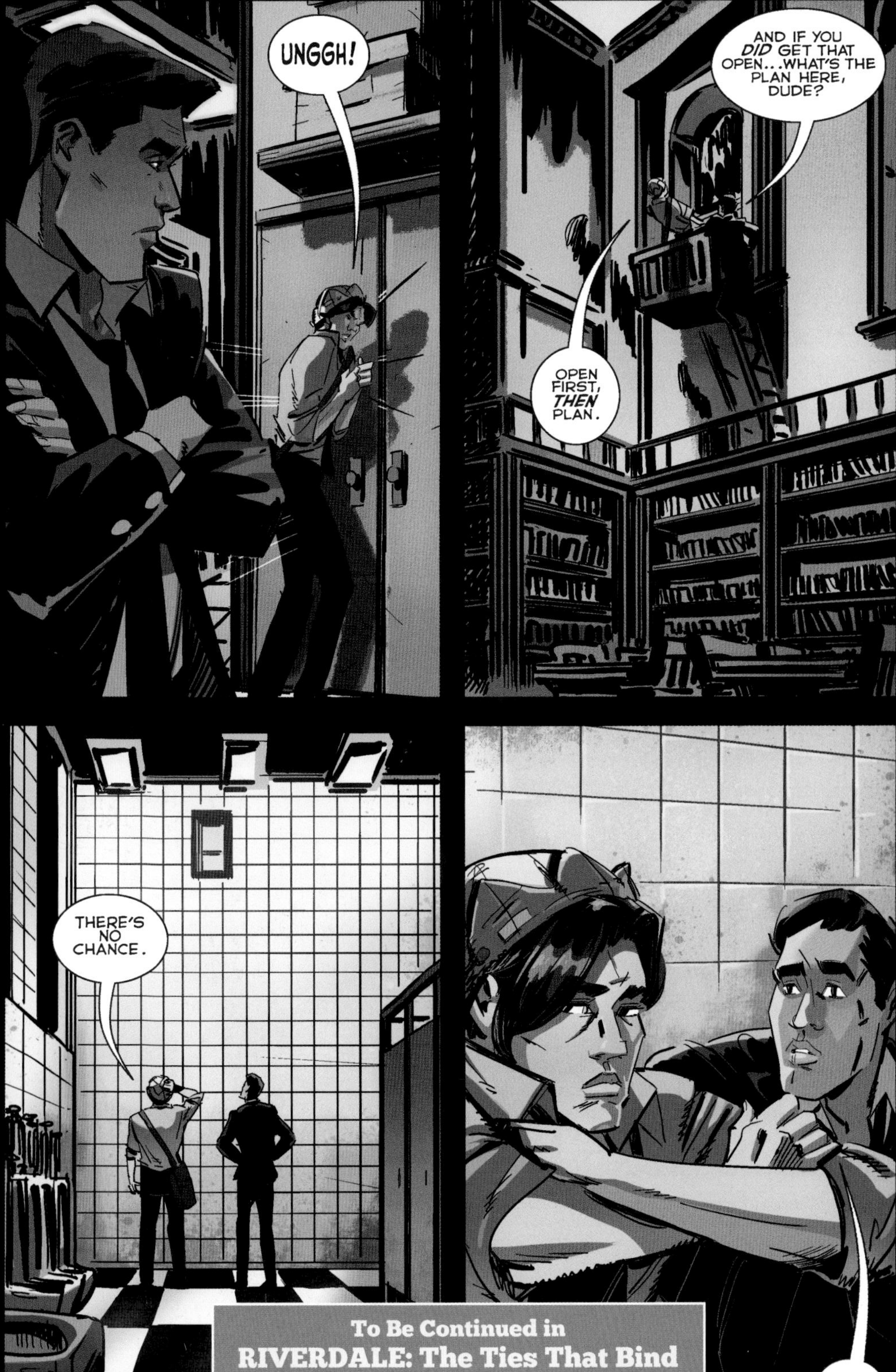
UNGGH!
AND IF YOU *DID* GET THAT OPEN...WHAT'S THE PLAN HERE, DUDE?
OPEN FIRST, *THEN* PLAN.
THERE'S NO CHANCE.
NOW WHAT?
To Be Continued in
RIVERDALE: The Ties That Bind
On Sale Fall 2020